Magemother

❖ Book Two ❖

The Paradise Twin

Austin J. Bailey

Cover design by James T. Egan, www.bookflydesign.com.

Edited by Crystal Watanabe, www.pikkoshouse.com.

Map of Aberdeen by Karl Vesterberg, www.traditionalmaps.com.

Printed in the United States of America

1043096

This book is dedicated to the four mothers who have influenced my life the most: my father's, my son's, my wife's, and my own.

Contents

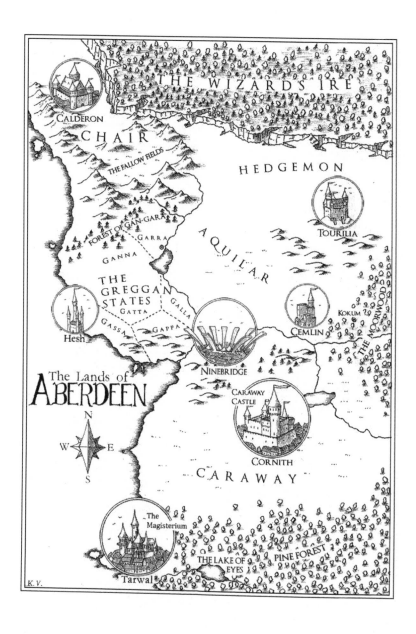

Prologue

In which there is darkness

IN THE DARK, HAUNTED HEART of the Wizard's Ire, four gnarled, evil-looking trees stood silent. They held something between them—a black box, hard and smooth, wedged into their intersecting branches. A voice boomed from it, breaking the silence and calling into the clearing.

"Gadjihalt!" it said, and a man appeared. He was a large, hulking figure with a rigidity to his movements that suggested both great strength and advanced age. He was a soldier, or had been, a knight of the High King of Aberdeen. But that was long ago. He was a traitor to the crown, and the king he had betrayed was long dead, fallen to the hands of time, the same hands that he had eluded now for five hundred years.

"I am here, master," he said, kneeling before the box.

"The Mage of Light and Darkness has awakened," the voice said. "The darkness calls to him."

"Shall I retrieve him for you, my lord?" Gadjihalt asked reverently.

"Send my daughter with a message for him. Tell him that he must listen to the darkness, and that I will instruct him. After that, there will be no need to force him. He will come to me."

Gadjihalt bowed his head. "And what of the Magemother? We have received word that she is searching for the lost mages. Soon their power may be restored. Their presence might make it difficult to conquer Aberdeen."

The box was silent for a moment. Then it said, "Send the Janrax. Tell him to release his haunts. In exchange for his service, he will receive his freedom. Go now."

Gadjihalt bowed again and moved away. When he reached the edge of the little clearing, a woman appeared at his side, hooded and cloaked in a robe the same dank color as the trees. "What did he say?" she asked.

"A message is to be sent to the Paradise prince," Gadjihalt grunted.

"Does he want me to take it?" she inquired.

He nodded.

She squinted at his face. "What?" she asked. "What else?"

"The Janrax is to be released and given his freedom in exchange for setting his haunts upon the mages." He considered her thoughtfully then gave a curt nod and turned on his heel. "Go fetch him from his hole and take him with you when you go."

March froze. "Me?" she whispered. "The Janrax? Why him?" But Gadjihalt said nothing, only disappeared into the trees.

❖ ❖ ❖

Hours later, March tossed a thin wooden wand over the narrow ledge that jutted out of the rock face on the side of a deep ravine. Then she swung herself over and hung, dropping the last few feet to the black valley floor. She was in the crater of a dormant volcano. She had only been there once before, and if she had not been ordered to do so, she would never have come again. The hard-packed ash beneath her feet smelled almost as putrid as the stagnant lake that ran beside her, but neither was as foul as the creature who inhabited this place.

She picked up the wand, careful not to touch the animal figures that were carved into the handle. The wand belonged to the creature that lived in here. He would need it if he was going to help free her father, but she did not like the idea of giving it to him. March did not consider herself a good person. At least, she understood that most people in the world rather she were dead. She had done terrible things in her time, as witches are often wont to do, and rubbed shoulders with the cruelest of characters, but she would prefer the company of any one of them to the Janrax. People who held such power as he once had could not easily be trusted. Her father trusted him—enough to use him—but she did not like to, no matter how much of his power he had lost in the long years since his demise and imprisonment.

A crude-smelling cloud of smoke curled from the top of a black pipe in the ground and told her that she had reached her destination. She lifted the steel grate to reveal a dark hole in the ground and jumped into it, leaving behind the dim light of the Wizard's Ire for an even darker setting: an intersection of long, low corridors lined with workbenches, cauldrons, hammers, and ore. Fire burned in a pit in the floor and cast dancing shadows across the walls.

There was a sudden hiss of steam and March ducked, letting a spell of light and water slip to the tip of her tongue before she realized who it was.

"Hold your tongue, witch!" a voice snapped. The air filled with an acrid smell as the steam cleared, revealing a thin, twisted wisp of a man. He swung his tongs brusquely over the workbench and dropped the little bronze disc that he had been quenching. As he moved, something jangled around his legs and March saw that he was shackled to the floor with a long chain as thick as a man's arm.

"What?" he asked. His face was small, his skin gray and pinched and taut around the edges, as if he had spent his life attempting to crawl backward into some invisible shell. "What does that tyrant want from me now?"

"The tyrant is my father," March said. "Watch your words."

"Do you know who I am?" the Janrax whispered, turning to face her straight on.

"Nobody knows who you are now," March said, leaning casually against a bench to show that she was not afraid. "No one remembers. How does that feel?"

The truth was she knew something of who he was. Once he had been the greatest sorcerer of all time, they said. The one who taught men to use magic. The very man who had taught her father, once upon a time.

The Janrax cocked his head and laughed. "I broke the bridge to heaven and cut this world off from the gods, little witch. And in return they stole my name and my power, but they did not take it all."

His face changed for the briefest instant, and she had a glimpse of something, flashing teeth and gaping maw and fierce eyes. It was gone as soon as it came, but it left her thinking about the powers that he was rumored to still possess: the ability to take any shape he liked, and the power to control some of his oldest weapons. His current powers were but frail shadows of his former glory, but his skill with the bridges of Aberdeen was unparalleled. It had taken him years, in his current state, to work out how the mages had constructed their line of warding on the bridge to the Wizard's Ire, and years more to successfully construct a key. Now he spent his time creating the enchanted coins that unlocked the barrier, a process that Shael would trust to no one else. The medallions weren't perfect, however. They were only strong enough for a single use, after which the power of the barrier would reduce it to dust. Luckily, this was only true for the particular medallion in use, so that a person could easily take a second for a return journey. She had used them several times now, and even she had to admit that his help had been indispensable.

He raised his hand and lifted a hammer into the air, bringing it down upon the metal disc. It cracked and peeled at the edges, and a thin, dull shell fell away to reveal a shining golden medallion within.

"Here is today's work," he said, dropping the coin into a large leather bag that hung from his desk. "I will have another tomorrow. And another the day after that. Go away and do not disturb my slavery until Shael has finally decided that he has enough of these coins."

"He has enough," March said. She raised her hand and pointed at the shackle around his leg. It fell away with a clatter. "I have been given authority to release you."

"Oh?" he said, turning slowly on the spot. He propped his leg up on a stool and began to rub it where the shackle had been. "You have, have you?" His eyes narrowed with new suspicion. "At what cost? What must I do to earn this new mercy?"

March raised the wand and proffered it to him, and he seemed to notice it for the first time. "Do you still have the power to wield this?" she asked.

He took it from her slowly and ran a careful hand over the caved creatures on the handle. "Oh, yes," he said. "I think so."

"Come with me, then," she said. "Help me bring down the mages. Set your haunts on them. Help my father go free, and you will have your freedom."

"Just that?" he said. His eyes widened in a look of surprise. "But that isn't work at all." He drew the cloak around his shoulders and lifted the hood, shrouding his features in shadow. "Haunting the mages of Aberdeen will be a pleasure."

Chapter One

IN THE MIDDLE OF THE NIGHT, deep inside Caraway Castle, something was very wrong.

Brinley shot out of bed as soon as she felt it. She got dressed and gathered the bag that held the things she never let out of her sight—a small crystal knife, a magical vial called a naptrap, a small silver summoning bell, a picture of her mother that she had made, and a small drawing notebook—and ran out the door. This seemed to happen every night now, waking up and searching the castle. Since becoming the Magemother, she found that she had an almost magical instinct whenever something was wrong. That was one of the few real changes she had felt in herself since embracing her new role.

There was never any telling what her instinct might be alerting her to. One night, a cat had been accidentally caught in a mousetrap. She found it wandering the castle halls in silent pain, dragging the mousetrap along behind it at the end of its tail. On another night, she found one of the cooks crying into an empty soup pot. Anything could happen in a castle at night, and now, it seemed, she was tuned in when things went wrong. She rounded a corner and the feeling of wrongness changed. It was different from the things she had felt before. Urgent. She needed to hurry.

She entertained the thought of sliding down the handrail of the four-story spiral staircase that led to the lower levels and decided against it. After all, being in a hurry wasn't reason enough to kill herself. When she reached the main level, one of the night guards nodded to her from his position at the main doors.

"Is anything the matter?" she asked him.

"Not here," he responded, moonlight gleaming off his helmet as he tipped it to her.

She nodded. No doubt the guards thought her crazy by now, what with her inevitable nightly prowl. She deciding against questioning him further. It was one thing to appear concerned, another to appear crazy or nosy, and she was already prowling the castle alone at night. At least she was dressed this time. The first time, she had run out in only her night shirt.

She turned slowly, wondering where she should go to find the source of the disturbance. Using a trick she had learned when she found the cat, she closed her eyes and imagined where the trouble was. Darkness and torches filled her mind's eye, so she took another staircase that led down.

A minute later she opened a door to a long, dank corridor lit softly by a single flickering torch. At the far end of it, directly across from her, there was a dark iron door with a little window set in the top of it, which could be opened and closed. That door was locked, she knew. She had been here before. She knew what the disturbance must be now. She had wondered how long it would take him to try and break through that door. She was glad that her instincts had led her here before he arrived. As softly as she could, she closed the door to the corridor behind her and nestled herself against the wall off to the side.

She didn't have to wait long before she heard soft footsteps approaching. With a small creak, the door swung open, hiding her from view. A boy about her own age stepped through it, his fair hair unkempt, probably from tossing and turning in his bed. He moved cautiously, slowly, without the confident strut that usually accompanied him in the halls of the castle. When he got to the locked door he simply stood there for a minute, staring. She could guess what he might be thinking. No doubt he was imagining the thing on the other side. Perhaps he was wondering whether it was wise for him to take it. He would be weighing the risks, thinking of what had happened to the ones who had come before.

She put out a hand and the door that hid her swung shut with a click, causing the boy to whirl about.

"Hi," Brinley said simply.

The look of worry melted from Hugo's face almost at once, replaced by a half smile. "You caught me."

Brinley shrugged. Inwardly, she marveled at the change that had taken place in him during the short time they had known each other. Not long ago he would have been angry or scared at being found out like this. He was the prince of Caraway, son of Remy,

High King of Aberdeen. There was a time when his pride would have been bruised by a situation like this, but things had changed. She was the Magemother now, and he was a mage. There was respect between them, and friendship, the bond of Magemother to mage.

Something fluttered out of the shadows behind Hugo, danced around the torchlight, and settled on Brinley's shoulder.

"There's a moth on you," he said, reaching to brush it away.

She swatted his hand. "Leave it."

He shrugged. "How did you know I would come?"

She yawned, covering her mouth with a hand. "You had to eventually. Remember that first day? I told you that it would call to you." Something flashed in Hugo's eyes. "Has it?" she asked.

Hugo shrugged. "Maybe. I haven't been able to think about anything else for a couple of days."

She nodded and approached the door. He was slightly taller than her, and she had to look up at him. "Are you ready?" she asked.

Some of the confidence left his face, but he maintained enough composure to nod just before she knocked on the door.

A small shutter opened behind a pair of vertical iron bars set into the door at eye level, revealing the face of a guard. "My lady?" the guard said, surprised.

"Sorry for the hour, Captain," Brinley said as he opened the door. She smiled kindly at him. "Thank you. We will be quite fine now. Please leave us."

"As you wish," the guard said, giving Hugo a small bow as he passed. She ducked inside the room and Hugo followed her, closing the door behind them.

It was a long, low storage room, packed from corner to corner with hundreds of years of things that nobody could find a place for in the castle above them. In the center of it all, propped against a tall stack of crates, was a long mirror shrouded in a protective cloth.

Brinley glanced at Hugo, who was staring, transfixed, at the mirror.

"What happens now?" Hugo asked.

Brinley's mouth tightened. She had been wondering the same thing for weeks now, ever since she had made Hugo the Mage of Light and Darkness. She had known, even then, that the darkness, the evil that was trapped in the mirror, would call out to him eventually. It could not stay confined forever—that much she knew. But there were many things that she did not know, like what exactly would happen when the Darkness entered Hugo. As the Mage of Light and Darkness, Hugo was one of the most important mages of Aberdeen, responsible for balancing the forces of good and evil, light and darkness, which flowed through every living creature. He was also the first mage that she, as the Magemother, had commissioned, and every part of his rise to power was going to be a learning experience for both of them.

"Practice with me one last time," Brinley said, catching the sleeve of Hugo's shirt as he moved toward the mirror.

He sighed. "Melding?" he asked.

She nodded.

Hugo closed his eyes and wiggled his shoulders, loosening his neck the way boxers do before a fight. His job was to feel a deep sense of what Animus called "allowing," something that Hugo had found to be particularly tricky so far. "Okay," he said.

Brinley squinted at him. Her job was to focus on him as strongly as possibly, so for her, keeping her eyes open was helpful. She took in every part of him, blond hair, face that looked like a young version of his father's, eyelids shut gently over eyes the color of the morning sky. She opened her heart to him completely. That was a part of the melding as well, the hardest part.

As usual, she felt vulnerable when she did it. But this time she felt something else. Something for *him,* something that she couldn't quite put a name to. It was part caring, part concern, part worry, all things that a mother would feel for a son, but there were other things, too. A fear of what he might become. A fear of what she might become without him. That part didn't make any sense. There were other feelings that didn't make any sense. They made her blush; she wished that they would go away. Beyond any doubt, though, he was a part of her, attached by invisible strings. It was like that with all of the mages, but more so with him.

For a moment, she was alone in the melding. Then Hugo opened up to her. She closed her eyes and saw the inside of his eyelids, heard the flickering snap of the torch through his ears, heard her own voice say "okay" from a few feet away. Hugo opened his eyes and she saw out of them.

Hugo looked at her. She wished he wouldn't do that. It felt strange, looking at herself like that. She knew that if she opened her own eyes she would lose the connection. There was something about looking into herself from two vantage points that boggled her mind. She had tried it once, even though Animus had warned her against it, and won a massive headache in the bargain.

"I'm ready," Hugo said. His voice was firm. She could feel the resolve in his heart. He switched off his fearful, doubting thoughts like a light inside himself, and she was jealous at the ability.

"Do it," she said, and Hugo raised his hand to the corner of the sheet, tugging it off the mirror with a smooth motion.

Brinley stared through Hugo's eyes at the figure waiting for them inside the mirror.

He stood there like a faceless body of darkness, suspended in the glass. Gently, like smoke bending through the night air, the featureless face shifted into a dark parody of Hugo's own. Two Paradise princes stood before her now, one dark, the other light, sizing each other up.

No one spoke.

Finally the darkness gave a tentative smile. "You have come for me?" it asked softly.

Hugo said nothing. He took a step forward and leaned in until he and his shadowy twin stood nose to nose. "Do you have a name?" he asked quietly.

"Let me inside," the darkness whispered, smiling hungrily. "Let me inside, and I will tell you."

Hugo set his jaw stubbornly. "You have no name unless I give you one."

The darkness mimicked his frown, but remained silent.

"You have no life unless I give it to you," Hugo said. "You have no power unless I give it to you."

The darkness lifted an eyebrow and gave a little bow. "As you say."

Hugo's frown deepened. "I will not give in to you like the others did."

The darkness gave a knowing smile. "Then you will be the first." It held out a hand and touched the inside of the mirror. Its palm flattened out like a tiny fog bank against the glassy surface. "Let me in," it said, "or I will never stop calling to you. Let me in. The world is starving for darkness."

Hugo took a long, deep breath before raising his hand to touch the glass opposite the smoky palm. When they met, the darkness shivered. A second later, the shadowy substance that composed its body began shrinking, narrowing, and pushing itself through the face of the mirror and into Hugo's hand. He thought it was going to take him over, try to control him right away, but it didn't. It didn't enter his mind and torture him. It didn't speak dark things to his heart or conjure up the worst of his memories. He felt nothing.

Brinley's eyes met Hugo's as she slipped out of the meld that had connected them. She felt like she should say something. "I wonder how long it will take," she said. That was the question:

How long before the darkness would try to corrupt him? Was it doing it already? Would he even be able to tell when it started, or would it be so subtle that he wouldn't be able to tell?

"I don't know," he answered.

"Don't worry," she said. "I think you'll notice it when it happens." She hoped that she was right. "Hugo?"

"Yeah?" He had a faraway look on his face that Brinley recognized as a sign that his mind was elsewhere—she was getting used to that look by now, spending so much time with Tabitha.

"Don't forget about the meeting later."

"Yeah," he said, not looking at her.

"We'll have to talk about this there."

"I know." There was a hint of irritation in his voice. No doubt the prospect of telling his father about how the evil of the world had entered him wasn't a thrilling idea. The king was, as a rule, suspicious of all things magical.

She grabbed his sleeve, holding him back from the door. "And don't forget," she said, "I want you to stay for the whole meeting so that you know what's going on." Hugo was famous for sneaking out of meetings, classes, and anything else he was supposed to be at as soon as he got bored.

He snatched his sleeve away irritably. "I told you I would," he said. He moved through the doorway, not looking back.

"Hugo?" she called, hurrying after him. "Do you want me to walk with you? Do you want to talk about what just happened? I mean, it's kind of a big deal, you know? And I don't want you to

think you're in this alone. Remember, I'm always here to help. We only have each other, and—oomph!" She ran right into Hugo, who had stopped walking suddenly. He turned slowly, one hand raised in emphasis, the irritation clear on his face. Right away she knew she had gone too far. Boys were so difficult sometimes, especially Hugo. He always wanted to be left alone right when he needed help the most.

"Brinley," he said, struggling to keep his voice down. "I know! I know because you keep telling me. I know you're there for me! But I just want to be alone right now, okay? I just want to think." He spun back around, the dark train of his shirt billowing gently in his wake. "I'll see you at the meeting," he called back, and he turned down a side passage.

Brinley didn't know where that went. Definitely not back upstairs. Most likely he would wander the belly of the castle for hours, brewing over his questions and worries alone . . . Maybe he hadn't changed that much after all.

"Go with him, Tabitha," she said quietly, taking the moth off her shoulder and cradling it in her hands. "Just watch out for him, please. I'm worried about him."

The moth fluttered away. Anyone watching might have thought it was a plain old moth (it got sidetracked dancing around the torchlight), but Brinley knew that it would follow her friend in the end, watching him when she could not.

❖ ❖ ❖

When Hugo finally realized that he was getting nowhere trying to make sense of what had happened, he made his way back to his rooms, taking a secret passage and a little-used stairway in order to avoid people. It was still early—at least an hour before the meeting—but the servants would be roaming about now and he wasn't in the mood to bump into people.

Unfortunately for Hugo, the apprentice to the Mage of Wind was lounging on Hugo's couch (completely uninvited) when he entered his rooms. Hugo didn't try too hard to hide his irritation. "Don't *ask* or anything, Cannon," he said. "Just come right in whenever you please."

Cannon smiled warmly. "Thank you. Tabitha said you wouldn't mind."

"Tabitha?" Hugo asked, looking around for the girl.

Cannon nodded toward Hugo's feet, and Hugo looked down to see a small brown rabbit sniffing his boot. The rabbit blinked at him and then erupted, growing skyward at an enormous rate, nose and feet and fluffy tail twisting into human form with a sound like fabric flapping in the breeze. In a moment the rabbit was gone and a girl of about thirteen stood before him. She had eyes the color of fresh tilled earth and a long braid of hair to match. She wore a bright yellow sun dress that made her look altogether older and more put together than the first time he had met her. Back then she had been living alone in her bird tower with little human contact.

Now, she was the apprentice to the Mage of Earth as well as the Magemother's Herald. Her time at the castle had done wonders for her, Hugo thought. Simply being around *people* had done wonders for her. She looked normal now.

"Hello, Hugo," she said brightly. "Are you evil now?"

He grinned. Maybe not *quite* normal. "I don't think it works like that," he said.

She shrugged and plopped down beside Cannon. "Just checking." She stretched her feet out and placed them on a low table. They were bare and dirty, as you might expect the underside of a rabbit's feet to be.

Hugo poured himself a glass of juice from a crystal pitcher on the table and sat down across from the others. He glanced questioningly at Cannon, and Tabitha said, "I told him everything."

Hugo choked on his juice. "You did? And I suppose you were along for the whole thing, were you? Spying on Brinley and me?"

"I wasn't spying," Tabitha said, sounding offended. "I was watching."

"As a bunny?" Hugo said incredulously. He couldn't believe that he hadn't noticed her bouncing around his feet.

Cannon laughed and Tabitha held up a finger to correct him. "A *rabbit*. And, no." She gave a sly smile. "I was a moth for a while, and then I was an ant. I sat on your boot all morning while you paced."

"*All* morning?" Hugo huffed, remembering the moth.

Tabitha folded her arms. "Well, not the *whole* time . . . I closed my eyes when you went to the bathroom. Your boots need to be washed, by the way."

"Tabitha!" Hugo and Cannon said together.

"What?" she said, taken aback. "They do! Just look at them."

"An ant?" Cannon said, trying not to laugh at Hugo's flushed cheeks. "Why an ant? He might have crushed you by accident. Your life could have been over like that!" He snapped his fingers.

"No," Tabitha said, nonplussed. "Ants are strong . . . Stronger than you think." She smiled. "Like me."

Hugo couldn't hold it in any longer. "Just listen to you two!" he exploded, standing up. "What about my privacy? I mean, coming in without asking is one thing, but spying on me too? How do you justify that?"

Tabitha looked confused. Finally she shrugged. "Brinley asked me to. She said you needed to be watched. Said that you might do something stupid, like try to sneak into the dungeons in the middle of the night to confront the darkness by yourself without telling her."

That stung. How did Brinley know him so well? She was the Magemother, of course, and he was a mage, and everyone said that mothers had an instinct about these things. Maybe this was what it was like to have a mother. All he knew was he liked things better before a girl took such an annoying interest in everything he did.

Cannon sat up, looking mildly surprised. "You're not arguing," he said to Hugo. "You really did do all that? Blast. I was banking

on you not being that stupid. Rumors are spreading around the castle already, but I thought they were exaggerated."

Tabitha held out a hand expectantly and Cannon withdrew a coin from the pocket of his robes.

"Were you *betting* on me?" Hugo asked, not sure whether he should be outraged or amused.

"Just a bit," Tabitha said, as if it wasn't any of his business, and Cannon said, "Don't feel bad, mate. Brinley's been waiting for you to sneak off to that room for a week. Now, do tell us all about it or we won't leave you alone. We still have a few minutes until the meeting starts."

"You were there," he said to Tabitha.

"I wasn't," Cannon said.

"Fine," Hugo blurted. The truth was he wasn't nearly as annoyed as he was pretending; Hugo was generally happy to be the center of attention. He told them the whole thing.

When he got to the part where the darkness entered him, Cannon shifted in his seat. "What did it feel like?" he asked. "Did it hurt?"

Hugo thought about it. "I didn't feel anything at all, really."

"Blast," Cannon said, taking another coin out of his pocket. Tabitha had her hand out again, wiggling her fingers impatiently.

Hugo gave them a dumbfounded look. Everyone had noticed Tabitha coming out of her shell over the last few weeks, but he had never seen the two of them carry on like this together. It made sense, though. After all, they were both apprenticed to mages.

Maybe there was some comradery in that which he was not privy to.

They had a few more questions for him—sincere questions, he guessed, since there were no more coins exchanged, and Cannon let himself out. On his way through the door, Cannon called back, "Watch out for ants." Hugo rolled his eyes.

Tabitha stepped to the open window.

"Are you going to see her now and report about me?" Hugo asked, knowing the answer.

"Yep," Tabitha said.

"Tabitha," Hugo said, making her pause. "Can ants really close their eyes?"

"Nope," she said. And she hopped out the window.

He crossed the room to look out after her. It was a hundred feet to the ground from there. No doubt she had changed shape after she jumped. He could just make out the shape of a robin winging toward the windows of the Magemother's quarters. She would tell Brinley everything, he knew. How he looked, how he acted, what he said. Was he afraid? Was he going crazy yet? Was the darkness taking control?

He went to the mirror and considered his reflection. Those were all good questions. He had been asking himself those, and a dozen others, for half the night.

Chapter Two

In which Brinley has a vision

LATER THAT DAY, Brinley was pacing in her room. It was time to be going. That much had been decided already, and now that the darkness had entered Hugo, there was nothing more to wait for. Hugo would be leaving too. The king hadn't been happy about that, but he was never happy at the prospect of his only heir leaving the safety of Caraway Castle. Overprotective, that's what he was, but in the end he had taken it better than she had anticipated.

Hugo would be going with Animus and Cannon on a fact-finding expedition that would take them anywhere and everywhere. A big part of the reason she wanted them together was because Animus was the oldest, wisest mage around. If anyone had a chance of helping Hugo learn how to be the Mage of Light and Darkness, it was him. She and Animus had discussed it at length over the past few weeks and agreed that if Hugo were overcome by the darkness, it was better that it happened on the road in the middle of nowhere, with Animus there to help, than here in the city with thousands of people around.

They hadn't told the king that part, of course, or Hugo. As far as they knew, the sole purpose of the mission was to discover some clue as to the whereabouts of the missing mages. They were going to the Magisterium and various royal libraries. They would be stopping in smaller places too, talking to the commoners, asking for rumors, stories, anything that might give them a hint in the right direction. It had been done before, true, but this time it was different. This time they had to succeed.

As for herself, her first order of business was to visit Cassis at the bridge to the Wizard's Ire. It was the king's wish that she examine the situation there, since the Magemother was said to control the magical gate there that kept the inhabitants of the Ire locked inside. If that was the case, she knew nothing about it. Just one more thing to ask her mother about when the time came . . . And she hoped the time came soon; the king was nearly hysterical with worry. In the past, creatures from the Ire had been coming in at random, one here and another there. But one week ago, that had changed. It was a monster a day now, every day at noon, coming across the bridge to challenge the king's armies. They were killed almost instantly by the soldiers waiting for them, but that didn't stop them from coming, and the fact that Shael was willing to throw away his forces day after day just to make a point was making everyone nervous. Such a show of force could mean only one thing: war was coming. The oldest enemy of Aberdeen still lived within the Wizard's Ire. Nobody thought that he could escape the prison that the mages had built for him, but nobody had thought the bridge could be breached either.

Brinley brought the little crystal vial out of her bag and twirled it between her fingers thoughtfully. She had been doing that a lot lately—too much, probably. But she didn't care.

Her mother was inside it. Trapped in the vial—the naptrap, it was called. She was wounded, mortally wounded, and if they released her she would die in moments.

She couldn't let that happen. Not just because Brinley had already gone through most of her life without knowing her. Her mother also held critical information. Information that they had to recover. That was why they needed the mages. The mages, she knew, could somehow save her mother, and she was going to need all of them if they were going to succeed.

Brinley squinted, holding the crystal vial up to the light. It looked empty to her. Habis, the witch who had made the naptrap, was supposed to report in earlier, but she had failed to do so. She had been researching fiercely over the past couple of weeks, looking for a way to save Brinley's mother. Finding Habis would be her second order of business then.

She hoped that her meeting with Habis would give her new ideas about what to do next. There were too many questions. Too many unknowns. She could still remember when she had lived a normal life back in Colorado, and all she ever worried about was her chores. She chuckled bitterly. In some ways, nothing had changed. She still had chores to do, things that had to get done. But now her chores were important. Now, if she messed up, people could die and the world could unravel at the edges. Being the Magemother wasn't all it was cracked up to be.

After she finished packing, she closed her eyes and reached out with her mind as Animus had taught her. She was supposed to practice this every morning when she woke up, but she had forgotten with all the excitement of leaving.

The mages were connected to the Magemother in many ways, and this was one of the most useful ones. She could communicate with them, and they with her, even across great distances. Touching the minds of the mages was something that the Magemother was supposed to be able to do easily, but so far it had proven a bit of a challenge.

She squinted in concentration. It felt odd, trying to reach out like this. She kept trying to throw her mind outside herself and it kept just slapping up against the inside of her own head. Finally, she broke through. She could feel Hugo on the other side of the castle. His mind was calm, slow. He must be asleep. She widened her awareness and reached out for the other mages, finding them one by one. Cassis was where she expected him to be, pacing back and forth across the bridge to the Wizard's Ire. Belterras, the Mage of Earth, was in the far north, tending to a herd of heartbeasts. She didn't even bother looking for the three missing mages. She *should* bother, she knew, but she didn't want to feel the disappointment of failure today. Wherever they were, they were beyond her reach. How many times did she need to be reminded of it?

She searched for Animus next. Strange that he should be so hard to find; he was usually the easiest. He was old and wise, and his brilliant, powerful mind usually stood out like a star in the darkness of the world. Where was he? She smiled. He was right outside her door.

She let him in and relaxed inside the bear hug he gave her, twitching her nose as his long white beard tickled her face. He was the closest thing she had to a father since her own father had disappeared trying to follow her into Aberdeen.

"I came to say good-bye," Animus said. He raised his snowy eyebrows. "I daresay there won't be time later. Will you continue to practice what I have taught you while I am away?"

"Of course!" she said. "I practice every morning."

"Indeed," he said, hiding a grin. "I noticed that you had quite a struggle locating me just now. Perhaps I was too far away?"

Brinley blushed.

He flashed a knowing smile, half hidden by his white moustache. "Sometimes," he said, "the hardest thing to see clearly is the thing right in front of us."

They sat together in silence for a moment, and then Animus asked, "Have you had any more nightmares?"

Brinley felt her chest tighten at the question. "Yes," she said, "last night. About my father. He was trapped in darkness again, trying to escape, calling to me, but I couldn't get to him." She lifted a hand to stop her lips from trembling. "Do you still think they are visions, Animus?"

He spread his arms. "I do not know," he said. "That is for you to discern." He put a hand on her shoulder. "Do not worry too much about it, though. You will know what to do when the time comes to act. You must trust your instincts."

She nodded.

"Why don't you practice your mind work with me?" he asked.

She welcomed the change of subject. Taking a deep breath, she closed her eyes again and spread her awareness outward, being careful to start with the space right around her body.

"Good," Animus said. "Now, look for them."

"What's the use?" she said. "I'm never going to find them this way."

"Try anyway," Animus said. "It's good for you."

She stretched her mind farther, as far as it would go, looking for some hint, some whisper of the mages that she could never find. Lignumis, the Mage of Wood. Chantra, Mage of Fire. Unda, Mage of Water. They had been young when Lux, the previous Mage of Light and Darkness, had been corrupted. She had been a baby at the time. Her own mother, Lewilyn, had been the Magemother. Lewilyn had hidden the three young mages, just as she had hidden Brinley. Hidden them so carefully that not even she could find them later, knowing that in time, when they were ready, they would return, just as Brinley had.

She could not feel them like she felt the others. No clear, soulful substance, no personality, no thoughts echoing out of the darkness between them, only weight. That was all she ever felt when she looked for them: emptiness and weight. The weight was more inside herself than out, and she knew it must be the weight of the lost mages' power that she still bore. She had taken away all of the mages' power weeks prior, and since she had yet to find them, she still held theirs. Normally it did not bother her, but when her whole being was focused on Chantra, or Unda, or Lignumis, the weight of Fire and Water and Wood began to bear down on her, as if in longing for their true bearers. She knew they must be out there still, if the power longed for them so, but she could not tell where. "Just like always," she muttered.

"Try again," Animus said. "Focus this time. Put your worries away. Just focus on one this time."

Summoning her patience, she closed her eyes again. Which one should she focus on? Almost automatically, her thoughts fell on Chantra, the Mage of Fire. How old was she? She couldn't be that much older than Brinley. She was a young girl when she went into hiding.

Brinley filled her mind with thoughts of fire, imagining the heat of it on her face, the smell of burning wood. Red and orange flames flashed across her imagination. She let them burn of their own accord, ignoring the impulse to stop them. She willed herself to believe that she was watching something more than an idle daydream of her own creation.

There was something in the flames now. A person. Her heart skipped a beat. That was new. She calmed herself, trying to keep her mind from wandering. A short man in a stately coat was peering at her from within the fire. He had a short beard and chiseled features. He was only there for a second, but she saw him clearly. "Animus!" she said, opening her eyes.

"What?" Animus said in a hushed voice. "What did you see?"

"I saw Tuck!" she said. "Thieutukar, I mean."

Animus's wispy eyebrows twitched in surprise. "The king of the gnomes?"

Brinley nodded. "I'm sure it was him. But I don't know why I would see him. I was concentrating on Chantra, just like you taught me, and then Tuck was there. I was concentrating so hard, Animus. Do you think it was a real vision?"

"Hmm," Animus said. "Perhaps. Worth looking into, for certain."

Brinley eyed him questioningly. "But why would I see him? Do you think he might know something about where Chantra is? If that's true then why hasn't he said anything? Tuck is my friend, Animus. I think he would tell me if he knew something like that."

"Perhaps he has forgotten," Animus said. "Or he does not realize what he knows. It could be some small piece of knowledge, insignificant in his own estimation. I think it is worth investigating."

Brinley nodded. "That is where you and Hugo will go, then."

Animus nodded. "I agree. This is the more promising lead." He smiled. "And no doubt Hugo will find it more exciting than searching distant libraries for clues to the whereabouts of the missing mages, as was our previous plan."

Brinley was still thinking about Chantra. "What is she like?" she asked.

Animus looked slightly startled. "Chantra? Well, she was . . . young." He held his hands up apologetically. "I was already very old by the time your mother selected her to be a mage. She spent more time around Cassis, but even he didn't know her well. I think she struggled a bit, growing up with Unda and Lignumis. They were both a bit older than her." He smiled. "Unda once told me he was going to have to get a troll to guard his room on Calypsis because she kept breaking in to jump on his bed and go through his things. I imagine he was joking, of course." He waved his hand. "You will get to know her yourself, I'm sure."

She hoped that Animus was right. She hoped Tuck would remember some secret bit of information that would help them. She hoped, but she couldn't help doubting. Tuck appearing in her mind might just as easily have been a mental hiccup as a real vision. That was something the Magemother was supposed to experience—visions. But she had imagined them being far more grandiose than what she had just experienced.

"I must be going now," he said. He placed a hand on her shoulder. "Have faith in yourself. And remember, never stop looking for them."

❖ ❖ ❖

Early the following morning, Brinley decided to say good-bye to Hugo. She had been arguing with herself about it for an hour now, going back and forth, unsure whether it would be worse to leave each other on the wrong foot or risk coming off as overbearing by checking in on him again. In the end she decided that the best thing would be to just call him with her mind and say her good-byes from a distance. That way he couldn't get mad at her for spying on him, but they would be able to talk before he left. She sat on her bed and reached out across the castle with her mind. She was surprised to find him still asleep, but nudged him awake anyway.

Hugo, she called to him. *Hugo!*

In his room, Hugo stirred.

HUGO!

The prince flipped over and tumbled out of bed, smashing his face against his bedside table.

Oh no! I'm so sorry!

Hi, Brinley, he said. *Can't you just knock like everyone else?* He had pushed himself up onto his hands and knees. *What is it? Is something wrong?*

No. Nothing. How are you feeling? Any changes?

Yes, he said. *My face hurts.*

Sorry about that. I wanted to say good-bye . . . and tell you I'm sorry.

Silence. Brinley cringed. She *was* sorry. Maybe not for caring about him so much, but she was sorry that Hugo kept getting angry about it. She felt a hint of frustration brewing within her. What did he want from her? She had to look after him, didn't she?

That was her responsibility. She was the Magemother and he was a mage!

Thanks, Hugo said finally.

She swallowed her next words, thoroughly stumped over what to say.

Is there anything else? Hugo asked.

Uh, well . . . no. But just be careful, Hugo, okay? And I want to make sure we talk even though we're going to be apart.

She felt something twitch inside him. A small movement. Had he rolled his eyes?

Fine, he said. *Bye, then.*

❖ ❖ ❖

Hugo felt Brinley slip out of his mind. What was her deal? Did she really need to check up on him every second? She had been pretending to be just saying good-bye, of course, but he knew the truth. She was being nosy.

He winced, listening to his own thoughts. What was wrong with him? Brinley was probably just worried. She cared about him. He squirmed. For some reason that made him feel uncomfortable. Uncomfortable and angry. He'd been feeling this way since the mirror . . . But he couldn't just tell her that, could he?

A moment later Hugo's thoughts were interrupted by a knock on his door.

Who could it be that this hour? It couldn't be time to leave already.

He opened the door to find Cannon in the hallway. Animus's apprentice stared down at him questioningly. Cannon had a way of doing that. Even though they were the same height and Hugo was a prince and a mage, Cannon could still look down at him somehow. Hugo had come to think of it as a side effect of Cannon's subconscious conviction that he was the smartest person in the world.

"Wow," Hugo said in mock wonder, "you knocked this time."

Cannon ignored the comment. "Are you ready to go?"

"Uh," Hugo said, looking down at himself stupidly. He was still in his pajamas.

"If I may offer a suggestion," Cannon said, eyeing Hugo's silky bedclothes. "Pants are a handy item to bring on trips like this. You could start there . . ." His face twitched in a small grin. "Would you like me to help you, Your Highness?"

Hugo's jaw tightened. "No thanks," he said. "I'll be out in a minute." With that, he shut the door in Cannon's face.

Several minutes later, Hugo lifted the steel plate on the floor of the chicken coop and climbed out. They wanted to leave quickly and quietly, so they had taken Hugo's favorite secret passage out of the castle. Several chickens clucked indignantly as Cannon followed him out.

"How ingenious," Cannon remarked, lifting the hem of his robe to avoid the mess. "You seem to have picked the only way out of the castle that is riddled with poo."

Hugo bit back a retort as they stepped into the open air. They were at the edge of the castle grounds now; Animus would be close. Sure enough, as they made their way toward the entrance to the city, Animus materialized out of thin air and fell into stride beside them. Hugo relaxed in the presence of the ancient mage, surprised at how tense he had been before. Animus, the Mage of Wind, was the sort of person that made you feel as if everything would work out right. He was the most knowledgeable and powerful of the mages, and by his own declaration actually older than dirt.

"So," Hugo asked to break the ice, "which stuffy old library are we off to first, eh? The Magisterium? Calderon?" The Magisterium was the pillar of the scholarly world in Aberdeen and had the biggest, oldest library around. Calderon was next in line after that, if you didn't count Caraway Castle itself.

"Neither," Animus said, winking from beneath bushy white eyebrows.

Hugo blinked. "I thought we were looking for clues about the mages."

Animus turned a sharp eye on Cannon. "Have you not informed the prince about the new development?"

Cannon looked down sheepishly.

"What new development?" Hugo said. It didn't surprise him that Cannon hadn't said anything. He could be a bit of a prat sometimes, especially around Hugo.

"The Magemother has had a vision," Animus said.

"I assumed she told you," Cannon muttered to Hugo.

Hugo felt his face flush with embarrassment. She hadn't. Why hadn't she? She had just spoken to him! Couldn't she have filled him in? Now Cannon, of all people, knew more than he did. It was insulting. "So where are we going?" he snapped.

"To Tourilia," Animus cut in, sensing Hugo's mood. "She feels there might be clues there about Chantra, and I agree." He gave Hugo a look that made him feel slightly ashamed of himself.

"Chantra," Hugo muttered thoughtfully. The Mage of Fire. She had been lost for years, since Hugo was only a small child. What could Brinley have seen that would give her a clue about Chantra's whereabouts?

"Is it a normal occurrence?" Cannon asked a moment later, clearly thinking along the same lines. "Such visions?"

"Normal?" Animus said airily. "For the Magemother, yes. At least, that is how it has been in times past. From time to time she will receive flashes of insight through dreams and visions, sometimes even direct communication from the gods. Part of her function is to be the connecting link between Aberdeen and the heavens above, though it can't be quite that simple. I remember our previous Magemother telling me she had rarely seen the gods in person. She claimed that her visions were little more than normal dreams, and difficult to distinguish as such." He chuckled. "I suppose we should be grateful that we do not have such challenges."

Hugo grunted. He wasn't in the mood to feel grateful just now. It felt good to be out of the castle and on the road again, but he wished he knew more about what they were doing. "Why doesn't Brinley—I mean, the Magemother, just go herself, Animus? I mean, isn't it her job to look after the mages?"

"She is," Cannon said, "by sending us."

Hugo rolled his eyes, then looked down when he saw Animus watching him.

"It is not wise to doubt the Magemother," Animus said.

Hugo bit his lip, wondering how much Brinley had told him. Maybe she had talked to him this morning. Maybe that's where Animus was before he joined them. "Uh," he said, "did Brinley— I mean, sorry, the Magemother—"

"You may call her by her name if you wish, Hugo."

"Oh. I thought you'd think it was rude," Hugo said.

"I do," Animus said pleasantly. "Or rather, I would, if you were not you. You have a very different relationship with her than I do, however. The two of you are . . . close."

Hugo felt his face flush. He didn't know what Animus meant by that, and he wasn't going to ask. It was true that he liked Brinley, if not lately. But that was the end of it. After all, he was a mage and she was the Magemother. (She *was* pretty, but she was pretty annoying too.) Besides, she was barely fourteen. That would just be . . . weird. "We're just friends," replied Hugo.

"As you say," Animus said.

Out of the corner of his eye, Hugo could see Cannon mouthing the word "close" thoughtfully to himself. But Animus was old, and odd. Maybe he meant something else by the word. Hugo asked another question to change the subject. "Are we taking horses?"

"No," Animus said.

Striding beside Hugo, Cannon stopped short. "Don't tell me we are going to walk just because His *Highness* here can't fly."

"Goodness!" Animus said. "I hope not."

Hugo shook his head, perplexed. "Then how are we going to get to Tourilia?"

"So many questions," Animus said. "Walking is good for the soul. That said, I hope that we can find a faster means of transportation. I intend for you to start learning how to use your powers. If you do not, then it may be difficult for you to survive the next few weeks, and a very long walk besides."

"We could just take him," Cannon said. "I can carry him, if I have to. Please don't make us walk, Animus."

Animus waved a hand. "This is not about you, Cannon. The time has come for Hugo to learn. I still remember the day when you couldn't even make a leaf rustle in the wind."

Hugo grinned, but it disappeared quickly as he realized how ignorant he still was. Animus could disappear into the wind and whisk away at a hundred miles an hour to anywhere at all. He had seen him do it. Cannon wasn't nearly as powerful as his master, but he could certainly get around fast enough. But he had no idea what Animus meant about him learning to travel quickly. "What do you mean?" he asked. "I can't disappear into the wind or anything . . ."

"Hugo," Animus said, "you are the Mage of Light and Darkness. How fast does light travel, do you suppose?"

Hugo shut his mouth. He hadn't thought about it like that before. "But light doesn't move," he protested a moment later. "It's just there. Isn't it?"

"Oh, no," Animus said, shaking his head. "I think you will find that light travels like any other substance, only much faster, and much more directly. Lux could slip into the light itself and be on the other side of the kingdom in a few seconds."

Hugo felt his stomach tighten. His discomfort must have shown on his face, for Animus said, "You don't like to talk about your predecessor."

Hugo shrugged. Generally, he tried to avoid even thinking about the previous Mage of Light and Darkness. Like the rest of Hugo's predecessors, Lux had failed in his role and become consumed by the darkness. On top of that, Lux had nearly killed Hugo once. That is who he would become, Hugo knew, if he wasn't careful.

"No," Hugo said finally. "I don't like talking about him."

"Hey," Cannon said, stopping sharply and poking him in the back of the head, "get over it. Just because he messed up doesn't mean that you will."

Hugo felt his face burn.

"Cannon," Animus said sharply.

Cannon dropped his hand and fell silent, but he didn't apologize.

"As you will learn," Animus said heavily, "my apprentice is brilliant, and almost always right, but tact frequently escapes him."

Cannon nodded thoughtfully.

"However," Animus went on, "we *will* need to speak of Lux Tennebris if you are to learn. The Magemother and I have discussed this at length, and we agree that as you have no master to teach you, your best chance at learning to be a mage is through my memories of your predecessor." He rapped a knuckle against his temple as he spoke.

"Fine," Hugo said. "How do we start? Do you want me to try to pretend that I'm made of light or something?" He looked to the east, imagining what the sun would look like shining over the distant landscape. They had just arrived at the edge of the city, and the lake stretched off to their right.

"Nothing as silly as that," Animus assured him. The mage straightened his belt in a self-conscious way. Perhaps, Hugo thought, *he* was as nervous about instructing Hugo as Hugo was about learning.

"Although this is not my area of expertise," Animus went on, "I had several detailed conversations with Lux on the subject. You might well remember that the Mage of Light and Darkness who preceded him was also corrupt. As such, Lux, like you, was left on his own to discover how to use his powers. Naturally, I was already old by the time he began this journey."

"I hadn't thought about it like that," Hugo said honestly. He kicked a stray rock into the lake and it sank beneath the surface with a loud burp. He was imagining a young Lux, as uncertain and ignorant as himself probably just as determined not to fail, just as afraid of his new calling. That didn't bode well.

"At any rate," Animus said, "the key to communing with the light, as I understand it, does not lie in thought or imagination, but in the senses themselves. Seeing and hearing in particular."

"Seeing and hearing?" Hugo echoed.

"Yes. You already see the light, obviously—though I doubt you see now the way that you will when you have come into your power—so we will start with hearing. Listening to something you are accustomed to merely seeing will force your mind to consider it anew. Your assignment for the remainder of the morning, then, is to listen to the light. Can you hear the moonlight? When the moon fades in a few hours and the sun climbs over the eastern hills, will you hear the change? What will it sound like? How does the noon sun differ from the midnight moon? I will require answers to these questions at dinner. Until then, there will be no talking. Only listening." Animus squinted up at the sky, taking in the wind and clouds with a practiced eye. "Best get to it right away. I think we'll be sorry if we're still walking the day after tomorrow . . ."

Right, listening. Sounds simple enough, Hugo thought, closing his eyes for a few steps as he followed Animus around the northern edge of the lake. He could hear the water moving gently, brushed along the surface by the early morning air. He could hear Cannon's footsteps, and his own. He could hear a bird in the distance.

Listen to the moon. Right . . .

That wasn't silly at all.

Chapter Three

In which there is treasure

BEFORE THE SUN HAD FINISHED rising, Brinley and Tabitha were on their way out of the castle.

"Don't you think you'll be hot in that big coat?" Brinley asked Tabitha, who was wearing a weathered leather coat over her dress. It was much too big for her, and along with her worn boots and bright socks, made her look like a street person.

"Oh, no," Tabitha said. "I couldn't leave my coat behind. Belsie gave it to me. Besides, I need the pockets." She opened it to reveal a plethora of pockets. There were over a dozen of them, and all in odd shapes and sizes. "I have anything we might need in here, you know," Tabitha said.

Brinley hid a grin and glanced at the sun. "I had hoped to leave sooner," she mumbled. People were already milling about in town and it was almost certain that someone would notice the Magemother leaving. Word was sure to get around. That wasn't exactly bad, but she liked being quiet about these things.

"But we still have time for me to say good-bye to someone, don't we?" Tabitha asked.

"What? No, I don't think so. I told you to say your good-byes yesterday, remember?" But Tabitha wasn't listening. She was skipping now, leaving the main road and heading toward the town square. Perfect. Just when she wanted to lay low, Tabitha was skipping through the center of town. This time of day it was sure to be packed with carts and horses and sellers breaking out their wares.

"Just one person," Tabitha called back in a singsong voice. "I just need to say good-bye to one person."

Brinley had learned that by the time Tabitha started singing her words, it was too late to change her mind. Tabitha had her own little world that she often disappeared into, and when she was in there, she was difficult to reason with. Brinley tugged the hood of her green traveling cloak down over her face and jogged to catch up. "Who are we going to see?"

Tabitha giggled. "Maggie. Mad Maggie."

"Mad Maggie?" Brinley asked.

"You'll see," Tabitha sang back, entering the square. "You'll like her."

Several people turned at the sound of her voice. Some smiled. Others rolled their eyes.

"This way," Tabitha called back, leading Brinley to a fountain on one edge of the square.

Next to the fountain, in a corner of the square, there was a small lean-to shelter stuffed under the low-hanging eaves of a blacksmith's shop. It looked like the makeshift shelter of a homeless person. Tabitha approached the door, which was nothing more than half a piece of scrap wood, and knocked loudly.

"She lives in *there*?" Brinley said.

Her question was answered as a wailing voice issued from inside the tiny house. "Go away or I'll bite your face off!"

"She's a bit crazy," Tabitha said matter-of-factly. "That's why we call her Mad Maggie, but she's wonderful." She turned back to the door and knocked again. "It's me!" she sang.

The door sprang open and the most ridiculous-looking woman that Brinley had ever seen stepped out. She was wearing several dresses, at least three, one on top of the other, along with long colorful socks and some tattered knitted mittens, which looked oddly dull against the rest. Brinley guessed that she was bald, but it was hard to be sure; she didn't seem old enough to be bald, and she was wearing what looked like a handmade cap of yellow fabric onto which she had sewn a generous amount of curly doll hair. Beneath her startling exterior were a pair of kind, smiling eyes. She seemed happy to see Tabitha.

"Hello, Apprentice Tabitha," the woman said formally. "Would you and your friend like to come in?"

Brinley glanced at the inside of the hut. It was just big enough to hold a large bucket, turned on its end, and a small, round pad of blankets. No doubt that was the woman's bed, and the bucket was her chair. What would it be like to live in such a place?

"No, thank you," Tabitha said. "But I would like to introduce my friend. This is Brinley."

Maggie waved her hand. "You know I don't speak with anybody but mages and kings, Tabitha," she said, waving her hand loftily. "Ordinary people are boring."

"Brinley isn't ordinary," Tabitha said. "She's the Magemother."

Grudgingly, Maggie turned her attention to Brinley. "Ooh, I see," she said. "Yes, you are quite right. Clearly the Magemother. I suppose I can talk with her. How do you do, Magemother Brinley?"

"Well, thank you," Brinley said with a curtsy. She eyed the drafty door of the hut. "Do you live here year-round?" Brinley was thinking of how cold it must be in the winter. Even now, it must be freezing at night.

Maggie's face fell slightly, but she propped it up with a smile a moment later. "Oh, yes, dear," she said proudly. "Built it myself, I did, and you won't find a finer home in all the city."

"I'm sure I wouldn't," Brinley said. She bit her lip, thinking of everything she had to do and wishing that there was more time to help the woman. "I'm afraid we don't have too much time to get to know one another today, as we are on our way out of town, but perhaps we can have you over for dinner at the castle in the future?"

"Ooh, yes. Food! That would be lovely. And indoors, no less." She turned back to Tabitha. "Can you imagine?"

Before Tabitha could answer, Maggie was speaking again. "You have time for a game of war hands before you go, of course." She spun on her heel and retrieved the bucket from within her hut. She then proceeded to place it on the ground in front of her door, sat down on it, and smoothed out several layers of dresses until they were flat again.

"I'm ready," she said when she had finished, and she held out her fist. "Oh." She plucked the sooty mitten off her hand. "*Now* I'm ready."

Brinley gasped loudly, but covered it by pretending to cough. When Maggie had taken her mitten off, she had revealed a horribly disfigured hand. Three fingers were gray and bloated from repeated frostbite. Brinley felt her gut twist as she looked at Maggie's hands.

Nothing that couldn't be fixed with a decent roof over her head, she thought bitterly.

Tabitha seemed not to notice. Without missing a beat, she sat down cross-legged across from Maggie. "Best out of three?" she asked.

Maggie nodded.

"Oh no," Brinley said with a groan. "You've finally found someone who will play with you."

Tabitha gave her a scathing look. "Of course I did," she said. "It's a fine game. You taught it to me, after all."

It was true. It had happened one night when the two of them had stayed up late, talking into the early hours of the morning. Tabitha had told her all about growing up in the Magisterium, and

Brinley had told her about living in Colorado and four-wheelers and how she had once tried to teach frogs how to do gymnastics.

It was an innocent thing, she had thought, a simple game of Rock-paper-scissors like she used to play with her dad, but for Tabitha it had become an addiction. She kept Brinley up for an hour the following night, and after that Brinley had absolutely refused to play with her again. Since then, Tabitha had been teaching anyone who would listen. Hugo had been her first victim. He lasted two hours before declaring that he would never play with her again. Several of the castle staff had likewise fallen victim to her trap before word had spread. Now most people knew to say no when the question was asked.

"Maggie likes to play," Tabitha said. "Don't you, Maggie?"

"Ooh, yes," the woman said enthusiastically. "Love it, love it, love it! Only best of three?"

Tabitha sighed, holding up her own hand. "It's all we have time for." She held a hand up to her mouth and whispered. "She won't let me stay any longer than that, and we have important things to do."

Maggie gave Brinley a suspicious look.

"Begin," Tabitha said. "Rock, paper, scissors! Paper covers rock. Again. Rock, paper, scissors! Ha! Scissors cuts paper!" She snipped Maggie's hand with her fingers and the woman drew them back in haste, inspecting them with a worried look on her face.

"Just a game, remember?" Tabitha said.

"Yes, of course," Maggie said, holding her hand out again.

They played three more rounds before Brinley finally convinced Tabitha that their original "best of three" were long over.

"But she's winning!" Tabitha objected frantically.

"We have to be going now, Maggie," Brinley told the older woman. "But I think I would like to come and visit you again, if that's all right."

Maggie sighed. Then her face brightened and she leapt from her bucket. "Gifts before you go!"

Brinley gave Tabitha a questioning look while Maggie rummaged in her shack, but the other girl just shrugged.

Maggie emerged with a metal box and presented it to them as if it were the most precious thing in the world. It was made of metal and shaped like an octagon, and reminded Brinley of the fancy tins full of Christmas cookies that she had seen back home. This one was bright red with bluebirds and daisies painted on the top. She turned her head from side to side as if she were checking whether it was safe to reveal her wares, then popped the lid open. "For your journey," she said.

The tin was full of odd baubles and pins, bits of string, a handful of marbles, strangely shaped swatches of fabric, and bits of shiny paper folded into animal shapes. There was a thimble, a mismatched set of dice, sparkling river rocks, bent strands of wire, a rough-looking egg-sized reddish stone, and a day-old apple core. There were a few old metallic objects whose function Brinley was not familiar with. Nothing that looked like it would be valuable to anyone other than Maggie.

"You can have anything your heart desires," Maggie said, "if you have something to give."

Tabitha immediately plucked a button off her dress and deposited it in the tin. "What do you recommend?" she asked, pinching her chin thoughtfully.

"This one," Maggie said, extracting a very old-looking bead of wood and brass. "It will protect you from harm."

"Thank you, Maggie," Tabitha said, then stepped aside and pushed Brinley forward.

"Oh, no, I'm okay," Brinley said, thinking that she didn't want to lose any of her buttons on the first day of the journey.

Tabitha flicked her on the back of the neck.

"Ouch. Okay, okay." She perused the tin and selected a thick wooden button. If nothing else, she thought, it might come in handy if something needed to be repaired on the road.

"Hmm," Maggie murmured, pursing her lips.

"What?" Brinley said.

"Nothing. A fine choice. Very lucky button. Just not what I would have picked for you."

Wondering how a button could be lucky, Brinley started to put it back.

"Oh, no," Maggie said, pulling the tin away. "Choices are final. Now, what will you give me?"

Brinley put the button in her bag and opened her traveling cloak. There was a golden thread that had come loose from the hem. She had noticed it when she was getting dressed. She wrapped the loose bit around her finger and broke it off, offering it to Maggie. "Is this okay? It's real gold, I think."

"Ooh, lovely!" Maggie said, placing it carefully in the tin. She stared at her treasure for a while, lost in thought, and then snapped the lid shut so suddenly that Brinley jumped. "Got to go. Water's on."

She put the tin back inside the hut and brushed past them to the door of the blacksmith's shop.

"She works for him," Tabitha explained.

Curious, Brinley stuck her head into the blacksmith's shop. There she was, on the other side of the room, sitting at a water-powered grinding wheel. She was shaping what appeared to be the cross guard for a sword.

"Can I help you?" a deep voice said.

"Oh," Brinley said, surprised. "No, thank you. Just saying good-bye to Maggie. She left in a hurry, that's all. Bye, Maggie!" she called, then ducked back outside.

The smith followed her out. "She spoke to you?" he asked, sounding surprised. Then he recognized her. "Oh, Magemother. Of course, I suppose she would speak to you, then." A look of apprehension crossed his face. "I try to take as good a care of her as I can, mind."

Brinley wondered if he thought she had come to rescue the woman. He was starting to sweat nervously now. The Magemother was supposed to do that sort of thing, she knew, rescue common people who needed it, right the wrongs of society.

"Honest," he went on. "I give her work to do and food to eat when she wants it. She won't take any money, and she won't take a room neither. Prefers her shanty."

"I believe you," Brinley said, glancing over at the shack. "It's a pity, though. I can't imagine that she is too comfortable in there."

The man took off his cap and wrung it between his hands. "Doesn't make a bit of sense to me. Very proud, that one. Won't accept any help from me beyond her employment."

"She told me that she likes having her own home," Tabitha said. "I expect that's just the best she can make."

The smith nodded slowly. "I suppose." He shook his head. "Any rate, good day to you, Magemother. Call on old Jaship if you're ever in need of a smith."

Brinley nodded.

"That was weird," Tabitha said as they walked back through the square. Brinley was leading them through the fastest route out of town.

"What, Maggie?"

"No," Tabitha said, "the smith. He was afraid you were going to call down fire on him or something."

"Or something," Brinley agreed. "The Magemother is supposed to be a guardian of the people," she explained.

"So?"

"Well," Brinley said as they approached the outer gate, "I have heard that the Magemother will sometimes intervene to help the common people when they get themselves into trouble. Sick, falsely imprisoned, being treated badly, things like that... Tabitha, do you think that Maggie would accept any help from me?"

"I bet she would," Tabitha said. "She has a soft spot for people she thinks are important, and she liked you." Just then Tabitha's coat made a strange squelching sound and Brinley glanced at it. "Tabitha, what was that?"

"Nothing," Tabitha said lightly. "So how is the Magemother supposed to know who needs help in the first place?"

Brinley rolled her eyes. "That's the hard part," she said. "Most people think the Magemother knows everything. Some actually think that she sees everything that happens. Everywhere."

Tabitha laughed. "That's silly." She stopped walking abruptly. "You don't, do you?"

"Of course not," Brinley said, pulling her towards the gate. "The only time anything remotely like that has happened was when I took the power back from the mages." She shivered, remembering. That had been the hardest moment of her life. In order to destroy the previous Mage of Light and Darkness, who had become corrupted by evil, she took back the power from all of the mages at once, which meant that for a short time she held all of it herself. "But that was just temporary," she went on. "After I gave the mages their power back I couldn't feel the air anymore, or the stones, or the animals. I'm more like a common person now than a mage."

Tabitha patted her on the back. "Don't worry," she said. "You'll figure it out eventually." She looked troubled at some thought. "We both will. I have so much to learn."

It was true, Tabitha was apprenticed to Belterras, the Mage of Earth, as well as being the Magemother's Herald, or protector. She had her own mountain of responsibility now, but she seemed to be taking to it better than Brinley was. Indeed, Brinley thought, if she could learn how to be the Magemother half as fast as Tabitha was learning how to be a mage, everything might turn out all right.

At the gate of the city, Brinley and Tabitha paused. Somebody was waiting for them.

"Archibald!" Tabitha said delightedly. "How wonderful! Have you come to see us off?"

Archibald stood with one hand on the city gate, leaning casually on his silver-handled cane with the other. He tipped his bowler hat to them and smiled. "Not exactly," he said. He motioned for them to follow and walked beside them under the gate.

He tapped Brinley on the shoulder with the handle of his cane as they walked, raising one eyebrow high. "A little bird told me about your secret problem," he said. "I have come to offer my services."

"What problem?" Brinley asked, confused.

"The matter of your missing father."

Brinley swung slowly around to face Tabitha, whose eyes had gone wider than she would have thought possible. Tabitha bit her lip, eyes rolling around to look at anything but Brinley.

"It could have been any little bird," Tabitha squeaked. "Not necessarily me."

"You are the only little bird I told, apart from Animus," Brinley said, poking Tabitha in the nose with her finger, which caused Tabitha's eyes to swing inward in an attempt to follow it.

"I couldn't help it!" Tabitha said, wincing as she attempted to uncross her eyes. "It just slipped out, and . . . well, I thought you'd be pleased. Archibald wants to help, and I know how stressed you've been because you want to just drop everything and look for your father, but you can't."

"But I can," Archibald added.

Tabitha cupped her hands over her mouth and leaned in tentatively to whisper in Brinley's ear. "And I know you had another nightmare about him last night. You were talking in your sleep. You have to let Archibald look for him. You just have to!"

"This," Brinley said, looking back and forth between the two of them, "is a conspiracy . . . But," she added to ease the look of panic on Tabitha's face, "it is a welcome one. I would be glad for your help, Archibald."

"Excellent," Archibald said. "Tabitha and I have planned things out already. We have devised a means for me to communicate with you while you're on the road, and I have my pony waiting, packed and ready to go. All that remains is some direction from you. Where should I begin my search?"

"Oh," Brinley said, startled. "I don't know." She proceeded to tell him the full story of her father's disappearance as they walked. She told how the gods had allowed him to accompany her back to Aberdeen from Earth, warning that it would be a dangerous trip for him. She told how his hand had slipped out of hers somehow as they crossed the black void that stretched between worlds, and how he had not come out the other side.

He put a hand on her shoulder when she had finished, pulling her into a hug. "I'm so sorry," he said. "I would have started looking earlier if I had known. No one deserves to lose a father, especially you. You've just lost your mother . . ." He looked down. A second later he cleared his throat with a cough. "At any rate, I believe I shall start my journey with a trip to Ninebridge. I have an old acquaintance there that might know something of this place, this in-between place where you think your father is."

"Really?" Brinley said, surprised that Archibald already had something to go on. "Who is it?"

"Oh," Archibald said, waving his cane dismissively. "An unsavory character. You wouldn't know him."

Brinley nodded. "Do you want us to take you with us? We're headed to Ninebridge right now." She patted Tabitha playfully on the back the way she would a horse. "It's much faster to fly."

Archibald gulped. "Ah, no, thank you. I much prefer to keep both feet firmly on the ground at all times. The back of my pony is as high as I go."

Brinley hugged him, filled with a sudden sense of appreciation. Someone was going to look for her father! True, it wouldn't be her, but it was getting done. She breathed a deep sigh of relief. For the first time in many days she felt her mind resting on the task ahead of her without any guilt in the background. She could focus on finding the mages now. Archibald would take care of things. "Thank you so much," she breathed, squeezing him once more before she let go. "You don't know how much this means to me!"

"Think nothing of it," he said. "It is my privilege." He nodded to them and smiled. For an instant Brinley thought she saw sorrow in his eyes, or maybe regret, but a moment later he had turned away from them.

"Archibald," she called.

Archibald turned.

"Ben," she said. "My father's name is Ben."

Chapter Four

In which a witch gets ants in her pants

CASSIS PACED BACK AND FORTH across the peak of the bridge to the Wizard's Ire, waiting for the Magemother to arrive. The city of Ninebridge was the magical marvel of Aberdeen. It got its name from the nine magical bridges that stood in a circle around the city. Each one rose high into the air and disappeared, and if a person walked past the midpoint they would be transported to the other half of the bridge, located a great distance away. Seven bridges connected seven distant cities in this manner. One bridge was broken and led to nowhere, while the bridge which Cassis stood upon led hundreds of miles to the north, to the most unwholesome place in the land. The Ire was far away, technically, but it felt strangely close when he was standing on the bridge. He stretched his neck restlessly. It wasn't a feeling that he enjoyed.

A horn sounded at the foot of the bridge. He looked down to the soldiers far below him and saw that several of them were facing south, hands shielding their eyes from the morning sun. A giant black swan was descending from the clouds, headed right for the bridge. The bird alighted on the stone railing of the bridge beside the mage and Brinley jumped down from her back.

"Hello, Cassis," she said warmly. "Let's get this over with." There would be no small talk today. She didn't have time for it, and Cassis wasn't the talkative type anyhow. The Mage of Metal was not unlike metal himself: hard, simple, and to the point.

He nodded, then led her to the gray curtain of mist which stretched from the floor of the bridge into the sky above. The side of the bridge that lay beyond the mist was not visible from here, or from the ground.

"This is the protection that your mother ordered the mages to place on the bridge," he said, approaching the mist. He was pointing at a line of gold bricks laid out across the center of the bridge before them. They were arranged such that if you wanted to walk through the mist, you would have to step over the line. "It is a warding line," Cassis said, folding his hands into the sleeves of his robes. "It was made long ago, by the mages of old. It was long before my time. Animus himself was not yet apprenticed. Its magic seems to hinge upon a keyword entrusted only to her. Without the keyword it cannot be removed or altered in any way."

"So my mother is the only one who knows about this now?"

The mage's brow furrowed. "There are rumors that the mages were helped by a wizard named Maazan Dow. He was exceptionally talented when it came to the bridges, and I do not doubt that the rumor is true, but he is of no use to us now. He is locked in the Ire himself, and most likely long dead."

Brinley nodded sullenly. "Okay. So is the line broken? How are the creatures getting across?"

Cassis shook his head. "It appears to be in good working order—except for the fact that Shael's servants continue to cross it, of course. It has long been a mystery as to how they have done so." He straightened his shoulders. "Now, I believe I have the answer."

Brinley raised an eyebrow.

"First I shall explain how it works." Cassis took something from inside his robes, a gold talisman the size of a flattened tangerine. "This medallion is one of a pair. They alone allow a person to cross the warding line." He stepped gingerly across the line to demonstrate, being careful not to step through the actual mist, then returned.

"And without it?" she asked.

"See for yourself."

She regarded the gold bricks hesitantly, judging the distance between them and the mist on the other side. The last thing she wanted to do was stumble accidentally through the mist and end up hundreds of miles away in the Wizard's Ire. She stepped over, and thought for a moment that she would be able to cross it, but as soon as her foot touched the ground on the other side, an invisible vice clamped down in the center of her thigh, causing her to cry out. Her shout was covered up by the deafening sound of a siren. It seemed to be coming from the bridge itself, and she knew that it was a part of the magic.

A troop of soldiers came sprinting up the bridge, swords drawn. Cassis reached out and touched her with the medallion. The thing holding her leg let her go, and to everyone's relief, the siren stopped.

Brinley had expected the soldiers to be alarmed, but instead they wore expressions of mild annoyance. The foremost one, a strong-looking man, spoke to Cassis in an accusing tone.

"Were you playing with the line again, my lord?"

"Not I," the mage said, pointing at Brinley. "The Magemother did it. You can lecture her, if you wish."

The officer coughed nervously. "Of course not," he said, shuffling his feet. "Just give us some warning of your intentions next time."

"Of course," Brinley said, feeling her cheeks go red.

As soon as the soldiers had turned their backs, Brinley rounded on Cassis. He held up his hands to stop her and said, "Now you know."

Brinley nodded, watching the soldiers march back down the bridge. "It is well guarded."

"Extremely well guarded," Cassis agreed. "Captain Mark commands an entire battalion of soldiers stationed at the foot of the bridge to deal with the creatures that have been crossing it every morning."

"I imagine so," Brinley said.

"You said the medallion was one of a pair," Tabitha cut in, addressing Cassis. "Where is the other one?"

"In the king's possession," Cassis said.

"And there is no other way to cross the line?" Brinley said.

"Not without the keyword," Cassis said.

"Which is known only to my mother."

"Perhaps," Cassis said. "There was the wizard who helped her with the spell. He might have known the keyword, or some other secret, which would allow him to replicate the medallions."

"But have you found medallions in the possession of the creatures that have crossed the bridge?" Brinley said.

"No," Cassis said. "There have been five crossings now, in five days. An ogre, an anthropoboar, a troll, a great-horned bear, and a Minotaur. It was the Minotaur yesterday that gave me the clue that I needed. He was the first beast that wore clothing, and in the pocket of his breeches, I found this." He pulled a small cloth bag from his own pocket and opened it to reveal a handful of fine gold dust.

Brinley looked at it doubtfully, unsure how this cleared up the mystery. "And you think this dust," she began, gesturing for him to elaborate.

"Works like our medallions," he said.

"It doesn't look like a medallion," Tabitha mumbled, leaning in to sniff at the dust.

Cassis closed the bag. "No, indeed," he said. "Nor does it have the power to get through the mist any longer." He tossed the dust at the veil of mist and it hit the gray curtain with a little puff and fell to the ground. "But I think it did once," he went on. "We have found this dust in the possession of every creature that has come over this bridge from the Ire. It seems likely to me that it is the dust that allows them to get across, as it seems to have no other function. It may be that it only works for Shael's servants, or perhaps it only works the one time."

"So," Brinley said, "Shael has his own keys now."

"I think so," Cassis agreed. "Keys that are strong enough to take the bearer at least once across. This could also explain how Animus was able to cross the line when he followed the Idris. The creature could have planted some of this dust on him, or he may have touched the Idris and got some on himself, which allowed him to cross over."

Brinley nodded. "You have done well, Cassis. Will you share your findings with the king? I think he sent me here to see if I could remember whatever power the Magemother has over the bridge, but the keyword is not magically occurring to me. I expect we will have to wait for my mother to pass it down to me. Until then, this should help to ease his mind."

Cassis nodded. "As we suspected, but the king has to be satisfied, eh?" He grinned at her and she smiled back, glad that he understood.

Brinley was suddenly serious. "Cassis," she said, "what about the other matter we discussed?"

Cassis looked confused for a moment, then smiled. "Of course," he said, and withdrew something from the pockets of his robes with a flourish. "Your—what do you call it?—pensill?"

"Pencil," Brinley said, grinning. She took the thin metal rod from his hand almost reverently. Art had been her passion back home, and she dearly missed drawing. There was nothing in Aberdeen but quills and ink and some terrible colored wax sticks worse than crayons. In what she considered a stroke of genius, however, she had described pencils to Cassis and set him to work on it.

"I think you'll find it meets all of your specifications," Cassis said. "Though I found it quite impossible to sheath the writing medium in wood as you described. I daresay we will need Lignumis for such a thing. However, I did come up with an alternative."

"It's brilliant!" Brinley beamed. She twisted one end of the metal tube and the lead eased out of the other. "They have these where I'm from," she said. "They're called *mechanical* pencils."

Cassis's face fell slightly. "Ah," he said. "And here I was thinking I had done something unique."

"Oh, no," Brinley spluttered. "But it's wonderful, Cassis. Simply wonderful!" She slipped the notebook from her bag and tried it out. "The lead is a bit hard, though."

Cassis cleared his throat. "Actually, it is not lead at all," he grumbled. "It's a simple planar carbon construction infused with clay for hardness . . . less clay would make it softer, I suppose, though I daresay it would change the shade."

"Exactly," Brinley said, beaming at him. She went up on tiptoes and kissed him on the cheek. "Thank you, Cassis. It really is wonderful."

Cassis's stern face went slightly pink, and he grumbled something unintelligible. Then he folded his arms. "Very well, Magemother," he said, his smile returning. "It shouldn't be hard to make you a veritable array of these . . . *pencils*." He glanced up at the sun. "It is nearing midday. We had best be off the bridge when the attack comes."

"I will leave you to it, then," Brinley said, and Cassis gave her a polite bow.

As soon as they were airborne again, Brinley relaxed. She was looking forward to seeing Habis, and to getting some of her questions answered. She was determined to give the woman a hard time for missing the meeting. No doubt she simply couldn't bring herself to visit with King Remy. She was a witch, after all, and had spent most of her life fighting against the Paradise kings.

Brinley examined her new pencil again, then wound her hair into a sloppy bun and stuck the pencil through it. She gave a relaxed sigh, feeling more like herself than she had in weeks.

They soared together across the city toward the seventh bridge, which would transport them to the city of Cemlin in Aquilar, which was near the forest of Kokum, where Habis lived. As they neared the bridge, Brinley heard a faint whining sound.

The siren again.

"I hope everything is okay," Brinley said, wondering if they should go back to investigate.

"Do you want to turn around?" Tabitha asked.

Brinley shook her head. "No. I'm sure they will be fine. None of the monsters seem to have been any trouble for them yet. Anyway, we've waited long enough to see Habis. She had better be home."

❖ ❖ ❖

When they found her, Habis was in her garden shelling peas. Brinley almost did not recognize her at first. The first time Brinley had seen her, Habis had been wearing an eerie cloak of thin, flesh-colored skin. Now a close-fitting set of gray cotton clothes gave her a clean, monk-like appearance.

Tabitha landed on a large stump in the middle of the garden and Brinley dismounted. Tabitha didn't bother changing back into herself. Instead she started munching on some nearby greenery in the garden.

"Get out of my cabbage, you blasted bird!" Habis shouted. "What kind of swan eats cabbage?"

With a small pop the swan was gone and Tabitha was there, her hands firmly planted on her hips. "I'll have you know," she said indignantly, "that swans eat all kinds of greenery, and though we do prefer spinach, we go for cabbage when we have to." Tabitha blinked, surprised at her own vehemence, and then turned to pick at another cabbage leaf.

"I know that," Habis said. "I just wanted to see if it was you. Tabitha, they call you, yes? I heard that Brinley picked a young shape-shifter as her herald. Stupid choice, I thought." She was circling Tabitha now, eyeing her critically from head to toe while Tabitha fidgeted nervously under her gaze.

"Leave my herald alone, Habis," Brinley said, and the witch turned to her as if she had just noticed Brinley was there.

"My goodness, if it isn't the Magemother herself! Come to lecture me for missing my meeting with the king, no doubt. Or perhaps she has come to strike another bargain. Well, I won't have it. Nope. Not again."

Brinley smiled. She had once crept into Habis's evil sister's lair and stolen a ring in exchange for some help. She held up her hands in surrender. "No deals," she said. "Though it looks like the last one worked out quite well for you."

Habis glanced around at her garden. The beautiful plants had grown up remarkably fast. They had not been there weeks before, when Brinley had first met the witch. Indeed, the exterior of Habis's lair was completely changed. There were flowers all around the edge of the garden. There was even a flower pot hanging from a nail in the sheer rock wall where her secret front door was concealed. "Habis," Brinley said, "I don't know how secret your secret house is anymore. You might as well hang up a welcome sign." Brinley was thinking of all the witches who, since Habis had clearly switched sides during the battle at Caraway Castle, would now be eager to see harm come to the woman.

"What?" Habis asked, looking up as she shelled the last of the peas. "Oh, don't be stupid. I don't live here anymore. The house is a trap. Take one step inside and you'll be in a world of hurt." She smiled deviously. "It seemed a pity to waste this place, so I have been keeping up appearances. I trap a witch a week, on average . . ." she trailed off regretfully. "Though most of them could hardly be called witches."

Brinley hid a smile, remembering the rather high opinion that Habis had of herself.

"Would you like to meet one of my prisoners?"

"Prisoners?" Brinley said.

"Dung!" Habis shouted at the top of her voice. "Get over here, Dung, the Magemother's here with her bird!"

At her shout, a very odd-looking young man came striding around the corner of the rock wall, carrying a bucket in each arm. He was remarkably lanky, as if Habis had somehow plucked a human string bean right out of her garden. He had a face like a mean fish, but beyond that he looked nice enough.

"Wheresa bird?" he asked, looking from Brinley to Tabitha to Habis. "Wheresa bird?"

"Here," Tabitha said brightly, becoming the swan again.

"Ooh, pretty," Dung said, reaching out to pet her long black tail feathers. "For dinner?" he asked eagerly.

"Absolutely not," Tabitha said, returning to her normal form.

Dung jumped back in surprise and glared at Tabitha for a long moment. "Abtholutely not," he said slowly, as if he had come to the conclusion on his own. He turned and began to empty the buckets into the garden. "Pretty bird," he muttered to himself. "Abtholutely don't eat it."

Habis chuckled. "He used to serve that rotten sister of mine. She came looking for me," she said, winking conspiratorially. "Unfortunately she had the good sense not to come into the house." She jabbed a finger at Dung. "She sent him in instead, just to test things out."

"Looks like he caught the brunt of it," Tabitha said, still watching the lanky man work.

Habis waved her hand. "He was like that before. I was able to repair the damage done to him by my little trap. Needless to say, he was glad to leave my sister's employ."

Brinley gave Habis a skeptical look. "And his name is really Dung?"

"I don't know," Habis said. "He couldn't remember what his name was after my living room hit him, so I started calling him Doug. He can't pronounce it though . . . kept getting confused, so I've given in to saying it like he does, and he's much happier now."

They were interrupted as Dung dropped his buckets and stared up at the tree line behind them. Tabitha laughed at the look on his face, and Brinley almost did the same. He looked not unlike a dog hearing the dinner bell. If he had ears made to perk up, she had no doubt that they would have.

"What is it, Dung?" Habis said, eyes narrowing.

"Baddies comin' this way."

"Baddies?" Brinley asked, searching the trees herself now.

"Dung is much like a watchdog," Habis explained. "Sensing the near future seems to be one of his little gifts—no doubt the reason my sister kept him around for so long."

"Should we hide?" Tabitha asked, taking a step closer to Brinley.

"No," Habis said. "His good and bad has been a bit mixed up since his accident. We don't have to worry unless he tells us friends are coming."

There was a crash from the tree line and a horse came flying out of it at a full gallop, carrying a soldier.

"Well, he's in a hurry," Habis said.

Brinley had never seen a horse move so fast. Horse and rider seemed to blur together as they raced across the field toward them. Both seemed bred for speed. The rider was short and lithe and wore no armor. Apart from the long, narrow, single-handed sword at his side, he carried no other gear.

"Magemother," the man said, dismounting smoothly before the horse had come to a stop.

"You are going to kill your horse!" Tabitha said, poking him roughly in the chest as she hurried to the animal. Sure enough, the large black horse was dripping with sweat. His breathing was coming in ragged gasps.

The soldier ignored her. "Magemother," he said, "I have pursued you since you left the bridge this morning. I am sent to you by Captain Mark with urgent news."

"What happened?" Brinley asked. "We heard the alarm sound as we passed out of Ninebridge, but we assumed it was the normal daily challenge."

"It was," the soldier said. "It was an ogre. Nothing we haven't seen before. But the first ogre was just a distraction."

"The *first* ogre?" Habis said.

The soldier nodded. "Just as we engaged the first, a second came hurtling through the mist. It caught us quite by surprise, I am afraid. We have had a breach."

"It got through?" Brinley asked, glancing back at the direction the soldier had come, half expecting to see the ogre burst out of the trees.

"Yes," the soldier said. "And it wasn't alone. There were two figures on its back. One of them was the March witch. Several of us recognized her from the attack on Caraway Castle.

"And the other?" Habis demanded.

"A man, or a boy, we couldn't tell. Wrapped in a black cloak."

"Did they make it out of the city?" Brinley asked.

The soldier nodded. "They are not more than a half an hour behind me. I caught a glimpse of the ogre in the distance. He looks formidable. He must have been, to make it out of Ninebridge alive. I was sent away as soon as he appeared, so I didn't see it happen."

"We haven't a moment to lose," Habis said. "I take it you were on the bridge before they came out, Brinley?"

"Yes," Brinley said, thinking of how close it must have been. "Moments before."

"Then we must assume you are the target."

They will probably not be fooled," she added to the soldier, "but it would be good if you get back on your horse and keep riding."

The soldier nodded his agreement. "Best case, they will follow me and we will be able to outpace them."

"Yes," Habis said, "though not likely."

"At least let him have some water before you go," Tabitha said, picking up one of Dung's half-empty buckets from the ground.

The soldier paused at the look on Tabitha's face. "Very well, but be quick."

The horse took three deep gulps, after which Tabitha tipped his head sideways and poured the remaining water under his lip.

"Where did you learn that?" the soldier asked, surprised. "I misjudged you."

"I know about horses," Tabitha said simply, "and a great many other things."

The soldier mounted his horse again. "Then you should know that a Gan-Garan stallion like this can run at a full gallop for nine hours straight, though he'll be wasted the rest of the week."

"There are no other Gan-Garans like this one, I think," Tabitha said shrewdly. She patted the horse appreciatively and whispered something in its ear. Like a rocket, the horse bolted away, causing the soldier to shout in surprise.

"What did you say to him?" Brinley asked, impressed. She was constantly amazed at Tabitha's ability with animals.

"I told him that an ogre was after him," Tabitha said darkly.

"Well, don't just stand there waiting to get eaten," Habis said, shoving them in the back. "Get inside."

"Inside what?" Brinley asked, looking around.

"My house!" Habis said. The witch had dropped to her hands and knees and was crawling straight at a large boulder. "Just pretend it's a hole," she said and disappeared into it.

Brinley closed her eyes and crawled after Habis, doing her best to pretend that the large, very solid-looking boulder before her was a hole. Sure enough, the impact never came. She kept crawling for a few strides, just to make sure, then opened her eyes to the most wonderful crystal room. It wasn't really crystal, she knew. Rather, it was made of some shimmering magical material which allowed them to see exactly what was happening outside. Apart from the strange nature of the walls, the space was quite cozy. There was a perfect little iron stove in the corner with a pot of tea boiling, and several comfortable chairs. Brinley was pleased to see that Habis's living room was no longer decorated like an apothecary.

"Wow," Tabitha said, appearing behind Brinley. "This is a very nice boulder, Habis."

"Thank you." Habis stuck her head back outside the boulder. "Get in here, Dung! What are you doing?"

Brinley, looking for the source of the problem, saw Dung standing in the middle of the garden, holding a pitchfork and trying to look threatening.

"Idiot," Habis spat. "He's going to get himself killed this time for sure. He fancies himself as my protector."

"I'll get him," Tabitha said.

"No, wait!" Habis began, but Tabitha was already through the boulder.

As it turned out, Dung needed quite a bit of convincing to come into hiding, and when they were halfway back to the boulder, the ogre burst through the trees.

At first glance, Brinley thought it looked like a mix between a large man and a dinosaur. It had thick, green, scaly skin, a bald head with human features, and legs as thick as tree trunks. Large as it was, it moved with remarkable precision as it crossed the field toward the two figures, now staring at it, motionless. The witch, March, sat upon its shoulders, draped in a deep green robe, but there was no sign of the cloaked figure that the soldier had mentioned. Tabitha glanced at the boulder and then back at the house, clearly wondering whether it was wise to lead her enemies back to her friends.

Brinley wanted to run out and help, despite the fact that she knew she would be of little aid, but Habis had an iron grip on her arm.

"Come on, girl," Habis whispered, watching Tabitha. "Go into the house." Then she said to Brinley, "If that empty-headed herald of yours doesn't head for the house I'm going to have to go out there."

Luckily, out in the field, Tabitha was thinking the same thing. "Let's go!" she cried when the ogre was halfway to them. "This way!"

Dung followed her to the edge of the garden, but when she opened the front door to the trap house and he realized what she was doing, he stopped dead in his tracks.

"Dung no go in there. No more!" Dung said, shaking his head. The ogre was only feet away now. Tabitha reached out and pulled him forcefully inside, slamming the door shut behind them. She looked around, careful not to take more than one step into the room. She did risk a step to the side, hoping that if the ogre barreled through, it wouldn't knock her forward into whatever trap awaited.

To her surprise, the ogre did not immediately follow them. She had expected the door to crash inward and the trap to spring, but there was nothing, only silence. Then she heard breathing, sniffing. He was on the other side of the door, smelling for them. There was a guttural growl as the ogre placed one large hand on the door and pushed inward. The door flexed a few inches, and Tabitha found herself looking right into the ogre's eyes. His nostrils flared when he saw her, and he let out a bellow.

"Follow them, you beast!" March yelled from outside.

She must have dismounted. He released the door, and a second later hit it so hard that it splintered as he barreled through.

As soon as he was through the door, Tabitha grabbed Dung and pushed him back outside. Better to be out in the open with a witch than inside a trap when it springs. They had only just cleared the threshold when an immense grinding, thrashing sound issued from behind them. Tabitha tumbled to the ground, turning to see the two sides of the house slamming together like the jaws of a mouth. The ogre bellowed.

"Blast! Where is the Magemother?" March asked. Tabitha jumped to her feet, turning to face her.

"Mistress!" Dung shouted, raising his hands and running towards March. "Go away! Go away!"

"Ah," March said, striding toward him. "My favorite fool. Serving my sister now, I see." She raised her hand and Dung was blasted from his feet, landing hard and hitting his head against a rock. He was still breathing, but he didn't get up. March raised her hand to finish the job, then paused as Tabitha shouted at her.

"Stop!"

March turned back. "What do you want, little girl? Are you going to try and stop me?"

"I'm not a little girl," Tabitha said, fists clenching at her sides. "I'm the Magemother's Herald." With a sound like a gunshot, Tabitha's body exploded into a thousand shimmering pieces. The pieces flashed and fluttered, catching the air. It took a moment for March to realize what they were.

"Butterflies?" she said with a little laugh. "Butterflies?"

The butterflies swarmed the witch, covering her in a cloud of soft, brightly colored wings. A flash of blue light erupted from the center of the cloud and several butterflies vanished. The light flashed again and again. Soon there were only a few butterflies left and Tabitha was forced to change back into herself. She was panting, clutching at her side.

"Impressive," March said, grinning at her, "but hardly effective."

"I don't know about that," Habis said, causing March to spin around in surprise. While March had been distracted by the butterflies, Habis had come up on her from behind. Before March could defend herself, a bolt of red light from Habis's hand struck her squarely in the stomach and she buckled over, grunting. Habis picked a little stone out of the stream that ran in front of the boulder she lived in and chucked it at her sister. It grew exponentially in the air so that it was ten feet across by the time it reached March. The witch ducked and rolled to the side to avoid it.

Meanwhile, Tabitha had become distracted by the house. The sounds coming from it were now punctuated by a vicious roaring from the ogre. The house seemed to be struggling to digest him. As she watched, one of the ogre's thick feet came crashing out of the kitchen window. Then it withdrew again. There was a low-pitched pounding noise and the house shook. The ogre was beating it from the inside. A moment later the jaws of the house opened and it gave a deep, sonorous belch.

"It's going to spit him back out!" Tabitha shouted. But Habis had her hands full with her sister. March was swinging a wicked-looking black sword that she had conjured out of thin air, hacking apart a small army of grass soldiers that Habis had created out of the field upon which they stood.

"Why are you hiding the Magemother from me?" March shouted angrily. "Are you so far gone as to help *her* over your own blood?"

Habis made no response other than to bend down and lift two more grass soldiers out of the ground with her hands. They saluted her and hurried off to join the fray. "And what is it you want with her, dear sister?" Habis said, bending over to lift another soldier out of the ground, this one a horseman.

March snarled, flicking her wrist in a complicated motion to produce a spear made out of what looked like smoke. She threw it at the approaching horseman and it hit him, evaporating as it touched him. The damage was done, however, and the grass that he was made from began to smoke at the edges, then flame. He stumbled among his peers, catching two of his fellow soldiers on fire before he fell apart. March gave a satisfied smile. "I need her help to open a certain box."

"You were the only one that ever wanted our father back," Habis said. "I like him just fine where he is."

March cut the last grass soldier in half and stepped over the pile of clippings to stand before her sister. Meanwhile, the house gave another loud belch. "You can't beat me," she whispered.

Habis shrugged. "Not alone, perhaps," she said. "Tabitha?"

Tabitha was looking at the boulder where Habis's real house was hidden. She thought she had seen something there—

someone—tapping on the rock. But there was nothing there, and Habis needed her help. Tabitha shrank out of sight. She became an ant. Not a very threatening opponent, perhaps, but it was the only thing that she could think of. The first thing she did was run for the house. If she was lucky, if she knew ants at all, they would be close by, near the foundation. She found them. She could smell the queen. Ants, like bees (and mages), could communicate and coordinate with each other over great distances without speaking. She called to them, every ant under the foundation, and they gathered to her. She kept calling and calling, until every ant within a hundred yards was scurrying to her aid. In under a minute, she had an army.

Above the soil, Habis and March were at it again. The house was positively churning now, struggling to keep the ogre inside.

Then the ants came. They burst from the ground at March's feet like a fountain, engulfing her. They were a foot thick around her ankles, biting her, swarming under her clothes. She screamed in horror, unsure how to defend herself, and began to dance about, trying to shake them off. Then the house shuddered, its jaws opening wide to release the biggest belch yet, the ogre along with it. It hit the ground not far from where March was dancing, and she ran for it, leaping onto its back.

"Run!" she bellowed.

There were ants rising out of the ground everywhere now, crawling up the ogre's legs. He stomped around for a moment, trying to crush them, then bolted for the trees. As he fled, one ant detached itself from the horde, falling to the earth. Tabitha popped back into her normal size, brushing her hands together in a satisfied way as she walked back to Habis.

"Very impressive," the witch said appreciatively. She turned and looked at the boulder. "And the Magemother actually stayed put like I told her to. Even more impressive."

Tabitha nodded. "She did, didn't she?"

"Of course, I *did* tie her up." Habis grinned. "Just in case."

Less than a mile away, March flung herself over the top of a waterfall and fell twenty feet into the churning plunge pool. Most of the ants released her when she hit the water, and those that did not were forced away as she stood in the waterfall's stream. When she was free of them, she waded to the bank and pulled her sopping body onto it, glancing up as the Janrax slipped out from behind a tree.

"Having fun?" he said.

She ignored him. "Did it work?"

"Yes," he said. "I was able to slip by quite unnoticed. I was able to locate the entrance to your sister's house before your little battle was over, and confirmed that the Magemother is indeed inside." He fingered one of the carved figures in the handle of his wand, a strange twisted man with the head of a snake. "It should be no trouble at all to sneak in during the night and release the first of my servants."

March eyed the wand uneasily. "What are they, these *haunts* of yours?"

"Different things," he said. "Birds and beasts and men, all of them desperate enough in life to make a terrible bargain."

"To serve you in death?" she asked, guessing the truth. "But why do you insist on targeting the Magemother when my father's instructions were for you to bring down the mages themselves?"

The Janrax twisted his wand, running his fingers along the figures. "My servants assault the psyche of their targets. They infiltrate the mind, poison the heart with fear. The Magemother would be sure to notice if all her mages became ... troubled, haunted at the same time. She would be sure to investigate. Likely she would liberate them with little trouble. So she must not notice. She must be haunted herself. Only if she takes the haunt herself will it be safe to proceed with the others.

"Takes the haunt?" March asked.

"Like a drug," the Janrax explained. "She must take it, accept it into herself, and believe the haunt for the effects to be real."

"How long until we can tell if she has taken the haunt?"

"Days," he said. "Maybe less."

March folded her arms, forcing herself to stop shivering. "You will watch her, I suppose?"

He shook his head. "I have no need to watch. I will know if she takes the haunting. I will accompany you in your work, if that is your desire, until the time comes for me to visit the mages."

"Very well," she said, wringing out her clothing as best she could. "We will leave in the morning, when your work is finished. We have a message to deliver to the Mage of Light and Darkness."

Chapter Five

In which Hugo tries to duel a chicken

A DAY AND A HALF after Hugo had begun listening to the moon, he was still walking in silence, and he was about to explode. He had been unable to answer Animus's questions at the end of the first day, but the older mage hadn't seemed surprised. Now Cannon was trying to cheer him up.

"It took me weeks to feel the wind for the first time after I really started trying."

Hugo cringed. *If I don't have some kind of breakthrough quick*, he thought, *I am going to go crazy*. It was the middle of the day, and it was hot, and they still had at least five more hours of walking. Hugo pulled a map out of his bag and consulted it. By his calculations, it would take another two weeks to get to Tourilia if they continued at this rate. He shoved the map into his bag angrily.

"What has that map done now?" Animus said seriously.

"I don't know why we didn't just go through Ninebridge," Hugo spat. "We could have been there in a couple days, even walking."

"As usual, the purpose of this particular journey does not depend solely on reaching our destination," Animus said.

"I figured you would say something like that," Hugo said.

Animus nodded. "That is because you are very wise. Can you tell me, then, what our other purpose is?"

"Training me, I suppose." *Or torturing me.* Hugo cleared his throat. "You picked a route that would take us forever, so that I would feel extra pressure to figure out my powers. You even made up an arbitrary deadline. 'The day after tomorrow,' you said. I suppose you thought that the pressure would make my powers slip out somehow." *But it didn't work.*

Animus winked pleasantly. "Very astute. Yes, I have often found that it is easier to succeed myself when the stakes are high. You are, however, incorrect on the last point. Your deadline was not arbitrary."

"What?" Hugo said. "Why a day and a half, then?"

"Ah," Animus said seriously, coming to a stop beside Hugo and straightening up. Hugo was surprised again at how tall the mage was. He was head and shoulders above Hugo, a fact that was easy to forget when they were separated by a few feet on the road. Animus was studying the sky again, twisting the end of his beard between his finger and thumb. "Because of the weather."

"What?"

"There will be terrible weather later today," Animus said. His eyes settled on a mass of clouds on the northern horizon. "I daresay you will not enjoy this evening at all."

As if in agreement, a peal of thunder sounded in the distance.

❖ ❖ ❖

Two hours later, Hugo was miserable. He was soaked through, but the rain wasn't the worst of it. The worst part was the cold. Being the king's son, he had the very best traveling clothes that money could buy. He had even taken his blanket out of his bedroll and put it around his shoulders under his cloak, but with enough wind and rain, it was impossible to stay warm. He clung to the thought that he was not cold enough to die.

Animus was just as soaked as Hugo, which was more than a bit surprising. No doubt Animus had the power to shield himself from the rain. He could probably make the whole storm blow away. But he didn't. He was suffering right alongside Hugo. He was probably doing it just to make Hugo feel guilty. Or maybe he wanted Hugo to experience the consequences of his actions but didn't think it was fair to spare himself the discomfort and leave Hugo to suffer by himself. Either way, they were both miserable.

Cannon, on the other hand, had no such qualms about staying dry. A halo of clear air hung about his shoulders, deflecting every raindrop before it could fall on him. He was even whistling. Whistling! *Curse him . . . What a nincompoop.*

Hugo liked him well enough, sometimes. Sometimes they got along just fine. And then there were times like today, when Cannon would annoy him for no reason. *He's probably jealous,* something whispered in his mind. That made sense. Cannon was used to being the smartest one around, the star pupil of the Wind Mage and all that. No doubt he felt a bit threatened around Hugo. After all, Hugo was younger than Cannon and he was a full mage already, while Cannon was still an apprentice.

Cannon's mouth moved then, but Hugo couldn't hear him over the screaming wind and rain and the occasional cracking of hail against his skull. "What?" Hugo shouted over the din.

"Can—you—hear—the—light—yet?" Cannon was laughing now. Laughing. That pig-headed, arrogant fool. How could someone laugh at a time like this? *This is the worst moment of my life*, Hugo thought bitterly. He stopped himself. No, there had been worse ones. But this was definitely a low point.

"Cheer up, Hugo!" Cannon shouted, stepping closer so that Hugo could hear him more easily. "Think of the stories."

"Stories?"

"This will make a great story someday, won't it? When you're a crotchety old king with grandchildren to entertain?"

"Maybe," Hugo said glumly. "But don't you think this is a bit much to go through just for a story?"

Cannon shook his head. "No way. This is what it's all about," he said. "Stories, Hugo . . . Stories."

❖ ❖ ❖

During a brief break in the storm, Hugo took his shirt off and wrung it out, shivering in the temporary sunlight.

"Enjoy it while it lasts," Cannon said, smirking.

"Hey," Hugo said, hitting Cannon in the shoulder. He hit him firmly, but not so hard that it couldn't be passed off as playful. "I'll tell you what I would enjoy." He stepped off the road and picked up two long, thin branches that had fallen from a tree in the storm. He handed one of them to Cannon. "Practice swordplay with me," Hugo said, unsheathing his real sword and laying aside his pack.

"No, thank you," Cannon said, handing the branch back.

Hugo didn't take it. "What?" he teased. "Chicken?"

Cannon dropped the branch at Hugo's feet. "I am not chicken," he said, as if he found the expression distasteful. "I am not poultry of any kind. I simply have no desire to engage in such a pointless exercise."

"It's not pointless," Hugo said. "I have to master the sword if I'm going to be a knight. And I'm *going* to be a knight. You have to be a knight to be a king. I mean, it's not actually in the rules, but everyone knows it. A king who can't use his own sword just looks like an idiot. You wouldn't want to be responsible for making the future king look like an idiot, would you, Cannon?"

Cannon smiled mischievously. "Here you are, shirtless, in the middle of nowhere, with your sword and your bag lying in the mud, holding a pair of sticks," he said. "The future king already looks like an idiot. I don't think my playing stick swords with him will make any difference."

Hugo cringed. Then he dropped the sticks and put his shirt back on. "Fine," he said. "But someday, when I'm a ridiculously powerful mage and the High King of Aberdeen, and you're a crotchety old Wind Mage, you're not going to be able to say no to me anymore, and then I'm going to kick your butt in a stick fight."

He had meant it to sound insulting, but Cannon started laughing, and Hugo found himself struggling not to smile.

"Excuse me," Animus said, walking over to them. "Did someone just call me old and crotchety?"

Hugo and Cannon looked at each other, then they both burst into laughter.

Hugo's good mood didn't last long, however.

The rain had started again.

❖ ❖ ❖

That night they camped beneath an old stone bridge. The bridge had been built over an old irrigation ditch, and water from the overflowing land coursed around them, but the little island in the center was dry, and dry spots were hard to come by at a time like this. In truth, it was more than Hugo had dared hope for. The cold wasn't as bad when you weren't being rained on.

With the three of them all huddled in together, there was no room to lie down. They could only sit there, back to back, and listen to the rain. Cannon was asleep, of course, though how a person could sleep sitting up was beyond Hugo. He doubted he was going to get five minutes of shut-eye tonight. On top of that, he was ravenously hungry, and there would be no fire, only dried meat from his pack for dinner. He reached in and pulled out a soaked piece of jerky.

Would you like some very wet cheese? Animus's voice sounded in his head, making him jump. *That meat smells quite nice, if you have some to spare.*

Sure, he responded, passing over a piece of meat. Animus deposited what looked like a sturdy white booger into his hand. If it had once been cheese, it was not any longer.

I still haven't gotten used to this mind talking thing that we do. I didn't even know about it before I was a mage, Hugo said conversationally.

Yes. It can be very useful in times like this.

They ate in silence for a while, and then Animus stirred. Hugo, who had left his mind open to the other mage, noticed a sense of discomfort emanating from him. *Sorry*, he said automatically.

For what?

Uh, well, I felt you getting uncomfortable. I didn't know that I could feel your feelings like that. I mean, Brinley feels mine from time to time, or so she tells me, but I didn't know that the mages could do it with each other.

Ah, yes, Animus said. *That can happen. Usually you will find that crotchety old mages like myself will keep their feelings quite guarded.*

Hugo didn't know how to take that. It didn't seem like a compliment by any means. He decided to say nothing. After a while, Animus stirred again, the same way he had done before. This time Hugo felt nothing from him. He had been shut out.

I have something for you, Animus said slowly. *I am not excited to give it to you, but I think you will need it.*

Hugo raised his head curiously. *What?*

See for yourself. Animus passed something over his shoulder and Hugo reached up to take it. It appeared to be a small folding pocket mirror. It was metal on the outside, and Hugo could tell that it was very old. On one side, the lid had been polished, but when he flipped it over, the opposite side was rough. It seemed to have developed a heavy patina, probably over a period of many years. He started to open it.

Take care, Animus said. *Do not forget yourself.*

Hugo stopped, the mirror halfway open, and snapped it shut. *Animus, whose mirror is this?*

The old mage sighed. *It is yours now, I suppose. It belonged to Lux . . . Every Mage of Light and Darkness has carried it, as far as I know.*

Hugo flipped it over again in his hands. One side was light, the other dark.

Where did you get it?

I took it from Lux's body on Calypsis. I thought that the next mage might need it at some point, though if I am being honest, I had hoped that I was wrong about that.

Why? Hugo asked. *Why have you waited so long to give this to me?*

Animus was silent for a while as the rain increased in volume again. *The Magemother gave this to Lux when he was old enough . . . He was never the same after that.*

Hugo felt a little chill. So this was it . . . This was how it began. This was the thing that would change him. He knew, of course, what would be inside— *who* would be inside. It would be the same person that he had seen in the mirror in the dungeons of Caraway Castle. His other half, as it were . . . his darkness.

Have you named him yet? Animus asked.

Named him? Hugo said.

Lux told me once that he had to name the darkness in order to control it.

Well, Hugo said coldly, *that didn't turn out so well for him. Maybe he was wrong.*

Maybe, Animus said. *Only you can decide, of course, but I think it is good to name the things that frighten us most. It makes them easier to deal with.*

What would you name him? Hugo asked.

That question, of course, is not appropriate for me to answer. Given that the governance of darkness is your affair, I cannot name the darkness any more than you can name the wind. It would be like naming another person's child. What would you name it?

Hugo folded his arms. *I don't know. I suppose I could just call him what he is.*

And what is he?

Darkness.

Animus shifted, bumping Cannon's knee and causing him to splutter mid-snore. *That is what Lux did, in a way. Tennebris is an old word for darkness.*

Great. So Lux had done the same thing he had been about to do? That made him want to do something else.

You do not have to decide now, of course, Animus said.

Hugo relaxed slightly. He flipped the mirror over again in his hands. What would happen if he opened it? Should he do it now? Or should he wait until later? Should he really open the mirror at all? It sounded dangerous. He turned it over in his hand again. It felt dangerous too. Evidently Animus thought that it was necessary. Perhaps it was.

Of course, there was only one way to find out. He flipped the mirror open and stared at the face that was staring back at him.

Chapter Six

In which there is some very nasty bread

"IF—YOU—EVER—DO—THAT—AGAIN," Brinley said as Habis cut the ropes that held her to the sofa.

"You'll what?" Habis asked defensively. "Make me a mage? Bah! If I hadn't restrained you, you would have rushed out there and probably been killed. I saved your life."

"I'm not completely helpless," Brinley said. She let out a puff of air, blowing the bangs out of her eyes. "Anyway, won't they come back?"

"Possibly," Habis said.

"The ants will not give up for a while," Tabitha assured them.

"We had better get a move on, then," Habis said. "They did not discover my new house, so we should be safe here, as long as we can lay a convincing trail for them to follow if they come back."

They followed her outside and met Dung, who was nursing a bruise on his head where he had landed on the rock, but otherwise appeared to be okay. Together, they set to work leaving a false trail of their departure. It was easy, really. They ran around a bit as if confused and deciding what to do, then they grouped up and walked through the field and past the tree line into the forest, opposite the way the ogre had come.

After Habis judged that they had gone far enough in to the woods, Tabitha, in swan form, ferried them back to the invisible house. This allowed them to get back without leaving any traces of their return.

"Now," Habis said, picking up a handful of shredded rope from her floor and glaring at Brinley, "what did you come here to ask me? Or is there some other calamity that you would like to bring upon me first?"

"No," Brinley said. "It's about this." She held up the naptrap.

"Ah," Habis said, walking over to take it. "Dung, leave us."

Dung, who had just followed them into the house, nodded his head and turned back for the door.

"Not that way!" Habis said. "Do you want to get eaten by an ogre?"

"No."

"Then just go sit in the cellar or something instead."

He nodded again and left the room through a small hallway at the back.

Habis inspected the vial. "It looks good. Seal intact, no signs of color change. You know, when they turn black, whatever you've placed in it has died, but this looks fine. I'm sure she is quite all right in here. Still in stasis." Habis handed the vial back. "You'll be happy to know that I did a little digging as you requested, to see if there is any easy way to heal her."

"And?" Brinley asked, trying not to get her hopes up.

"There is definitely no easy way."

Brinley sighed. "The hard way, then."

"I'm afraid so."

"What's the hard way?" Tabitha asked.

Habis retrieved a large brass-bound book from her shelf and laid it on the table. She opened it to a page near the center and showed them an illuminated picture of four of the most horrible-looking trees that Brinley had ever seen. They were short and stocky and completely bereft of leaves. Their color was black, and a face was drawn onto each of them with bark twisting out of the center of the trees to form the features. The one on the left had a very sad face, its eyes downcast, while the tree on the right looked like something from a horror movie. Its eyes were wide open and straining, its mouth gaping, teeth bared, tongue sticking out in a grotesque way, as if it was being tortured. The third tree looked incredibly angry, while the fourth, the shortest of the four, wore a blank expression.

Brinley shivered.

"These," Habis said solemnly, "are the twistwood trees."

"I've heard of those," Tabitha said. "When Belsie was teaching me about trees I asked him what the worst tree was. He said the twistwood, and he said if I ever saw it to run, because I was in a very bad place."

"Indeed," Habis said. "A very bad place. The twistwood trees are located in the very heart of the Wizard's Ire, created and planted there by my father.

"The trees are evil. The seeds were originally from a willow, the Weeping Willow of the Fallow Fields, upon which thousands were executed by hanging in the old days. The bark of the trees, if eaten, will kill a person slowly and painfully, and there is no cure. The wood itself is deadly, as well. A sliver will kill in under a day, while a wound made from a weapon fashioned out of the wood will have a more terrible effect, torturing the victim with a subtle increase of pain until they can stand it no longer."

"And then they die?" Tabitha asked.

"No," Habis said grimly. "Nothing as easy as that. It is as if their soul becomes infected. They lose the will to live. They are unable to feel happiness. Never again is there laughter, enthusiasm, satisfaction in their heart. Documented victims describe feeling no will to live and no desire to die. Most end up taking their own lives in the end. Though if they can hold out, the day will come when their body becomes so depressed that it is unable to form nutrients from food, their desire and enjoyment of food having long since left them. They eventually wither and die of starvation."

Tabitha looked horrified; Brinley was feeling a bit queasy herself. She hoped that they were getting to the end of it.

"Shael originally planted the trees to make weapons of war, which he gave to his most trusted servants. During the war many a knight or noble was slain by a twistwood blade, but the only person to suffer the trees' evil in the last one hundred years is your mother."

Tabitha's eyes grew wide. "So that is what was wrong with her . . ." she said. "I tried to treat her when she came to me as a magpie in my tower," she said, blushing. "I thought it was just a scratch. I treated her for a topical infection."

Habis smiled kindly. "In a way that is what it was. I'm sure she was grateful for your help. In the form of a bird, she was able to slow the effects of the wood. In the naptrap, time is suspended for her, or very nearly so, but if she were to come back out now it would take her quickly. She was cut by the bark of the tree, not the wood itself, so the effects should be reduced somewhat. Wounds of this nature are less common, however. There is no documentation of similar cases that I can find."

"And there's no cure?" Brinley asked.

"If the bark is *eaten*, there is no cure," Habis corrected. "For one who is merely cut by the bark, there may be a cure. There is some speculation on the subject, some by my uncle, who wrote this book, and some by me, as I have been pondering it since our last meeting."

"And?" Tabitha and Brinley said together.

"If I am right," she said cautiously, "a tincture brewed from the bark of a twistwood tree may heal her. It would be best if the bark came from the same tree as the weapon that injured her, but if necessary, any tree will do."

Tabitha brightened. "That's easy enough," she said. "There's bound to be some old bark weapons lying around somewhere. We'll just get one!"

"I'm afraid not," Habis said. "Great care was taken to destroy all such weapons after the war."

"Oh," Tabitha said. "Well, then we'll just have to go into the Wizard's Ire and get some ourselves."

Brinley bit back a smile, but she couldn't help feeling the same way. She had expected it to be much worse than that. It would be a long and difficult journey to reach the twistwood trees, but at least it sounded possible.

"Not so fast," Habis said, holding up a hand. Tabitha was on her feet and halfway to the door.

"I knew it," Brinley said dully.

"The tincture will be the easy part," Habis continued. "But the only way it will work is if we have all of the mages in attendance when your mother drinks it."

"I don't understand," Brinley said.

Habis gave her a stern look. "That is because I'm not finished explaining yet."

Brinley flopped back into her chair with a huff and placed her head in her hands. "Listening."

"Will it take much longer?" Tabitha said, "I'm getting quite hungry. It must be nearly lunchtime."

"True, true," Habis said. Then she shouted, "Dung, potatoes!" She turned back and motioned for them to follow her into the kitchen. "Help me cook. It is unwise to talk so much on an empty stomach."

The gangly servant appeared a moment later with a small bucket full of potatoes, and Brinley and Tabitha began to help Habis peel them. When they were finished, Habis tipped the potatoes into a pot of boiling water together with chopped carrots, onions, parsley, beets, and some sort of meat that Brinley did not recognize.

"The twistwood trees," Habis went on, "originally created by Shael, are born of a magic that is designed to elude all attempts at healing, even by the mages themselves. Shael grew the trees with polluted specimens from each of the seven elements. The wood, the seeds themselves, I already told you of. He planted them in soil imbued with stone dust ground from a piece of the Hezarack Stone."

Tabitha gasped.

"The what-arack?" Brinley asked.

"The Hezarack Stone," Habis repeated. "An ancient altar in Aquilar where the witches once made human sacrifices."

"Everyone avoids it," Tabitha explained. "Birds won't even fly over it. I've seen it before, once." She stopped talking abruptly and looked down. Evidently the memory was not pleasant.

"So what?" Brinley said. "I mean, that's horrible, but what does it have to do with—"

Habis cut her off with a wave of her hand. "As the trees grew they were watered with the tears of tortured men, breathed upon daily by Shael himself, and scorched with fire taken from the heart of a dragon."

"Ech!" Brinley said, disgusted. "That sounds like a lot of nasty work."

Habis nodded. "It was worth it. He was able to arm his soldiers with the most deadly weapons known to mankind. They were a force to be reckoned with."

Tabitha was frowning skeptically. "Habis, what do you mean, the heart of a dragon?"

"Oh, yes," Habis said, nodding. "The heart of a dragon will burn for weeks outside its body. One of the very last dragons was slain for this purpose."

Brinley shivered. "There are dragons in Aberdeen?"

"Possibly," Tabitha said.

"Definitely not," Habis corrected. She stirred the stew, checking the potatoes, then dished them each a bowl and served it alongside a red and yellow bread with a strange smell. "Not anymore, that is. A thousand years ago there were only two, a male and a female. Shael killed Anorre, the female, for her heart. In his anger, her partner Kuzo attacked Shael's fortress in the Ire but was wounded badly. He died from his wounds somewhere in the wild. That's rotoberry bread," she added proudly as she watched Brinley inspect it. "My own recipe."

Brinley took a bite of it and froze. It was horrible.

"His body was never found," Tabitha pointed out, not noticing Brinley's face.

"He is dead," Habis said dismissively. "You forget that Shael is my father. I was at the battle in question. I saw the monster's wings burning with my father's fire as it retreated into the northern sky."

Tabitha set her jaw stubbornly but said nothing.

Brinley flicked a piece of rotoberry bread across the table at her when Habis wasn't looking.

"Look here," Habis said. Brinley jumped and dropped the rest of her bread, but Habis was pointing at the book again. She indicated the space between the trees where their branches almost touched each other. Brinley took the opportunity to sneak the rest of the rotoberry bread off her plate and into her pocket.

"There's something wedged between the tree branches," Tabitha said. Brinley could see it too now. A small box of some sort.

"It's called a Panthion. A prison box. This particular one was forged of mage steel, that is, steel drawn from the earth by the Mage of Metal, by Cassis's predecessor. It is of strange design. It has no exit, only an entrance, and it cannot be broken or melted. It can only be opened by the Magemother."

"Wonderful," Brinley said sarcastically.

"Indeed," Habis agreed. "Life is full of responsibility."

Tabitha, who had picked up the piece of rotoberry bread that Brinley flicked at her, suddenly clamped her hand over her mouth in disgust. Before Habis realized what had happened, she covered it up by saying, "You mean he's locked in there? Isn't he out? He sent March after us. And he sent the two Idris before that."

Habis laughed. "If he were out, we would all be dead or at war. No. He seems to have found a way to communicate with his servants, but it is safe to say that he has not escaped the Panthion."

Tabitha leaned in to inspect the picture more closely. "It looks so small," she said. "How could it hold an entire person?"

"It is a *magical* prison," Habis said. "There is no telling how big it is on the inside, or what it could hold. For all we know there could be a whole world inside. Or he might be crammed into a single tiny room. The only way to find out would be to go inside."

Brinley frowned. "But—"

"We have strayed from the point," Habis said briskly. "I have told you all of this to explain the power of the twistwood trees. As you see, Shael created them so that their power could not be undone by one mage alone. Just as he used every element to curse the tree, every mage will need to do their part in lifting the curse."

"So that is why I must find the mages first," Brinley said. "That is what you meant when you told me that on Calypsis."

"That was my guess," Habis said. "Now I am more certain. I feel confident that together, they can lift the curse of the twistwood tree on a single piece of bark. If we then feed her a tincture of the healed bark, it should do the trick."

They sat in silence for a moment, pondering the magnitude of the task before them. Brinley was about to say something when a loud, rumbling belch issued from Tabitha's general direction. Brinley stared at her and Tabitha's eyebrows went up slowly. Habis was staring intently at Tabitha's coat.

Brinley cleared her throat. "Um, Habis, I don't suppose you know where the lost mages are hiding?"

Habis snorted. "Hardly."

"Well, then maybe you can help me with something else," she said. "Do you know what the Void is?"

"Excuse me?" Habis said. "What kind of ridiculous question is that?"

"It's not ridiculous," Brinley said. "When I was with my mother in the lightfall on Calypsis, before you arrived, I traveled back to Earth for a few moments."

Habis sat up straighter. "Really? Intriguing."

Brinley nodded. "When I came back, someone came with me . . . my father. He came through the portal with me, but when I got back, he was gone. We were holding hands. I didn't even feel him leave."

"Describe this portal to me," Habis said.

"It was the door of an old church on one side—the Earth side—and a door of light inside the lightfall on the other."

"And between them?"

"Like a dark tunnel."

Habis raised an eyebrow. "Portals are not precisely my specialty . . . in fact, as far as I know, only the Magemother has ever used them. It is a magic beyond anyone in this world," she said thoughtfully. "It may not be magic at all, technically speaking."

Brinley didn't know what she meant by that, nor did she particularly care. At the look on her face, Habis returned to the matter at hand. "Perhaps he slipped back to his own world," she said doubtfully.

Brinley shook her head. "My mother told me that he must have gotten lost in the Void."

"Ah," Habis said almost excitedly, tapping her fingers together. "Interesting." She studied them carefully for a moment, and then said, "I have no idea."

"What do you mean?" Brinley exclaimed.

"I mean I have no idea. You can't expect me to know everything. I know of the Void only as a theoretical state of being." She picked up a peanut from the table. "If I vanish this nut, for example, where will it go?"

"I don't know," Brinley said. "Nowhere?"

"Precisely," Habis said. She snapped her fingers and the peanut vanished into thin air. "Nowhere. Or, as some would say, the Void. I have always thought of it as representing nonexistence. I had not thought of it as a place that a person could go to physically before now."

Tabitha looked at Brinley. "Does your father like peanuts?" Brinley gave her a weird look.

Habis was tapping her fingers thoughtfully. "If you did indeed walk through the void between worlds, then perhaps it is a place that you can visit. If so, I have no idea how you would get there, unless you open another portal."

Tabitha looked at Brinley curiously. "Can you do that?"

Brinley shrugged. "How should I know? It's not like I got much training at this whole Magemother thing."

Habis smiled. "Indeed. Well, don't be too hard on yourself. I am sure that you will find a way."

"I do have one idea, actually," Brinley said shyly. It was the only thing that she could think of, apart from learning how to open a portal herself, and it had been gnawing at her for days.

"Go on," Habis encouraged.

"The summoning bell you made brought me here from another world—across the Void, I guess. So I thought, maybe . . . you could make another summoning bell, but for my father . . ."

Habis cocked her head thoughtfully. "Not a bad idea. That could bring him here, theoretically, no matter where he was. But I'm afraid it is not possible."

Brinley's heart sank. That had been her only idea. Over the last few days, she had convinced herself that Habis would be able to do it. "Are you sure?" she asked.

Habis nodded. "Unfortunately, yes. A summoning bell is crafted for a specific individual, or in your case, a specific *type* of individual, the Magemother . . . I could try to make one for him based on your description, but it would almost certainly not work. They are very hard to make, and they are very complicated. As far as I know, I am the only person ever to succeed, and even I do not understand them fully."

"What do you mean?"

"Take the Magemother's summoning bell, for instance. It summoned you, even though your mother was still alive. She was technically still the Magemother, so I would think it would have summoned her. However, you were the Magemother that Aberdeen needed at the time, the new Magemother. Somehow, the bell knew to bring you instead of her. How? Nobody can say. Summoning bells are extremely powerful objects. I will not attempt to make one for a person that I have never met."

They sat in silence for a minute as Brinley ran over everything Habis had said. At length, a thought struck her. "Habis, could you make a summoning bell for your father and summon him out of that box?"

Habis went pale. Slowly, she nodded. "Perhaps . . . It is helpful if the subject is actually present at the making while their essence is aligned to the bell . . . but then, I know him well enough that I could very likely do it from memory. A dark idea. Of course, I would never do so."

"You hate him that much?"

Habis's eyes shifted around the room, coming to rest on her hands. "I did not always," she said simply.

Brinley nodded, studying her own hands. She loved her own father very much. He was probably the best person she had ever known. The best father in the world, in her opinion. She couldn't think of what it would be like to have a bad one.

"What if someone tried to force you to make one?" Tabitha asked presently.

Habis laughed. "I would like to see them try." She shook her head, motioning for them to get up. "We have been talking about heavy things for too long now and your heads are beginning to spin. It is time for you to get some rest. Will you be leaving in the morning?"

"Yes," Brinley said. "As early as we can. There is much to do."

❖ ❖ ❖

Brinley walked alone across the central square before Caraway Castle, stone tiles cold with new snow, muffling the sound of her footsteps. She wanted to visit Maggie. She had been thinking about her, worrying about her living in that tiny house all by herself. It must get cold in there at night.

But when she arrived at the place where Maggie's shack should have been, there was nothing there. Where could it have gone? She heard a moaning sound behind her and turned. Maggie was there, lying prostrate on the ground, fingers black with cold, clutching at the frozen stone.

"I'm so cold," Maggie whispered. "So cold."

Brinley's breath caught in her throat, and the scene changed. Tabitha was high on the battlements of the castle, running as if her life depended on it, but from whom? She got to the edge and stopped, with no place else to run, and changed into a butterfly. Then Hugo was there, reaching for the frail, fluttering creature. But he did not look like the Hugo she knew. His face was creased and lined, and his eyes were black and cold. He caught the butterfly by the wings and ripped them off, laughing.

Brinley screamed, but no sound came out.

The scene changed again, and she was walking with her father through the trees at Morley. He would make everything better. She was telling him about Maggie, about Hugo, about Tabitha. It felt good to talk to him again. She hadn't realized how much she missed that. He passed beneath the door of Morley Church and fell into blackness. It was like quicksand, but the color of the night sky, and it was pulling him down, down. He called to her, reached out, and she tried to lift him, knees braced against the steps of the church, but he was too heavy. She dropped him, and he was sucked in. She was crying now. She could still hear his voice calling to her.

No, not his voice. The voice of children. Children she had never met. She opened her eyes and found herself in a maze. Thick green bushes shot skyward on every side. She could hear their voices—Chantra, Unda, and Lignumis. They were calling to her, begging her to save them, help them. They were lost. They needed her. How was she supposed to find them? She ran through the maze, but every turn she took was a dead end. A silver orb swung out of the corner of her vision, obliterating the bushes with a cleaving swing. It began to chase her, swinging back and forth, back and forth, until there was nowhere to run.

Brinley jolted awake, at first unsure of where she was. Then it came back to her. She was in a tiny bedroom in Habis's invisible house.

A voice spoke inside her mind. *Are you all right?* It was Hugo. *I couldn't sleep, so I thought I would reach out and see if you were up, and you were screaming.*

It was just a dream, she said. *Just a bad dream.*

Was I in it?

She grinned, feeling the terror melt away. *Like I would tell you if you were. Honestly.* She felt Hugo's mood start to radiate warmth. He was smiling, she realized. *Had a hard day?*

You could say that. Animus isn't any fun at all to travel with. All he wants to do is teach me, and he won't let me talk until I learn the last thing he taught me, which would be okay if it was simple stuff, but no. He's picked something a bit more challenging. Not that it should be, for the Mage of Light and Darkness. Should be easy, I expect, but it's not.

Aww, Brinley said in the most patronizing thought-voice she could summon, *do you miss your castle, Hugo?*

Hey! Hugo protested. *If there was an ancient mage trying to get you to travel at the speed of light, you wouldn't be happy either.*

Huh. I bet I could manage it if I were the Mage of Light and Darkness.

Hugo laughed. *It's good to talk to you. Animus hasn't let me say a word all day. Even to Cannon. I'm supposed to be listening to the moon or something.*

You should probably be doing it, then.

I know. Don't worry. I think I'm finally getting the hang of it.

Really?

No. How was your day?

She thought about it. *Long.*

I hear you there . . . Well, I'll let you sleep then.

Hugo?

Yeah?

How are things going with our . . . mutual friend? It sounded silly to say it like that, but she was trying to avoid calling it "darkness." He didn't answer right away. *Hugo?*

The same, I guess. I mean, I really haven't felt much different.

Brinley had the feeling that he was holding something back, but she didn't want to push it. *You'll tell me when something happens, though, won't you?*

Silence.

Hugo?

It really isn't your problem, you know, his voice came back. *Whatever's going to happen, you shouldn't have to deal with it.*

Brinley stood up and began to pace. This was exactly what she was afraid of hearing from him. It would be just like him to try and deal with the darkness all by himself without involving anybody else, and that was probably what would get him into trouble. Without warning, the Hugo from her dream flashed in her mind, and she struggled for a moment to dismiss it.

I'm the Magemother, Hugo, was all she could think of to say. *And you're a mage. Your problems are my problems.* She searched around the empty room, looking for some way to explain her feelings. *Hugo, you never knew your mother, did you?*

No.

Well, let me tell you something about mothers in general. We want to know everything. We want to help you even when we shouldn't.

Hugo was silent for a while, but eventually his voice came back to her, more loudly this time. *All right, all right,* he said. *I'll keep you informed when I have visits from Dark Hugo, and you can stop asking me about it. Fair?*

Fair. As long as he kept up his end of the bargain, that is.

They said their good nights, and Brinley was left to her own thoughts. It was going to be a long night. It felt like a few hours before dawn still, and she knew that there would be no getting back to sleep. Pulling her warm clothes back on, she decided to go for a walk. Maybe she would grab a snack in the kitchen.

She peeked into the room next door to check on Tabitha, but the girl was gone. Brinley felt a tinge of worry, but calmed herself. This was normal for Tabitha. She seemed to need little sleep these days, and would often be out walking in the woods at night or patrolling the skies as a bird or filching food from the kitchen. Brinley decided she would look there first.

A moment later she opened the door to the kitchen and froze. A small man stood there, cloaked and hooded, brandishing a short stick at her. A shape that was half man, half snake, tore from the end of it, flying across the room at her. Then it was gone, all of it, the man, the stick, the snake-man flying toward her; it had vanished as quickly as it appeared, and her scream died on her lips. She stood, rooted to the spot for a moment, wondering if any of it had happened, or if it was a figment of her imagination, the trick of a sleepy mind.

Brinley ducked her head outside, partly to check for Tabitha, and partly to rule out the possibility of that man being real. What she saw struck her as very strange. Habis and Tabitha were crouched beside a little stream just outside the entrance, tossing stones into it. But that wasn't the strangest part. There was some sort of creature on the other side of the stream, half hidden in shadows. It took her a moment to realize what it was.

The ogre.

Brinley covered her mouth to stop a shout when she realized that Tabitha and Habis didn't seem to be afraid at all. They were laughing. Laughing as they threw the stones, one by one, into the brook. Almost without her noticing, the memory of the man and the stick faded from her mind with their laughter, replaced with curiosity. As she watched a stone plunk into the water, Brinley caught a better look at the ogre. He was sniffing the water, walking along the opposite bank. Occasionally, he would dip his foot into the stream and Tabitha or Habis would toss a stone into the water in front of him, after which he would snatch his foot out, stomp in frustration, and start pacing again.

Brinley took a few steps closer. She could just make out what Tabitha and Habis were saying now. They were whispering.

Whispering to the rocks, it seemed. They held them up to their faces and whispered before they threw them.

"A rash and a canker sore," Tabitha was saying, but Habis cut her off.

"No, no, no. Rhyme it, rhyme it!"

Tabitha nodded vigorously and began again. "Warts and rashes and hammer toes, and a canker sore the size of a rose," she said, holding a stone in her hand. She was squatting barefoot, her dress pulled up over her knees, looking very much like a toddler, and drawing on the stone with the mud-covered finger of her left hand. When she had finished, she stood up and threw the stone into the brook. The ogre, who had made it halfway across the stream, snarled as the rock slapped the water in front of him. He reared up and twisted around, retreating back onto the bank.

"Seeds stuck in your teeth," Habis was saying, painting mud onto a stone of her own, "and sour honey for painful pee." She laughed and then threw it into the stream.

Tabitha giggled. "Oh, Habis. That was a terrible rhyme."

The ogre gave up trying to cross the stream and sat on the far bank. Now that she could see him better, Brinley realized that he bore no marks of the ferocious temperament that he exhibited during their battle with March. He looked quite frightened now.

"What on earth are you doing?" Brinley said. Tabitha dropped her stone. Habis hid her own stone behind her back.

"We're not on Earth, Magemother," Habis said defensively.

"Let me see that," Brinley said, holding out her hand for the stone.

Habis gave her a stubborn look, but handed it over. It had a strange pattern of swirls and lines painted across it with mud. The writing was unlike anything Brinley had seen before. "What is it?" she asked.

"A curse rock," Tabitha said brightly, having recovered from the shock of Brinley's appearance. "Habis has been teaching me how to make them."

Brinley raised her eyebrows at Habis.

"What?" the witch said, reaching out to snatch the stone back. She turned then, and hurled it into the brook, causing the ogre to scurry farther back from the edge of the stream.

"Dark magic?" Brinley asked. She knew, of course, that Habis had spent most of her life as a witch, and that much of her magic was what people would call questionable, if not downright unsavory.

"Pish posh," Habis said, waving her hand. "Magic is magic. Only what you do with it is good or bad, and this," she said, picking up another stone and handing it to Brinley, "is good. Unless you want to get eaten by an ogre."

"No," Brinley said. "I don't. But he doesn't look very hungry."

"Ogres can always eat," Habis said. "He wandered in an hour ago. Looking for help, I think. That sister of mine probably abandoned him. Ogres aren't much use on their own after they've been domesticated, you know. Not too different from a horse. I expect he sensed that I would take care of him."

"Will you?" Brinley asked.

"Yes," Habis said. "But he'll have to wait until morning. It's not worth the risk messing with ogres at night." She tossed another curse rock into the stream and dusted her hands off on her pants. "I think that will hold him for now, Tabitha."

"Uh oh," Tabitha said, and Brinley glanced up at the ogre. It was walking away from them now, back toward the woods.

"No matter," Habis said. "He is probably just going to look for March again. When he doesn't find her, he will be back."

"What if he does find her?"

Habis shrugged. "Then we have lost nothing. Ogres are not very communicative creatures. Useful in a fight, but hard to get information out of. He will not be able to tell her that he saw us. Why don't we go back inside for some tea before you leave . . . and I do believe I have some rotoberry bread for the road."

Tabitha gagged softly.

Chapter Seven

In which Brinley challenges a troll to a battle of wits

OUTSIDE HABIS'S HOUSE, Tabitha changed into her favorite shape, a large jet-black swan. Brinley climbed onto her back.

"Be careful," Habis said. She had crawled halfway out of the opening and then stopped so that the whole back half of her body was completely invisible, her face and hands sticking out as if from nowhere. "You never know what you will find on Calypsis. That place is a mystery known only to the Magemother, and you have not been the Magemother long enough to learn it yet."

Brinley nodded. "Thanks for all your help," she said, and Tabitha leapt into the air, her great black wings beating powerfully.

They flew higher and higher, rising above the clouds. The air grew thin and cold and eventually Brinley had to stop breathing, holding her breath for the last leg of the journey. This was the part that always scared her. It seemed like it would take hours to cover the distance that remained between them and the moon, but whenever they got high enough for the air to grow thin, they crossed the remaining distance in a few seconds. That was the magic of it: only the Magemother, the mages, and those with their permission could make that journey. Anyone else would freeze to death or suffocate in the distance between Aberdeen and its moon.

Moments later, they landed on the white sandy surface of the moon, and Tabitha changed back into herself. The great crystal palace jutted out of the sand in front of them, its clear glass spires twisting gracefully around ramparts of silver. No matter how many times Brinley saw it, she never got over the sheer size of it. "I wonder if this is what it's like to be an astronaut on the moon," Brinley said.

"What is an astro nut?" Tabitha asked, cocking her head.

"Never mind," Brinley said, chuckling to herself as she walked up the castle steps. Tabitha skipped after her.

"I like it here," Tabitha said. "Do you really think that we will find clues about the mages?"

"Dunno," Brinley said honestly. "I hope so. Can you think of a better idea?"

"Oh, no," Tabitha said, startled at the thought. She patted Brinley's arm. "I'm sure you're right."

The tall ivory doors swung inward at Brinley's touch to reveal a golden floor. It looked like clear glass with honey flowing beneath it, and it lit up from corner to corner at the touch of her foot. It was warm, and she swore she could feel it pulsing beneath her feet as if it were a living thing.

"Wow," Tabitha said, "it didn't do that last time."

"I think it's because I'm the Magemother now," Brinley said.

Tabitha nodded. "That makes sense." She stared up at the fifty-foot ceiling of sculpted glass. "I like this place," she said again. "But it needs more plants."

Brinley laughed. "Let's just hope that it's not filled with enemies this time." She felt her pulse quicken at the memory. The Magemother's home was the safest place on Aberdeen—except that it wasn't actually on Aberdeen—but the first time they had been there they had been in a heated battle with the previous Mage of Light and Darkness, Lux Tennebris, who had lost control of the balance he was charged with keeping and became evil. Now, she knew, it was completely safe, but she had avoided coming here because of the bad memories.

"You know what, Tabitha?" Brinley said, trying to think positively. "I think you're right. The entrance hall should be happier. Greener." She raised her hand, wondering if what she had in mind would work. She had no real magic to speak of as the Magemother, but then, this place was built for her, and she had the sneaking suspicion that things would be different here. "Four big golden palm trees!" she said in a commanding tone.

Nothing happened.

Tabitha covered her mouth, laughing. "That's embarrassing. At least you didn't do it in front of Hugo."

"What are you talking about?" Brinley said, feeling her face go red.

"You know," Tabitha said. "Word on the street is you two like each other."

"Word on the street!" Brinley exclaimed.

"Well, do you?"

"Tabitha, you are around me all the time. If I liked a boy, don't you think you'd be the first to notice?"

Tabitha looked suddenly confused. "Oh, yeah. I forgot . . . Well, I think he likes you."

Brinley shook her head, striding across the entrance hall. "I'm the Magemother and he's a mage. Plus, I'm barely fourteen . . . That would just be—"

Suddenly the floor began to shake. There was a rumbling sound, and then the glass floor began rippling like water, starting at the corners so that the golden ripples converged under their feet in the center of the room. Four beautiful palm trees, at least thirty feet tall, rose from the floor in the corner of the room. At the same time, the domed glass ceiling sparkled and changed as if an invisible hand were drawing on it. A second later, there was a beautiful scene carved into the glass: four palm trees mirroring the ones on the floor, surrounding a mother with a child in her arms.

"Wow!" Tabitha said. "How did you do that?"

Brinley shook her head, still staring up at it. "I don't know . . ."

Tabitha grinned. "I guess being the Magemother has some perks!"

They took a curved staircase to the second floor and stepped into a long hallway interspersed with tall windows and pillars and a dozen doors.

"This is going to take forever," Tabitha said. "We should have brought Belsie to give us a tour or something. It could take us all day to find the mages' rooms."

"You're right," Brinley said. "I wish we had a map."

At her words, a sculpted pillar burst from the floor in front of them, rising to the height of a pedestal. On it, carved into the smoky glass surface, were detailed diagrams of the various floors and wings of the palace.

"Well, that's handy," Brinley said, grinning. She pointed to a golden dot pulsing on the map. "Look, here we are on the second floor."

"Show us where the mages' rooms are located, please," Tabitha asked.

Nothing happened.

Tabitha sighed. "You ask it."

Brinley repeated her question, and several rooms lit up on the drawing. There were far more than the seven that Brinley had expected. There had to be more than twenty of them. "Oh my. I guess whoever built this place was planning ahead. Show us Chantra's room, please."

A large round room lit up on all three levels. Apparently, the room was three stories tall.

"Let's go!" Tabitha said excitedly, and she sped off down the hall.

When they reached Chantra's room, they discovered that it was indeed very tall, but if Brinley were to sum the room up in one word it would have been "red." The walls were painted, and the windows had little rubies set into them so that the light from outside played across the red walls in shimmering patterns. A large round bed was set off to one side like a giant apple that had sunk partway into the floor. And there was a long oval window seat under the largest window.

"Oh," Tabitha said, "this one is definitely going to be my favorite." She skipped off to the bed, pushed her fist into it, and then stepped onto it and started jumping. "Yep! I can tell I'm going to like Chantra when we find her." That last thought made her stop bouncing and she added, "What are we looking for in here?"

"I wish I knew. Clues, I guess. Anything that could give us an idea about where she might be hidden."

"But did the mages choose where they were going to hide?" Tabitha asked, jumping down from the bed.

"I don't know," Brinley said. "I think so. But even if they didn't, I'm sure my mother would have picked someplace that they would like to spend a lot of time in. That's what I would have done."

Tabitha stared at her. "You're really good at this Magemother stuff," she said with a nod of her head.

Brinley blushed. "I don't know about that." She definitely didn't feel like it. "I should be able to find them more easily than this."

"That's okay," Tabitha said, shaking her head. "I'm not a very good herald either."

"What do you mean?"

Tabitha sat down on a cushion and put her face in her hands sullenly. "I'm not good at protecting you. Belsie said so himself."

"He did not!" Brinley said, shocked.

"No," Tabitha said, looking up, "he didn't, but that's what he thinks. That's what everyone thinks." She stared despondently at the floor. "I'm not vicious . . . I'm not a lion like Peridot. I'm a . . . butterfly. I mean, I could be vicious, if I really wanted to be." A look of panic crossed her face at a memory. "But I don't want to be. I can't!"

Brinley threw her arm around the other girl, pulling her to her feet. "Now you listen to me, Tabitha," she said. "Why do you think I picked you to be my herald?"

Tabitha stared at her blankly.

"It's not because you are terribly vicious looking," Brinley said, bringing a smile out of the other girl. "It's not because you are the biggest, scariest, strongest bodyguard in all the land." Tabitha laughed at that. "It's because you were the right person to pick. Sometimes you just know a thing is right, even when you can't tell why."

Tabitha smiled. "See," she said. "You're good at this Magemother stuff." She sniffed proudly. "Told you so."

"Come on," Brinley said, "let's search this room."

❖ ❖ ❖

Four hours later they were sprawled on Chantra's bedroom floor, exhausted from their search. Tabitha had gone through all of her drawers and books and papers before finally settling down to help Brinley read the journals. There were five of them, each one a different size, but all of them red, like most everything in her room. Chantra, it seemed, had a love for all things red, especially rubies, which apart from being in the windows they had noticed earlier, also decorated many of her other possessions including her bed frame, desk chair, and all five of her journals. Brinley had made it all the way through Chantra's first journal and halfway through the second, and she was finally starting to feel like she was getting to know her.

"Listen to this," Brinley said, picking up the second journal and beginning to read,

Today I went with Mom to visit the king of Caraway. He just got married, and there was lots of food left over, so Belsie was there too.

"Did you hear that, Tabitha? She calls Belterras Belsie, just like you!"

Tabitha forced a weak smile. "And she knows how Belsie likes food."

Anyway, Cassis was there too and he gave me a beautiful ruby that he found in the ground while he was working, and he said he

was going to cut it and polish it for me. I asked him if he would set it into a new diary for me and he said that he would do it!

Brinley held up a different journal. It was shaped like a heart, with a great red ruby set into the center of it so that all of the pages were cut out around the ruby. "See?" she said, tapping the ruby. "I bet this is the ruby that she was talking about. Isn't that interesting?"

Tabitha was holding her hands in front of her face as she lay on her back, making animal shapes against the ceiling, clearly not interested in the least. "I suppose," she said. "But what does it mean?"

"Well," Brinley said slowly, "we've learned that she likes red things..." Slowly, the enthusiasm drained from Brinley's face until finally she slumped down beside Tabitha. "Oh, you're right. Maybe we're wasting our time here."

Tabitha cocked her head, letting her hand-bird fall apart. "Yes. And she liked Cassis. I read a bit too, and it doesn't sound like she got along very well with the other mages."

"Yeah," Brinley agreed. "Animus told me that she used to snoop through their things."

Tabitha sat up abruptly. "I guess we *have* learned something."

Brinley nodded. "Let's go find Unda's room."

Back at the map, two rooms lit up when Brinley asked for directions. Lignumis's room was a tiny thing on the top floor, while Unda's was several floors down, far below ground level, and incredibly large. After some debate they decided to start with Lignumis's and leave the larger one for last.

The door to Lignumis's room was made of a rich, dark wood and was covered from top to bottom in intricate carvings of trees and rocks and birds, with a great lion in the center.

Brinley tried to open it and it didn't budge. "Oh. Please open up." She tried the handle again confidently, assuming that the castle would obey her wish, but the result was the same as before.

Tabitha put her hands on her hips indignantly. "It should let you in," she said. "You're the Magemother!"

"Hmm," Brinley returned. "Well, Lignumis was a boy, you know, and boys like their privacy."

"What's this?" Tabitha asked, pointing to something on the door handle.

Brinley bent down to inspect it. It was a very ornate brass handle with trees and a river stamped into it, and it took her a minute to see what Tabitha was talking about. There was a tiny line of writing scratched around the outside of the handle. "A lion's roar will open the door," she read. "What do you suppose that means?"

"Lignumis couldn't turn into a lion, could he?" Tabitha asked.

"I don't think so," Brinley said. "That sounds more like something that Belsie—I mean, Belterras, could do. Lignumis is the Mage of Wood. Forests, trees, plants, you know . . ."

Tabitha was staring stubbornly at the door. Suddenly, she let out a bellowing roar in her own voice, eyes bulging from the effort.

Brinley jumped, then started to laugh. Tabitha was bent over with the effort now, face straining with her roar, staring madly at the door handle. The roar grew fainter and fainter until Tabitha was completely deflated, gasping for breath.

The door clicked and swung open.

Tabitha smiled in a self-satisfied way and strode through the door. "I'm definitely doing that to my door when I get a room here. I can, can't I?" she said as an afterthought.

"Of course you can," Brinley said, following her through. The room was small—barely long enough for a grown man to lie down in, but it was impeccably well organized. There was a small cot on a ledge built into the wall above their head, where Lignumis must have slept. The space behind the door had been made into a tiny desk, on which a pad of paper, a feather quill, and a pen knife still lay parallel to one another in the center. The whole opposite wall, apart from the small round window, was taken up by tiny doors and drawers with brass hinges and handles with little paper labels of varying colors. Walking over to the window, Brinley had the thought that it would be very bad to fall out of it; the ground looked very, very far away from up here.

Tabitha began reading the labels. "*Lignum vite* (Ironwood), Garra. *Quercus alba* (White Oak), Caraway." After each name, there was a date printed. She moved down the line of drawers. "*Dalbergia latifolia* (Rosewood), Tarwal Coast. *Malus domestica* (Rose Apple), Gan-Gara." She opened one of them. "Oh," she said tenderly. "How beautiful." The drawer was filled with wood shavings, a small twig that had been sliced from a branch, an apple blossom, and a drawing of the fruit. As she opened the drawer, the small room filled with the scent of ripe apples. "Look," Tabitha said, closing the drawer, "there's a little door beside every drawer, and each one is labeled the same as the drawer that it corresponds to."

"Open one," Brinley said, wondering what other wonders Lignumis was hiding.

Tabitha opened the tiny wooden door to reveal a single miniature apple tree. It was the most beautiful apple tree Brinley had ever seen, and although it was only two inches tall, it appeared to be fully grown. Its tiny roots wound down in a round table of black soil on the floor of the little compartment. There was even a tiny little toy shack at the foot of the apple tree. It reminded Brinley of the little houses that people on Earth put in the bottom of fish tanks.

"Amazing," Tabitha whispered, shutting the tiny door carefully.

"It must have taken him years to collect all of these," Brinley said appreciatively. "Do you think this can help us?"

Tabitha shrugged. "At least we know he loved trees."

Brinley nodded. She pulled a small three-legged stool out from under the desk and sat down, taking up the paper and quill. She opened the desk drawer and removed the ink. "Okay," she said, wetting the pen. "Let's start from the beginning. Read all the names to me in date order, earliest first. Maybe we can find out what he was working on when he disappeared. I don't think it will mean anything to me or you, but maybe Belterras might see some pattern in it."

Tabitha nodded eagerly. "I think I should probably check on all the trees as we go too," she said. "Just to see them. You don't think he'll mind, do you?"

It took them over an hour to copy them all down. When Tabitha had come to the very end of the last row she said, "This is the last one. Oh my."

"What?" Brinley asked.

"*Olea europaea* (Twistwood), the Ire."

Brinley felt a twinge of excitement.

Tabitha opened the drawer. It was empty. There was nothing behind the door either.

"This is what he must have been working on when he disappeared," Brinley said.

"But why would he want that tree?" Tabitha asked. "You don't think he actually went looking for it, do you?"

"Look at this wall," Brinley said. "I think he probably did."

"You don't think he's still there, do you?" Tabitha said.

"Maybe," Brinley said. "Maybe he went in and never came back out."

❖ ❖ ❖

On the lowest level of the castle, where Unda's room should have been, there was nothing but a long, white marble ledge with a pillar on each end supporting the castle above them. Beyond, empty space stretched out in all directions. Carved into one of the pillars were the words, "The true path lies in emptiness."

"Hmm," Brinley said. "He must have been quite a thinker."

Tabitha was reading the pillar on the other side of the landing and chuckling. It read, "Go away, Chantra. I know you hate heights."

"What do you think it means?" Brinley asked.

Tabitha shrugged. "Maybe we have to take a leap of faith? Just step out there and hope we step into his room?" She walked to the edge and, holding Brinley's hand for balance, reached into the void with one foot, searching for some purchase. "I don't feel anything."

Brinley pulled her back. "I think you're right, though," she said. "We probably have to just step off for real. It says the path is in emptiness, and that is definitely emptiness."

"I'll do it," Tabitha said, facing the edge.

"No," Brinley insisted. "I should. If it's the wrong thing to do, if it's dangerous . . . well, I don't think the castle will let me die or anything. It seems to respect me, being the Magemother and all."

Tabitha waved Brinley away. "I can just change into a bird if I fall too far. I'll do it." And with that she stepped off the edge. Brinley reached out to grab her but missed, and Tabitha fell out of sight. A split second later she screamed, and then there was a splash.

"Tabitha!" Brinley shouted, leaning over the edge. She couldn't see anything below.

"It's okay," Tabitha said out of the darkness. "Come down!" Her voice sounded very far away. "Don't worry, just jump off!"

Brinley rolled her eyes, cringing. Trying not to think about what she was doing, she stepped off the ledge. She fell farther than she anticipated, then plunged into warm water. When she surfaced, she could see again; the void had disappeared. They were wading in a deep, clear azure pool under semi-bright light. She could see the white marble ledge above them clearly now; there was a ladder carved into the rock face beside them, which they could use to climb back out. In the center of the pool, a small stone island rose out of the water, which was connected to a high, floating walkway of stone by means of a beautiful bridge. They climbed onto the island and stepped onto the bridge, only to find it guarded at the center by a troll.

"Ooh," Tabitha said. "Isn't she lovely?"

"She?" Brinley said incredulously, searching the troll for some hint of femininity.

"Obviously," Tabitha said. "She's the prettiest troll I've ever seen."

Brinley wished that she could agree. The troll was almost nine feet tall and built like a house. Its face was covered with a mass of shriveled skin that obscured its features. Brinley was trying her very hardest not to simply turn and run.

"Greetings," the troll said in a husky voice. It said nothing else. Just stood there, in the way, waiting.

"Ooh," Tabitha said excitedly, grabbing Brinley's arm. "It's a troll bridge! Maybe we'll have to answer a riddle to pass!"

"Great," Brinley said, giving the troll a wary look. She hoped that all it would do to them was ask a riddle . . . Then again, what would it do if they got it wrong?

"Uh," Brinley said to the troll, "do we have to answer a riddle to pass?"

The troll nodded once.

"And if we fail?"

The troll pointed at the sparkling water twenty feet below. It was a long drop, but the water looked deep. It probably wouldn't hurt too badly.

"Oh," Tabitha said. "She throws us in the water!" She seemed to relish the thought. "I'll go first." She danced away from Brinley, practically skipping up the bridge. "Tell me your riddle," she said, placing her hands on her hips defiantly.

The troll cleared its throat. "I grow green. Trees within trees. Taller than peas, shorter than knees. Our heads are the same size, but I fit in your mouth. What am I?"

"Socks!" Tabitha said without pause, and then gave an ecstatic scream as the troll picked her up and threw her over the side of the bridge. She came out of the water laughing and swam back to where Brinley was waiting for her at the base of the bridge.

"Socks?" Brinley asked incredulously.

"I wanted to be thrown! I like Unda," she added. "He's fun." She stepped past Brinley and approached the troll again. This time she whispered, "Broccoli," and the troll stepped aside. Tabitha, looking slightly disappointed, crossed the remainder of the bridge and waited as Brinley approached the troll.

"What had nine lives?" the troll asked.

Brinley waited for the rest of it. Then, when nothing more was forthcoming, said, "What, that's it?"

The troll nodded.

She thought for a moment. It couldn't be that simple, surely, but she couldn't think of any other answers. "A cat?" she offered. The troll reached for her and she danced backwards. "Agh! No, wait! I get it. Had! Had! A *dead* cat!"

The troll, who had already picked Brinley up, lowered her back onto the bridge sullenly and stepped aside.

"Aw," Tabitha said, watching the troll with a sympathetic look. "You could have let her throw you just once . . ."

The bridge led to a circular stone room situated high above the water. The room itself had an open feeling, with low stone walls interspersed by marble columns that held up a domed roof. There was a round bed in the center, and a simple table beside it. Looking around the space, Brinley could see why Unda might have liked it. It was like being in the ocean. Suspended in space with water all around. Compared to Chantra's room, however, there was a notable lack of personal possessions. "Tabitha," Brinley said. "I need your help, you know."

Tabitha had taken a running start at the bed. "I just want to see if it's as good as Chantra's," she called, and then launched herself into the air. She landed with a solid thump on the bed that made her knees buckle. "Ouch! It is definitely *not* as good as Chantra's." Tabitha got off the bed, glaring at it suspiciously, and then pulled off the covers. A second later she had peeled back the thin mattress pad as well.

"Tabitha," Brinley said. "What are you—oh, my."

Beneath the mattress, Unda's bed was little more than a giant box full of identical black books. They had hard covers, with no writing on the spines.

"There has to be a hundred of them," Tabitha said, picking one up.

"More than that," Brinley said. "What's in it?"

The cover was completely blank, but when Tabitha opened to the title page, they found the word "Thoughts" written in blue, flowing letters. Tabitha turned to the first page and read aloud:

I think that life may be symbolic of something greater. What we call life exists because of language, and all language is symbolic. The word "understanding," written here, is obviously not the thing itself. Thoughts are symbolic also—perhaps because they are so imbued with language. The thought "I can fly" is not the thing itself; I cannot fly. Religions then, are symbolic also, because they are—when they are not being anything else—structured systems of thought and belief. Perhaps life is symbolic. Is it too far-fetched to dream that a world built of symbols may be, when viewed from some celestial height, no more than a symbol itself? A cosmic expression of deity? A note from one god to another, or, more likely, a play written by the only being that truly exists to create a story in which he is not alone . . .

When Tabitha finished reading they stared at one another in silence. "Do you have any idea what that means?" Tabitha said.

"It means that Unda was a thinker," Brinley said. "Beyond that, I don't have a clue."

"I'm not a thinker," Tabitha said with a sigh, and she put the book back as if she were suddenly worried that it might be dangerous. "We had better cover these back up."

Brinley laughed and helped her replace the mattress. "You're probably right, Tabitha. Maybe if we had a year or two, we could read all those, but I doubt even that would be enough time to understand them."

Brinley sat on the bed and put her head in her hand thoughtfully. They needed something else. Something simpler. She glanced around the room again, noting its emptiness. "There's not much else to see here, is there?" she said.

"Oh, I don't know," Tabitha said. "Look at this."

Tabitha was pointing to what was by far the most interesting thing about the room. Namely, that every square inch of walls, pillars, and ceiling was covered in a giant mural. The mural had clearly been drawn by Unda himself over a period of years, as the complexity and realism improved dramatically from one side to the other. Tabitha was pointing at what looked like his best work, on a pillar next to his bed.

Brinley chuckled. "Well, butter my buns and call me a biscuit," Brinley said.

"Do what?" Tabitha asked, looking startled.

"Never mind. It's just something my dad says." As she said it she thought of the nightmare of him sinking into a black hole. She shook the thought away and returned her attention to the mural.

There on the pillar beside his bed, Unda had painted the likeness of himself in a little forest clearing, playing a game like chess with a creature that looked very much like—

"The troll," Tabitha said. "The bridge troll." Tabitha's face fell. "Unda must not have had many friends. That *is* Unda, isn't it?"

Brinley nodded. She recognized him from the vision she had seen a few weeks prior when she had been with her mother in the throne room below them.

"Oh my," Tabitha said. "Look at this!" She had lowered herself gingerly onto the firm bed and folded her arms behind her head.

"Tabitha, this is no time for a nap."

"No, look!" Tabitha grabbed her arm and pulled her onto the bed beside her. She pointed at the ceiling. "See?"

There was a mural on the ceiling above them inside the dome, around which the pillars were set. The mural depicted a very beautiful lake surrounded by trees. It reminded Brinley of the intricately painted ceilings in medieval castles.

"Well," Brinley said, "it is pretty."

"It's important," Tabitha insisted. "I'm sure it is. If this was my room, I would paint my very favorite thing on the ceiling. I'd paint a swan, of course, or maybe a unicorn, though there aren't any unicorns left in the world, but they're still one of my favorite—"

"Tabitha," Brinley interrupted, "what are you talking about?"

"Well," Tabitha said, "if you were painting your own room, where would you put your very favorite picture?"

Brinley thought about her bedroom back on Earth. She had several of her own drawings pinned up around the walls, but her favorite was pinned to the ceiling above her bed. It was a drawing of her father bending over their old GMC, wrenching on the engine. The shading in that piece was some of her best ever. She'd put it there because she liked looking at it right before she fell asleep.

"You're right," she said to Tabitha. "I don't know why I didn't think of it. What is it, then?"

"It's a lake, silly," Tabitha said, giggling.

Brinley punched her playfully. "I know it's a lake. But which one? Did he make it up or was this his favorite lake? If it was his favorite, and my mother knew that, then it would have been a good place to hide him, don't you think?"

"Hmm, maybe. Except for the fact that it's painted on the ceiling in his bedroom."

"Right," Brinley said. "That might give away the secret to anyone trying to find him. But then, nobody can come here except the Magemother and the mages, and, you know, people I say can come here."

"But the Magemother was hiding him *from* one of the mages. Lux," Tabitha pointed out.

"Right."

They stared at the lake for a while, deep in thought.

Finally, Tabitha said, "I don't recognize it. Do you?"

"Nope."

"Do you think that Animus or Belsie might recognize it?"

"Nope."

"Why?" Tabitha asked. "They've lived on Aberdeen longer than anybody."

"Because," Brinley said, "the painting has been changed."

"What?"

"Look." She showed several places where the paint was heavier, around the bottom of the lake and across the whole left side. If it hadn't been for her own artistic talents, she would never have noticed the subtle changes in the color.

"Part of it was painted over by someone else long after the original work," she finished.

Tabitha looked very impressed. "Do you think that the Magemother did it to throw off Tennebris and hide where she really put him?"

Brinley shrugged. "Maybe. Probably. Or Unda did it himself."

Tabitha was inspecting the lake again. "We still have the whole right side of the painting," she said. "That has to help, doesn't it? You could show it to Animus and Belsie and everyone and maybe they will be able to tell which lake it is. And you can draw it too, so that we can have a copy with us when we go looking for it. We are going to look for it, aren't we?"

"Yes," Brinley said. "I guess those rocks on the right are pretty unique. It's better than nothing." She plucked the pencil from her hair, took out her notebook, and settled down to draw.

Tabitha nodded. "Much better."

It felt good to draw. She was worried at first. It had been a while since she had done it. So much had changed in her life that she hardly felt like the same person anymore. She would not have been surprised if she had forgotten how to draw altogether, but luckily that wasn't the case. In a minute the page was covered in a rough outline of the lake, and she could tell that it was good. An hour later she had a near perfect copy of the right half of the painting. Hopefully it would be good enough for someone to identify it. If not, it was going to be a long, boring chore to visit every single lake in Aberdeen.

"What do you think?" Brinley said, turning her drawing around and glancing up at Tabitha.

Tabitha was fishing for something in her coat, and froze as a large belching croak echoed out of it.

"Tabitha!" Brinley said. "What on earth do you have in there?"

Tabitha looked startled, but quickly brightened. "This is as good a time as any," she said. "Look who I brought, Brinley! It was going to be a surprise, but, well, surprise!" And she stuck her hand into one of the larger pockets, withdrawing a very fat and dizzy-looking toad. "This is Miah," she said. "Short for Jeremiah." She gave the toad a sympathetic look. "Doesn't like his real name at all, poor thing, so I had to shorten it." She placed him on the bed theatrically, and he flopped over sideways.

"Tabitha," Brinley said slowly, keeping her eyes on the creature. "Why do you have a toad?"

"To cheer you up," Tabitha said brightly. "I remembered how you told me about the frogs where you come from and, well, I couldn't find any frogs that wanted to come, but toads are always keen for a good journey and they don't mind bouncing around a bit inside a coat and—"

"Tabitha."

Tabitha nodded several times and then threw her arms in the air, dropping into a straddle and bellowing in her most enthusiastic singsong voice, "We're going to teach him ginastics!"

Brinley grinned. "Gymnastics," she corrected.

"Oh," Tabitha said. "Yes, that. I know how you've always wanted to, and I've been practicing my Toadish just so I can translate for you. Your dream's finally going to come true, Brinley!"

Brinley stared at her in amazement and then their eyes went to the toad together. He attempted to sit up, belching loudly again, then swayed on the spot and toppled over.

He was asleep as soon as he hit the covers.

Chapter Eight

In which Hugo hits an old man with a stick

ON THE FOURTH DAY of their travels, Hugo shook Animus awake in the early hours of the morning.

"What time is it?" Animus said. "Is something wrong?" He squinted at the brightening sky. The sun was not quite up, and the moon was not quite down.

"No," Hugo said. "I heard it. I heard it, Animus!"

Animus smiled, got to his feet, and began to pack up their campsite. "Tell me," he said.

Hugo recounted the story. He had awakened several minutes earlier with his eyes locked on the moon. It looked incredibly large to him when he woke; the moon had filled his whole vision, as if he could have reached out and touched it. "And then I heard it," he said. "I didn't realize what it was at first. I thought it was just the sound of my own head, you know? It was beautiful. Like a wind chime—no, it wasn't like that. It was like, like . . ." he trailed off, at a complete loss for words.

"Like a glass violin," Animus offered, nodding knowingly. "But as bright as a bell."

Hugo's expression went blank as he remembered it. "Yes," he said. "That's it exactly. Animus, how did you know that?"

"Lux described it to me once. Did it change when the sun came out?"

"Yeah—yes," Hugo said. "It sounded different when the sunlight started to brighten the sky. Quieter . . . almost sad."

Animus nodded. "You have done well. But moonlight is the easiest to hear. When you train your mind to be quiet enough to hear the sunlight, you may begin to learn to feel it as well, and use its power. That is your next assignment."

"Fine," Hugo said, rolling up his blanket. "But you have to help me with something else first."

"Oh? What is that?"

Hugo held up two long sticks.

❖ ❖ ❖

"Is this really necessary?" Cannon asked, holding one of the sticks before him with disdain. "Animus, I demand to know why you insist on subjecting me to this."

"Because I do," Animus said simply, settling himself down beside their little cookfire and checking on his tea.

Hugo grinned and Cannon swallowed whatever retort he had been preparing.

"It's all in the footwork," Hugo said, dancing around to illustrate. "Though you shouldn't let me hit you, either."

"Indeed," Cannon said, and without further ado lunged at Hugo, swinging the stick harder than was really necessary.

"Hey!" Hugo exclaimed, dancing away from the tip of Cannon's stick. Then he was laughing, parrying Cannon's blows easily. He went on the offensive then, smiling at how effortless it was to control the fight. It wasn't much of a challenge. He could tell that he would beat Cannon quickly if he gave it his full effort, but he wanted to drag this out as long as he could. Cannon's face had broken into a sweat, and Hugo was pushing him back, forcing him towards the cookfire.

"Hugo," Animus warned. "If you make him spill my tea . . ." He raised a threatening finger and Hugo got the message, swooping around Cannon in an attempt to disarm him instead. Cannon, to Hugo's surprise, moved away in time to avoid him.

"Very good," Hugo said, grinning.

"Don't patronize me," Cannon said, and he lunged at Hugo, attacking with a haphazard barrage of downward cuts. Hugo had to concentrate a bit harder to parry them all, and the last one caught him slightly by surprise, unbalancing him. An overpowering gust of wind struck him broadside at that moment, sending the stick out of his hand and flinging his body to the ground.

Hugo gasped for breath, looking around in the grass for his stick and trying to ignore the sound of Cannon chuckling. "Hey," he said, getting to his feet, "no powers."

Cannon shrugged. "Whatever."

Hugo picked up his stick, flashed Cannon a friendly smile and then darted forward, unleashing a series of jabs in quick succession and forcing Cannon to retreat again. Hugo didn't hold anything back this time, and in a matter of seconds he was holding both of the sticks while Cannon stood there, empty-handed.

Animus laughed and slapped his thigh enthusiastically, nearly spilling his tea. "A good lesson for you, my apprentice," he said. "It seems that you do not know everything after all. Not yet, at least."

Cannon flopped beside the fire and poured himself a cup of tea, grumbling something under his breath.

"What's that?" Animus asked pleasantly.

Cannon glanced at his master out of the corner of his eye. "I don't suppose you could show me how it's done?"

Animus sipped at his tea. "I daresay, I could," he said. "But I will refrain."

Cannon nodded knowingly. "Of course," he said. "No doubt you're feeling a bit unsteady at your age, master. We wouldn't want you getting hurt."

Animus frowned. "Point your manipulation elsewhere, young man."

"Oh, come on," Hugo said. "I'm just getting warmed up. One of you has to give me another bout. Please? I promise I'll whine all day if you don't."

"Oh, very well," Animus said. "Though I daresay you'll whine all day anyway." He stood and stretched so that his back popped in several places. He walked over to Hugo and took a stick, whispering under his breath as he did so. "I really *am* too old for things like this, Hugo. Not that I ever had much interest in them. I pray, do not injure me too badly."

Hugo held his own stick up enthusiastically. It felt good to use his muscles for something other than walking. It was awfully sporting for Animus to join in the fun, but he would have to be careful not to injure the old man. He lunged at the mage, who sidestepped with more dexterity than Hugo expected and knocked him on the back of the head.

"Ow!" Hugo said in surprise.

Animus shrugged. "I said I was uninterested, not ignorant."

Hugo smiled, bringing his stick around again and advancing more carefully. "When did you learn swordplay?" he asked.

"Long ago," Animus said. "Gadjihalt taught me. We were good friends in those days."

Hugo's sword arm went limp in surprise and Animus smacked his left knee sharply.

"Ouch! Wait—Gadjihalt? The Betrayer? You knew him?"

Animus raised an eyebrow. "Of course."

"But then, how old are you?" Hugo said. "I mean, I knew you were old, but . . ."

Cannon snorted from the direction of the fire. "Subtle."

Animus raised his stick again and Hugo countered the attack. "I was born," Animus said, "just before the first Paradise king." He smiled reminiscently. "When Gadjihalt taught me the sword, I was still a young man. Not yet twenty years old—barely more than a child, and not yet an apprentice to the Mage of Wind. Gadjihalt was the first knight of King Rhendin Paradise. That was many years before he betrayed the king."

"Wow," Hugo mumbled, trying to count the years. Animus really *was* old.

Animus struck him another blow on the arm. "Focus."

"How exactly did Gadjihalt betray the king?" Hugo asked. "You must know. The history books never say. They all avoid the subject, like it's something you should not speak of."

"True enough," Animus said. "What do you know already?"

"I know that he was Rhendin's most trusted knight, and that he betrayed him to Shael. He let him into the city, I think. Opened the gate and just let Shael's army in. But I don't understand why he would do that. Was he always evil? Oh, sorry." He had slipped past Animus's guard and knocked him a firm blow in the ribs.

Animus stopped to rub the spot, leaning on his stick. "No," he said, "I think not. But he always had his own demons . . . Shael had great power then. He made Gadjihalt an offer that he couldn't refuse."

Hugo sat on the ground to stretch. He was breathing hard. "What was it?"

"Eternal life."

Hugo stopped, glancing up. "Really?

Animus shrugged. "That he actually had it in his power to give, I doubt. But it was just the thing that would twist Gadjihalt's mind, play off his demons. His parents died when he was young, you see—in a fire, I believe. I do not think that he ever overcame the pain of their passing, the pain that death had brought into his life. The fear of death is common, but Gadjihalt was uncommonly afraid."

Hugo nodded. "Is he still alive?"

"Very likely. He became Shael's most trusted servant, and the leader of his armies during the war. If he is still alive, he must be feeling his age, as Shael would not be able to sustain whatever spell kept Gadjihalt young from inside his prison. I expect that he is hiding somewhere in the Wizard's Ire. He was wounded, I believe, when he defeated the dragon, Kuzo. As far as I know, he has not left the Ire since then."

"He killed a dragon?" Hugo said, looking impressed.

Animus looked sorrowful. "Yes . . . the last dragon. He came one day, to avenge the death of his companion, who died at the hands of Shael. Gadjihalt killed him, so the rumor goes. How, I cannot imagine . . . but then there was never another fighter that could match Gadjihalt's skill.

Hugo was frowning. "I still don't understand how he broke his vow of loyalty to King Rhendin. Even in those days the knights took oaths to the king, didn't they? And sacred oaths to the king are binding. They have magic in them. There are other knights in history who broke their oaths—lied to the king and other stuff—and died on the spot. Why didn't his oath bind him?"

Animus held up a finger. "That was the most troublesome part, especially to Rhendin. However, such magic has little to do with the wind, and as such I am not an expert. If I had to hazard a guess, I would say that Shael was powerful enough to protect Gadjihalt from the effects of breaking his oath. But, if that is true, while Shael's imprisonment keeps his magic at bay, then Gadjihalt may indeed be dead, or at least suffering greatly."

Hugo shivered. "I don't like the idea of knights being able to betray the king."

Animus laughed. "I should think not, seeing as how you will be the king someday." He tossed the stick aside and rubbed his ribs again. "That will have to be enough. An old man can only take so many bruises." Animus shouldered his pack. "I have enjoyed our conversation, but in the best interest of my feet, I think we need silence again. You should practice listening to the sun. There is still the matter of learning to travel like a proper mage."

Chapter Nine

In which Tabitha is mistaken for dinner

BRINLEY WALKED THROUGH a land of endless lakes. They looked golden in the evening light as the sun hit them from a steep angle. Why was she alone? How did she get here? She couldn't remember. All she remembered was that she was looking for Unda.

She came up to the edge of an especially large lake and brushed the surface of the water. "Unda?" she called. Nothing happened. Then hands shot out of the water, grabbed her, and pulled her under before she could scream.

The water changed to leaves and she climbed out of a tall pile beneath a giant oak. Why was she in the leaves? She couldn't remember.

She heard a tapping sound and went to investigate. She found Lignumis next to a horrible, black, twisted tree. He was cutting a thin shaving of wood from the tree with a silver knife. "What are you doing?" she asked. "We shouldn't be here."

"I had to," he said, not looking up at her. "You're not doing anything, so I had to."

"No," she pleaded. "Come back with me." She glanced back at the woods behind her, looking for a safe path out, but the forest was gone.

She saw a silver orb shine through the darkness. It swung back and forth before her, and then it swung away. Her father was standing there behind it, calling for her. He couldn't see her, couldn't hear her. She ran to him, but as she ran she began to shrink. The closer she got to him, the smaller she became. She was the size of a football, a baseball, a plum, a toothpick. When she was the size of an ant, someone scooped her into a small crystal vial. It was the man with the head of a snake that she had seen in Habis's kitchen. He corked the end of the vial and held her up, bringing her close to his beady black eye. "Let me in," he said. Then he dropped the vial and she fell into oblivion.

Brinley jolted awake. Her body was covered in cold sweat and she was breathing hard.

"It was just a dream," she told herself. "Just a dream." She forced herself to lie back down and found herself staring at Unda's painting on the ceiling above her. She and Tabitha had decided to sleep in Unda's bed, but she wished they hadn't; it was small and hard, and Tabitha moved around and made small animal noises in her sleep. She wondered how Unda got any sleep at all. Maybe he didn't. Maybe he just lay there and thought about deep things and wrote in his journals.

She stared at the lake above her, wondering where it might be. She took a few moments to contact the mages and share the image with them, but nobody recognized it, not even Belterras. She didn't know what to do next. Fly all over Aberdeen looking for a phantom lake, she guessed.

What she needed was some direction.

She closed her eyes as the images from her dream came back to her. Did they mean anything? Were these the visions she was supposed to receive? She dismissed the thought. Most likely it was just a dream, a nightmare like any other. She shivered, remembering how it felt to be trapped in that tiny vial. Without thinking, she pulled the crystal vial out of her bag and turned it over in her hand. Was she still alive in there? She shook her head.

I have to stop thinking like that, she thought, and put the vial away. As she did so, her fingers brushed something. It was the button that Maggie had given her. She smiled faintly at it, and then her smile disappeared. Winter was coming. It would bring the cold southern winds down the streets of Caraway, into Maggie's shack. Then the snow would come. How had she survived for so many years on her own? Surely it could not have been comfortable. She wished there was something she could do. She was supposed to look out for people in need. Her jaw tensed. She couldn't even get *that* part right.

She pulled the button out of her bag and put it in her pocket for safekeeping, then rolled out of bed and followed her feet out of Unda's chambers. Wandering alone seemed like the thing to do, especially since she couldn't get anything else right. Aimless wandering was a hard thing to mess up.

As she walked, she became vaguely aware that a deep part of her must have accepted the castle as home. It was the only thing that accounted for her being so comfortable in it. Eventually, she stumbled out of her thoughts and realized that she had found her way into the Magemother's throne room. It was a beautiful space with tall ceilings and the same polished glass floor that ran through the rest of the castle. On the opposite end of the room, behind the Magemother's throne, a waterfall of light fell from the ceiling.

She looked around warily. The last time she had been in here, she had not been alone. Her mother had been there, and Habis, and Hugo . . . and Tennebris. She shook her head, dismissing the memory. He was dead now. Hugo was the new Mage of Light and Darkness, and he was okay. The darkness was still in check.

She strode across the room then, realizing why she had come. What she needed was some direction. She walked into the strands of falling light and closed her eyes at the sensation. Everything bad fell away from her, and she realized that just by living, she had acquired some sort of mortal tarnish made of fear and loneliness.

She breathed deeply. Her body felt warm and strong. Her mind was sharp, clear. She opened her eyes to a strange scene. A chestnut horse stood beside her, and a road stretched ahead. On the far side of the road, across from her, there was a black rider on a black horse. His head was covered, his face veiled. He gestured to her, indicating that she should mount the horse to her side.

She closed her eyes. This was not what she wanted. She wanted to speak with the gods. She didn't know why she hadn't thought of this earlier. She wanted to ask them what she should do. She focused on that thought, prayed that as she opened her eyes again the horse and rider would be gone, that she would see the golden room and archway like she had last time. But it was not to be. The black rider still stared at her from beneath his hood.

She wondered if this might be a different kind of portal, that instead of walking through an archway, she had to ride a horse—no, *race* a horse—before she could gain an audience with the gods.

She mounted her horse and immediately it lurched into motion, speeding down the road at a full gallop. She glanced across the road and saw the dark rider bent over his own steed, pressing ahead. They were coming up on the end of the road. The dark rider beat her there and dismounted. He left his horse as she rode up. He walked to a large black tub of water with a familiar, arrogant stride. Who did it remind her of?

The tub was tall and deep and it shone with a clear iridescence, as if it had been hewn out of a single black crystal. He paused at the water, looking confused, then returned to his horse. The veil fell from his face as he mounted, and she gasped. It was Hugo, and yet not Hugo. His features were dark, twisted, as if she were seeing them through a nightmarish lens. She blinked, and she was back at the beginning of the road. They were starting the race over again, and the rider was not Hugo, but the man with the snake's head.

She lost track of how many times her opponent beat her, how many times he dismounted eagerly, only to puzzle at the tub of water and return to his horse. Sometimes he was Hugo, sometimes he was the snake-man. She tried to win every time; every time, she failed. It was as if her opponents were just faster, stronger.

On the tenth race (or maybe it was twentieth), she felt a sort of rage, a sense of desperation. She *had* to win. She had to beat him to the pool. She didn't know why, but she knew that she must do it. She felt something well up inside her, releasing like a spring uncoiling in her gut. The force of it rushed out of her body like an invisible wave, and then into her horse. It was the force of pure will, perhaps, or the need of her heart. She didn't know, but whatever it was, it worked.

She beat Dark Hugo to the water and dismounted. As soon as she stood before the tub she knew instinctively what she had to do. She wondered why Hugo had not. She placed her cupped hands in the water, filled them, brought them to her lips, and drank.

Flat black steps like slabs of stone rose out of the water and curved around and above her. She climbed the first one, then the second. She fought back a fear of falling as she climbed the third and fourth, for the steps floated freely in the air with nothing around them to hold onto, and nothing between them to prevent her from falling. With each new step they were a little farther apart until on the sixth and seventh, she had to reach up with her arms and let her legs dangle in the air as she pulled herself up. She had to jump to reach the last one.

She was easily twenty feet up now. A fall could seriously injure her, but she pressed on. Need drove her. She knew instinctively what was waiting at the top of the steps. She jumped, slipped, grabbed at the smooth face of the stone, and slid backwards. Hands caught her, pulled her up, set her on her feet. Arms embraced her, held her close.

"Why did it take you so long to come?" a warm voice asked, holding her tightly as she trembled.

She pulled back from him, looked into the face of the god that had created Aberdeen. His eyes were blue; his brown hair sat on a high forehead. His wife stood beside him. She had the same clear blue eyes. She reached out and squeezed Brinley's shoulder.

"I don't know," Brinley said. "I forgot. I don't know how."

"It is easy to forget who you are," he said. "The challenge of life is to live in remembrance."

She nodded. "I'm sorry. I have questions. I have so many questions. Where are the mages hidden? Where is my father? How can I find them? What is the keyword for the bridge?"

His blue eyes flashed, but he said nothing.

"Tell me what to do," she begged.

His wife smiled. "That is not the way," she said. "The answers that you seek are all before you. You will find them when you need them."

And he said, "What else do you seek?"

She felt her mind go blank. What else was there? After all that, was he really going to tell her nothing? Do nothing for her? She felt a silent anger seize her heart. "What about my dreams?"

"Dreams are there to reveal your own mind to you," he said, giving her a significant look. "Yours are filled with fear."

"What am I afraid of?" she asked.

"You fear that you are not enough." he said, touching her heart. "You fear that your friends will abandon you, as your mother did when you were a child. You fear that you will fail her, and your father."

His words cut like glass. "That's not true," she said. "I know my mother left me because she loved me."

He raised his eyebrows. "Your *mind* knows that," he said. "Your heart does not."

She glared at him. "You aren't helping," she said. "I'm the Magemother. You're supposed to help me."

He smiled at her again, his blue eyes reflecting some inner fire that she could not see. "I have given you everything that you need to succeed. What else do you want?" He touched her head with his hand and light fell from it like liquid gold, falling over her, enfolding her with warmth. She closed her eyes, breathing it in, and felt her questions seep out of her like sand. Her mind relaxed. She couldn't remember why she had been troubled at all. Everything was just as it should be.

She opened her eyes, took a step, and was back in the throne room. Her mind fell over the things that she had seen, the things that she had heard. She wasn't sure she had really learned anything useful, but she did feel better. If nothing else, it was a relief that the gods were not as worried as she was. They didn't seem worried at all, in fact.

There was something else that was bothering her: she knew she would not be able to hold on to the peace that lingered in her now. Her fears, her worries, they would return soon, as they always did.

She kicked a stone, and it skidded across the hard floor. She picked it up, thinking that it was an odd place for a stone to be. It was smooth, black, perfectly round, and flat. It fit perfectly into the palm of her hand. It was solid, warm. It reminded her of the way the gods had made her feel. Solid. Warm. Fearless. She put it in her pocket. Maybe carrying a reminder would help.

She found Tabitha looking for her in the entrance hall. She met the other girl at the front doors. "Oh, there you are. Are we done?" Tabitha said. "Where are we going next?"

"To search," Brinley said.

"For Unda's lake?" Tabitha asked. She grinned excitedly, absently turning one shoulder into a wing momentarily; she was ready to be a bird again.

"For Unda's lake."

❖ ❖ ❖

Later, on the shore of the sixteenth lake that they had checked that day, Brinley was crouched on a flat rock that jutted out over the water, comparing her drawing to the view before her. Tabitha stood behind her, changing out of the swan shape and into her own.

Brinley sighed, letting the notebook drop to the ground. "This isn't it either," she said.

"But it is a very lovely lake, isn't it?" the other girl said pleasantly. She held up her hand to block the sun, which was low in the western sky. "And it is such a hot day. Come and put your feet in the water."

"No," Brinley said. "We can do a couple more before the sun goes down. Let's go."

Tabitha shook her head and sat down. "I'm tired," she said. "I've been flying all day, you know." She rubbed her arms. "I think they need a break."

Brinley put a hand to her head and sat down beside Tabitha at the water's edge. "Oh, geez. I forgot! I'm sorry, Tabitha." She was glad for the rest herself, and she knew the water was going to feel good on her feet. She took her boots off, then laid her socks out on the rock and dipped her toes in the water; it was ice cold, in a refreshing sort of way.

"What else have you got in here?" Tabitha asked, picking up the notebook and thumbing through it.

"Nothing," Brinley said, lunging for it, but Tabitha held it out of reach. "Brinley, it's beautiful," she said, staring in awe at a page. "It's me!"

Brinley had drawn a quick portrait of Tabitha one night, just to experiment, and it hadn't turned out too badly, but she didn't know about beautiful.

"Ooh ooh," Tabitha cooed eagerly, handing the book back. "Do another one!" She struck a ridiculous pose and fluttered her eyes in what Brinley guessed was supposed to be an alluring fashion.

Brinley laughed and began to draw. A few minutes later she handed the completed sketch to Tabitha, who shrieked and dropped it. "You gave me antlers! And a mane!" She put a hand to the top of her head and grinned. "Actually, I look pretty good in antlers. Brinley, can you give me feathers?"

After feathering Tabitha, Brinley drew Cassis, then Belterras, then Animus, and then the world came crashing back down on her as she began to sketch Unda. She had forgotten her worries as she played with Tabitha.

She drew Unda from memory, but made him older. When she finished, there was something in his eyes that she had not intended to put there. Worry, she thought, and before she closed the book she wondered if the worry belonged to him, or if some of her own had leaked out onto the page.

"Tabitha?" she said, looking up.

Tabitha was fishing in the pockets of her coat for something. Finally, she drew out a small paper bag filled with tiny cut-up apple pieces. They were so old now that they were brown and nearly dry, but Tabitha didn't seem to mind. She popped one in her mouth and threw several others into the lake.

Brinley sighed. Tabitha had done this at every single lake, claiming that it was the best way to test for sea dragons. "I don't think there are any here," Brinley said patiently, but Tabitha waved her into silence.

"You never know what you will find in a lake," she said. "There are sea dragons here somewhere. There have to be! Belsie said a whole family of them came up the river from the sea and were never heard from again!" She plopped back down beside Brinley and dropped her feet in the water, then slipped into the lake.

"Tabitha, you'll freeze!" Brinley said.

Tabitha shrugged. "I doubt it," she said. She twisted in the water and vanished. In the space where she had been, a tiny minnow leapt twice above the water. Brinley stretched and crossed her legs, settling down on the warm rock to watch the minnow swim. The water was clear, and she could track its movements from a surprising distance. It moved to and fro, darting under rocks, exploring, then diving into the depths of the lake. It returned after a few minutes and began to circle lazily.

Brinley stretched out on the warm rock and rested her head in her hands. She wondered what it would be like to have that kind of power. If she could be a fish or a bird, she would disappear for a week just to think. Well, maybe when she was younger she would have done that. Now she had too many responsibilities to disappear. She thought of her mother, trapped in the naptrap, and of her father, trapped who knew where. She thought of Shael and his dark forest and his monsters and his malice, and how they threatened to pour over a bridge into her world.

Finally, she let her worries slip away and watched the fish. It swam with a perfect, relaxed rhythm. Left, right, left, right, left. She watched it for a long time, longer than she realized, and drifted off to sleep in the rays of the setting sun.

Brinley woke in the little bedroom of Habis's invisible house and couldn't remember how she had gotten there. "Tabitha?" she called, and jumped out of bed to check the room next door. She wasn't in there.

"Tabitha?" she called, walking down the hallway. The door to Habis's storage room was open. She thought she heard a faint tinkling sound coming from within. She entered it, walked past the rows and rows of jars and boxes and books, looking for the source of the noise. Finally, she found it and stopped in her tracks. In the very center of the massive room there was a veritable mountain of naptraps: tiny crystal bottles stacked ten feet high in the shape of a giant pyramid. There were thousands of them.

"Gotcha," a voice whispered in her ear, and she screamed.

She felt something brush her bag and turned to see Hugo backing away from her. There was a wicked grin on his strange, darkened face, and in his hand he held her mother's naptrap.

"No!" Brinley cried, feeling in her bag for the naptrap, but sure enough, it was gone. He had stolen it!

Hugo laughed and tossed it over his shoulder so that it landed on the pyramid. She thought maybe, just maybe, she might find it. She had seen where it had landed.

Then Hugo gave a high, cold laugh and kicked the pyramid. It toppled over, falling into itself and flowing across the floor in a cacophony of shattering glass.

"NO!" Brinley screamed. "NO! MOTHER!"

The stream of crystal vials grew, forming into a wave. It chased her across the floor. She searched for the door, but couldn't find it. The wave swallowed shelf after shelf as it chased her. Finally, when there was no place else to run, it swallowed her too, and sunlight blinded her.

She blinked and held her hand up to block the sun. She was standing on the bridge to the Wizard's Ire. Cassis was there, along with Animus, Archibald, and Cannon. They were all staring at her gravely. Archibald looked sad.

"We've figured it out," Cassis said. "We know why the bridge is failing."

Cannon gave her a disgusted look. "It's you," he said. "The Magemother is in charge of these things."

"No," she whispered. "I'm sorry."

Archibald placed a hand on her shoulder. He looked sad. "I'm afraid it is all your fault, my dear," he said. He looked at the others. "We shouldn't blame her. Not everyone is cut out to be a good Magemother."

Animus nodded. "True, true," he said. "Nothing she can do about that. Just a bad egg. A pity she is not more like her mother."

Tears were rolling down Brinley's face. "I'm sorry!" she said. "I'm so sorry. I didn't know. I didn't know." She squeezed her eyes tightly against the disappointment in their faces, and when she opened them again she was in Cornith.

The king's city was empty, covered in a blanket of winter snow. She shivered, wishing that she had a coat, and then found that she had one on. That was nice. But what was she doing here? She couldn't remember. She shrugged it off, walking towards the castle. There would be warm fires there. She could stay up all night talking with Hugo and Tabitha and they could get hot chocolate in the kitchen.

She stopped as a faint sound reached her ears. She turned, looking for the source, but heard only the soft, feathery sound of snowflakes landing on the ground with a whisper. She took another few steps to the castle and heard it again, more clearly this time.

Whimpering.

Who on earth would be out at this hour? She followed the noise and stopped in an alley between two tall buildings. The whimpering came again, directly below her, filtering faintly through the piled snow. She dropped to her hands and knees and dug at the snow until she hit the cold, hard stone of the street. Her hands moved, searching, digging, until they hit metal. In another minute she had dug out a drain grate. A dark, frostbitten hand slid through the grate slowly and wrapped itself around the cold metal. A face peered out at her, pale, sickly.

"Maggie," Brinley whispered. "What are you doing down there?"

"It's the only place I could find," she said. "My shed burned down. I couldn't build another." A tear pooled in one eye and she raised her hands. "The season was over. I couldn't make any money." She squinted, and then her face changed in sudden recognition. "Magemother, I thought you cared. Why did you leave me? I don't have anyone."

"I know," Brinley said, bending over to tug on the grate. "I'm sorry. I'm so sorry. I'm here now." She tugged on the grate again but it would not budge.

Maggie shook her head. "It's too late," she said. "I died." As she said it, the life went out of her body and she fell onto the frozen floor of the sewer hole.

Brinley stared at her motionless form in disbelief, and then it changed. Maggie's worn face changed into the flat, calculating face of a snake, its beady eyes glowing with life. The man with the head of a snake shifted in Maggie's empty grave and lunged for her. "Let me in," he cried.

Brinley woke. The sun was nearly down now. There was a miniature yellow songbird perched on her hand. The tiny minnow that was Tabitha swam in a small circle in the water next to her. Brinley felt herself relax. It was just a dream, she told herself. Just a dream, like the others. She closed her eyes, willing the image of Maggie in the frozen sewer to leave her mind, but it wouldn't. She had to do something.

Brinley's eyes shot open again. There was a bird on her hand! She jumped in surprise, sending the little bird fluttering, but it righted itself with a few quick beats of its wings and returned to her wrist, where she stared at it warily. "Tabitha?" she said. But the bird simply cocked its head and ruffled its feathers impatiently. "Uh, Tabitha," Brinley called, glancing at the minnow in the water. "I need you." The minnow didn't respond. Holding the bird carefully on her hand, Brinley cast about for a stone or something to kick into the water.

She felt a rush of air on her shoulder and glanced up to see a large bird gliding toward the water. It was very large, with a deep, round bill like a pelican, and it was . . . hunting.

"Oh, no!" she said aloud. "Don't!"

But it was too late. The bird snatched Tabitha from the water and circled away. Then several things happened at once: the minnow grew and the bird slipped in the air and Tabitha was hanging onto the bird's legs with both hands, at which point the bird gave a startled squawk and fell out of the sky.

Tabitha rolled on the soft grass as she landed.

"Well, I never!" she said, wagging her finger at the bird, who looked like it might die of fright. "You need to be more careful, or what you catch might end up catching you." When she was finished, the poor thing scuttled away to a safe distance on foot before taking off again.

"Brinley," Tabitha said, brushing herself off. "Don't tell Belsie about that, okay? Oh, what do you have there?" She picked up the little bird from Brinley's wrist and became instantly excited. "Why, it's Peanut!"

"Who?" Brinley asked, peering at the bird.

"Peanut," Tabitha said. "I trained him to carry messages between us and Archibald."

Brinley blinked, remembering how Archibald had said they had devised a way to communicate with each other. "Archibald can talk to birds?"

Tabitha gave a weary sigh. "Not very well, though I've been coaching him. But Peanut is a wonderful listener, aren't you, Peanut?" she said, smiling at him. She dug into the pocket of her dress and brought out a small handful of seed, which the bird took to at once.

"Well," Brinley said after a moment. "What does he say?"

"Give him a minute," Tabitha said protectively.

Brinley sighed and began to tap her foot, but the bird finished the seeds quickly and then began to sing.

"Oh, my," Tabitha said, nodding encouragingly. "And then what happened?"

After what seemed like an incredible amount of time, Tabitha began to translate. "He says that Archibald arrived in Ninebridge and found his acquaintance, but that the person—a cat, yes?—ran from him, and now he's chasing it."

"A cat?" Brinley asked, bewildered. "What is he doing chasing a cat?"

Tabitha tweeted something to the bird and it sang a reply. "Oh," she said, nodding. "It's a magical cat."

"Is he in any danger?" Brinley asked.

"It sounds like it," Tabitha returned a moment later.

"Well, then send Peanut back and make sure he's okay."

Tabitha nodded. She chatted with the bird for another minute and then released it to the sky. "What now?" she asked, looking around. "Are we going to camp?"

Brinley shook her head. "I'm not tired. I just had a nap. You?"

"No," Tabitha said. "Being a fish is very restful."

"Hey, that's right," Brinley said, remembering. "I didn't even know you could be a fish! When did you learn that?"

Tabitha's eyes went wide. She had never told Brinley about her accidental trip into the nymph kingdom to rescue Archibald. There were many things that she had learned there, about Archibald being Brinley's father, about Brinley's mother growing up in the nymph kingdom. She had promised Archibald that she would say nothing about it. It was his business anyway, finding a way to tell his daughter. She hadn't known how to tell Brinley how she had promised to find the old Magemother, either. It didn't seem necessary to talk about it, since that's what they were doing anyway. It hadn't seemed necessary to talk about any of it, in fact.

Brinley waved a hand in front of her face. "Tabitha? There you are. I was just saying how I didn't know you could turn into a fish. That's very hard, isn't it? I thought you wouldn't learn fish for a while yet."

Tabitha nodded. "Belsie taught me," she said simply.

Brinley beamed at her. "You never cease to amaze me, Tabitha. I never know what you'll turn into next."

Tabitha's face went blank again. She was thinking of another creature she had formed, a shape she had taken in that dream world of the nymphs. She rarely let herself think about it. She never wanted to take that shape again, but at the same time she couldn't wait for the moment when it would be necessary. The power of it, the freedom. It was exhilarating, unlike any other creature she had formed . . . and it was terrifying. She didn't trust herself as much in that shape. Even now, she remembered the ancient craving for flight, for fire, and for death.

"Tabitha?"

Tabitha snapped back, seeing Brinley again. "Oh," she said. "What?"

Brinley just smiled.

Tabitha shook herself, trying to remember what they had been talking about. "So," she said. "Since we're not tired, what will we do? Look at more lakes?"

"No more lakes," Brinley said. She pulled out the wooden button that Maggie had given her and twirled it between her fingers. "I want to do something. Let's fly."

Tabitha took the swan shape again and they took flight, banking high over the lake. "Where do you want to go?"

"Back to Caraway," she said. "I have an idea."

Chapter Ten

In which Hugo skips rocks

HUGO AND HIS COMPANIONS camped on a little hill overlooking a lake. The sun was going down and Hugo sat apart from the other two in a foul mood. The day had not gone well at all. Animus had insisted on silence so that Hugo could listen to the sun, but for all his listening, he hadn't heard a thing. He knew that Animus expected more progress, given his breakthrough that morning, but it just hadn't come.

Hugo picked up a rock and chucked it into the lake. The sunset was beautiful, but he couldn't see it, focused as he was on his frustrations. The only good thing that had happened that day, other than showing Cannon a thing or two about swordplay, was when Brinley had contacted him.

Shortly after they were on the road that morning she had reached out to him with a story about the Mage of Water. Apparently she had been searching Calypsis when she had come across a painting of a lake in Unda's room. For whatever reason, she thought that's where he might be hiding. She wanted to know if anyone recognized it, but no one had. Since then Hugo couldn't shake the feeling that he knew where that lake was. He had been wrestling with it all day without success, like a forgotten word stuck on the tip of his tongue.

He tossed another rock at the water, skipping it across the surface this time. He smiled. Nine skips. Not bad.

A bird floated down from the evening air and alighted upon the water, and Hugo watched it, letting his mind go blank. The bird circled the little lake and dipped its head in, splashed water on its back, and dove for its dinner as Hugo watched. Finally, when the bird had glided around to the bank nearest him, it turned an eye on Hugo. Something in the gesture, the eye staring at him from the lake, triggered something. He sat bolt upright and gave a small shout. The bird squawked and darted away, glancing over its shoulder at him in annoyance.

From the fire, Animus called, "Everything okay?"

"Yeah," Hugo said, waving his hand. "Everything's fine." He forced himself to sit back down, struggling to contain his excitement.

BRINLEY! he shouted, throwing his mind across the distance between himself and the Magemother.

Hugo? her voice came back quietly. *Is that you?*

I just realized where your lake is, he said, excitement bubbling out in his words. *I was just sitting here, staring at this little lake, and it reminded me of another lake, and it hit me. Brinley, Unda's lake is the Lake of Eyes!*

Really? she asked. *Are you sure?*

I think so, he said. *And it doesn't surprise me either. Brinley, I never told you—I forgot, I guess, with everything that happened—but on the night that we met Peridot at the Lake of Eyes, I saw something . . .*

What? she prompted.

Eyes. Big ones . . . They came up out of the lake and sort of watched me—I know it sounds ridiculous, but that's what I saw— I mean, it's called the Lake of Eyes, after all, so why shouldn't it watch you, right? I think there is something living in that lake, Brinley, and I'm almost certain it's the lake in the painting.

Hmm, she said, and Hugo guessed that she was studying the picture. *Well, it doesn't really look like the Lake of Eyes to me. I've only been there once, though. We'll go check it out. I think Tabitha will want to go anyway, just because of the eyes. She'll want to know what sort of creature has eyes like that. I expect she'll think it's her sea dragon. How many eyes did you see? Please don't say two.*

Dozens, Hugo said, grinning.

Poor Tabitha. Maybe I won't tell her.

Poor you if those creatures are mean, and their bodies are as big as their eyes, Hugo said. *Be careful.*

I will, she said. *Hugo, how are you feeling? Has anything new happened with our mutual friend?*

Hugo thought about it. About the mirror, and what Animus had said about the name.

No, he said before he could stop himself. *I mean, yes. But I don't want to talk about it. I don't think I can talk about it yet. I need to figure it out first. How about you? Learn anything new?*

Brinley told him of her suspicions about where Lignumis might be and filled him in about what she had learned from Habis about the bark. He probably didn't need to know, but she was talking and he was listening, so she rambled on as long as she could. When she had run out of things to say, she was silent, but neither of them broke the connection.

After a while, Brinley said, *Hugo, if being a mage without a master to train you is anything like being the Magemother without a Magemother to teach me, then I think it must be very hard. But we still have each other. Don't forget that.*

Hugo nodded, then said, *Yeah,* when he remembered that she couldn't see him nodding. At her words, something moved inside him, something like gratitude, friendship, kindness, but different. He was glad that she understood.

Good night, Brinley, he said, and made his way to the fire to join the others.

He felt better. It was talking to Brinley that had done it; he would be able to sleep now. "Hey," he said, sitting down, "it turns out today wasn't a total waste of time. Brinley and I just figured out where Unda's lake is."

Chapter Eleven

In which a foundation is laid

"I NEED YOU TO HELP ME build a house," Brinley said. She was standing with Cassis and Tabitha in a little secluded clearing in the trees outside the city of Cornith, with Caraway Castle gleaming in the valley beyond.

Cassis looked wary. Evidently this was not what he was expecting. "A house?"

Brinley nodded. "A house. I want you teach me about rock and metal, and help me build a house. It will be a special house. Each of the mages will help me. It will be a gift that only the Magemother could give."

Tabitha beamed in sudden comprehension. "For Mad Maggie!" she exclaimed. "Oh, this is wonderful! I'm going to build birdhouses for her garden." She scampered off into the trees in search of supplies.

Cassis cocked an eyebrow. "*Mad* Maggie?"

Brinley nodded. "A homeless woman in the city."

Cassis fiddled with his robe thoughtfully, avoiding her gaze. "I will honor your wishes, of course," he said. "But you should know that I do not approve of giving things to people for free. I think that they are better served by learning how to provide for themselves."

Brinley nodded thoughtfully. "I don't think she's that kind of person. She works for her keep now, little as it is. She works the grinding wheels in a blacksmith's shop."

Cassis brightened. "She works with metal? That is good."

Brinley nodded. "We can build her a workshop here."

Cassis was rolling up his sleeves. "Yes. If her work is good, she'll be close enough to the city to bring in business."

"Where do we begin?" she asked.

Cassis smiled. "At the beginning," he said. And with that, he began to teach her of stone.

She learned that every stone had its own consciousness, and that a new mind was born when a stone was broken or chipped or hewn away from its former self. Death, she found, was a thing that stone knew nothing of. Each piece remembered where it had come from, its lineage from mountain to boulder to river rock.

"Stones have long memories," Cassis explained, and he taught her how to feel the life in a rock and place a memory inside of it so that she could carry it with her always.

She watched him as he drew hard, pure stone out of the earth in the center of the clearing and spread it across the ground like quicksilver. The liquid stone melded twigs and leaves as it passed, and it smelled like burning chalk. She guided him sometimes, and other times he created as he saw fit. They laid the foundation of a root cellar and gave her a round, comfortably sized living room and a short, narrow kitchen with a round stone window overlooking the city. On the side of the house Cassis drew out a long flat table of stone on the ground. Walls grew out of it on three sides, with the fourth left open, a pillar rising out of it to support the roof.

"It's beautiful," Brinley said appreciatively, laying a hand on his shoulder.

He breathed in deeply. "Ah, it feels good to create again. My mind has been riddled with questions of bridges and stone for too long."

Brinley smiled. "I'm glad you had fun."

"Fun?" he said thoughtfully, as if he was trying to remember what the word meant. "Yes. I suppose I did." He gave a sharp laugh like a dog barking. "I can't say that I've had this much fun since Chantra left."

Brinley's ears perked up. "Chantra?" she asked. "Were you two close?"

He shrugged. "Close enough," he said. "It is hard to be very close with someone so much younger than yourself, but we spent a fair amount of time together. I was her favorite, I think."

Brinley sat down on the now cool stone of Maggie's new home. "I didn't know that," she said. "Can you tell me about her?"

Cassis leaned against the corner of the house thoughtfully. A hand strayed to his pointed gray beard, twisting it. "She was always on the move, Chantra. Always learning. Always wanting to see something new." He barked a laugh. "And she loved rubies. I was always bringing them to her when I found them, and she was always wanting more. I remember the last time I saw her she was trying to get me to teach her how to see inside one."

"See inside it?"

Cassis nodded. "There is a whole world inside of a stone," he said. "Most never learn to find it. It is simple for me, being what I am, but it is a great feat of wizardry for others to see inside of a stone, much less enter it."

Brinley blinked, startled. "What do you mean? Go inside it?" she asked.

He nodded, grinning. "Like I said, there is a whole world inside of a stone. If you could enter a cut gemstone you would find yourself in a place like a palace of glass, full of memory, patience, and peace." The corner of his mouth twitched. "I spent a whole winter inside the emerald ring of the king of Caraway once, when I was young. I never told him."

Brinley laughed. "And Chantra wanted to go inside a ruby? That makes sense. Her whole room was red. In fact, almost everything she owned was red. And she did have several rubies, come to think of it."

Cassis nodded. "If there is any stone with fire in it, it is a ruby. I think she saw it as the bridge between our worlds, hers and mine. She wanted desperately to live in one. She said she would carry her house with her wherever she went." He laughed again. "I think she would have figured it out too, if I'd had more time to teach her." His face fell.

Brinley put a hand on his arm. "You will," she said. "You'll still get your chance."

"Is she alive?" he asked, giving her a piercing look. "Can you feel her out there?"

"Yes," Brinley said. "I can't find her, but she's definitely there."

Cassis relaxed, looking up at the house. It looked like a ruin, nothing but a stone skeleton, but it had promise. "You are off to a good start," he said. He glanced at her out of the corner of his eye. "This is a kind thing to do," he said quietly. "Something your mother would have done."

Brinley felt her heart swell. *Like my mother,* she thought. Maybe things would turn okay after all. She surveyed the house. It was going to work, she thought. If nothing else, she could do *this* right.

A scraping sound made them both jump. Brinley turned and saw there was a bear walking towards them. A giant pile of twigs and bark and river rock was lashed to his back with string, and he grunted under the weight of it. Brinley's eyes grew wide, staring as the beast grunted under the heavy load. When he reached them, he raised a sharp claw and severed the string, dumping his burden on the ground.

Tabitha trotted out of the woods behind it and patted it on the back. "Thanks," she said brightly. "I couldn't have done it without you!"

The bear sauntered back into the woods without a backward glance.

"I got supplies!" Tabitha said. "Oh, are we done? It's beautiful! It looks cold, though." She rubbed her arms with her hands, eyeing the open roof and the empty doors and windows. "Drafty."

Cassis gave her a wry smile. "Doors of stone are difficult to open," he said, "but there will be windows later, I think." He glanced sideways at Brinley. "And a roof of glass, if need be."

Brinley shook her head. "Windows, yes. But I will need to find Lignumis to build the roof. We will need wood. There's no way around that. We'll find him," she added firmly, and Cassis nodded.

"I'm sure you will," he said.

"Tabitha," Brinley said, "the birdhouses will have to wait. We need to return Cassis to Ninebridge, and then we need to go to the Lake of Eyes. Hugo has remembered where Unda's lake is."

"Really?" Tabitha said. "The Lake of Eyes?" She clapped her hands. "That's wonderful!" Then she yawned, and as her mouth opened it changed into the open beak of the black swan again. She turned, allowing Brinley to climb onto her back. Brinley fingered a small pebble in her hand as they rose into the sky.

Chapter Twelve

In which Hugo talks to himself in a mirror

HUGO SPENT THE NEXT DAY of his journey walking through field after field of sunflowers. The flowers were small at first, coming up to their knees, but by afternoon they were passing through fields in which the flowers stood taller than a man. They produced the best seeds in the land, Hugo knew. He had heard of their size, but had never seen them in person. He bent a stalk as they walked and began to pick seeds out of the flower's face.

"Careful there," Animus said.

"Why? AGH!" Hugo released the flower and backed away, gagging.

"A toxic gas is emitted by the flower if the seeds are picked prematurely," Animus explained. "That one is not quite ripe."

"I can see that," Hugo said between coughs, waving a hand around his face. "How long does it take to wear off?"

Animus shrugged. He raised his hands and a warm breeze washed over Hugo, ruffling his hair and tossing the edges of his clothing before it subsided. He sniffed; the smell was gone.

"Thanks." Hugo studied the seeds in his hand. He dropped them, unwilling to risk further surprises.

"Wise," Animus said, turning back to the road.

The road, which was little more than a footpath, wound through the sunflowers so that they had to part a couple of plants in order to step through.

Hugo sniffed himself again just to make sure. Thankfully, the smell was truly gone. "No harm done," he said.

"Unless the Magemother's ogre is after us," Animus's voice came. "They have a remarkable sense of smell."

Hugo did some quick calculations in his head. "He would have found us by now if he was after us. Where do you suppose it went after it attacked Brinley with that witch?"

"Who knows?" Animus said. "But we should probably keep our guard up."

A few moments later, Hugo nearly ran into Animus. He and Cannon had stopped right in front of him. "Hey, why did we stop?"

"Shh," Animus said, then he vanished. A summer wind fluttered away from the spot through the sunflowers and Hugo and Cannon were left alone.

"Excellent," Hugo muttered. But Cannon waved him into silence.

"I think he sensed something," Cannon whispered.

Hugo was trying to decide whether they should stay put or continue on when he heard what must have stopped Animus: a thrashing sound, like something large moving through the field. It was coming straight toward them. He and Cannon darted down the path. Whatever it was, it didn't sound friendly. Hopefully Animus was out there, watching its progress. The fact that the mage had not returned was a good thing, he hoped. It meant that he wasn't in any real danger just yet.

With a final crash, something broke through the line of sunflower stalks. It was an ogre, all right, and a big one, too. Hugo had never seen one himself, but he had spent a fair amount of time reading about them. He drew his sword, wishing bitterly that he had worked harder on listening to the light. If he had figured out his powers by now this probably wouldn't be such a stressful situation. Hugo hoped that Cannon was a match for the ogre if Animus did not reappear.

The ogre had seen them now, and they darted off the path, zigzagging through the sunflowers.

"Split up!" Hugo cried. "Confuse him!"

He heard the crashing resume behind him and smelled the putrid gas again; evidently the ogre was knocking seeds out in his rampage. He heard heavy footfalls, and then something massive crashed into his right shoulder, jarring his teeth and lifting him off his feet. He landed painfully and glanced up at the ogre.

The beast smiled. A slight breeze made his hair flutter slightly, then made him frown. The flowers around him were stirring in the wind now too. He took a step toward Hugo and the wind increased tenfold. His skin was flapping in the wind now. With a great effort, he took another step.

The wind doubled. The stalks around him bent over, laid flat against the ground, and Animus materialized out of the wind in front of the ogre. The ogre sneered at Animus and took another step. Animus held up a hand, a vortex of wind pouring from it, enveloping the ogre. The beast dropped to all fours, sinking his claws into the earth. The muscles on his arms and legs rippled. Small cuts began to form on his face where the wind tore at his skin. He lifted one leg slowly as if to take another step, and Animus brought up his other hand. There was a sound like a thunderclap and the ogre was blasted into the air, along with several feet of dirt and rocks and sunflowers. He flew a long way before landing with a distant thump on the other side of the field, out of sight. Animus looked as calm as ever.

"Cannon!" Animus shouted, looking around for his apprentice.

Cannon emerged from the sunflowers. "I'm here! Oh, well done. Wow, he is a big one. Bigger up close."

Animus nodded. "Big, and strong too, if a little bit stupid. I am surprised that he attacked you with me nearby. Very ambitious of him, don't you think?" He jerked his thumb in the general direction of the ogre. They could all hear him now, huffing through the sunflowers toward them. "I think it best if I take him back to Ninebridge. Captain Mark might benefit greatly from questioning him. Continue on this course until I meet up with you."

"How long will you be?" Hugo asked, dreading the thought of spending the rest of the day alone with Cannon.

"Not too long," Animus said. "Not too short, either. Stick together, you two, and don't do anything foolish."

With that, Animus vanished. He must have reappeared near the ogre, because Hugo heard the crashing sounds a second later. Then a funnel cloud formed over the field in front of him. The ogre was sucked up into it, and the cloud sped off across the sky.

Cannon and Hugo glanced at one another. "So," Hugo said conversationally, starting back towards the path, "reckon we could have taken him ourselves?"

Cannon snorted. "I reckon *I* might have, though I don't know what you would have had to do with the process."

"Whatever," Hugo said, his voice rising. "I bet you would have had your hands full by yourself. You're not as powerful as Animus yet, no matter what you say."

Cannon coughed. "And I suppose you think you could have taken that ogre all alone, do you?"

Hugo scowled. He couldn't have. He knew that, and he knew that Cannon knew it too. Why was Cannon so grumpy all the time? It was his pride, that's what it was. He had the biggest head of anyone Hugo had ever known.

"Maybe I couldn't have," he said, "but it would have been a lot better than trying to fight him with you."

"Whatever," Cannon said, echoing Hugo's snippy tone. "I'm hungry. You?"

"No," Hugo said flatly. He was, but he didn't feel like agreeing with Cannon about anything right now.

"Fine," Cannon said. He pointed into the distance. "I'm going to go make lunch. You can have some when you catch up. If you're hungry by then."

Hugo scowled at Cannon's back as he lifted himself into the air and sped into the distance.

"Whatever," Hugo grumbled, kicking a rock. He was better off on his own for a while anyway. At least this way he wouldn't have to listen to Cannon whine about everything.

"All alone at last," a voice said.

Hugo spun around, gawking at the small form that had stepped onto the path. It was a kudri, a small, slender, dwarf-like creature that served Shael. They had been used as spies and assassins in the days of the war, and were renowned for their speed and stealth.

"I thought he'd never leave," a woman's voice said behind him. Hugo turned again, drawing his sword.

"You," he said. It was the witch, March.

"Me," she agreed, cocking her head to the side. "We've come to have a word with you, Hugo. I hope you don't mind."

Hugo backed away from them, trying to put sufficient distance between them to keep an eye on both. "You brought that ogre here," he said. "You lured Animus away."

"Yes," the kudri said with a dark grin. "I'm afraid he would not have approved of our meeting with you."

Hugo's face went blank. He reached out with his mind. *Animus!* he called.

The kudri leapt forward and trapped Hugo's sword between his two daggers. At the same moment, March slammed something hard onto his head.

"None of that," she said as the kudri twisted the daggers, ripping Hugo's sword away. "Let's keep this meeting private."

Hugo grunted and dropped to his knees, hands going to the cap on his head. The pain was unbearable, but it let up after a moment. His fingers ran over it, trying to figure out what it was. It was made of steel, and it was small, not much bigger than his hand, but it was clamped down tightly on the crown of his head, and it seemed to be blocking the connection that he had to the other mages.

"Don't struggle," the kudri advised, picking up Hugo's sword and stepping away.

Hugo got the tip of a finger under the edge of the cap and attempted to pry if off, but the cap only tightened in response, squeezing his head so hard he thought it was going to crack. Numbly, he dropped his hands, wincing. "Are you here to kill me?" he asked. March laughed.

The kudri waved Hugo's sword dismissively. "Obviously not," he said, "or you would already be dead. I bring a message from Lord Shael."

Hugo grimaced. "I don't want any messages from Lord Shael," he said. "I thought he would have known that, but I guess he's dimmer than I thought."

March slapped him across the face. "It is not wise to insult my father," she hissed. "Especially when he has been gracious enough to spare your life."

The kudri nodded in agreement. "You may not be interested in him," he said, "but he is interested in you. Believe me, it's a predicament I understand well."

March scowled at the kudri and he stopped talking abruptly. "Ahem," she coughed. "Shael has sent us to offer you some advice."

"Advice?" Hugo said, glancing in the direction that Cannon had gone. Why had they not stuck together? "What advice?"

March smiled. "Talk to the darkness."

Hugo felt a shiver run down his spine.

March nodded. "Yes. You can feel the power in it, can't you? The truth of it? You are the Mage of Light and Darkness. You must give the darkness room inside yourself. You have to face it, or it will destroy you. That is the message from Shael."

"I won't," Hugo said.

"Then it will destroy you," March said, taking a step forward. "Shael knows this. He has known your predecessors well—better than anyone. He has watched your efforts as you have tried to learn from Animus. He says that you will make no progress that way."

"But I have made progress," Hugo said.

March swept his comment aside. "If you wish to find your true power, then you must look to the darkness as well as the light. You cannot find one without the other."

Hugo squinted suspiciously at her. "Why would Shael want to help me?"

"Because you hold the balance," March said. "The powers of darkness in this world flow though you. The dark has as much interest in your success as the light does. Our survival depends on yours. Our power flows through you."

Hugo shook his head. "No. Not if I don't choose it."

The kudri laughed. "That is not how it works. If it were, you could kill me with a thought. Try it. You can't. The power of light and darkness flows through you, but you do not control it, no more than Animus controls the wind."

"But he does control it," Hugo insisted.

"Control is an illusion," March spat. "There is something else you should know: stop trying to control everything. It will get you nowhere."

The kudri tossed Hugo's sword into the sunflowers and backed away into the tall stalks.

"Shael has as much invested in your success as anyone," March called as they retreated into the sunflowers. "His counsel is a gift to you," she called out of them. "You would do well to heed it."

Hugo sighed, rubbing his head where the cap still bit into it. How was he going to get it off? He tried to distract himself from the thing that had entered his mind like an animal, crouching in the corner of his thoughts like a bitter truth: he had to speak to the darkness. He knew it was the truth. He didn't know whether hearing it from Shael made it less true, but it made him want to hide from it.

"Where did you go, sword?" he said out loud, hiding from the thought again.

It took him several minutes to find it. He had mumbled to himself throughout the search, hiding from what he knew he had to do.

Animus! he shouted with his mind, and the sound reverberated in his own head, reflected back to him by the cap. "ANIMUS!" he shouted. But there was no response. The mage would be halfway to Ninebridge by now.

Blast. He glanced up the path, searching for some sign of Cannon, but saw nothing. No doubt he'd gone a good long way. He probably wanted Hugo to be starving by the time he got there for lunch. He was on his own for a while.

He withdrew the little mirror from his pocket and turned it over in his hands, settling down in the middle of a wide patch of flattened stalks. Yellow heads peeked out of the verdure around him as if watching him, waiting for him to open the mirror. Maybe he should wait, he thought. Maybe he should get back on the trail and walk and wait until Animus came back. Animus would know what to do.

He almost got up, then remembered something that made him stay put: Animus was the one who had given him the mirror. He had known already. He had known that he would have to speak with the darkness. Why else would he have given him the mirror? But then, why didn't Animus just say that? Maybe he didn't want to be responsible for pointing Hugo toward the darkness.

He turned the mirror over in his hand again. He had not opened it since the previous night. He had snapped it closed then, as soon as he had opened it and seen his own face peering back at him. It wasn't exactly his face, of course—that was the scary part. It was him, but it was dark, twisted. It was the dark side of him. He put his thumb on the latch and remembered something. Animus had suggested naming it. He said it might help.

Hugo thought about what he should name it. It was like his shadow.

"Shadow," he said aloud, testing the name. He rolled his eyes. What a stupid name. That was a bad name even for a dog. He thought of doing his own name backwards.

"Oguh."

Terrible. And it sounded like ogre. He shook his head. This was a part of himself he was trying to name. It should be easy. He felt his train of thought grind to a stop. He was the Mage of Light and Darkness. He scraped the sunflower stalks apart between his feet, searching for earth. When he found it, he wrote with his finger: M.O.L.A.D.

He opened the mirror.

The twisted shade of himself was there, waiting for him.

"I am Hugo," he said formally. "The Prince of Aberdeen, and the Mage of Light and Darkness. You are my darkness. You are Molad."

Molad mouthed the name silently, trying it out. "Good," he said. "It's about time you—"

Hugo snapped the mirror shut. Molad had spoken. He had known that was going to happen, of course, but he hadn't known that it would feel so . . . normal. It felt like talking to anyone. That terrified him. He steadied himself and opened the mirror again.

"As I was saying, before you panicked, it's about time you started talking to me." Molad spoke in a mocking tone that seemed eerily familiar. It was his own, he realized. Was that really what he sounded like?

Molad sat down inside the mirror and Hugo recognized the room around him. "Hey," he said, "you're in my room!"

Molad rolled his eyes. "Our room," he said. He smiled. "So, I heard what the kudri was saying. Finally talked some sense into you, eh? I hoped he would. I can help you. What do you want?"

"Nothing," Hugo said.

"Liar. You want to travel like a mage. You want your power. You forget," he said, tapping his head. "I see everything you see. Your life is my life. We're the same. Equals."

"No," Hugo said. "Remember, I named you. I'm in charge."

Molad chuckled. "Okay, Hugo. You're right. You're in charge. What do you want, then?"

Hugo glared at the tiny dark vision of himself in the mirror. "I want to learn to move like a mage," he said.

Molad nodded. "You've been holding Animus back."

"Yes."

"Good. It's simple. I know how to do it."

"Tell me," Hugo said.

Molad smiled wickedly. "I can't. "Don't get me wrong," he went on smoothly, "I can help you. I just can't tell you how to do it." He winked. "I have to show you."

Realization dawned on Hugo. He had been wondering what the price would be. "I have to give you control." It wasn't a question.

Molad chuckled again. "Control is an illusion," he said. "But yes, that's the price of my knowledge. That is the price of power, you see? Relinquishing control. Don't be afraid," he pressed as Hugo began to close the lid of the mirror again. "You're only giving power to yourself." He opened his arms. "After all, I'm you."

Hugo snapped the mirror shut again and closed his eyes. There had to be another way, he thought. Any other way. He wanted to talk to Brinley, not that it mattered; the cap wouldn't allow it. But he wanted to hear her thoughts. He wished that he could. He thought of simply waiting. Animus, no doubt, would be able to help him get the cap off, and then he would have others willing to help him make these decisions.

Something welled up inside him: loneliness and determination mixed together. Facing the darkness was *his* fate, his responsibility alone. He alone was the Mage of Light and Darkness. He alone had to face this and learn how to deal with it. In the end, nobody would be able to help him.

He opened the mirror again and said, "What do I have to do?"

Letting Molad take control of his body turned out to be just like falling asleep—simple and difficult at the same time. Eventually he managed it. When it happened, he felt distanced from his body, powerless. He could still feel, still see, but he sensed that he was merely along for the ride.

Molad stretched deeply and laughed, then darted off the path and into the sunflowers. He ran for what seemed like an hour, like a dog that had been penned up for the whole summer and then finally released to stretch his legs. He stopped at the edge of a winding brook and drank deeply from it, and Hugo saw their flickering reflection in an eddy of the stream. His face looked different with Molad in control. Handsome still, but devious, haunted. He didn't want to think about what would happen to him if he couldn't learn how to control Molad. There had to be a better way to balance light and dark than giving his other half free rein like this.

Something made a noise in the underbrush and his head snapped upward. Molad peered into the tall flowers and smiled. He crossed the stream and crept softly on the pads of his feet, parting the stalks silently as he passed between them. Suddenly a bird shot out of the flowers. A quail, he thought. Moving faster than Hugo would have thought possible, Molad jumped and snatched the bird out of the air.

What are you going to do with it? Hugo asked.

Play, Molad said. Hugo felt excitement flutter through them and winced. Molad squeezed the bird tightly, trapping its wings, and then released it. He caught it expertly before it got out of arm's reach. *Are you paying attention, Hugo?*

He released the bird again. He did not catch it right away this time. He watched it fly. He watched it in a way that Hugo had never watched anything before. The bird seemed to slow under his gaze. He could see the feathers bending on the air as the wings moved up, down, up. He saw the way the light changed as the bird turned, tipping this way and that. He was aware of every feather, each shape and shade.

You have to see as the light sees, if you want to see the light, Molad whispered. *You must be moved by what moves the light, if you want to move in the light.*

What moves the light? Hugo asked, mesmerized by the way they had seemingly stepped out of time. The bird was still just ten feet away. Everything seemed to have slowed down.

Truth, Molad said. *The truth that all light is connected.* His eyes glinted. *Like the darkness . . . Light is here, and light is there, but there is only one Light, just as there is only one Darkness. It's all the same light. It's all the same darkness. Light is one. Darkness is one.*

Molad closed his eyes and Hugo felt a subtle tipping, a shifting in the region of their middle. Molad took a single step, and then they were floating in the air. The bird was in their hands again, except they didn't have hands. They didn't have a body at all. Rather, everything felt like their body. The air itself swam across the surface of their body. The bird flew through it. They surrounded the bird, holding it tightly, and stepped back to the ground. They were back where they started, across from the little brook, and the quail was clamped firmly in Molad's hand again.

Let it go, Hugo said. *You've taught me what I wanted to learn, and you've had your fun.*

Hugo felt their hand tighten around the bird, crushing it slowly. Molad smiled and dropped the bird's body on the ground. *Now I've had my fun.*

Hugo blinked at the sudden return of power. His body tingled. It was *his* body again, and he never wanted to give it up again. He picked up the bird and walked back to the trail, where he built a small fire. He cleaned the quail with the small knife from his belt and then cooked it. He wasn't hungry anymore, but at least now it hadn't died for nothing. He finished the quail and doused the fire.

When he went to retrieve his sword, he found it covered in mud, so he wiped the blade on his shirt and proceeded to polish the gleaming emerald salamander on the hilt thoughtfully. The symbol of the Paradise kings. His family. His mind drifted over the long line of men who had held that name before him. What would they think of him now, the boy king who could not find his power, who had a darkness inside him that was more powerful than his own will?

Hugo's eyes went wide. *I have a devil inside me*, he thought. How was he going to tell Brinley? He shook away the thought, sheathing his sword. What had happened was done. He would never let Molad have control again. He might as well make the best of it, though. There was no sense in ignoring the power that Molad had shared with him, the things he had learned.

He made his way back to the trail and focused on a distant point on the landscape. He tried to see it the way Molad had seen the quail. He took a single step, felt a tiny inkling of the turning around his middle, and fell on his face in the dirt ten feet from where he'd started.

"Ugh," he growled, getting to his feet again. What did Molad say? See as the light sees. Hear what it hears. He picked another spot on the trail, closer this time, and tried again, only to be met with the same result. Facedown in the dirt, he groaned again. His hand scraped a rock as he pushed himself up, and he scowled at it. Then he picked it up and threw it as far as he could.

It happened almost by accident. The rock, flying through the air, reminded him of the quail. Then he was seeing the rock as Molad had seen the quail: in perfect, slow-motion detail. He felt the rock moving through the body of the light, and then it was his body. He was the light and the light was him. There was that subtle tipping around his middle again and the rock was there, in his hand, and he was . . .

Where was he? He fell from ten feet up and hit the dirt hard. He was a long stone's throw from where he had begun, though. His leg hurt badly; he thought he might have sprained his knee. He smiled. The knee didn't matter now. He had felt the subtle shifting more clearly this time. That was the key, he knew, to know the light and still know yourself. It was like being here and everywhere at the same time. He moved down the path with the speed of light until he found Cannon. He stopped just out of sight, then decided he didn't want any company just yet. He glanced at a large oak tree a mile down the path and tipped himself toward it, losing himself in the light, then weaved back out of it at the foot of the oak. He placed a hand upon the warm, sunlit bark and smiled.

Wonderful, isn't it? Molad's voice said in his head.

Hugo bristled. *I didn't give you permission to enter my mind.*

Molad laughed. *Your mind? Your mind is not your own any more than your body is. It is ours. Our mind. Our body.*

"Liar!" Hugo said aloud. *My mind is me. And I am not you.*

Molad chuckled darkly. *So much to learn,* he said. *You are not your mind. You will understand that soon enough, if you don't believe me.*

"Get out of my head!" Hugo shouted, squeezing his head between his hands in frustration. A terrible thought struck him then. What if everything Molad had said was true? He panicked and began to scratch at his head, clawing at the steel cap until one of his fingers began to bleed.

Don't do that, Molad said sharply, and Hugo stopped. *There is no getting me out. I was always here. But there is no reason that we can't figure this out together.*

Hugo leaned back on his hands, breathing hard. *Yes, there is,* he said. *I don't trust you. Is that the same speech you gave the others?*

What others?

The other mages. The ones that came before me.

You are the only Mage of Light and Darkness that concerns me, Molad said. *Or rather, the only Mage of Light.*

Mage of Light?

You are the Mage of Light, Molad explained. *I am the Mage of Darkness. Together, we are what you seek to become.*

Hugo shook his head. *No,* he said. *I will not accept that.*

You will, Molad said simply. *You will have to.*

❖ ❖ ❖

Just out of sight, hiding in the trees, two forms huddled together, watching Hugo.

"It appears to have worked," March said.

The kudri beside her nodded and changed back into the Janrax.

"Good," he said. "What next? Do we drive him into the Ire?"

"No." March rose to her feet and turned to leave. "He will find his own way there."

Chapter Thirteen

In which has to learn how to dance

BY THE TIME CANNON came along, Hugo had settled down beside the path at a spot that would make it easy to be found.

"Hugo?" Cannon said, concern flashing across his face as he came near. All of the anger that he had left with seemed to have dissipated. "How did you get all the way over here? It took me forever to find you again. What the . . . What's that thing on your head?"

"It was a diversion," Hugo said, tapping the cap on his head. "The ogre, I mean. It was led here by a kudri, and that witch, March."

Cannon paled. "You're joking."

Hugo tapped the cap on his head again. "Nope. They put this thing on me so that I couldn't communicate with the other mages and call for help."

"You spoke with them?"

"Yep. Apparently Shael is so eager to give me advice that he's sending it by messenger now."

"Hugo," Cannon said, "this is no time to joke. You could have been killed!"

Hugo shrugged. "I don't think Shael wants me dead. In fact, I don't think he wants me to think of him as an enemy. Shael could have just had them take me if he wanted." Hugo stretched his legs out, doing his best to look as if he'd had a relaxing afternoon. "I guess you didn't pick a very good time to abandon me, eh?"

At that, Cannon looked positively sick.

"He's going to kill me," Cannon said. "I can't believe I did that." He was muttering to himself now, as if he'd forgotten Hugo was there. "Could have died. Stupid. Stupid. Hothead, just like he said." He glanced up. "I'm sorry, Hugo."

"Don't worry about it," Hugo said. "Every cloud has a silver lining."

"What do you mean?"

Hugo shifted, moving from one spot on the grass to another in the blink of an eye.

Cannon's face split into an involuntary smile. "So you've arrived at last."

Hugo shrugged, tapping the cap. "Yes, well, apparently I'm still not powerful enough to get this thing off my head."

Cannon waved a hand. "Not to worry," he said. "I've got you covered."

"Are you sure?" Hugo said. "It hurts like death if you pull on it. Just gets tighter."

"Hmm," said Cannon. He put a hand on the cap and tilted it to one side, then the other. Then, to Hugo's horror, he smacked it with a knuckle.

The cap gave a loud, bell-like tone and then tightened slightly. "Ouch!" Hugo exclaimed. "Don't do that!"

Cannon whistled. "It is on there pretty tight, isn't it . . . Well," he said, rolling up his sleeves, "There's only one thing to do."

Before Hugo could ask what the one thing was, Cannon raised his arm in front of Hugo's head and flattened his hand like a knife. Then he drew it straight through the air from left to right, just far enough away to avoid touching the cap. Hugo felt a thin blade of air whip across his scalp. The cap slipped, but then tightened down again, causing him to wince in pain.

"Oops," Cannon said, turning bright red. "Oh, wow. That was my mistake, Hugo."

"Don't sweat it," Hugo said. "I couldn't get it off, either. I'm sure Animus can."

"No," Cannon said. "I mean . . . Oh boy . . . How do I say this?"

"What?" Hugo said. He raised his hand to his head self-consciously, thinking that Cannon might have cut him. No, it felt fine. His scalp was entirely intact. There wasn't even a nick in his skin . . . His skin. Hugo's hand went to his shoulders, then to his shirt. There was hair on both. *His* hair. He rose up slowly, the realization dawning on him.

"CANNON, YOU IDIOT! YOU SHAVED MY HEAD!"

Hugo lunged, but Cannon ducked away from him.

"Look at the silver lining, Hugo," Cannon said, dancing out of reach. "You still have hair under the cap."

Hugo threw a wild punch and it went wide. The second one connected, sinking into Cannon's gut.

Cannon grunted, falling down hard. Hugo charged in for more, but Cannon held up a hand and a wall of wind knocked him to the ground.

"One's enough," Cannon said.

"You deserved it," Hugo protested, trying to make himself believe it.

"Yeah, probably."

They contemplated one another for a brief moment, and then Cannon broke into a grin. "Hey," he said. "You're looking a little bald there."

Hugo stared at him, speechless for a moment, then began to shake with laughter.

❖ ❖ ❖

Animus didn't find the situation very funny at all.

"You split up?" he growled. "After I specifically told you to keep an eye on each other?" Animus leveled a finger at his apprentice. "You left him?"

Cannon started to say something, but Animus held up his hand, cutting him off.

"No excuses," he snapped. Then he rounded on Hugo. "You should be wary of whatever those two said to you, Hugo. The devil will tell nine truths to sell a single lie, so they say. Since they left you unharmed, I expect Shael's aim is to gain your trust by helping you."

"That's what I figured," Hugo said.

Animus nodded. "Of course you did. Well, let's get this thing off your head, shall we?"

"Uh . . ." Hugo said nervously.

"Don't fret," Animus said. He grabbed Cannon and pulled him in front of Hugo. "I see you tried to cut it off first." His voice was soft, but Cannon winced as if he were shouting. "After you discovered that you were a poor barber, what were you going to try next?"

Cannon closed one eye, thinking hard. "Suction?"

Animus gave an exasperated sigh. "Then it is a good thing he was wise enough to stop you. A Horocular Cap gets tighter the harder you pull. If you had tried to pull it off with the wind, I'm afraid our friend would have ended up with a very long neck, or none at all."

Cannon went so pale that Hugo very nearly felt sorry for him.

"Heat!" Animus barked. Cannon jumped. "Heat creates what?"

"Pressure," Cannon said, looking slightly confused.

"And in metal?"

Cannon exhaled slowly, deflating. "Expansion," he muttered.

"Exactly," Animus said. He waved his hand at Hugo. At once the air around Hugo's head became very hot. Hugo felt a sudden increase of pressure against his crown. Then, just when he thought his head would burst into flames, the heat turned into a sharp, freezing cold and the cap cracked in several places, tumbling away.

Several voices entered Hugo's head right away.

Are you okay?

Hugo, are you there?

Why aren't you answering me?

Hugo, I know you're a boy, but if you don't start talking to me this instant, I swear I will make Tabitha turn into a lion and eat your pants. This last voice was Brinley's.

YES! Hugo shouted. *I'm here. You can all stop worrying now. Or being mad at me, or whatever is going on. A kudri attacked me and March put a magical helmet on my head so that I couldn't communicate with you.*

A Horocular Cap, Animus added to the group.

Why didn't you just take it off? Brinley asked.

Ah! Hugo said. *Why didn't I think of that? It was stuck, Brinley. Animus had to get it off.*

Interesting, Cassis said. *I hope you didn't destroy it, Animus.*

And Belterras said, *Oh, poor boy. Happened to me once, during the war. Make sure you put some ointment on the cuts; you never know where a thing like that has been.*

Cuts? Hugo touched his head, wincing as his fingers brushed the area where the rim of the cap had dug into his skin. Sure enough, there was a deep circular cut. It was oozing blood slowly, and he dug around in his pack for a cloth.

Well, I'm glad you're okay, Brinley said, just to Hugo this time. *It sounds like you're not having a very good day, either.*

You too, huh? Hugo said, eager to change the subject. The less he told her about March and the kudri, the less she was likely to worry and ask him difficult questions.

Yes, she said. *Tabitha and I are having some difficulty at the Lake of Eyes.*

You'll figure it out, Hugo assured her.

Thanks, Brinley said. *And be careful.* Then she was gone.

Animus was eyeing Hugo thoughtfully. "If you are finished, I would like to ask the question that no one else did: What did they say?"

Hugo winced. He had spent a good while thinking about what he should tell Animus, and he had yet to make up his mind.

"The truth will do nicely," Animus said, reading his thoughts.

Hugo shrugged. "The kudri basically said that the key to my power was in talking to the darkness."

"And did you believe him?"

Hugo shrugged. "He said he was a messenger from Shael. He said that Shael wanted me to learn how to use my powers so that there could be balance."

Animus nodded. "The kudri have long served Shael as messengers . . . and assassins. I am sorry that I left you alone with him. It was a terrible risk."

"I don't think he meant me any harm," Hugo said. "He just wanted to talk to me."

Animus held up a finger. "Do not underestimate the harm that words can do, especially when they come from Shael. You should not believe everything that was said."

"I think he told me the truth," Hugo said. "At least, it felt like the truth when he was saying it." He rushed on, hoping that telling Animus would make himself feel more justified. "I did what he said. I spoke with the darkness. I used the mirror you gave me. I took your advice too. I named him."

"What?" Cannon said, but Animus waved him away.

He eyed Hugo with an unreadable expression on his face. "And?"

Hugo looked at his boots thoughtfully. "He taught me . . . things."

"Show me," Animus said.

Hugo threw a rock as hard as he could and caught it, moving several yards in the blink of an eye. Then he shot back to his starting position.

Animus gave one small laugh and then smiled kindly at him, though Hugo saw sadness hiding behind it. "Well done." Animus hesitated. "However he taught you, I am sure that it could not have been easy." He gave Hugo a significant look.

I hope you did not pay too high a price for your knowledge.

Hugo said nothing. Animus waved a hand dismissively. "No matter," he said. "We can easily make it to Tourilia now. We should be off at once."

Hugo blinked in surprise at the abrupt dismissal. "But ... I thought you would have more questions for me."

Animus held up a hand. "I am curious about many things, but the balance of light and darkness is yours to strike. You cannot lecture me on the workings of the wind, nor can I teach you what you must learn of light and darkness. If you have questions for me, I am happy to listen. As for me, there is only one question in my mind now, and you cannot answer it."

Hugo nodded. He felt surprised at how much Animus trusted him, and a little apprehensive.

Animus stretched, preparing himself for the journey. "Off we go, then. Wait for us when you get there, will you? I'm afraid light travels much more quickly than air ..."

"Animus," Hugo said. "What's the one question in your mind?"

Animus sighed. "If Shael is still imprisoned as we assume, then how is he sending messages to you? For that matter, how is he communicating with anyone at all?"

Hugo's eyes went wide. "He must be out."

"Perhaps," he said. "Perhaps not." Animus raised an eyebrow. "I will go ahead and wait for you. Give me a few moments to get there before you come. Cannon will stay here with you. This way we will not have to leave you alone again."

Hugo nodded and Animus vanished in a sudden breeze from the south. Hugo watched him go, imagining that he could see the wind winding its way through the hills, climbing to the clouds.

Cannon was still watching Hugo. There was something in his expression that Hugo had not seen before, as if he were reexamining some of the assumptions he had made about the prince of Caraway. He looked like he had several things that he wanted to say, but kept his mouth shut instead, causing Hugo to look away awkwardly, searching for something to distract himself with while they waited. The little brook wound its way peacefully through a forest of sunflowers, and it seemed strange to think that somewhere north of them, a terrible evil might be free. A cloud moved in front of the sun and covered him in shadow. He shivered, looking up at it, and then shifted into light.

❖ ❖ ❖

An hour after Hugo, Animus, and Cannon had been talking on the road, they bowed together before the king of the gnome kingdom. Hugo had arrived several minutes before Animus and Cannon. Luckily, he had caught sight of his reflection in a pane of glass and noticed the ridiculous circle of hair that the Horocular Cap had left on his head. He had just enough time to shave it off before the others arrived. Now, in front of the king, he was feeling very bald.

The great hall of the king's castle stood five stories tall and was built of polished stone the color of ripe apples. In contrast, the king of gnomes himself was diminutive by human standards, though he looked downright burly next to some of his servants.

Thieutukar Manisse inclined his head and said, "Animus, you are welcome. And Hugo Paradise. This is your first time venturing into our lands, so let me start by saying it is an honor to have the prince of Caraway in our halls." He had strong, chiseled features and a neatly trimmed beard. His eyes were soft, the eyes of a man accustomed to doing a lot of listening. "This day began like any other, and lo, it has ended with two mages under my roof, and an apprentice besides. How may I be of service to you?"

Animus inclined his head again. "Thank you, King Thieutukar. We are on an errand of some importance. We were sent here by the Magemother herself. She had a ... feeling. An intuition, if you will, that we might find some clues here as to the whereabouts of the Mage of Fire. She was searching for her, and saw your face in her mind."

Thieutukar looked startled. "My face?" he said, frowning thoughtfully. "That is a strange thing. The Mage of Fire, you say? Chantra ..." He looked as if he was going to say something more, but changed his mind. He waved an arm and said loudly, "Clear the hall."

Cannon and Hugo exchanged glances, but Animus was still waiting patiently for the king to speak. After several moments of shuffling feet and closing doors, they were alone.

"The Mage of Fire," he prompted.

"Yes," Thieutukar said, settling back into his chair. "I remember her well. It is true that she came here often. That is a well-known fact ..." He folded and unfolded his fingers on the table before him. "What is not well known, is that she was not coming to visit me." He looked at Animus. "I thought perhaps you were aware, but I take it from your questioning that you weren't. She came here seeking someone that we do not speak of. Someone that is presumed to be dead. A prisoner, if you will, of my kingdom."

"A prisoner?" Animus said, startled. "Who can you be talking about, Thieutukar?"

The king shifted. "Perhaps I should not have introduced them, but she was a very persuasive child, and I was convinced she would have found a way to talk to him with or without my help."

"With whom?" Animus pressed.

Hugo froze. Something was clutching at his mind. It had caught him unawares, wrenching control away from him. He leapt to his feet, drawing all eyes towards him as he approached the king.

"Thieutukar," Molad said, and at his words, several torches sputtered out around them, casting them into shadow.

Animus, who had been about to say something, stilled in his chair.

The gnome king looked up at him, not trying to hide the surprise on his face. "Yes, Hugo?"

"I am Molad," he said evenly.

The king's face blanched, but his expression remained unchanged. "I see. What is it you want?"

"I seek an audience with the dragon."

The king's inscrutable face unraveled at the edges, dissolving into a look of astonishment.

"What dragon?" Animus asked.

"The prisoner," Thieutukar said. "But how can you know? Nobody knows. We kept the secret for our own safety, and his."

"I know," Molad said simply. "There is a great darkness beneath this fortress, and the dragon was last seen in the skies of Hedgemon. He is here."

The king nodded slowly, disbelieving. "He is. But to speak with him is no light endeavor. Only the kings of Hedgemon have approached him and lived. Only the kings of Hedgemon."

"And Chantra?" Animus said.

The king inclined his head. "And Chantra."

Molad nodded curtly, as if these facts did not concern him. "I must see him." He jabbed a finger imperiously at the king. "I will speak to the dragon."

Molad closed his eyes and Hugo opened them. He blinked at the faces of the mage and the king as the torches flickered to life again. Cannon was staring at him, open-mouthed.

"Hugo?" Animus asked.

Hugo cleared his throat, unsure of what to say. "Yeah."

King Thieutukar shook his head solemnly. "It has begun for you. I remember when the quickening began for Lux."

"The quickening?" Hugo asked.

Thieutukar nodded, motioning for Hugo to take his seat again. "That is what my people call it when a new mage begins to come into his power. For the Mage of Light and Darkness, of course, it is not always easy to watch. Lux became something of a split being for a time, before he learned to live in balance."

"I don't think he ever learned," Hugo muttered under his breath.

"I assume the dragon in question is Kuzo? The beast that attacked Shael's stronghold in the Ire?" Animus asked. Thieutukar nodded, and Animus turned to Hugo. "Do you know why Molad desires to speak with him?"

Hugo shook his head. "I think the dragon must have something that he wants."

"Knowledge," the king said. "That is the only wealth the dragon has now." He turned to Hugo. "You cannot see him right away, I'm afraid. One cannot just walk up to a dragon and live to tell the tale. There is a ceremony involved. Dragons are very old creatures. If you approach him as a man, you will die like a fly. Only by approaching him on his own terms will you survive."

"His own terms?"

Thieutukar nodded. "To approach the dragon you must learn an ancient ceremony in which, more or less, you demonstrate your ability to fight like a dragon. The dragon will then decide whether you are worthy to speak to him."

"But I don't want to see him at all!" Hugo exclaimed.

Animus smiled bitterly. "Part of you does," he said. "And I have a feeling that part of you will win out. Besides, I am confident that this is the reason the Magemother was drawn to this place. No doubt the dragon holds the clue that we are looking for. You had better learn what you need to learn, Hugo. I would just as well let King Thieutukar speak with this dragon for us, but Molad seems very determined to have his own audience. Unless you think you can change his mind?"

Hugo thought for a moment, then shook his head. "I don't think so. I can't even keep him quiet."

And I don't know how I ever will, he thought bitterly. His stomach growled loudly, echoing the angst in his mind. "We can still have dinner, right?" he asked.

"Of course!" the king said. "Food before fighting!"

❖ ❖ ❖

A little less than an hour later, Hugo's belly was filled to bursting with roast beef, hot corn on the cob, fruit tarts, soft-baked sweet potato chips, fresh bread with orange marmalade, and a bowl of cauliflower soup, which had looked very questionable but turned out to be quite good. After the final course was cleared, the king emptied the great hall again. Even Animus was asked to leave; only Hugo and Thieutukar remained. The king had changed out of his regular clothing and now wore a form-fitting black tunic and light cotton pants of the same color. He walked to his throne and picked up the longsword that leaned against it. "Draw your sword," the king said.

The king began to circle him meditatively as he spoke, words flowing out of him slowly, methodically, as if he had memorized them years ago.

"The secret of gaining an audience with a dragon is to prove to him that you are kin."

"Kin?" Hugo said. He was trying not to look down at the king. It felt awkward to look down at someone, especially when they were teaching you, and especially when that someone was a king, but he couldn't find a way around it. The man was three feet tall.

"Kin," the king repeated, apparently unaware of Hugo's discomfort. "Brothers. You must show him that the same passion and power that lives in him lives in you. All of his grace, all of his poise, all of his terrible rage . . ."

The king slipped into a slight crouch, raising the sword lightly above his head like an extension of his arm. He pivoted from foot to foot, tracing out some secret shape upon the ground. Hugo watched in awe as he moved; his feet never seemed to leave the floor. His arms and legs moved as one, floating, calm, as if he were a creature of water instead of flesh and bone.

Thieutukar slipped out of the dance and pointed at Hugo. "The dragon dance should be effortless," he said. "Invigorating. You should feel empty afterwards. Spent, as if you have given your whole soul to it."

Hugo balked. "I don't know how to do that!" he said. "If I had years to practice, maybe. How long have you been practicing it?"

"Years."

Hugo gestured with an open hand, proving his point.

Thieutukar shook his head patiently. "The amount of time is not the problem," he said. "You are the problem."

"Me?" Hugo said.

The king nodded gravely. "You. You cannot dance it. Only the dragon within can perform it." He tapped Hugo firmly in the center of the forehead. "For the dragon within to come forth, you must step aside." He waved his hand. "The dragon dance cannot be learned, at any rate. It can only be danced."

Hugo gave him a blank look. It sounded like complete nonsense, but he might as well make the best of it. "Okay," he said. "I guess it doesn't hurt to try." The king nodded his approval and moved away to give him the floor.

Feeling incredibly awkward, Hugo crouched down as he had seen the king do. He remembered how the king had moved, how he had traced the invisible shape with his feet, and he tried to imagine the most beautiful shape he could think of. A salamander was the first thing that came to mind, and the feel of that shape steadied him as he began to trace it. The salamander was the symbol of the Paradise kings; if there was anything that should feel natural, it should be that. As he finished tracing it he realized that he had given little thought for what his sword hand was doing. He hoped the king hadn't noticed that bit. He finished and stepped out of the dance. It didn't feel graceful at all.

He knew how he had done before he looked at the king. Thieutukar shook his head, his expression inscrutable, and pointed at the center of the floor. "Again."

Hugo sighed, moving back to the center.

"Hugo."

"What?" Hugo replied, eyes closed in concentration as he began to move again.

"You're trying too hard."

Hugo sighed and began once more.

Chapter Fourteen

In which there is a magical talking cat

BRINLEY AND TABITHA reached the Lake of Eyes early in the morning. The black swan settled onto the shore and Brinley slid down from its back as it changed into Tabitha. Brinley took the drawing from her bag and together they held it up against the lake in the background to compare.

"It looks different," Tabitha said, and Brinley had to agree.

"But look at that boulder," Brinley said, pointing. "It's exactly the same as the one in the painting. What are the chances of that?"

Tabitha shrugged. "I suppose so," she said. "What now?"

That was the very thing that Brinley had been wondering since their search began. She walked to the edge of the water and opened her mind to the lake. She reached out mentally, summoning up an image of Unda in her mind and probing the lake for signs of him. She felt again the sudden awareness of a great weight. It was as if all the water in the lake had been set on her shoulders in a giant bucket. She released the image of him with a gasp, and the weight faded too.

"He's here," she said. "He must be. It's never felt that heavy before. It's like his power wants to get back to him."

Tabitha stooped over the water's edge and slapped the water brusquely, making Brinley jump. "Unda!" she shouted.

Brinley grinned. "I don't think that's how it works," she said.

Tabitha shrugged. "I'm going to make breakfast," she said, and started gathering twigs for a fire.

Brinley walked around the edge of the lake thoughtfully, searching—for what, she did not know. When she came back around from the other side of the lake, Tabitha had food roasting over the fire (a zucchini from Habis's garden, cut in half and stuffed with mushrooms from the forest). It smelled wonderful.

"Wow," Brinley said.

"I know," Tabitha said, sniffing the aroma. "Smells wonderful, doesn't it? Belsie teaches me all sorts of things."

As they sat waiting for breakfast to finish, a yellow songbird settled on the rock next to them.

"Peanut!" Tabitha exclaimed, reaching a hand out. The bird hopped onto her fingers and began singing to her, and when it was finished, Tabitha passed along the message. "He says Archibald caught the cat. Apparently the cat can make the journey into the Void. Archibald says they are on their way there right now and that he's going to send the cat in to look for your father! He wants to know where he can find you if he needs to speak to you in person."

Brinley was speechless. "I don't know. Here, I guess."

Tabitha nodded, gave the message to the bird, and waved as it flew away.

"That's quite impressive, don't you think?" Tabitha said, watching the bird fade into the sky. "Finding your dad so fast, I mean."

"Yes," Brinley said thoughtfully. "Though it sounds like he hasn't found him yet . . . What kind of magical cat can travel to the Void? Maybe we should go meet it."

Tabitha glanced out at the lake. "Unda, though," she said.

Brinley nodded. "Of course. Of course, I know we can't go. We need to find Unda. And we're here already."

Tabitha pulled the zucchini off the spit and divided it between them, and they spoke of the lake as they ate, trading ideas about how to contact Unda.

"Do you think he can breathe under water?" Tabitha wondered.

"I don't know. I guess so. He is the Mage of Water, after all."

"But can he hear us through the water?"

Brinley shook her head. "I don't know."

"You can't sense him. Do you think he can sense you?"

"I don't know that either," Brinley said. She leaned against a log and stared dejectedly at her feet. She was starting to feel silly for coming here. She should have found out more about how the mages were hidden.

"Don't worry," Tabitha said, watching her closely. "I'm sure we'll figure it out." Tabitha's face brightened suddenly. "Maybe we can send him a message."

Brinley sat up. "What do you mean?"

"Maybe he's down there, but he can't speak to us. Maybe he can't hear us, but if we send him a message, he will be able to read it." Tabitha was combing the shore for something. Finally she picked up a large, flat rock and set it down beside Brinley. Using another small rock like a pencil, she began to scratch a message on the face of the flat one.

Dear Unda,

You can come out now. Everything is okay.

-Brinley (The Magemother)

When she was done she looked up at Brinley expectantly. "What do you think?" she said.

"I like it," Brinley said.

Tabitha clapped happily. "Oh, good. See? I told you we would think of something. Now you throw it in."

Brinley took the stone and eyed the lake. She wondered where she should throw it, or if it even mattered. In the end she decided to just throw it as far as she could. It landed about halfway to the center, disappearing beneath the surface with a loud *plop*.

Tabitha appeared at her side, frowning. "What if that's not where he is?" she asked. "Or what if he just thinks it's any old rock falling into the lake and he doesn't bother to check it?"

They stared at each other for a moment, and then Brinley grinned. "More rocks?"

Tabitha nodded fervently, handing her the sharp writing stone.

They split up and walked around the lake on opposite sides, stopping whenever they found a rock flat enough to write on. Brinley had thrown in eleven rocks by the time she met up with Tabitha on the opposite side from where they had started.

"What now?" Tabitha asked.

"We wait, I guess," Brinley said, and they sat down together on the shore. Tabitha took her shoes off and dipped her feet in the water. After a few minutes, she scowled.

"I don't think it worked," she said. "He wouldn't ignore you, would he?"

"Maybe he didn't get the message," Brinley said.

"Or maybe he's not in there." Tabitha sighed. "Maybe this is the wrong lake after all." She yawned. "I'm very tired. I think I'm going to lie down for a while."

Brinley nodded, starting to yawn herself now. They found a place with soft grass and shade on the shore of the lake and laid down, and before they knew it they were out.

❖ ❖ ❖

Brinley was surprised at how much time had passed when she awoke. She was even more surprised by Tabitha's excitement. The other girl was babbling about something that Brinley couldn't quite follow, pointing to the shore.

"Slow down, Tabitha," she said. "What happened?"

Tabitha was on her feet now. "There were these huge eyes!" she said, making her hands into circles and holding them in front of her own eyes to illustrate. "They were right there, staring at us!" She pointed to the water near the shore where several ripples were still dissipating.

"That's what Hugo said he saw," Brinley said, getting to her feet.

"Do you think it was Unda?" Tabitha asked, a worried look crossing her face.

"Who else could it be?" Brinley said, excited. She searched around, found another flat stone, and wrote on it:

Hello, Unda, I am the new Magemother. We are your friends. We need you to come out so that we can speak with you. Please don't be afraid.

She tossed it into the water and was pleased to see that it landed right on the spot that the ripples had come from.

Nothing happened.

"Maybe I should write one too," Tabitha said, and she began scratching away on another stone. When she was done she threw it at the same spot in the water. Before it landed, an arm shot into the air and caught it with a slimy hand. The arm looked like it could have been made of seaweed, all brown and green and twisted. Brinley gasped and Tabitha waved and shouted, "Hi, Unda! Oh, good catch!"

For a split second, the arm froze, as if the person it belonged to was listening. Then it whipped around and hurled the stone back at them.

"Ack!" Brinley cried, sidestepping to dodge the stone.

Tabitha shook her finger at the lake. "Now, Unda. That's not nice at all! Please don't throw rocks at us." Then her hands shot to her mouth. "Oh my! We threw rocks at you, didn't we?"

Brinley patted her on the shoulder to calm her. "Tabitha, I don't think that was Unda."

Tabitha looked confused for a moment, then wrapped her arms around herself protectively and mumbled, "Oh my," several times.

"Don't worry," Brinley assured her. "Whoever it is, I don't think they mean us any real harm."

"But they threw a rock at us," Tabitha said. "And we threw rocks at it! Never throw rocks at strangers!" She slapped herself on the forehead. "Why do I always forget that?"

Brinley hid a grin. She bent and picked up another rock. On this one she wrote:

I am the Magemother. I am looking for the Mage of Water. Who are you?

This time, instead of tossing it, she bent down and skipped the stone across the surface of the lake. It skipped five times and then sunk, and a moment later the water thrashed where the stone stopped, as if a fish had jumped—or an underwater hand had snatched it suddenly.

A moment later, the arm appeared again and another rock sailed towards them.

"Watch out," Brinley said, ducking. But Tabitha reached out and made a move to catch it. It hit her hand but slipped through her fingers and fell to the ground. When Brinley looked at it, she could see why—it was covered with green and brown slime, as if it had been sitting on the bottom of the lake for a long time. It didn't look like there was any writing on it, however. She reached out to pick it up and dropped it abruptly, for the moment she touched it an image flashed across her mind. She saw a city beneath the lake, with teal towers and long stone halls covered in green-gray moss, and in front of the city she saw a crowd of people with short, lithe bodies.

"What is it?" Tabitha asked, watching Brinley's expression.

"Tabitha, last night Cassis taught me about the memory of stones. He taught me that they can hold thoughts."

"Oh," Tabitha said, looking confused. "That's interesting . . ."

Brinley shook her head. "I think that the creature from the lake did that with this stone. I touched it and I saw . . . something. Lake people that live under the water."

Tabitha picked up the stone. "I don't see anything. Can you send the lake person something like he sent you?"

Brinley nodded, and Tabitha handed it to her. "I think so."

She held the stone and reached out to it with her mind, feeling for the space inside. Cassis had said that there was a whole world in there if you looked closely enough, but she could only sense a small space, just large enough to hold a thought. She placed in it an image of Unda from the memory of her vision with her mother on Calypsis. Then she threw the stone into the lake. A moment later it came flying back out to land at their feet. Brinley picked it up and winced as the sound of a thousand voices reverberated through her mind. It took a moment for her to realize that the voices, high pitched and angry, were all shouting the same word: *No.*

Brinley told Tabitha what she had learned, and they agreed that "no" was quite a confusing answer. Tabitha summed the problem up.

"Does that mean that they don't know where Unda is, or that they do know, but don't want to help us?"

"I don't know," Brinley said.

"Ask them."

Brinley scratched on the stone, *Do you know where Unda is?* She threw it into the lake.

It was several minutes before anything happened. Then the same stone came back out. Brinley picked it up and saw in her mind a tall, round, underwater cell with bars of black metal. A faint light glowed at the center of it, and she could make out a scrunched figure curled on the floor. The cell itself was surrounded by a vast darkness that made her shiver even in the sunlight.

"Oh no," she whispered. She told Tabitha what she had seen.

Tabitha gasped. "They have him prisoner? But why?" She looked suddenly angry. "What did he ever do to them?"

"I don't know," Brinley said, and started scratching another message on the rock. "I'm asking them to release him."

When she had finished, she tossed it back in the water, and it came back almost immediately. Brinley caught it this time, and the chorus of voices shouted inside her head again: *NO!*

"But why?" Tabitha said. "You're the Magemother. They have to do what you say, don't they?"

Brinley laughed bitterly. "Apparently not. I'm going to ask Belterras if he knows who these people are." She retreated a few steps from the water's edge. "Don't go in there," she called to Tabitha, who was crouched on the shore, about to jump. She froze and then flopped to the ground instead.

Brinley called Belterras and told him what had happened.

Merfolk . . . he said, sounding surprised.

Merfolk? Brinley asked. *You mean like mermaids?*

Yes and no. The merfolk inhabit the deeper parts of Aberdeen's oceans, and are very seldom encountered, except by sailors. I cannot think of how a group might have come to live in a freshwater lake. They have Unda, you say? Then you should be careful. The merfolk are a magical species. You will not find them unless they want to be found. Even I could not force them to do anything.

Then what should I do? Brinley asked. *I have to get Unda back. Should I have Tabitha search the lake for him?*

No! Belterras said. *She should not enter it. No one should enter it until we have an agreement with the merfolk. If you jumped in,*

I think it likely that you too would become a prisoner. The merfolk are a strange people. We should be able to reason with them, but we need to understand what they want first. Let me think on it for a bit.

Can you meet me tonight? Brinley asked. *We can discuss the merfolk, and then maybe you can come and talk to them yourself.*

I can try, he said, *but I doubt that it will do any good. The merfolk are creatures of the sea. You really need Unda for something like this. Hardly a helpful suggestion, I know . . .*

In the end he agreed to meet her and she sent him an image of the hill where Maggie's house was. When she finished speaking with him, she returned to the beach, where Tabitha was waiting impatiently.

"Can I go in now?" she asked. "Maybe I can make them understand if I just go down there and talk to them."

Brinley shook her head firmly. "No. It's too dangerous. Belterras agrees. They might take you prisoner too. We need to find out what they want first." She scratched that exact question on a rock and threw it into the water. It came back quickly, containing the same image that she had seen before, of Unda in his cell, deep under the water.

"You already have what you want," Brinley whispered. "But why? Why do you want that?"

Tabitha took the still-wet rock from Brinley and wrote *Why?* on the other side before throwing it in.

It came back a moment later. This time the arm that threw it rose out of the water only a few feet from them, making Brinley jump in surprise. Tabitha caught it and handed it to Brinley, who saw a picture of the ocean in her mind when she did.

"The ocean?" Tabitha said when Brinley told her. "What does that mean?"

"I don't know," Brinley said. "Maybe Belterras will." She scratched another question on a rock, asking what the ocean had to do with it, and they waited for a response. When none came after ten minutes, Tabitha said that she was hungry and wandered off in search of berries. Brinley stayed by the lake just in case.

Half an hour later, Tabitha returned with several handfuls of blackberries, and they ate them while tossing more stones into the lake. Each stone bore the same question on its face: *What do you mean?* But nothing came back.

Long after they had finished the berries, when the sun was beginning to set over the forest, they were still waiting for an answer.

"Brinley," Tabitha said, "are we going to stay up all night working on Maggie's house again, or are we going to sleep like normal people?"

Brinley smiled, removing the wooden button from her pocket and fingering it. "What do you think?"

❖ ❖ ❖

When night had came, they alighted in the little clearing where Maggie's house stood and found Belterras waiting for them.

"What is this place?" he asked. "Did you find out anything more?"

Tabitha skipped to his side and he embraced her while Brinley told him what they had learned.

"The ocean . . ." he murmured. "The obvious interpretation is that they want to get back to the ocean. They are ocean creatures, after all. It cannot be easy for them to live in a freshwater lake. In fact, I would not have thought it possible."

Brinley wondered why she had not thought of that. It was so simple. "But then why did they leave it in the first place?" she asked.

"I cannot guess," Belterras said. "Unless the answer has something to do with Unda. If he took them from the ocean, then that would certainly give them cause to hate him."

"But he's much more powerful than they are, isn't he?" asked Tabitha. "Why would he let them keep him as a prisoner?"

"I do not know that either," Belterras said. "It is true that when a mage comes into his power there is nothing in his own kingdom more powerful than he, but Unda was very young when he was lost. Perhaps he had not yet discovered the extent of his powers." He trailed off, and Brinley remained quiet so that he could think. "If I were you," he said finally, "I would offer to return them to the ocean in exchange for releasing Unda. He is the only one who could actually do it, but they don't need to know that, and if the ocean is what they really want, then that may be your only bargaining tool. I'm afraid that is my only idea."

"It's a good one," Brinley said gratefully. "We'll try it in the morning."

Belterras nodded. "But what is this place?" he asked, turning to look at the empty stone house. "Does someone live here?"

Brinley felt her mood lighten. "No one yet," she said. "I am building it for a friend. Cassis helped with the foundation. I was hoping that you would help with the garden."

Belterras smiled. "Gardens are not my specialty. How about an aviary?"

"A what?" Brinley said, but Tabitha looked excited at his words.

"A house for birds," Belterras explained, rubbing his hands together, and Tabitha said, "I've already got things ready for birdhouses!"

Belterras smiled in approval and had them sit in a circle. He showed Brinley how to build a birdhouse quickly out of bark and grass and twigs, and Tabitha told her all about what kind of birds liked what kinds of houses, and soon they had seven lovely birdhouses. Tabitha disappeared into the woods to hunt for poles while Brinley and Belterras built more houses, and sometime later she returned with several long branches and began to strip the bark off of them with a sharp knife.

When Tabitha was done, they fastened the houses to the poles and planted them in the ground so that she could see them from the kitchen window. Together, they stepped back to survey their work. Brinley couldn't help feeling disappointed. The ten handcrafted birdhouses were slightly crooked and misshapen, and they looked very unimpressive in the half light, empty and colorless.

"Don't worry," Belterras said, catching the look on her face. "We're not done yet. Birds just need a little inspiration, you see. They do the rest."

He took them inside the house so that they looked out on the yard through the empty kitchen window. "What now?" Tabitha asked.

"Now we call the birds," said Belterras.

"Will you teach me?" Brinley asked, and Belterras smiled kindly.

"I will teach you, but have patience with yourself if you do not learn right away. Few ever do, though they try for a lifetime."

Belterras began to sing then, a tune that felt familiar to Brinley, though she knew that she had never heard it before. It was a birdsong, and like all birdsong, it was both new and old at the same time. He sang with the voice of a man in the language of birds, and the birds came. Robins and finches and jays, three of each to three of the birdhouses. A large hawk came next and claimed two of the birdhouses at once. It flew away and returned with large sticks that it set carefully on top of the two houses, spanning them for the foundation of its nest.

Tabitha began to sing to them, and her voice mingled pleasantly with Belterras's. Brinley wondered if they had practiced this before. A cardinal came down out of the trees as if it had been watching, waiting to be called, and claimed the sixth house. He brought a small family with him, and together they decorated the house with berries and filled it with leaves and wound a strand of live green vines down the pole and buried the root of it in the ground.

"Now you try," Tabitha said, pausing in her song to urge Brinley along.

"How?" she said. "I don't know how to sing like that."

"Perfect!" Belterras said. "Neither do the birds, but they still do it."

"Open your mouth," Tabitha said. "Pretend you're a bird."

Brinley did so, feeling very foolish, and to her surprise, a tune sprung out of her that complemented the song that the other two were weaving. She smiled and then realized she did not know what to sing next, and shut her mouth quickly. Before she did, a magpie flitted down from the night sky and claimed the seventh birdhouse. Brinley grinned, wondering if it had been her song that had called the magpie. She did not try to sing again, and neither Belterras nor Tabitha asked her to. They just sang together until there was a family of birds in each house, and then they stopped.

"Thank you," Brinley said. "She will love it. I know she will. And thank you for teaching me." She blushed. "Maybe someday you can teach me to change shape into a bird, like my mother."

"I have no doubt," Belterras said seriously. "You sang the birdsong on your first try. That is not common. You called the magpie."

Brinley felt her heart warm slightly. She had done something right. Finally! She looked out at the birds and watched as they all rose from their houses at the same time and flew into the early morning sky. She wondered where they were going, what they would build, and then imagined the look on Maggie's face when she saw it. She was doing something right. Maggie's house, at least, would turn out well. She turned around to find Belterras whispering fervently to Tabitha, who had her head down, eyes downcast. She looked very much like a child being scolded, and Brinley turned back around, not wanting to watch. She wondered what Belterras could be saying to her.

"I must go now," Belterras said from behind her, and when she turned back around Tabitha looked normal again. "I still have much work to do tonight. They're harvesting early in Gappa this week because of the weather, and it has been a dismal harvest thus far. Duke Kendrin is beside himself with nervousness, so I said I'd look in and see if there was anything I could do."

"Good luck," Brinley said. "We should be getting back to the lake, too." She yawned. "But I think I'm going to need to sleep when we get there."

Belterras bid them farewell and said to Tabitha, "Remember what I told you." Then he changed into a bright yellow meadowlark and winged away into the early morning light.

"What did he tell you?" Brinley asked.

"Nothing," Tabitha said.

"That's not true," Brinley said.

Tabitha's eyes widened in horror. "I lied just now, didn't I?"

Brinley laughed. "That's okay, Tabitha," she said, placing a hand on the other girl's shoulder. "You don't have to tell me if you don't want to."

Tabitha looked at the ground and kicked a stone. "He heard about the butterflies, and the ants."

Brinley remembered how Tabitha had summoned the ants to overwhelm the ogre that had cornered them at Habis's house. "Well, what about them?"

"It's nothing," Tabitha said, slumping down against the house.

Brinley sat beside her. "He didn't like the butterflies?" she asked, trying to understand what Belterras could possibly be displeased about.

Tabitha shook her head. "He said that I could have done better. He said that I took a terrible risk. He said I risked your life."

Brinley frowned. "He said that?"

Tabitha nodded vigorously and wiped a tear from her cheek. "He's right. If I became a lion instead, or a bear or a dragon, I could have protected you better."

"Tabitha," Brinley said, putting a hand on her shoulder. "Belterras is the Mage of Earth. He can teach you how to be the Mage of Earth. He can't teach you how to be the Magemother's Herald."

Tabitha was shaking her head again. "But he's right! Peridot told me the same thing, and she *was* the Magemother's Herald, so you know she has to be right! She told me I had to be vicious sometimes in order to protect you! She told me!" Tabitha sniffed several times and then said softly, "She told me, and I tried to ignore her."

"Peridot?" Brinley asked. "When did you speak with Peridot? Before she died?"

Tabitha shook her head. "I had a–a vision," she said. "Except that it wasn't really a vision. I can't tell you, because I promised that I wouldn't, so don't ask me, but I *did* talk to her, and she told me that I had to be vicious sometimes, and I promised that I would help rescue your mother."

Tabitha started crying again and Brinley pulled her into a hug. "Don't worry," she said. "We will. Don't think about all of that right now. We can't fix everything all at once."

Tabitha looked at her gratefully and Brinley felt suddenly warm. She was surprised how quickly she and Tabitha had become friends, how much they cared for each other after a few short weeks. Then they were startled by a singsong voice calling to them out of the trees.

"Who's there?" Brinley asked. Her heart was pounding loudly in her ears as she turned on the spot, peering into the trees for the source of the voice.

"Don't flee," the voice said. "It's me." A blood-red cat stepped from the trees on their left and settled down on its haunches to lick a paw.

Brinley gasped. "You're that cat that Archibald was telling me about, aren't you? What did you find out about my father? And where's Archibald?" Her eyes narrowed in suspicion, scanning the trees for a sign of the man.

"What's your name?" Tabitha said sharply. Brinley could tell from the tone of her voice that Tabitha was just as startled by this new arrival as she was.

The cat ignored Tabitha, but its green eyes flashed up to meet Brinley's. "My name is Tobias, servant of Cyus."

Tabitha snorted. "No, you're not," she said. Then, at the confused look on Brinley's face, she explained. "Cyus is just a children's tale—a legend that mothers use to scare their children. He lives in a glass kingdom where he sees and records everything that happens in Aberdeen. He is supposed to record everything that everyone does. And he has a magical cat—the Swelter Cat— that can run messages to your mother if you're bad, or he can set your toys on fire." She grinned at the cat. "So don't be bad, Brinley," she said in a mocking tone, "or the Swelter Cat will burn your toys." She jabbed a finger at the cat. "It's just a story, though.

This poor cat seems to have been bewitched so that it speaks in rhymes."

The cat shot Tabitha a dark look and raised a paw, sticking a long, sharp claw out. "You're not the first to ridicule, but all are dead who played the fool."

Tabitha frowned at the cat, but remained silent.

The Swelter Cat, satisfied, went on. "A Swelter Cat's words must always rhyme. Every sentence, every time. I can say whatever I please. I can even lie. But it's lucky I can rhyme with ease, for if I don't, I die.

"If you are who you say you are," Brinley broke in, "why are you here?"

The cat drew itself up a little taller. "I have come with a message of greatest import. Sent to you as a last resort."

Tabitha harrumphed. "There's nothing about him rhyming in the stories," she said. "How can we trust him?"

Brinley placed a calming hand on her. She wasn't sure why Tabitha was overreacting. It wasn't like her to be rude or skeptical. In truth, the cat had done nothing suspicious yet, apart from appearing out of nowhere. "What is your message?" she asked the cat.

The cat cleared its throat. "Your father is trapped in Inveress. Fear not, he suffers no distress. He cannot get out on his own; he needs his daughter and the crone."

Brinley felt her pulse quicken. Her father! It knew where her father was!

"Where is he?" Brinley asked. "What's Inveress?"

Tabitha sighed. "It's the magical glass kingdom that doesn't exist."

Brinley turned on her. "Why do you doubt all of this, Tabitha? Is it really a children's tale? Do you know for certain?"

"No," Tabitha said, defensively. "But it's just a story."

"Well, the cat's right here," Brinley said, pointing at Tobias. "And it says it knows where my father is."

"*He*, please," the Swelter Cat said.

"*He* says he knows where my father is. Do you know where my father is, Tabitha? Why are you making fun of him?"

Tabitha's mouth clamped shut on something before she could say it, her jaw quivering with emotion. Then, without warning, she started to cry.

Brinley froze, uncertain what to do.

The Swelter Cat took a few steps forward. "The mother of Tabitha, long since dead, told her stories when she put her to bed. She took to the streets when her parents died, and searched for Inveress to hide."

"What?" Brinley said. "What do you mean?"

"It's true," Tabitha said through her hands. "My mother told me stories about Inveress when I was little. Cyus and the Swelter Cat in the city of glass. But she told the stories different. Inveress was a happy place. The best. And when they died . . ."

"You went looking for it," Brinley finished, beginning to understand.

"But it was just a story," Tabitha mumbled.

"But it's not, as you will see," the Swelter Cat said. "You'll surely see, if you follow me."

Tabitha came out from behind her hands and gave the cat a thoughtful look, as if she wasn't sure what to believe.

Just then, Archibald appeared. He came crashing through trees into the clearing, panting loudly. His hat had fallen off and his hair was disheveled. He limped slightly, using his cane for support. "There you are," he grunted.

"Archibald!" Brinley exclaimed. "Are you all right?" She hurried over to him and he put a hand on her shoulder for balance.

"I'm fine. Twisted my ankle is all." He pointed his cane at the Swelter Cat and Tobias glared back at him. "Bolted away from me as soon as he came back from the Void, the devil. I've been chasing him all afternoon. Practically killed poor Pilfur, running him all day. I had to leave him back at a stream to rest." He pointed in the direction he had come from.

"Sit down and rest," Brinley told him. "I was just about to ask Tobias to repeat his message."

"Good," Archibald said. "I would like to hear it myself, after all that."

The Swelter Cat ignored Archibald. "Your father is trapped in Inveress. Fear not, he suffers no distress. He cannot get out on his own; he needs his daughter and the crone."

"What's a crone?" Tabitha asked.

"An ugly old lady," Archibald said. He turned to the Swelter Cat. "Now, which one?"

"The witch," Tobias said. "The witch that is white, who was born in the dark but has come to the light."

Brinley squinted at him in confusion. "Uh . . . who now?"

The Swelter Cat sighed and cleared his throat. "Habis, her name is."

"Oh," Brinley said with a nod. "Habis. We know her . . . Born in the dark but has come to the light. She's going to love that."

Tobias got to his feet, stretching. "Excellent," he said, "the choice is made. Leave now, or you might be delayed."

"What?" Brinley asked. "I can't—we can't leave now! We have to save Unda. We can't just leave him there, now that we know where he is."

The Swelter Cat coughed. "So, you'll just let your father be? That isn't very daughterly."

"No!" Brinley said, going red in the face. "Of course not! But you said he isn't in any danger, didn't you?" She rubbed her face with her hands. Her head hurt. How could she be putting her father off now that she knew where he was? What had happened to her? She hadn't even thought about it, hadn't even considered abandoning Unda to go and save her father. What was happening to her? "Tabitha!" she snapped. "What are you laughing about? This isn't funny."

"Sorry, Brinley," Tabitha said, giggling. "It's just . . . daughterly . . . It isn't a very good rhyme."

"Oh," Brinley said, "No, I suppose not."

The Swelter Cat flicked his tail loftily and turned his butt to them.

"Now you see here," Archibald said, rising to his feet painfully and wagging a finger at the cat. "You'll show Brinley the respect she deserves."

"I need some time," Brinley told Tobias. "Can you come back later? Will my father be okay just a little longer? I can't leave just now. A friend of mine is in trouble and I need to help him."

The Swelter Cat gave a bemused expression. "Three days more you'll have to burn, then with or without you, I must return."

"Three days," Brinley murmured. It was better than nothing, she supposed.

"Um," Tabitha said. "And what are you going to do for three days?"

"If you like, I'll tag along. Leaving you would just be wrong."

Tabitha grimaced. "What if we don't like?"

The Swelter Cat just smiled.

"Well," Brinley said, "I guess he's coming with us."

"Then I am too," Archibald said. "If it's all the same to you."

"Archibald," Tabitha said, "he's got you rhyming now."

Archibald pursed his lips and the Swelter Cat grinned. Brinley turned to Tabitha. "Well, Tabitha, we had better get going. I hope you can carry all of us."

Chapter Fifteen

In which there is a dragon

HUGO WOKE IN THE MIDDLE of the night because someone was staring at him. His voice caught in his throat around the name. "Molad."

His own dark reflection smiled back at him deviously. Hugo wondered how that was possible, then remembered that he had fallen asleep with the mirror open. He fought the urge to run, and snapped the mirror shut instead.

I can dance the dance, Molad said in his head, his voice dripping with pride, confident he had an offer that Hugo could not resist.

Hugo's mind quieted. This was just himself he was speaking to, after all. Besides, it was a lie. *No, you can't.*

Hugo could almost feel Molad smile. *No,* he agreed, *you're right. I can't. That's good. You're learning . . . but you can't dance it either.*

Hugo nodded. The truth was clear to him now. *Neither of us can by ourselves.*

I will help you today, Molad said. *I will give you whatever help you need, for a price.*

Hugo closed his eyes. He didn't want to ask, didn't want to even consider it, but he didn't see what choice he had. Without Molad's help, he didn't stand a chance of meeting with the dragon and living to tell the tale. *What price?*

I want one hour, Molad said. *One hour of freedom.*

Hugo laughed. *After what you did last time? Do you think I'm stupid?*

That is my price, Molad said. *Pay it or play with the dragon yourself. We both know how that will end.*

Hugo punched the bed in frustration. *Fine!* he snapped. *But you get ten minutes. Ten minutes or no deal, and you can't hurt anyone this time.*

Hugo felt Molad glow with satisfaction. *Very well. Ten minutes. No hurting. You have a deal.*

Hugo sighed. He swung his legs over the edge of the bed and felt Molad skulk away into the recesses of his mind. *I will learn to do things without you someday,* Hugo promised. Molad didn't bother answering.

They both knew it wasn't true.

❖ ❖ ❖

Hugo was surprised to find the king waiting for him in the throne room. He was sitting cross-legged in the center of the floor, his eyes closed, his sword lying naked on his lap. His eyes fluttered open when Hugo entered, and he rose, sheathed his sword with a subtle motion, and bowed. "I thought you would come back," he said.

"Why?"

The king's shoulder twitched with the ghost of a shrug. "Dragons love the night."

Hugo took his place in the center of the floor. He felt Molad's emotions bubbling at the edges of his consciousness, sifting into his thoughts, his heart. He bristled at the sensation, then forced himself to surrender.

Good, Molad said. *We will share.*

Hugo could still feel their body. He could still move it too, as long as Molad allowed, just as Molad could move it with his permission. Their thoughts and emotions ran together as well. Hugo felt alarm at the emptiness running through Molad's heart, like a river that ran unchanging across the face of a fluctuating world. The darkness in it unsettled him. It was like peering into a black abyss. But there was beauty there too, unlike anything he had felt before, and freedom like a dark, soaring anarchy of thought.

Yes, Molad said. *Yes. I will move the body. You will silence the mind.*

Molad took a step and Hugo let him do it, choosing to trust, choosing to allow. He did not try to still their thoughts. It was too difficult. There was too much to process. He simply allowed them to come and go as they pleased. They were sporadic at first, his own fears and nervousness whirling together with Molad's dark dreams of power, of joy, of secrets held in a dragon's mind beneath the earth.

They moved together, but it was a different dance than the one the king of the gnomes had made. It was their own: the dance of the Mage of Light and Darkness. Then that too faded away. The place where Hugo ended and Molad began became hazy, indistinct, until neither of them could find it, until neither of them could remember being separate from each other.

And when their separate selves were forgotten, a new being was born, a being with no name, no beginning, no end, and no identity beyond the dance. It lunged, pivoting with a quickness that would have defied the human prince. Its sword licked out, catching the low light of the dwindling fire in a bead, sent it flying with a flick across the room at the silent watcher, the small man with an inhuman strength in his bones, the gnome king. The dancer moved across the room, blending into darkness, flying out of it with the strength of the earth and a raised sword. Passion filled the dancer, an anger older than the stars, and it struck.

There was the loud, crisp ringing of steel, and Hugo shook his head, trying to regain his thoughts, trying to remember what had happened. His own long sword rested against the king's shorter one, upraised to block a death blow that he could not remember making.

The king lowered his sword slowly, and sheathed it again. He looked at Hugo as if he had not seen him properly before.

"You are ready."

❖ ❖ ❖

When morning came, Hugo, Animus, and Cannon followed Thieutukar into the depths of the castle. They descended stair after twisting stone stair until Hugo decided that the ancient fortress must have been started on the bottom of a canyon and then built up; nobody could have dug a foundation so deep. Minutes passed, and still more, until they came upon the dungeons. Hugo was relieved to find them empty, but could not miss the signs that they had been full before. There were scratches on the walls, and dark spots in the stone that could not be cleaned out.

At the lowest level of the dungeon, the king came to a door of solid stone. It bore no markings, no handle or hinges. Hugo wondered for an instant how he knew it was a door at all, and then dismissed the thought. After all, sometimes when you least expect it, you see things for what they really are without trying at all.

The king placed his hand on the door and whispered something—his name, Hugo thought—and the door swung inward, revealing a steep, narrow stairway of black stone, clear as glass, leading into darkness.

"It goes down for a very long way," the king said. "It is a couple hours' walk, and I'm afraid you will have to go in darkness . . . Unless you can make light yourself. The space becomes too tight to have a smoking torch. You have no need to fear getting lost, however. There is only one tunnel. All you have to do is continue on until you reach the end of it. It would be dangerous for us to follow you. We will close the door behind you, but we will be here when you return."

Hugo nodded. He had been expecting that. He peered down the steep staircase into the cold, stone darkness beyond. "And there's a fire-breathing dragon at the end of it," he said darkly.

Thieutukar brightened. "No, in fact. His fire is gone."

Cannon slapped Hugo on the back. "See? One less thing to worry about."

"Great," Hugo said nervously, inching down the first couple of steps. The air tasted stale in his mouth. He didn't like the idea of them closing the door behind him.

"Good luck, Hugo," Animus said. "Trust in yourself." And he shut the door. Just before he did, Hugo felt a rush of air move past him. Then someone was beside him, coughing loudly.

"Phew!" Cannon's voice said, and then he started to laugh jubilantly. "Come on, Hugo," Cannon bellowed. "Let's get away before they catch me!"

A hand reached out in the darkness and pulled Hugo down the stairs. He tumbled down three steps and then found his footing, struggling to move fast enough to keep the arm from pulling him over. "Cannon?"

"Yes!" Cannon said. "Can you believe it?"

"No," Hugo said, swatting Cannon's hand away. "How did you do that? Did you turn into air?"

Cannon laughed. "Impressive, isn't it? Animus doesn't even know I can do it. I've been trying for years, of course, but I only figured it out last week. I've been saving it for a surprise."

Hugo couldn't help grinning. "Well, I bet he's pretty surprised right about now."

Cannon laughed. "Couldn't let you go by yourself, of course. Not after what happened the other day." Cannon grunted. "Be careful, the stairs end right there. Better slow down a bit, I'd hate to find the next staircase too abruptly."

"Right," Hugo said, slowing down. "Admit it, though, you just came to see the dragon."

"Well," Cannon admitted, "I can't let you have all the fun, can I?"

Truth be told, Hugo was more than glad to have some company in the darkness. He didn't know how much help Cannon would be with the dragon, but it would have been a long, lonely journey in the dark by himself. Not that he cared to tell Cannon that, of course.

"Agh!" Cannon yelped. "There's another staircase. Better keep your hands up in case it turns. Don't want to locate the wall with your face. How long did the king say it was to the bottom?"

"A couple of hours."

Cannon muttered something under his breath that Hugo didn't catch.

Hugo could guess at his thoughts. Two hours in a place like this would be a very long time. He searched for something to take his mind off the darkness around them and his mind settled on an amusing memory from the castle. Life had been simpler back then, when all he had to worry about was how to get out of his schoolwork. "Did you ever hear the story of Den and the pot of beans?" he said.

"Who?"

"Den. He's a squire in Cornith, in service to Sir Getwist."

"No," Cannon said.

Hugo cleared his throat. "Well, we were having a bit of a party—the squires and me, and a few of the serving girls—after we beat Sir Mallory's men in the knight's tournament. It was an unauthorized party, to be honest, so it was in the middle of the night. Anyway, Den was in charge of bringing the food, but all he could find in the kitchen was a big pot full of beans, and he couldn't figure out how he was going to smuggle them out. In the end he had the bright idea to dump them in a bag and hide them under his tunic."

"He didn't," Cannon said, and Hugo could tell by his voice that he was smiling.

"He did! He was halfway down the hall when the cook caught him. Totally lost his head then. Ran down three flights of stairs trying to get away from her and ended up tripping down the last one. He fell flat on his face and that bag of beans exploded right inside his tunic. Beans everywhere! Oozing out his sleeves, down his pants. A whole line of it shot out the neck of his shirt and covered his face. The cook thought it was *him* that exploded. She was dancing around, screaming her head off when, to her horror, Den got up and tried to comfort her. That's when she passed out."

Cannon roared with laughter, filling the black tunnel with echoes.

"Best part was when the king's physician got there. He thought Den had soiled himself. Wanted to pump him full of fluids and give him something to stop up the flow, so Den had to run for it. By the time he got to us, we didn't care that there wasn't any food, story like that . . ."

Cannon was wiping his eyes, sputtering now and then with little bursts of laughter. "You know, Hugo," he said, "you're all right. Sorry I'm such a prat sometimes."

Hugo smiled. Maybe having Cannon around wouldn't be terrible, as long as he could refrain from being so . . . *Cannon.*

Cannon clapped him on the back. "Hugo, your story has inspired me. I have thought of the perfect name for your nemesis. This darkness of yours. We shall call him . . . 'Mr. Poopy Pants.'"

Well, that didn't last very long, Hugo thought.

"It's perfect!" Cannon went on proudly. "You can't go calling him *Molad.* You'll end up taking him too seriously. This is demeaning, disrespectful, but not too serious. A little reminder not to be afraid of him, see? Also, I'm sure he's going to be a very stinky sort of person, so this fits."

"Cannon," Hugo said sternly. "You can't call it that."

"It's perfect." Cannon said, dismissively. He stopped short. "Look! The darkness looks different there. Maybe we've reached the bottom."

"Maybe," Hugo said, squinting. It was impossible to tell. Then, abruptly, the stairs ended and they had their answer. There was some kind of chamber ahead. Hugo could almost sense it in the darkness, like a foreboding, something sleeping that did not want to be disturbed. Cannon must have sensed it too, for he grabbed Hugo's arm.

"Hugo, we're sure that his fire's gone?"

"Afraid we're going to be burnt to a crisp?"

"I'm afraid *I* will," Cannon said. "You'll be much less flammable without your hair." He patted Hugo's bald head and pushed him into the chamber, where Hugo found himself in a darkness more absolute than anything he had ever before experienced. It was like being in a cave, or in the heart of a mountain (which they were, of course), except blacker. This darkness was thicker, older, eternally cut off from light and fresh air. It had been unsettling enough to make the descent in darkness, but it was far less scary to be in the darkness when the space around him was relatively small. Now he could sense that he was in an immense cavern, and it was unsettling. Anything might be out there.

"Sure would be nice to have some light right about now, Mr. Mage of Light and Darkness," Cannon said. His voice echoed into the space around them, convincing them of its size.

Hugo thought about it. If he let Molad out again, would he know how to make light out of nothing? If not for the leering possibility of a dragon in the shadows around him, he would have smiled at the irony of the Mage of Light being stuck in the darkness.

They heard a whisper from somewhere ahead of him.

"Hello?" Hugo called softly. He swallowed, found his voice, and called again, more loudly this time.

The whisper answered him again.

"I . . ."

Hugo squinted into the darkness. It seemed to be lifting, brightening by degrees somewhere ahead of him.

"Oh, boy," Cannon said. "Here we go."

"I . . ."

The brightness had condensed now, a small orb in the blackness right in front of him. It unfolded, stretched, lengthened, until it was the height of a man. Arms emerged from its sides as if an artist were painting them right before his eyes.

In the space of a heartbeat, the image sharpened and a man stood before Hugo, their faces mere inches apart. He was taller than Hugo and his hair was the color of fire. It didn't just look like fire, it burned. His body shone like amber.

"I am Kuzo," the dragon said. "Who are you?"

"I am Hugo," Hugo said, swallowing hard. And in the same instant Molad said, *I am Molad.*

"Uh," Cannon said, stepping back slightly, "I'm just here to watch."

Kuzo smiled. His arm lashed out and caught Cannon in the center of his chest.

The apprentice tumbled to the floor. He did not get up.

Kuzo's eyes snapped back to Hugo, holding his gaze with a pair of vibrant, fiery eyes and driving all concern for Cannon out of his mind. His voice was as deep as the darkness around them. "Hugo. Molad. You do not yet know yourself. Is that why you have come? I cannot give you that. Your journey was in vain." The dragon lifted his hand, reaching for Hugo's throat.

Molad moved faster than Hugo could, bending away into the dance. Hugo nearly stopped him, surprised, and then caught himself, allowing it to happen.

They bent and twisted, dancing around the dragon, and Hugo felt a feeling of liberation, of power, pure and unquestioned. He drew his sword and it blazed like a miniature sun. The sword spun through the air, now shrouded in darkness, now revealed, painting clean light across the dragon's pit. He brought the blade down swiftly toward the dragon's heart, and a blade of fire and diamond sent it glancing away, showering the void with violet sparks where the two swords met. The dancer twisted, spreading himself around the room, refracting the light from his sword until there were five swords, ten, a hundred. They dipped and scooped, collecting the violet sparks before they could fade.

Then the hundred blades coalesced into a single one again, twirling in the hands of the dancer, a single violet spark glimmering on its tip like a jewel. Kuzo lunged for it. Their swords gleamed, red on white as they met in the air, with violet dancing from blade to blade. Kuzo leapt into the air and Hugo rolled to the side as the red blade cleaved the air where his head had been moments before. Their blades met again and Kuzo stole the spark from Hugo's blade. Hugo wove around him and retrieved it. The sound of diamond and steel and flame echoed through the vast darkness as they traded the spark back and forth, back and forth.

Molad worked to keep them alive. Hugo worked to keep possession of the spark, and together they danced with the dragon. Finally their blades met for the final time—the spark hovered between them as they struggled against each other, then inched toward the tip of Hugo's blade. The dancer stopped, Hugo and Molad melding again into one, and with the swiftness of silence itself, they threw back their head and blew fire at the tip of the upraised sword.

The violet spark shimmered in the flames and became stone, a flawless gem the size of an egg. It slid down the dancer's blade and they caught it. Kuzo stared at it hungrily, and then, to the dragon's surprise, they handed it to him.

The dragon took it, speechless, and bowed. Then there was a sound like the howling of wind through stone, so loud it was overwhelming. Hugo covered his ears and winced, and when he opened his eyes Kuzo was in his true form: a great dragon, red and black, with eyes of pure gold and wings like iron sails. It regarded him wordlessly for a moment and then settled down, its golden eyes coming to rest on the purple jewel that was pinched delicately between two claws.

Hugo stumbled slightly as the dancer died again, went back to wherever he had come from. He eyed the purple stone in the dragon's hands and tried to remember where it had come from. They had made it, he thought, Molad and himself. How, he did not know.

"You have brought me battle," the dragon whispered in a voice like the east wind. "And treasure. What do you desire?"

Hugo fumbled for an answer, reaching for Molad, but encountered only his own thoughts. He thought of asking the dragon about Chantra, and then didn't. It was probably a good idea to ease into things.

"You are magnificent," he said. "How is it possible that the king can keep you a prisoner here?"

Kuzo flicked the tip of his tail restlessly. "That is a long, sad tale. I do not wish to tell it again so soon."

"Again?" Hugo asked. "Who did you tell the first time?"

"Someone who thought they could help me," the dragon said. "A mage . . . She was young, new to her powers. I did not wish to tell her, but I could not resist. She was the Mage of Fire, after all, and I am a dragon."

"Chantra," Hugo said. He felt a bubble of excitement from Molad.

The dragon nodded wearily. "I lost my fire," he said. "She hoped to restore it to me one day."

"Where is she now?" Hugo asked, and the dragon closed his eyes.

"Beyond my reach," he said, and there was something in his tone that said the subject was closed. Hugo was about to press him anyway, but Molad interrupted him.

"How did you lose your fire?"

Kuzo beat the ground with his clawed foreleg and growled viciously. "The Betrayer," he spat. "Gadjihalt. He stole my fire."

"How?" Molad urged, taking a step back as Kuzo's tail twitched again.

"He mocked our laws," the dragon said. "He desecrated the body of my Anorre."

"What do you mean? What laws?"

The dragon growled impatiently "Dragons live by laws of their own—deep magic from the dawn of time. We mate for life; our fire is bound to the life force of our mate. If one dies, its body must be burned or the mated dragon's fire will wither until there is nothing left." Kuzo gave him a hard look. "Do you know of Anorre?"

Hugo shook his head.

"Anorre was my mate. Shael slaughtered her for some dark purpose, and then Gadjihalt burned her body, all of it, except for her heart, and one spike from the crown of her head. The heart, Shael used to work his magic, and with the spike, Gadjihalt fashioned the hilt of a great sword."

The dragon paused, and Hugo looked up at him, but his face was hidden.

"I came seeking my revenge," Kuzo said, "but my flame was already waning. Gadjihalt killed me with the sword that he made from the body of my mate."

Hugo waited, listening for the rest of the story, but none came. "But you're not dead," he said.

"I am close enough," he said. "My fire is gone. Without it, I cannot fly. I cannot even break the small magic of the gnomes that keeps me bound in the heart of this mountain."

Hugo was silent for a moment, studying the blackness that surrounded them. There was a silence in the darkness, a reverence for the long, sorrowful wait that Kuzo had endured.

"Why did Thieutukar lock you in here?" he asked finally.

"It was his father," the dragon said. "I was wounded badly when I finally fell from the sky in my retreat. I landed in the gnome city. I was beyond anger then. My judgement was gone. I killed many of his people, even those that tried to help me. He was not wrong to imprison me . . ."

Hugo stifled his surprise. "You're not mad?"

The dragon growled. "Few live long enough to find the hatred I have found . . . But it is not for the gnomes. They did nothing to me. They put a dead dragon in a tomb of his own making."

"You want to kill Gadjihalt," Hugo said, feeling relief at discovering they shared the same enemies.

"I did once," the dragon said. "Now, I wish only for my waiting to be over. I am weary of living in the dark, and I cannot seem to die."

Hugo felt Molad's determination, his clear certainty surfacing inside of him. "I will help you," said Hugo, but the dragon said nothing.

He bent his long neck until his large golden eye was level with Hugo and said, "You are young. You should not make promises lightly to a dragon."

"I don't," Molad said. "I will get you what you need, and you will get me what I need."

"And what do you need?" Kuzo said, his voice a whisper.

"Chantra."

The dragon stared at him silently. "Very well," he said. "I will tell you where to find her when you have brought me what I require."

"And what is that?" Hugo said, as Molad reveled in self-satisfaction.

"A small thing," the dragon said. "The last part of my beloved Anorre." His eyes settled on Hugo, heavy and dim, as if the weight of an ancient world rested inside them. His words were low and quick, as if by speaking them aloud he feared that the hope they held would fade into the darkness. "Bring me the spike-hilt sword of Gadjihalt the Betrayer."

Hugo nodded cautiously. "It's a deal," he said.

"Good." The dragon's tail whipped around in the air like a long, fiery rope, razor sharp spikes glinting on the end of it. "I have something to give you before you go. Something to remember me by. Something to remind you why you must not return empty-handed." The tail lashed again, flicking out of the darkness and glancing off Hugo's thigh.

Hugo shouted and stumbled. He scrambled backwards, the pain in his leg threatening to block out the world. He put his hand over the wound and felt hot, wet blood there.

"*Why?*" Hugo shouted angrily. "Why would you do that?"

But the dragon was gone.

Chapter Sixteen

In which Tabitha boils some water

BY THE TIME THEY ARRIVED back at the Lake of Eyes, Brinley was exhausted. The trip had taken a couple of hours, and it had been so cramped on Tabitha's back with Archibald and the Swelter Cat riding behind her that she had been unable to sleep. Of course, if she were honest with herself, it wasn't just cramped quarters that kept her awake. She was afraid of what dreams might come if she drifted off. She had grown wary of letting herself sleep. She didn't like getting lost in worlds that seemed so real, so terrible, only to wake and wonder what it meant. When she slid off Tabitha's back and onto the shore of the lake, her legs nearly collapsed beneath her.

Archibald reached out a hand to steady her. "Easy," he said. "You've had a long couple of days."

Brinley put a hand to her head. "Thank you, Archibald. Yes, I suppose I have."

"What are we going to write this time?" Tabitha asked, producing a good flat stone from the shore and handing it to Brinley.

"Something about the sea," Brinley said, taking the stone. After a moment's thought, she wrote:

Give us the Mage of Water, and we will give you the sea.

She let Tabitha throw it into the water. A moment later, a plain brown stone landed on the shore next to them. Archibald picked it up and handed it to Brinley, who jumped as the chorus of voices shouted in her mind again, *NO!*

"Agh!" she growled in frustration, and threw the stone back into the lake. "They still say no." She put a hand to her head to steady herself again. "I think I'm going to lie down. I'm too tired to think what to do next."

Archibald nodded. "A good idea. Sleep for a while. We still have the whole morning. Tobias and I can circle the lake while you rest and see if we find anything. Though I don't doubt that whatever success we have here will have to do with the creature who has been throwing these." He picked up a stone, frowning at it thoughtfully, then tossed it into the water and began to circle the lake slowly. The Swelter Cat followed him grudgingly, complaining all the while.

"Tobias and I can circle the lake," the cat mimicked. "Because the Swelter Cat doesn't deserve a break." The cat stepped in front of Archibald's foot, causing him to trip and stumble into the water.

"Argh! Stop it, you!" Archibald snapped, waving his cane at the cat and making it spring away.

The Swelter Cat sniffed and licked a paw indifferently. "You get what you get, and you don't throw a fit."

Brinley grinned at them. What a pair they made. Archibald had explained on the way over that Tobias had indeed once been the servant of Cyus, but had left his service and the Void several years ago, against his master's will. Archibald had heard rumors of where the cat had been hiding and decided that Tobias would make the ideal messenger for them. However, he had been strangely silent on the topic of how one actually gets into the Void. She made a mental note to ask him about it later.

"Wake me up if anything happens," Brinley said, watching Tabitha search the beach for other suitable message rocks. "I just need to rest awhile."

Tabitha nodded, not really hearing her. She was staring at the lake again. She waited as Brinley moved away to lie down on a soft patch of grass, then turned to stare at the water disapprovingly. She spoke softly so that Brinley would not hear. "You know, it's really not nice of you to be like this. The Magemother deserves everyone's respect. She's one of the most important people in the world. You are supposed to help her. We are all supposed to help her." She eyed the water patiently, waiting for a response, and when none came she wrote her words on a rock and threw it in.

A moment later a plain rock came back and she picked it up, but nothing happened.

I can't read your thought rocks like the Magemother, Tabitha scratched into the rock. She threw it back.

A moment later another rock came out with one word written on it: "Can't."

"You can't help her?" Tabitha asked. "You mean you can't give Unda back?"

Why? She wrote on another stone.

The stone came back with words scratched haltingly on the opposite side: "Give the sun."

"Give you the sun?" Tabitha said, perplexed. "Trade? But you can't have the sun. We need it. And it's too big to fit in the lake." She scratched the word "Can't" on another rock and threw it into the lake, and it came back a moment later with nothing new added to it, just her original message.

"I see," Tabitha said, though she knew she probably didn't. "You can't help us? Fine." She sat down on the shore and stared at the lake, and her mind drifted to another lake, and the journey that she had made to the kingdom of the nymph queens. She thought of the promise that she had made to them, that she would help find their sister, Brinley's mother, the old Magemother. The only way that was going to happen was if they found the mages. Habis said that without all of the mages, Brinley's mother would not be able to be healed. They had to get Unda back. They simply had to.

She glowered at the lake, thinking of the merfolk within it who held the person that she needed, and refused to give him up. She felt helpless, stuck at the edge of a problem that she couldn't solve for Brinley. She thought of Belsie and his disappointment. She thought of Peridot and how she had ignored her counsel. She thought of how she had risked Brinley's life running from her own fear of violence.

She felt something tighten inside her. She thought of the arm coming out of the lake, throwing stone after unhelpful stone out at them, speaking in riddles and barring their way to Unda, to Brinley's mother. The thing that had been tightening inside her broke suddenly, and she picked up stone after stone, drawing on them, small curses, spells, hexes like the ones that Habis had taught her. One by one, she threw them into the water.

When she had exhausted the supply of stones near her, she moved down the shore and started over again. She cursed the water to dry up, to be thirsty for rain and never receive it, to grow stale and warm and dank, for the fish to leave it, for people to never find it again. She cursed it to never be touched again by the sun, never to feed a stream, never to be fed by one. She cursed it to die. She threw the last stone in and left to find more. She had seen some good flat ones, perfect curse rocks, up in the patch of trees where she had found the berries.

❖ ❖ ❖

Brinley awakened. She had shifted in her sleep and now the little black stone from Calypsis was pinching her leg painfully. She drew it out of her pocket and ran a finger across the smooth, black surface. A sudden idea struck her then, and she reached into the stone with her mind. She thought back to the lightfall, to the words spoken there, to the peace that had filled her, and tried to fill the stone with it.

It sort of worked, she thought. Not perfectly, but there was a sense of peace inside it now that hadn't been there before. She withdrew from the stone and hefted it. It felt the same, and yet, without a doubt, something had changed. It had an almost soothing quality now. Just holding it made her feel better about things. She wondered if Tabitha would be able to feel the difference as well.

"Tabitha?" she called. She put the stone back in her pocket and walked to the water's edge. She could see Archibald and the Swelter Cat on the other side of the lake, but where was Tabitha? An uneasy feeling struck her.

Oh no . . . She knew that feeling. Where was Tabitha? What had she done? Why had she gone to sleep and left Tabitha alone with the water? Something had happened. The lake had taken her too, perhaps. And now she had two people to rescue.

"TABITHA!" she called, and the water rippled. A man with strong arms of braided seaweed rose from the water. His face was pale, white, and his hair was the color of the water. He wore a rusted steel breastplate on his chest and an empty sword scabbard on his left hip. In one hand he carried a wooden shield that was half rotted away, and in the other he held a bag of netted seaweed full of stones.

"I am Dram," he said simply, glaring at her as if she had done something terrible.

"You are the one who caught our stones," Brinley said, recognizing his arm.

"Yes," he said, dropping the bag on the shore. He leveled a finger at her. "You attacked us. You pay the price."

"Attacked?" Brinley asked nervously. "What do you mean?"

"We talk with you. You talk with us. You ask. We say no." He gestured with his empty hand. "And then you curse us."

Brinley's eyes narrowed, thinking that the merman must be trying to trick her in some way. "I did no such thing," she said firmly. "Tell me, where is Unda? Why won't you give him back to me? Why won't you let us return you to the ocean?"

The merman pointed to the bag of stones that he had brought. "You have cursed us." Then his expression darkened. "Yes. I will take you to the mage. You will become our prisoner, as he did." He leapt forward and grabbed her around the waist, walking back towards the water. She struggled, punching him in the side.

"Archibald!" she cried. "Help!"

If Archibald heard her, she never found out, for even as she struggled to get free, the merman knocked her on the head with the flat of his shield, and everything went dark.

When Tabitha returned to the shore with the hem of her dress full of flat stones, she found a bag full of her curse rocks sitting there. Brinley was gone.

"Oh, no," she whispered, and then shouted for Brinley. She ran back to where Brinley had been resting but found her nowhere. She knew that she wouldn't, but she tried anyway, even though she knew—the lake had taken her. It had been angry, she thought, about the curses. It had gotten angry and taken Brinley instead of her. Why did she leave? What had she been thinking?

She dove into the lake, changing into a fish. She wished, in that moment, that she could take the shape of a shark instead, something menacing, something scary. She searched the whole lake from top to bottom, side to side, and all around the edges. It was deeper than she thought, and colder, but it was empty. There were fish, of course, and rocks and plants, but nothing else. No kingdom of merfolk, no towers and halls like Brinley had said. And no Brinley.

She rose from the lake bitterly and glowered at the water. It had taken Unda. It had taken Brinley. And it was all her fault. If she hadn't lost her temper and cursed the water, this wouldn't have happened. If she was a better herald, this wouldn't have happened. If she had been a good protector, they would have known to be afraid of her. They would have known not to ever harm Brinley.

"Bring her back!" she shouted, stomping into the water, but nothing happened.

"Bring her back or I will burn you up," she whispered. The water remained motionless, still and silent at her threats. "I will make you hear me," she said, twisting around. She took everything that was in her heart and channeled it into her shaping. She shaped fire out of her fear. She took the anger she felt at herself and formed wings, and a great white dragon stomped a clawed foot into the lake and bellowed so loudly that the earth shook. Then it bent its head to the water and red fire burst from it, bathing the lake in light, making the water hiss and scream as it turned to steam.

❖ ❖ ❖

Brinley came to on the sandy floor of the lake with a hundred feet of water pressing down on her. She panicked, thrashing for air, then realized that she was breathing water. The merfolk must have done something to her, changed her so that she could breathe in their world.

She was inside the dream that she had seen in the stone. She was in a round cell with black bars stretching all around her, as high as she could see, and through the bars there was nothing but darkness. Darkness and guards, that is. Four mermen with muscular arms and glistening red tails stood just beyond the bars, watching her. They carried no weapons that Brinley could see, but they looked menacing enough. Something made a ringing sound against the bars and Brinley peered into the half-light behind her. Sure enough, there was a figure there, sprawled on the ground and leaning against the bars. She stepped closer and saw that it was a boy. He was a few years older than she was, and had dark hair and blue eyes and a face that seemed to be always thinking hard about something else. Even now, he seemed not to see her, his eyes glazed over in some strange sort of trance as he tapped the bars again with his hand. There was a dull silver ring on his forefinger (which accounted for the noise), and it caught the light as he tapped again and again, a steady, feeble call for help into the darkness.

"Unda?" she said, and his hand froze. His face, however, did not change.

"Unda? Can you hear me?"

Unda's eyes came back into focus for a moment, and his face twisted in agony. He fell forward onto his knees, hands pressed against the sides of his head. He reached out to her, hand shaking, clutching at the water desperately.

"Give it to me," he groaned.

She took a half step back, unsure of what to do, but at his words, something moved inside her. It was as if a great weight had been cut loose from its moorings in her heart and shifted, swinging slowly away from her, toward him, and she recognized it for what it was. She crossed the distance between them and placed her hands on his head, whispering into his ear. When she finished saying the words, she felt the weight tear away from her and settle into him, and at the same moment he seemed to straighten up.

"Unda," she said.

"Yes," he said. "That is my name. I had forgotten."

"You forgot who you are?"

"I forgot many things," he said wearily. "When I ran."

"When you came here, you mean?" she asked, indicating the cell.

He shook his head. "When I hid from the pain," he said. "There was great pain, when I lost the connection to the water." He glanced at her questioningly. "When you took it from me . . . You did take it, didn't you? And now you have given it back."

She nodded. "I did. I'm sorry, but I had to, to defeat Lux. You remember him, don't you? And my mother, the last Magemother? She was the Magemother that you knew."

He squinted as if struggling to remember. "Yes," he said. "I forgot their faces. I had to forget everything, to forget the pain." His face went oddly blank, and she put a hand on his arm.

"Unda," Brinley said, "can you get us out of here?"

Unda glanced around at the bars of their cell casually. "That will not be a problem," he said. He gave her a searching look and began to circle their cell, reminding her of the giant cats that she had seen in a zoo once, pacing back and forth across their enclosure. "Is your mother dead?"

"No, she's alive. But she will die if we do not save her. We need all of the mages in order to save her. That is one of the reasons I came to find you."

He nodded. "One of the reasons?"

Brinley hesitated. "I think that there may be a war soon. Lux is dead, but I have called a new Mage of Light and Darkness, and he is being tested. Shael has found a way to send creatures across the bridge from the Ire. We are going to need all of the mages again, though you may be in just as much danger now as when you went into hiding."

He shrugged. "Hiding us was the Magemother's idea. Not mine. Who else have you found? Chantra? Lignumis?"

She shook her head. "You're the first."

"It's Chantra that you should look for next," he said, folding his arms behind his back thoughtfully. "I had the skill to forget my mind and hide from the pain. Lignumis may have succeeded in this also, but she will not have. She was young, wild, never willing to apply herself to the boring exercises that build that kind of strength. She would not have been able to cope well with the loss of her powers. She will need you." He tapped the bar with his ring again and closed his eyes, listening to the sound. Then he swept his arms up and the bars peeled away, ripped away as easily as if they had been made of cloth.

One of the four guards gave a shout and they rushed from the room. Not at all what you would expect guards to do when a prisoner was escaping, Brinley thought, but maybe they knew they were no match for him.

"Why did they lock you up?" she asked.

"I asked them to," he said simply. "I wanted them to hide me, lock me away somewhere where I would be safe. They have guarded me, but they knew I would break out when I was ready." He paused suddenly, raising a hand. "Do you feel that?" He closed his eyes as if listening hard.

"What?" Brinley asked.

His eyes snapped open again. "The lake is under attack. The water is evaporating . . . A great beast burns the lake. A dragon." He glanced at Brinley. "Did you bring a dragon?"

"Um," Brinley said uncertainly. She thought suddenly of Tabitha. She couldn't turn into a dragon, could she? Then she thought of Tabitha watching her get dragged into the lake, taken captive by merfolk. Suddenly it didn't seem so out of the question. "Yes. I think I might have."

❖ ❖ ❖

Archibald grasped the dragon's tail, tugging on it violently, but to no avail. Rivers of fire continued to pour out of the dragon's mouth and into the lake. Finally, in desperation, he drew back his cane and brought it down heavily on one of the dragon's clawed, white feet. He wiped his brow and stepped back as the dragon slowly turned its head to look at him.

"Tabitha," Archibald said sternly, "what are you doing? Where is Brinley? Is she in the lake?"

The dragon blinked and shook its head in annoyance, then turned back to the lake and roared, blowing another deep line of flames into the lake to make a great, frothing cloud of steam.

Archibald picked his hat up from where it had fallen in his struggle with Tabitha and placed it back on his head. He had never seen Tabitha like this. Truth be told, he hadn't known she had it in her. She was out of control, beyond reasoning with. She had nearly killed him earlier, when he had come up on her from behind. His vest was badly burned from the experience.

He only hoped that whatever had happened, she had a good reason to be this way, and that she was making things better instead of worse. The lake had already receded noticeably. In another couple of hours she would likely succeed in reducing the lake to a puddle, not to mention cooking whatever happened to be living down there.

He stumbled backward as a wave of heat hit him, retreating behind a tall, upright rock. The Swelter Cat was sitting on the other side of it, preening a paw as if it hadn't a care in the world.

"Quite a temper that one's got," the cat muttered. "Things are getting pretty hot."

Archibald scowled at him, then peered cautiously around the edge of the stone.

❖ ❖ ❖

The dragon did not notice right away when Brinley's head broke the surface of the water.

"Tabitha!" she shouted, swimming away from the flames and towards the shore. "Tabitha!"

The dragon shook its head, baring its white teeth between spouts of fire. "Don't worry, Brinley!" it growled. "I'm coming. I'll boil them out. They can't ignore me forever. I'll—Oh, Brinley!" The dragon had spotted her now, and Brinley relaxed. For a moment she had wondered if she might be accidentally boiled alive.

The dragon extended a paw to her and Brinley grabbed on to one of the curling white claws, careful not to cut herself as she was drawn toward the shore.

The dragon shrank out of sight as soon as Brinley was back on dry ground, replaced by a frazzled-looking Tabitha, bobbing up and down on tiptoes anxiously.

"Oh, Brinley!" she said, rushing forward and hugging her tightly. "I'm so glad you're all right."

"Me too," Brinley spluttered.

"But where's Unda?" Tabitha asked, craning her neck over Brinley's shoulder as if she might be hiding him in her back pocket. Tabitha began to roll up her sleeves angrily. "They have to give him back, too. First they take him. Then they take you! I'll make them give him back. I'll—"

"Tabitha!" Brinley said sternly. "Calm down." She placed a hand on the girl's arm.

"Oh," Tabitha said. "I'm sorry. I don't know what came over me."

Brinley patted her arm, walking her toward the shore of the lake. "Unda is on his way up," she said. "He's just talking with the merking."

"The king?" Tabitha exclaimed, raising her hands to her mouth in horror, "I hope he's not angry with me. I've burned up his lake!"

"Not all of it," Brinley said, grinning. "Besides, you didn't really hurt any of the merfolk, though they were getting quite nervous."

"Oh, good," Tabitha said, relaxing. "That's wonderful."

"Are you okay?" Archibald asked, coming up to them. He placed his hands on Brinley's shoulders and looked her over for damage. When he was satisfied that she was all right, he asked, "What did you find out?"

"Unda came to the merking," Brinley explained. "The king agreed to use his magic to hide Unda if Unda would return their people to the sea, but the food they fed him made him sick. It made him lose his memory, I think. I don't think it was meant for humans. But the merfolk thought that he was faking, and they got angry with him, so they locked him up."

"That's terrible!" Tabitha exclaimed.

Archibald shook his head. "It was just a big misunderstanding?" he said. "Who would have thought?"

"Unda remembered in time, though," Brinley said. "I gave his power back and it all came back to him. He's working it out with the king now."

At her words, two shapes emerged from the water. One was a young man with dark hair and eyes the color of the sea. The other was a burly fellow with a watery green beard. Brinley could see the spot on his belly where skin turned into scales. Unda and the king were still chatting in a strange, cooing language that sounded like nonsense. Then Unda shook the king's hand and walked the rest of the way out of the water. Brinley noticed that his clothes were completely dry the moment they left the water. She, on the other hand was freezing, now that her damp clothes had cooled in the air.

"I do not have the time to move their whole city now," Unda said. "But I promised them that when the war is over, I will."

"How did they get here in the first place?" Brinley asked.

"They came out of the sea long ago, searching for a quiet place to live, I think, and they found it. But now the sea calls to them, and they cannot find their way back. The rivers have changed since then. Some have dried up altogether. And always they must fear the nymphs who rule the waters of Aberdeen. They would not be pleased to find a city of merfolk. Several of their people have left to find the path but none have returned." He waved at the king and the large man nodded and slipped back into the water. "Soon they'll be back where they belong." he said.

"Speaking of soon, it's well after noon," the Swelter Cat said to Brinley. "Your time's running out while you just stand about."

Brinley sighed. "Come, Unda. I want you to meet my friends."

Chapter Seventeen

In which Molad crosses a line

THE FIRST THING HUGO noticed was the horrible taste in his mouth. He wondered for a moment how it got there. He hadn't eaten anything strange for breakfast, had he? Then the pain in his leg surged to the forefront of his awareness and he gave an involuntary gasp.

"It's okay," a voice said.

He felt a cold compress cover his forehead, and someone squeezed his hand. He squeezed it back automatically, then released it and reached for his leg. He needed to touch it, to feel it. It must be ripped in two to feel like that. Hands stopped him, holding him back.

"No, Hugo," the voice said. "You mustn't touch it. They said you'll feel much better in a couple of hours."

"Brinley?" Hugo asked blearily, opening his eyes to make sure. Yes, it was her. What was she doing here? "Where am I?" he asked, realizing that he didn't actually know where here was.

"You're still in the castle," Brinley said. "Tuck's castle, in Tourilia. You fought a dragon this morning, so they tell me."

"But how did you get here?" Hugo asked. He racked his brain in vain, but the last thing he remembered was Kuzo's tail coming out of nowhere.

"I felt your pain," Brinley said. "So I came."

"Where were you?" Hugo asked, trying to take his mind off his leg.

"I was with Unda," Brinley said.

Hugo opened his eyes again. "Really?"

"See for yourself," Brinley answered, shifting aside to reveal a young man sitting in a chair. He was of medium height and build with dark hair and a thoughtful expression, even in sleep.

"He's very tired," Brinley explained, looking very tired herself. Her hair was askew and there were lines under her eyes. "We had a long day."

Hugo gave a low whistle. "I guess so." He glanced around the room, taking in his surroundings. He had been placed in what looked like a room designed for sick people. His bed was adjustable, and there were chairs all around it so that many people could visit him at once. He remembered a couple such rooms at Caraway Castle, but he had never been unfortunate enough to stay in them. He gave Unda another glance. "How did you find him?" He shifted onto his elbow so that he could look her in the face and winced as the pain in his leg doubled.

"You shouldn't move," Brinley said, pushing him back onto the bed.

"Yeah," Hugo said through gritted teeth. "Got it."

"I'll tell you my story," Brinley said, "if you tell me yours. Nobody really knows how you got like this. Cannon was knocked out, and nobody else was there."

"Right. Okay." He glanced around the room. "Where is everyone else?"

"Dinner," Brinley said.

Hugo's stomach grumbled loudly at the mention of food, and he looked hopefully at the table beside his bed, but it was empty.

"They gave you a special medicine," Brinley said. "They say you will be mostly better by tomorrow, but you can't eat anything until then."

Hugo grimaced. "Figures." He shifted his weight more carefully this time and began to tell Brinley the story of his confrontation with the dragon, but was careful to leave out the parts about Molad. When he was finished, she sat back in her chair thoughtfully and folded her arms across her chest.

"It's amazing that you were able to learn how to do that dragon dance thing so quickly," she said.

He shrugged, not meeting her eye. "I got by, I guess."

"That's not what Tuck says," Brinley said. "He says that you did it as well as he could have, and after just a day's practice . . ." She waited for him to explain.

Hugo was staring very hard at a small knot in the wood of his bed frame. He could tell Brinley knew he was holding back. How did she do that? It didn't matter. He had to find a way to satisfy her without explaining all about Molad. She wouldn't like that, he knew. She wouldn't like the way he had bartered with him, but what did she know about it?

"Well," Brinley said, "if you're not going to tell me how you did it, then I had better tell you about my day."

Hugo brightened. "Yeah?" He wished that he had kept his mouth shut instead. Now he looked like an idiot.

Brinley shrugged. "I'd rather you keep the truth to yourself instead of lying to me," she said, then launched into the account of finding Unda. When she got to the part where Tabitha threw the cursed rocks into the lake, Hugo burst out laughing.

"It's funny now," Brinley said, "but it wasn't funny at the time. You might not want to mention it to Tabitha. She feels pretty bad."

"I bet," Hugo said, chuckling.

When Brinley had finished her story, Hugo leaned back and closed his eyes. "I can't imagine Tabitha as a dragon," he said. "Where do you suppose she learned to do that? It doesn't sound like a very easy thing to do."

"I think it is quite hard," Brinley said, smiling. "Animus almost didn't believe it when he heard, and later he told me that not even Belterras can take the shape of a dragon. Tabitha said it happened by accident once, and now she can do it whenever she wants."

"I wish I could do that," Hugo said. "It would have come in handy today."

Brinley laughed.

At that moment, the door to the room burst open and Tabitha walked in, followed by Cannon and Animus. Behind him came an elderly female gnome wearing a white apron, then Archibald and a strange-looking cat.

"Hugo!" Tabitha cried. "Where is your hair? Your head is *so* shiny now! Can I touch it?"

Hugo was spared from answering when the king of the gnomes entered the room. "Ah!" Tuck said. "The hero has awakened! How is your leg?"

"A bit better," Hugo said. It actually did feel better than it had when he had woken up. He didn't know what kind of medicine they had used, but it must have some sort of magical properties. When Kuzo's spiked tail had struck his thigh, he hadn't expected to walk on it for several weeks. Now he felt like he might be able to do it by the end of the night.

"Does this hurt?" Tabitha asked, slapping the bottom of his foot with the flat of her hand.

Hugo screamed, and Tabitha leapt back in surprise.

"Ah, good," the gnome in the apron said. "No nerve damage."

Hugo gave the old gnome a scowl, and Tuck said, "Hugo, this is Armesa. She is my chief physician. She thinks that you might be up and about as soon as tomorrow."

"Can you wiggle your toes?" Armesa asked.

Hugo glanced down at his toes. He could just see them protruding from the heavy white bandage that was wrapped around his entire leg. "I can barely even move my leg," Hugo protested.

Armesa coughed. "Your leg is immobilized," she said shortly. "I asked you to move your toes."

Hugo tried. He felt a sharp pain in his leg, but he was able to flex his big toe. Tabitha must have thought that his toe looked funny wiggling at the end of the bandage, for her fingers moved almost automatically, reaching out to pinch it. Luckily, Armesa swatted her away.

"Now the others," Armesa said, and Hugo winced as he tried to wiggle his remaining toes.

"How are you healing me so fast?" Hugo asked. "What did you give me?"

"A special concoction," Armesa said. "Brewed together and taken orally every hour, also wrapped on the wound."

"What's in it?" Hugo asked, intrigued.

Armesa recited the list of ingredients, ticking them off on her fingers one by one.

"Taro root, balewyrth, jagunda, yumis, and tobacco. Brewed together."

"That's it?" Hugo asked, disappointed. He had been expecting some sort of magical elixir.

Armesa waved a hand. "Mages are easy to heal when the Magemother is around to bless their medicine. Makes it all work ten times better than on normal people." The physician sounded almost annoyed.

Hugo turned to Brinley, who was blushing slightly. "You blessed my medicine?" Hugo asked, pushing himself onto one arm again.

Armesa slapped his arm at the elbow, causing him to fall back down. "She sat by your bedside all afternoon, too. The least you can do is sit still long enough for the medicine to work."

"Sorry," Hugo mumbled. He risked another glance at Brinley but found her staring at the floor. He wondered why. And why was he so afraid to look at her, anyway? She was just the Magemother, after all. He thought suddenly of the look on her face when he had awakened. She had been relieved, like she was really worried about him, and she had been holding his hand. Cannon caught his eye from the corner of the room and winked. He hoped nobody noticed that.

When Armesa was finished, the others wanted to hear the full story, since, as Tabitha put it, Cannon was knocked out for the good parts.

He told much the same version again, and he was slightly surprised when no one commented about his strange success with the dragon dance like Brinley had. Mages were always accomplishing strange things, he reminded himself. Most likely they all suspected that there was something else to the story, but unlike Brinley, they all realized that it was none of their business.

"Well," Archibald said when he had finished, "you are picking up all sorts of new skills. A job well done, if I may say so."

"Thanks," Hugo said, trying not to let on how much it meant to him to receive praise from his old tutor. "Archibald, when did you get a cat?"

"I am not his possession, Paradise brat," the cat snapped. "I could leave this procession at the drop of a hat."

Archibald grimaced at the Swelter Cat. "How he came to be with us is a long story, Hugo. And not a very pleasant one. Better for another time."

"Indeed," Animus said, raising an eyebrow. "I believe the most pressing business is to come up with a plan to retrieve Gadjihalt's sword."

"Really?" Hugo said, hoping that the fear he felt didn't come across in his voice.

Animus nodded. "There are two difficulties. The first is that he is in the Ire. A few of us—a small group, I should say—might enter the Ire and succeed in finding him, but that leaves the other difficulty."

"You mean that he won't just hand over his sword . . ." Brinley said.

"Precisely. There are two possibilities. The first is that we may get lucky. Gadjihalt swore loyalty to the Paradise kings. He took sacred vows, which cannot be broken lightly. He is, in fact, bound by magic to fulfill them." He nodded to Hugo. "We have discussed this previously. At the height of his power, Shael made it possible for Gadjihalt to break these vows and live, but it seems unlikely that he will enjoy the same freedom from his obligations now that

Shael is imprisoned. Given this, Hugo, as a member of the Paradise line, should be able to challenge him to a duel that he cannot refuse. There are laws regarding this in the knight's code that Gadjihalt once swore to uphold. If it works, we are in luck, for it means that Hugo, as the younger duelist—"

"Will get to pick the weapons," Hugo finished, his eyes going wide. "I could request to use his own sword to fight him."

Animus nodded. "Correct. If this happens, we can retreat the moment Hugo has Gadjihalt's sword, and there may be no need to actually fight him."

"Thank goodness," Hugo said, leaning back. "I like this plan . . . Other than the whole sneaking into the Wizard's Ire and challenging Gadjihalt to a duel thing."

There were a few chuckles, but Archibald was frowning. "You said there were two possibilities," he said to Animus. "What happens if we aren't lucky?"

Animus nodded ponderously. "If we don't get lucky, Gadjihalt will still be exempt from the magic that binds him to honor his vows, and he will simply refuse. At that point we would be forced to actually fight him."

"That doesn't sound good," Brinley said.

"I should think not. As Shael's second-in-command, he will have many resources at his disposal. Also, he will be surrounded by guards wherever he goes. Should we have to fight him, he will not be fighting alone."

"You're more than a match for him though, aren't you, Animus?" Hugo said.

"Hmm," Animus murmured. "Perhaps, under normal circumstances. But in this case, I will not merely be fighting. I will also be protecting you and whoever else goes with us. Also, we will be within the Wizard's Ire, and that place sometimes has a strange effect on magical powers. I went there once to save the Magemother, but I took a great risk doing it, and I do not relish the idea of repeating the experience."

Hugo nodded slowly. "Either way, I guess you and I have to go."

Animus nodded. "Cannon should come too, I think, and no one else."

There was a chorus of objections from around the room, but Animus held up his hand. "No one else is essential to this quest," Animus said. "And every person who comes risks a great deal. It does not make sense for those to venture in who do not absolutely need to."

Nobody had anything to say to that, and after a moment of silence Hugo decided to break the ice with a question that had been troubling him. "Hey, how did I get out of that dungeon?"

Animus brightened. To Hugo's surprise, he slapped Cannon on the back. "My apprentice here carried you out."

Hugo blinked at Cannon. "Really?"

Cannon pursed his lips pompously. "Well," he said, "I figured it was the least I could do after you just stood by and let that dragon knock me out."

Hugo blushed, but left the comment alone.

"All right, people," Armesa said, "everybody out." And the room emptied, leaving Hugo alone with Brinley again. For a moment, the thoughts he'd had earlier crowded in on him again, but he pushed them away, focusing on the present moment, and looked at her.

"You didn't answer my question earlier," she said. "You don't have to tell me if you don't want to, but I think that you do."

"*They* didn't ask," Hugo noted, looking down.

"Because they know that's my place," Brinley said. "Also, they all know what the answer is anyway, and they know there's nothing they can do to help you."

He glanced up at her and found her eyes searching him. It made him feel uncomfortable, but he didn't want to look away either. She had pretty eyes. How had he never noticed that before?

"It's the darkness, isn't it?" Brinley asked. "That's how you were able to do it."

Hugo stared at his hands. "Molad."

Brinley straightened. "You named it?" she asked, sounding afraid.

Hugo sighed. "You wouldn't understand, Brinley," he said, more sharply than he intended. "I mean . . . I just don't want to talk about it right now, okay?"

She nodded, not looking at him. "I'll just leave you to rest, then," she said, turning to leave. At the door, she stopped and came back, taking something from her pocket. "I have something for you," she said, holding it up. It was a smooth stone. Hugo noticed that it felt oddly warm when she dropped it in his hand. "Animus told me about Molad. I can only imagine what you have been going through."

Hugo stared at the stone, not meeting her eyes. So she had known all along. She had no doubt guessed that his success with the dragon was due to Molad. She had just been giving him an opportunity to come clean.

"Hugo," she said, drawing his gaze. "You don't have to tell me everything, you know. I'm just here to help when you need it. That's what friends do."

He glanced down again. "What's the rock for?"

"It's something I made. Cassis taught me how to put things inside of stones. Memories, feelings."

"What's in it?" Hugo asked, holding it up to his ear and shaking it.

Brinley laughed. "Peace," she said, and turned for the door again.

He tried to think of something to say. A way to say thank you, or to make her understand, but the door had shut behind her before he could.

❖ ❖ ❖

Several hours after Brinley had left him alone to think, Molad woke Hugo. It was the dead of night, and a mirror image of himself darker than death or night was staring at Hugo from behind his own eyes.

"What?" Hugo said out loud.

The time has come for you to repay your debt.

What are you talking about? Hugo asked. *Leave me alone. We need to sleep. Can't you feel it? We're injured.*

Your debt, Molad said. *My ten minutes of freedom. The time has come.*

Hugo felt his neck prickle as Molad's words from early that morning came back to him.

Not now, he said. *Any time but now.* He was thinking of Brinley. She could be staying in the room next door for all he knew. And Tabitha and Cannon and Animus were there too. He couldn't let Molad loose in the middle of all of his friends. He wouldn't do it.

You don't have a choice, Molad said.

I always have a choice.

You made a deal, Molad insisted.

You mean you can take control of me just because I made you a deal? Hugo asked. *I won't let you free. You can't have control, not here, not now.*

Don't you trust me, Hugo? Molad simpered. *I'm just you, after all. You and me, we're the same.*

No, Hugo said, ignoring the rest of the question. *I don't trust you.*

Don't make me force you, Hugo. Let me out.

You can't make me, Hugo said defiantly, and for a moment he thought that Molad had given up. His mind felt like his own again, his body felt strangely vacant, like he had the place all to his own again after sharing it for so long. Then something hit him with the force of a brick wall. He tried to scream, but no sound came out. He tried to run, but his muscles wouldn't move. This was the battle, he realized, this was the struggle for control. His sense of awareness faded, then returned. It was like being in an arm-wrestling match with someone just a bit stronger than he was, except that it wasn't just his pride on the line, it was his mind and body.

After a moment, it became clear he would lose. Molad was simply stronger than he was. It surprised him, in a way. He had secretly been hoping that when this moment finally came he would prove the stronger, that this would be the answer for how to control the darkness. But he wasn't stronger. Brute force was not going to work. He felt control slipping away from him before he had finished the thought, and then it was completely gone.

Hugo found himself confined to a small, dark chamber inside what he would previously have called "himself." Now, however, that self was in the control of Molad. Molad's thoughts flowed before him like a glowing river running by the window to his little prison. He could see them, but he couldn't influence them. He tried to speak, but no sound came out. That didn't make any sense. Molad had been able to speak with him. Why couldn't he do the same now that they had traded places? Maybe Molad was more adept at this inside world than he was.

Something flashed in the darkness outside his window and it took him a moment to realize what he was seeing. It was the world. The world through Molad's eyes. He was seeing again. He could see the little room that he had been lying in. He watched as Molad got out of the bed and got dressed. He saw himself cross the room to the little wash basin and splash water on his face. Something uncomfortable bit at the tension in Molad's mind. It was coming from his pocket. That was odd. Molad took out the stone that Brinley had given him and tossed it onto the bed with a look of disgust, and Hugo realized that it must truly have a sort of peace inside, to bother Molad like that. Then Molad looked into the mirror and smiled. There was something different behind the eyes, Hugo thought, but otherwise it looked just like him. It was the same body afterall. Only the body's master had changed.

"Good-bye, Hugo," Molad said, and everything went dark again.

Molad was free.

❖ ❖ ❖

It did not take Molad long to find what he was looking for. The Magemother slept in the room next to his, and he located her bag quickly. She stirred when he opened it. He froze. It would not do to wake her just now. It would be easier, faster, if he went undetected. When the steady breathing resumed, he took the small crystal vial out of the bag and put it in his pocket. Then he moved to the open window. He reached out across the night, feeling for the city of Ninebridge. He would make the journey in a single step.

"Hugo, what are you doing?"

The soft, curious voice made him turn. It was Tabitha. Of course. That fumbling idiot child that "protected" the Magemother. How had he forgotten her? He considered whether he should answer her at all or just step out of the window and into Ninebridge.

Tabitha started when she saw his face clearly in the moonlight from the window, letting out a little squawk and rising briskly from the chair where she had been sitting. The chair clattered to the ground, making more noise than he would have liked, but the look of terror on her face was satisfying, and he decided to admire it for a while. It wouldn't hurt to indulge himself for just a moment. He had ten minutes to get to the Ire before Hugo would find the strength to return. That had been their agreement. Ten whole, glorious minutes.

"Hugo," Tabitha gasped, "what's happened to you? Your face, it's . . . wrong."

Molad smiled. It felt good to be recognized. The door creaked open and a young man poked his head through the opening. It was that annoying apprentice of the Wind Mage, Cannon.

"Everything all right in here?" he asked. "I heard—" He broke off, catching sight of Molad. "Hugo!" he said in surprise. "Up and about already? What are you—" He stopped short again, no doubt seeing Molad clearly, as Tabitha had.

"That's not Hugo," a voice said. Molad turned. The Magemother was sitting up in bed, watching him warily.

"Not Hugo?" Tabitha asked.

Molad frowned. He had stayed too long. He was just wasting time now. He reached out again to the night, feeling for his destination. He leaned farther out the window, ready to step.

"Oh," Cannon said quietly. "Mr. Poopy Pants."

Molad eyed him sharply. "What?"

Cannon shrugged. "It's what I call you. Don't feel bad. Hugo doesn't approve."

Molad's eyes narrowed.

"Speaking of Hugo," Cannon went on, taking a step into the room. "I don't think it's quite fair, you kidnapping him like this, taking his body wherever you want. Where are you going, anyway?"

Molad smiled and moved to step to Ninebridge. Before he was out the window, however, he felt a hand grab him from behind. A split second later, at the other end of his step, Cannon toppled onto the stones beside him, at the top of the bridge to the Wizard's Ire.

"Ouch." The mage's apprentice was holding his head. "How far did we come?" He got to his feet, glancing at the lights of the city around them. It was just light enough to make out the shadows of the large stone bridges rising out of the city beneath them. "Ninebridge?" he said in disbelief. "Ugh." He was pulling on his ears now. "So far, so fast. I think I left part of my brain back in Tourilia. Let's not do that again, okay, Mr. Poopy Pants?"

Molad punched him hard in the jaw as he turned, lifting him off his feet and sending him crashing to the stones with a satisfying *thump*. He didn't get up.

There, Molad thought. *That's better.* He turned and walked to the top of the bridge.

When he reached the apex of the bridge, he slowed. He was close enough to see the line of gold bricks that marked the midpoint of the bridge. All he had to do was cross that, and he would be on his way to the Ire.

"And just what do you think you are doing, Hugo?"

Molad turned to see Cassis stepping out of solid stone. "I came to see you," he said quickly.

"Unlikely," Cassis said. The mage's eyes were narrowed in suspicion, and Molad guessed that the other man was already drawing the correct conclusion. "You're not Hugo."

Molad shrugged. "Yes and no."

Cassis nodded. "So, the dark one has come out to play . . . What have you done with Hugo?"

Molad cocked his head. "He will be back shortly. He . . . owed me a favor . . . ten minutes' worth."

Cassis gave him a dark glare. "I suppose you want to go into the Wizard's Ire?"

Molad smiled. "And you have the key, Cassis. Don't you? I would, if I were in your position."

Cassis laughed. "You don't think I'm foolish enough to carry it with me."

"I do." His hand darted into Cassis's robes with lightning speed and emerged with the medallion.

"Don't!" Cassis cried, catching Molad's wrist in an iron grip. His grip literally became iron, an immovable vice that held Hugo in place. Then his arm turned to metal as well, and his leg. The whole left side of his body turned hard, rooted to the bridge.

"You can't hold me forever," Molad sneered, holding the medallion out of Cassis's reach.

"I only need to hold you for ten minutes," Cassis said. "Less now, I'll wager."

"Let me go," Molad ordered.

"No."

"Very well," Molad said darkly, "but Hugo won't like it when he finds out what I had to do to you." He reached out and grabbed the other mage by the throat, his own hand turning black as night.

The darkness spread from his fingers to the other mage's skin as they tightened around his throat.

Cassis clenched his jaw, the muscles in his neck bulging against Molad's grip. He clenched his free hand into a rock hard fist and clubbed Molad in the head, but it was not enough. The boy's grip remained tight. He could feel the blackness that was spreading from Molad's skin to his own. Finally, he cursed and released Molad's wrist. He folded his arms tightly across his chest, wincing as the darkness spread to his face. Then, with a groan, he turned to stone. The stone began to glow a second later, faintly at first, then more strongly, and then he was a solid metal statue. The soldiers below were sure to see the light and come to investigate. It was time for Molad to be going.

"That's right," Molad whispered before turning to leave. "You go ahead and heal yourself. I have what I came for."

Flashing a smile that no one could see, Molad put the medallion in his pocket and strode to the golden line of warding.

"Hey!" someone shouted. Molad turned to see Cannon hurtling at him. The apprentice hit him before he could react, bent over double, shoulder connecting with Molad's gut.

And together, they tumbled across the line.

Chapter Eighteen

In which Cannon falls into a bog

HUGO WOKE TO A STRANGE stinging sensation: his head was rocking back and forth, back and forth, and someone was slapping him.

"Hugo!" a voice shouted. He received another slap. "Hugo!"

Where was he? He tried to open his eyes, but they were too heavy. He felt sluggish all over, unwieldy. His body felt like a foreign place. How long had he been gone from it?

Another slap hit him and his face stung sharply, and his eyes snapped open on their own.

"Oh," Cannon said, stepping back from him. "There you are. Finally. You won't believe what you did, Hugo. Or do you know already?"

Hugo pushed himself to his feet, wincing at the pain in his leg. "Know what?" he asked blearily. He rubbed his eyes. What had happened? He had been talking with Brinley. No. He had been talking with Molad. Molad . . .

"Oh, no," he said. The memory came back to him with sudden clarity, and he struggled to his feet, grabbing at Cannon. "What did he do?"

"See for yourself," Cannon said, taking him by the shoulders and spinning him around. A vast forest of dark trees stretched beneath him; the bridge at his feet descended into the heart of it. The night was darker here, as if a curtain had been drawn over the face of the moon. Dark. Too dark. A darkness he could feel was emanating from the forest, diluting the natural light of the night. He felt a chill run down his spine. Somewhere inside himself he felt Molad shiver with anticipation.

"Uh oh."

"Yep," Cannon said gravely, sticking his fingers in his belt. "The Wizard's Ire." He gave Hugo a sidelong glance. "I sure do hope we have a good reason for being here."

"Well," Hugo said, "there are certainly things to do, if we want to stay a while. Like getting Gadjihalt's sword, for example."

"Just the two of us?" Cannon said. "Wonderful."

Hugo turned to look at Cannon, his sore head filling with questions. "Why did you follow me here? *How* did you follow me here? What happened? Argh!" He winced. He had been feeling the side of his head and his hand came away bloody. He gave Cannon an accusatory look.

Cannon held up his hands. "That wasn't me," he said. "That was Cassis. He clocked you right in the face when you were stealing the medallion from him. I came to just in time to see it."

"Came to?"

"Yes. Came to," Cannon said icily. "After you knocked me out."

"Oh," Hugo said. "I, uh ... Sorry." Hugo was rubbing his stomach now. It was tender to the touch, and he thought a couple ribs might be bruised. "Did I fall or something?"

Cannon grinned. "*That* was me." Cannon glanced around uneasily. "Can you contact the Magemother?"

Hugo reached out with his mind, searching for Brinley. *Brinley? BRINLEY!* But there was no response. "No. It's like I'm being blocked out."

"It must be the Ire," Cannon said, as if he had expected it. "Well, let's get out of here."

"Fine," Hugo said. "Um, do you have that medallion, or do I have it?" He tapped his pockets, looking for a bulge.

"I don't have it," Cannon said. "And you don't either." He jammed a finger into the air, indicating the edge of the bridge. "Mr. Poopy Pants threw it over the side the second we got through. I tried to stop you, but you were too quick."

"You're joking," Hugo said. He limped to the edge, grimacing at the pain in his leg. It was several hundred feet down, with a river at the bottom. Hugo cursed softly, and Cannon patted him on the back.

"Yep," Cannon said. "I guess he wanted us to stay. We're definitely not going back the way we came."

"Then how?" Hugo said. "Do we wait here for someone to come get us? Are there more medallions?"

Cannon shrugged. "How should I know?" He glanced around them, then down at the forest. "I, for one, don't like the idea of just standing here."

Hugo shivered. He was right, of course. They were way too exposed here. "Hey," he said. "People have been getting through this portal, right? So there must be a way through."

"No doubt," Cannon said, sticking his boot into the mist. His foot touched something solid. "But it's obviously not as simple as just walking through." He eyed the forest below them warily. "I guess we'll have to go in before we get out."

"Right," Hugo said nervously. There was a prolonged silence, during which they both waited for the other to come up with a better plan.

"Well," Cannon said, starting down the bridge, "there is a bright side, I suppose."

"What?" Hugo said, pulling alongside him.

Cannon winked conspiratorially. "Stories, Hugo. Stories."

❖ ❖ ❖

Minutes later, Hugo trembled as something new poured into his consciousness from Molad. Urges, strong and desperate, spilled out of him. He wanted to leave the tiny path he and Cannon were on and run into the forest, screaming at the top of his lungs to announce his presence. He wanted to melt into the darkness that surrounded him, explore the depths of it and never return. He was hungry too, terribly hungry. He needed to devour something, cover it in his darkness until it became a part of him. He felt his mind tipping, sliding away from his control and into Molad's hands.

"Look at this," Cannon said, stooping down.

Hugo shook himself, maintaining control somehow. He scratched at his chest, digging through his shirt with his fingernails, until the pain of it brought clarity back to him. "What is it?" he asked.

"A footprint. See?"

Hugo squinted down at it. "Bear?" He glanced around them, searching the trees. "Shouldn't bother us, right?"

Cannon raised his eyebrows. "Maybe. Maybe not. Depends."

Hugo sighed. "Depends on what?"

Cannon lifted a leaf, sniffed it, and dropped it back to the earth. Then he started down the path again. Hugo followed him. He was still limping, but he noticed that the pain had lessened somewhat since their journey began. That old gnome's magic medicine still seemed to be working on him.

"Do you know the four terrors of the Wizard's Ire?" Cannon asked.

"Obviously," Hugo said, racking his brain. They were the four most deadly things in the Ire. The things that you really didn't want to find, should you have the misfortune of getting into the

Ire at all. He coughed awkwardly. "I mean, I don't know if I could name all of them."

"Right," Cannon said, hiding a half-smile. "Well, first is the Slugbear."

"Oh, yeah," Hugo said. "Giant bear. Lives in a swamp, right?"

Cannon nodded. "And it eats you, of course."

"Of course." Hugo had remembered the second one now. "And the Hoarfrost Forest," he said.

"Yes. It's supposed to be a particularly nasty place. A grove of perpetually frozen trees. You wander into them and freeze so fast that you can't get out before you die . . . Though why you would go strolling through a bunch of frozen trees in the first place escapes me."

Hugo shrugged. "Maybe you're looking for a nice place to picnic? Very pretty, probably. That'll be the one that gets the girls."

Cannon chuckled. "Number three is the Janrax." He didn't say anything else, and he didn't need to. Everyone knew what the Janrax was. The shape-shifter. Probably the scariest creature in the whole world—apart from Shael—since it could be standing right in front of your face at any moment and you wouldn't know. The Janrax could take any shape, it was said, and if it wanted you dead, that's when your life came to an end.

"I hope we don't meet that," Hugo said darkly.

Cannon nodded. "Could just be a myth."

Hugo frowned. "Not with our luck," he said. There were too many rumors, too many myths and accusations for all of them to be false. In the old days, they said the Janrax would impersonate people. It would appear to you after your brother died, looking just like your brother, until you went mad from fright. Or it would appear as the king in a meeting and create some terrible new law. The Janrax lived to create chaos, large and small . . . But that was before it was locked away in the Ire. The mages had trapped it long ago, it was said. No one had seen it since.

"Number four, though," Cannon said. "The Sea King. He's just a myth for sure."

"I don't remember much about him," Hugo said.

Cannon waved a hand. "Crazy stuff. They say the great North Sea flows right out of the night sky to touch the northern border of the Ire, far beyond the edge of the map. They say a creature lives on the shore, half in the water, half out, and half god, no doubt. He has the head and arms of a goat and the body of a fish, but he speaks the language of men."

Hugo laughed. "That's right. I remember him now. You go crazy if you set eyes on him or something like that."

"He tells you your future," Cannon said. "That's what makes you go crazy."

Hugo stopped smiling.

"Oh," Cannon said. "I didn't mean . . ."

"What?" Hugo said. "That I'll go crazy?" He gave Cannon a sharp look and then shrugged. "It's okay. You're probably right. I don't think we need to worry about this Sea King, though. My future's probably the same as every other Mage of Light and Darkness. You know, madness, death, and all that. Can't imagine that hearing it from a crazy goat-fish would make it any worse."

"See?" Cannon laughed. "That's the spirit."

They walked for a few minutes in silence, then Cannon clamped a hand over his nose and glared at Hugo. "Ugh! Wow!"

"It wasn't me," Hugo said, raising his hands innocently.

They rounded a corner and Cannon stopped short, ducking down to study the dirt. "Looks like the same tracks again. More of them this time."

"It's the Slugbear," Hugo said.

Cannon bent lower over the tracks. "Hmm." He waved at the air around his nose absently. "Phew, wow, that's bad."

"It's the Slugbear," Hugo said again, more quietly this time.

Cannon matched his quiet tone, eyes still intent on the tracks. "I don't think you can blame *that* on the Slugbear, Hugo."

"How much you want to bet?" Hugo tapped Cannon on the shoulder, careful not to take his eyes off the creature that was watching them.

Cannon looked up, and when he followed Hugo's eyes, he leapt to his feet. "Ah," he said, voice straining. "Okay. Maybe it is the Slugbear."

The ground before them sloped sharply into a murky bog. It looked like a long valley filled with rotten egg soup, and it smelled like it too. In the center of the bog, a large, gangly creature, covered in fur and mud, was leering at them. It looked vaguely like a squirrel, Hugo thought, but was sized more like a grizzly bear. It made no noise. It didn't move, either. It just sat there, staring. But that was threatening enough, in Hugo's opinion. He could sense what would happen if they ventured into the bog. The creature had razor sharp claws and fangs that protruded slightly from its closed mouth. Its long, bushy tail was laced with thick, spike-like hair.

"Well," Cannon said, "good thing we're mages, eh? Meet you on the other side." Cannon leapt into the air the way Hugo had seen him do numerous times now . . . and fell face first into the bog. He surfaced, spitting bog mush and cursing. If Cannon hadn't been in danger, Hugo would have loved to sit back and laugh for a while, but as it was, the Slugbear was speeding toward his friend.

"Oy!" Hugo shouted, dropping to the ground and reaching for Cannon. He caught him by the arm and pulled him quickly onto firm ground again, just in time to avoid being lunch.

"Agh, ouch, Hugo," Canon spluttered, wiping the gunk out of his eyes. When he could open them again he gave a yelp and jumped back. The Slugbear was wading back and forth right in front of them, sniffing the edge of the ground.

"He's fast," Hugo said. "Very fast." He'd never seen an animal move like that before.

"So I see," Cannon muttered, squinting at the bog to judge the distance the Slugbear had covered. "Must be magic."

"Nice belly flop."

Cannon scowled. "An accident," he snapped. "You distracted me."

"Okay," Hugo said. "Try again, then."

Cannon nodded, then jumped into the air, this time sideways instead of out over the bog. He landed a few feet away. "I don't understand it," he said. He lifted his arms and twirled them around, but nothing happened. "It's like it's gone." Hugo could hear the panic in his voice. "Just gone!"

"Why, though?" Hugo said. "Is it the Ire?"

"Could be," Cannon said. "Could be that my magic just doesn't work here. It happens sometimes. I'm not a mage, you know, and in some very magical places, lesser magic can malfunction. You try."

Hugo closed his eyes. It seemed like ages since he had moved in the light, but he thought he could remember how. He opened his eyes and looked down at their shadows. They were standing close enough together that their shadows touched. Hugo slipped out of himself, into his shadow, then into Cannon's, then emerged, standing on the other side of his friend.

Cannon turned. "I guess yours still works," he said bitterly. "Typical."

"What's the plan now?" Hugo asked. They turned back to the bog to find the Slugbear staring up at them. The beast backed away slowly, putting more distance between them. "Why doesn't he come out?"

"He can move like lightning in there," Cannon said. "Faster than a slug, that's for sure. Maybe he's really slow on dry ground. That would explain the name."

Hugo nodded. "I'm going to try and get across. I'll take you with me."

"No, thanks," Cannon said. "I've already tried that light-traveling thing, remember? Didn't care for it."

"What choice do we have?" Hugo said. "We have to at least try."

"Fine."

"Give me a second," Hugo said. Then he focused his thoughts inward.

You will not come out tonight, he told Molad. He built a prison in his mind. He built it out of need and will and determination. He built an iron floor out of his iron will, fixed and determined to remain in control. He built an impenetrable roof out of the truth of who he was, good and loving and decent. He fashioned bars out of his brightest memories: learning secrets in the castle library as a boy, meeting Brinley for the first time, being called as the Mage of Light and Darkness, and his only memory of his mother (that one may have just been a dream). He built bars instead of walls because he was not sure, truly, if it was right to build a prison at all.

You will not come out tonight, he whispered again, ignoring the feeling of betrayal that was emanating from Molad. If they were going to do this, Hugo was determined not to accidentally let Molad loose halfway through and ruin the whole thing.

I will, Molad whispered out of the cell.

No, he said, setting his jaw firmly. *Not here. Not in this place.*

"Ready?" Cannon said.

"Ready."

Cannon gripped Hugo's arm, and he shifted into shadow, speeding around the edge of the bog. He was hoping to skirt it quickly instead of going through it at all, but there was no end in sight.

Magic, he thought, *an enchanted bog.* He glanced into it and saw the Slugbear keeping pace with him. He dropped out of shadow and stood on the bank, thinking.

Cannon reeled at his side, clutching at his gut, moaning. "Did we make it?"

"No," Hugo said, and he grabbed Cannon's arm again, slipping back into the shadows. This time he moved right out over the bog. Instead of trying to speed across it in one step, he oozed over it like a night shadow. Somewhere, beneath him, in the physical world that he had left, the Slugbear twisted and struck out at him with its bushy, spiked tail. Somehow it caught Hugo right in the chest and he tumbled out of thin air and into the bog.

This was not good. Cannon made a gurgling noise, half submerged in the stinking mud beside him. Something bristly brushed his leg, but he couldn't see it. Then the Slugbear's gaping mouth opened out of the murk in front of his face and lunged for him. Hugo slipped into the shadows again, but he did so alone. He looked on, helpless, as the Slugbear latched onto Cannon and started dragging him towards the opposite shore.

His friend's screams lit the night, and Hugo didn't know what to do.

I can help, Molad's voice whispered, but Hugo ignored it. He moved, slipping through darkness, becoming a part of it. He followed the Slugbear, watched as it dragged Cannon, still screaming, onto the shore.

Hugo slipped out of the shadows and drew his sword. The bushy tail slammed across his body, tossing his sword from his hand and throwing him against the ground. He blinked up at the beast in surprise and it opened its mouth, revealing a long line of pale incisors.

To his surprise, it did not eat him. It merely breathed in his face.

Odd, he thought, and then he felt his body go limp. He could still see, still breathe, but he could not move. The beast lifted him, set him on its back, and carried him to a nearby den. It was little more than a hole dug out under a rock outcropping. There were faint sounds coming out of it. Scuffling, whining. A pale nose poked out of the hole, then another, and another, and Hugo realized suddenly that he was about to be the guest of honor at a family dinner.

He panicked then, and his fear unlocked the prison in his mind. Molad slipped out of it, and then forced Hugo in. He found himself helpless, locked in a prison of his own making.

Molad breathed deeply, inhaling the darkness from the shadows around him. He held his breath, forcing the darkness into his blood. He waited as the blood was purified, cleared of the toxin from the Slugbear's breath, and then rose to his feet. The great beast growled at him, reaching out with a clawed hand, but the hand never touched him. The beast froze in fear, seeing nothing but darkness, feeling at once every fear that had plagued its life of hunting and digging and swimming in the bog. It screamed and scrambled blindly for its hole, its children.

Molad laughed at the Slugbear's fear, glorying in his power to scare such a beast, then turned and laid his eyes on Cannon. The Wind Mage's apprentice was lying on the ground, clutching his arm where the Slugbear had been pulling him, eyeing Molad contemptuously.

"Hello again, Mr. Poopy Pants," he said. "What are you going to do now?"

Molad was impressed by the lack of fear in his voice. There was nothing of panic either, or despair. Just contempt. Hatred. He could respect that. He picked the other man up without a word, slung him over his shoulder, and walked into the woods.

When he found a suitable spot, he set the apprentice down and began gathering wood. The wood came to him out of the darkness, old branches and deadwood, carried by the shadows. Then he did something he did not mean to do. He reached out and touched the pile of wood with light. Pure light, a tiny sunbeam from one finger. It set the wood ablaze. He shook his head in confusion. Why had he done that? He looked at Cannon. Why had he carried him all the way here? What was wrong with him?

"Hugo?" Cannon said tentatively, searching his face.

Molad's face split in a slow grin. No. He was not Hugo. The apprentice raised a thick branch with his good hand, more quickly than Molad had expected, and cracked him on the side of the head.

❖ ❖ ❖

Hugo woke to another splitting headache. He groaned.

"Ah, you're back." Cannon said. "Sorry about the head. It is you, Hugo, isn't it?"

Hugo opened his eyes to see Cannon sitting over him, a thick branch held high, ready to strike. Strike *again*, he realized. "Yes!" he croaked. "Yes! It's me." He rolled into a sitting position, rubbing his head again. "Did you hit me with that thing?"

"I didn't like the way you were looking at me," Cannon said, tossing the branch onto the fire. "Though I have to say, it was thoughtful of you to carry me here and build this fire before you decided to kill me."

"Yeah," Hugo said. "Yeah! You know, I think I was controlling him a bit this time."

"Wonderful," Cannon said with a snort. "That just puts me right at ease."

They stared into the fire for a while. It felt good as the fire dried away the damp and cold of the bog. Cannon obviously needed a bit of a rest. He ripped a strip from his shirt and bandaged his shoulder. Hugo's stomach grumbled.

"Got anything to eat?" he said hopefully.

"Nope. Didn't think to pack a lunch in the middle of the night."

Hugo nodded. "Right. You know, you never did tell me the whole story about how we got to the Ire."

"Very well," Cannon said. "I've got nothing better to do, I suppose."

When Cannon had finished, Hugo asked the question that had been nagging at the back of his mind. "Why did you do it? Why did you follow me?"

"Oh, that," Cannon said. "Well, you know. I left you on the road the other day and you got into trouble. I was supposed to be with you, you know . . ."

"Cannon," Hugo said, touching his chest dramatically, "I didn't know you cared so much."

"Ha!" Cannon barked. "More like I don't want to get in trouble with Animus again. He doesn't like it when you're in danger, and you obviously can't take care of yourself."

"Right," Hugo said. He glanced at Cannon's injured arm, then out into the black, menacing expanse of trees. "Well, at least we're not in any danger."

"Right," Cannon said, grinning weakly.

Hugo mulled Cannon's story over in his mind, wondering what Molad had been up to. Why he had brought them here. Was it really to get the sword? Was Molad helping them? He found it hard to believe. He squinted at Cannon thoughtfully, poking the fire with a stray stick.

"Cannon, what was I doing in Brinley's room?" he asked, trying to remember. "Why didn't I just go out my own window?"

Cannon propped himself up on his good arm, frowning. "Good question. You don't remember anything?"

Hugo shook his head.

Cannon closed his eyes, thinking back. "Well, when I came in, you were already by the window. Tabitha was talking to you, Brinley was sitting up in bed." He pursed his lips. "What else? The room was empty otherwise, except for Tabitha's boots. Those were on the floor by the bed. And the Magemother's bag. It was on the bed." His eyes snapped open. "Hugo, what does she keep in that bag?"

Hugo's eyes went wide. He had a sudden sinking feeling in his gut. He had done something bad. Very bad. He just couldn't remember what.

"Check your pockets," Cannon said.

Hugo did. He had patted them on the bridge, but he'd been looking for a heavy medallion. He found it in the right front pocket of his pants and pulled it out. The small crystal vial flashed in the firelight.

"The naptrap," Cannon whispered.

Hugo groaned. That's what Molad had been doing. They had brought the Magemother into the Wizard's Ire. "How could I have been so stupid?"

"Just poor breeding, I suppose," a deep voice said behind them. "The Paradise kings have always been a bit dim."

Hugo shoved the naptrap back into his pocket and spun around to discover the source of the voice. To his horror, a group of soldiers stood there. At least, he assumed they were soldiers. They were not the kind of soldiers he was used to seeing, clean cut and dressed in polished suits of armor with bright weapons. These men, if they were indeed men, were the exact opposite. Their clothing was the color of mud, their hair was long, their faces were bearded, and they were covered in sweat and grime. Hugo was amazed that he had not smelled them coming. They were big, too, bigger than most men Hugo had seen, and they carried an array of weapons—axes, clubs, bows, hammers, but not a sword among them, except for the one their leader was carrying. It was huge, and it had a hilt like a dragon's spike.

"Hugo," their leader said, pointing at him with his sword. His face looked like it might have been carved from stone, the features hacked into it with a dull blade. "It was very kind of you to join us here. It would have been terribly difficult to force you here. My master has sent me to collect you." His voice was firm, as if daring anyone to contradict him. This was a man that was used to being obeyed.

"Gadjihalt," Hugo said, resting his hand on the hilt of his own sword nervously. He couldn't tell how old the man was. His face looked old, but it might just be the scars. He moved slowly, carefully, but it was hard to say whether that was due to creaking joints or a warrior's self-awareness.

The big man chuckled, casting sidelong glances at his companions. "Knows my name," he muttered.

"Yes," Hugo said, "I know your name." His mind was racing. This was, sort of, exactly what Animus had been planning, wasn't it? At least the part about luring Gadjihalt out, confronting him, challenging him to a duel ... in a way, everything was going according to plan ... apart from the fact that Hugo and Cannon were here alone, without the support of their friends, and they had no way of escaping after Hugo got the sword. Minor details.

Hugo gulped. Gadjihalt's forearms were the size of his thighs, and his own thigh was still hurting. He tested it and grimaced. If he ended up fighting Gadjihalt for real, it wasn't going to be pretty.

"You're coming with us," Gadjihalt said. "You can walk on your own two feet or go in a bag. Your choice."

"Of course," Hugo said. "Going with you sounds like a wonderful time, but before we go, I'd like to challenge you to a duel."

"What?" Gadjihalt croaked, a smile twitching on his beaten face.

"A duel," Hugo said easily. "You know, mortal combat. You and me, fight to the death and all that. As a knight of the king, you are bound to accept. I'm sure you remember that."

Something twitched again in Gadjihalt's face, not a smile this time. He did not look pleased at all.

"What are you doing?" Cannon hissed. "Is this really the right time?"

Gadjihalt was shaking his head. "I think not, boy. I admire your courage, of course, but I'm afraid that if I accepted, I would be forced to kill you." He cocked his head. "My master would not appreciate that."

"You don't have a choice," Hugo said, hoping he was right. "I demand to meet you, now, in mortal combat. You are bound by your oath to honor my wishes."

Gadjihalt cursed. "So I am," he whispered. "Who concocted this little plan? Not you. You are too young to realize what you're playing with." His eyes scanned the trees, thinking, perhaps, that it was some kind of trap. He raised his hands and made a couple of quick gestures to his men, who fanned out and disappeared into the forest, all save one.

"If this is a trap," Gadjihalt said, "then your friends had better spring it quickly, for you are about to die." He drew the big sword at his side. "I'll fight you on one condition: that it is not to the death. Like I said, my master would be displeased with me if I returned with a corpse instead of a mage."

Hugo nodded. His courage was quickly dissolving now that Gadjihalt had drawn his sword. He was big, bigger than the others, and he moved like a man who had been fighting for a very, very long time. It was obvious how this fight was going to end, if it ever began, of course.

"Hold on a minute," Cannon said, coming to his feet. "Doesn't Hugo here get to pick the weapons?"

Gadjihalt laughed. "So he does. But he doesn't have many choices."

"I'll take your sword," Hugo said quickly. "You take mine."

Gadjihalt shot him a dubious look. "An odd request," he spat. "Trying to disarm me before the fight, eh?"

"Not at all," Hugo said, drawing his own sword and offering it, hilt first, to the big man.

Gadjihalt took it with a grimace and swung his own to Hugo. "Whatever you like," he spat. "It will make no difference."

Hugo glanced down at the sword in his hand. The spiked hilt was warm beneath his fingers, and he couldn't help wondering why. Was it something of the dragon that kept it warm all these years after it had died? He turned to Cannon.

"Now?" Cannon asked.

Hugo nodded. He put a hand on Cannon's shoulder and stepped away from Gadjihalt and into the night. He didn't know where they were going. He didn't have enough time to think about it or search for a safe direction, but it didn't matter. Anywhere other than where Gadjihalt was would be just fine.

"Argh," Cannon grumbled, rubbing his head and leaning against a tree. They had landed in some random spot in the Ire. "I guess that went pretty well. Hugo, are you okay?"

He wasn't. Hugo's head was spinning. Molad had nearly taken over when he had traveled just now. He didn't understand why. He had done it earlier just fine, but this time when he moved through the darkness, it felt like offering Molad an invitation to join him.

"He almost got out," he muttered. "I can't do that again. Not for a while, at least."

Cannon put a hand on his shoulder. "Okay. Don't worry about it. We won't need it." He glanced around them. "Where are we now?"

There was no way to tell. A forest at night looks pretty much the same on one end as it does on the other.

"How far did you take us?" Cannon asked.

Their question was answered when a chorus of rough voices sounded through the trees. "Heard something this way. Couldn't have gone far. Come on!"

"Excellent," Cannon whispered.

"Sorry," Hugo said. "I didn't exactly have time to chart a course."

"You can't travel again?" Cannon asked.

"Maybe," Hugo said, frustration mounting. "I don't know. All I know is he almost got out just now."

"Then don't do it again," Cannon said. "Follow me." He crept into the trees in the opposite direction of the voices and Hugo followed. He was surprised at how quietly Cannon could move through the forest. Soon the voices behind them had died down considerably, then they were gone altogether. Eventually, Cannon paused to rest against a tree.

"Good. I think we got away."

"What's that up ahead?" Hugo asked. There was something bright in front of them. They had caught sight of it now and then for the last few minutes, but neither one of them had bothered mentioning it. It didn't really matter what it was. It was in the direction that they needed to go.

"Guess we'll find out," Cannon said.

It was the Hoarfrost Forest. It couldn't possibly be anything else. A huge expanse of gray trees and hard ground, still rivers, and frozen waterfalls, all of it covered in a thin, icy frost.

"We can't go this way," Cannon said.

"Come on back, then," Gadjihalt said, stepping out from behind a tree to their rear. "They're over here, boys!" he shouted behind him.

Hugo dashed into the frozen wood with Cannon right behind him. To their surprise, Gadjihalt did not follow them. One by one his men emerged from the forest, each one coming to stand silently beside him.

"You can't stay in there forever!" Gadjihalt shouted after them. "I'll be waiting for you here when you come back out."

❖ ❖ ❖

Hugo shivered, clutching his chest with his arms. Cannon stood beside him. They were both staring, yet again, at one of Gadjihalt's soldiers blocking their way out of the frozen patch of trees. They had crossed the little wasteland quickly; it was only a half mile across. But when they came to the other side, Gadjihalt was there, waiting for them, and they were forced to turn back. They had tried several times now, coming out of the center of the wood in new directions, hoping to find the way open for their escape, but each time, they had been disappointed. Now they were getting seriously cold.

Cannon collapsed beside Hugo, shivering so badly that his teeth chattered. "Can't go on," Cannon said through the cold. "I'm done. T-they can take us."

"They'll kill us," Hugo said.

"Then at least we'll die w-warm."

Hugo lifted Cannon to his feet. "I'm just going to have to travel again," he said. "We don't have any other choice."

Cannon's head jerked in a nod. "But what if Mr. P-poopy Pants comes out?"

Hugo handed Gadjihalt's sword over to Cannon. "Take this," he said. "Keep it away from me, if you can. If I run off or something, make sure it gets out of the Ire."

Cannon's head jerked again.

Hugo closed his eyes, reaching into the night, feeling after the darkness of the Ire, looking for a safe place to move to. Almost at once, he felt Molad stirring in his mind. The world spun for a moment, and he lost track of what was going on. Then he released the darkness, and reality returned.

"He's definitely going to come out if I move us," Hugo said. "I may not even be able to."

Cannon didn't respond. He was shivering harder now.

"Here," he said, giving Cannon his cloak. "I'm not as cold as you are."

"You're c-crazy," Cannon said, but he took the cloak.

Hugo? Brinley's voice said in his head.

Brinley? he answered. *Where are you?*

Here in the Ire. We followed you. We used the king's medallion to get in. Tabitha and I are here, and Tobias too. Animus wanted to come too, but I wouldn't let him. Where are you?

Hugo couldn't believe his good luck. Just when he was about to mess everything up again by releasing Molad.

Brinley, he said, *I'm so glad you're here. I mean, seriously, you got here just in time. We're surrounded by Gadjihalt and his men. I have his sword!*

You're kidding! Where are you?

In the Hoarfrost Forest.

The what?

It's this little patch of enchanted trees. It's freezing here, like winter. You have to hurry, Cannon isn't looking good.

But where is it? Brinley asked. *I can't feel you in here. I didn't know where you had gone at all until Cassis told me what happened. I can't sense you at all in this place.*

It has something to do with the Ire, Hugo said. *Cannon's powers don't work here either.*

How am I going to find you? Brinley said. *We're flying over the trees. Can you climb one?*

No . . . Hugo said, looking around desperately. Even if he could grip the slippery, ice-covered trees, there were no branches low enough to grab hold of, the canopy above was too thick to climb through. He would never reach the top before it was too late. He racked his brain. There had to be a way. Something simple, probably. He told Cannon what was going on.

"Build a fire," Cannon said.

"With what?" Everything around them was frozen solid.

I can help, came Molad's voice.

I don't want your help. Hugo said fiercely. *I don't need your help.*

Yes, you do, Molad said. *Look around you.*

Hugo heard a twig crack somewhere off to his left and looked up to see one of Gadjihalt's men advancing through the frozen trees. They were finally coming in after them. He turned around, looking for more, and found them. There were men advancing on all sides now. They were a long way off still, moving slowly, cautiously.

"They're afraid w-we'll run again," Cannon said.

Where are you, Hugo? Brinley called. Her voice sounded farther away now.

I think you're going the wrong way, Hugo said. *Come back.*

Another twig cracked. Hugo turned to see the man who had blocked their escape earlier. He, too, had entered the frozen trees now. There was someone beside him. It looked like Gadjihalt. He would be on them soon.

Hugo placed the flat of his hand against the frosty bark of a tree. He focused all his thoughts on it, willing it to burst into flame, to give Brinley a light in the darkness, but nothing happened.

Laughter filled his mind. Molad. *Light and Darkness are two halves of the same coin, Hugo. You can't have one without the other.*

Hugo groaned. "Fine!"

Help me, he said, opening the prison that he had locked Molad in earlier. Suddenly his chest was filled with fire, light, and the power that he had been looking for. Even as he felt the darkness engulf him, the light was there. He touched the tree and it erupted into flame, leaping from branch to branch until there were five, ten, fifteen trees alight around them.

"Ooh," Cannon said dimly, holding up his hands to warm them by the fire. "That's n-nice."

We see you! Brinley shouted. *We're coming!*

Cannon pulled himself up with an effort, holding onto Hugo's shoulder. "Hey," he said seriously. "If we get out of this alive, I think you and I might have to just give in and be friends."

Hugo barely heard either of them. Molad was not going quietly back into his cell. For a moment, Hugo thought he might be able to win the struggle, but then he heard a shout and turned to see Gadjihalt lumbering towards him, and his mind filled with fear.

"I mean it Hugo," Cannon went on, oblivious to the silent struggle that raged inside his friend. "I promise to help you, if I can. I don't want to see you go nuts and die, you know. That's friendship, eh?" He jabbed Hugo in the ribs with an elbow as Brinley descended on them, but Hugo neither heard nor felt any of this. He was in the dark cell of his own mind again, locked out of the world he had been a part of only moments before. He beat his fist against the inside of his own head furiously, mad at Molad for being so strong, mad at himself for being so weak, so ignorant, mad at Gadjihalt for distracting him, mad at the whole world.

Molad sniffed the air, smelled fire. Burning. Was it his doing? He couldn't remember. He took it all in quickly, Gadjihalt running at him, Cannon standing up beside him looking at the sky, the Magemother descending on them from above on a great black swan. He sniffed the air again, smelled fire, and something behind it. Something deep in the woods. Darkness, shadow, the thing that he had come for. He stepped into the night and was gone.

Chapter Nineteen

In which there is no way out

MOLAD STOOD BENEATH four tall, twisted trees. Their great arms met in front of him at shoulder height, cradling a black box. The darkness was coming from in there. Yes . . . he remembered this box. It was old, very old. The Panthion, it was called, made by the mages and locked by the Magemother herself. This was what he had come for.

He took a step toward it and crushed something with his boot. He looked down. There was something green under his foot. As he watched, it grew into a bush, blocking his path to the box. He tried to skirt it, but the bush grew into a hedge and swept around him with a sound like leaves rustling in the wind. Before he knew it, he was surrounded on all sides by a green wall ten feet tall. He drew the dagger from his boot and hacked at it. Wherever he struck it, the hedge regrew.

He twisted into shadow and seeped through the leaves, but the branches tightened around him, growing so thick that not a sliver of light could penetrate them. He returned to his own shape and began to walk along the hedge wall. There were three openings that led out of the little clearing that held him. One directly across from where he knew the box was and two on the sides. He took one of the side exits, hoping that the hedge would veer back toward the box. It did, at first, then led him in a different direction. Then there was another intersection, and he took the path that seemed to be going back toward the box. He came across another intersection, then another. Soon he had made so many turns that he lost track of which direction he was headed, and where the box might be.

He wove his way into the maze until all thought of finding the box had vanished from his mind, and all that was left was a desire to be free. Then, at last, he took another turn and found himself on a wide green field. He could not see the end of it in any direction, just emptiness before him and the hedge behind. He turned to look at the maze, wondering if he should stay in it and exit somewhere else, someplace less empty, but the maze was gone. A single tree now stood behind him, a tall oak, ramrod straight, its leaves splayed against the faint moonlight. One eye opened in the bark halfway up, then another.

Wooden lips parted and spoke to him. "What are you?" it said. "I have not seen you in this forest before."

Molad stiffened. "You're the hedge," he said. It wasn't a question, and the tree didn't answer. "I am the Mage of Light and Darkness. Who are you?"

"False," the tree whispered. "I have met the Mage of Light and Darkness. You are not him."

Molad grimaced. "Lux Tennebris is no more. I am Molad."

"Prove it," the tree said. "Show me your other side. Show me your twin."

Molad sneered. "I think not. He locks me away. I lock him away. I will not let him out just to convince a tree of who I am." He glanced around himself again, searching for something in the emptiness of the plain, but found nothing. "Where am I?" he demanded. "I must get back to the box."

The tree swayed slightly, though there was no wind. "I do not think that is a good idea," it said.

Molad squinted darkly at the tree. "Who are you to tell me what to do?" he said, and he twisted into darkness. He seeped into the bark of the tree, into the leaves, searching out the life that was in it. He poured darkness into the mind of the tree, attacking it as he had attacked the beast from the bog, but the tree just laughed. The laughter startled Molad, shaking him to his core. He felt Hugo bend a bar in the wall of his cell, and Molad straightened it quickly, calming himself.

The tree was still chuckling. "I have lived in the darkness too long to be frightened of the darkness that lives in me," it said. It stopped laughing abruptly. "You are indeed the Mage of Light and Darkness. Why have you come here?"

Molad considered answering the question and then decided not to. He simply turned and twisted into darkness again, sliding across the field. He stopped short. The tree was in front of him again. He looked back. Only the empty plain was there. Had he turned around without realizing it? He went off in a new direction and the tree appeared before him. He turned, and again the tree blocked his path. Feeling a sudden rush of anger, he charged the tree. With a motion that he barely saw coming, the arms of the great oak caught him and slammed him against the ground. He stared up at it, dazed, and the oak stared down at him.

"Molad?" it asked.

"Let go of me," Molad hissed. When he spoke, the tree lifted him skyward and slammed him into the ground a second time, and all went black.

Hugo woke up. His body cried out in discomfort, gripped in the hard, bark-covered hands of the oak. The tree was staring down at him. "Molad?" it asked.

Hugo shook his head.

"Good," the tree said, and it set him on the grass.

Hugo rubbed his back. It felt like he'd fallen from a great height. He couldn't keep doing this. He needed to find a less painful way to switch places with Molad. Something sparked in Hugo's mind as he studied the tree … the talking tree … He remembered what Brinley had said about Lignumis and the tree bark, and the last tree that he had been looking for, here in the Wizard's Ire. He whispered a name so softly that neither of them heard it.

"What did you say?" the tree asked, bending closer.

"Lignumis," Hugo repeated. The tree shivered. Hugo watched, dumbfounded, as the tree moved through a year of seasons in a single moment. Spring leaves widened, seeds sprouted from the buds at their base and fell to the earth. The branches sighed toward the ground and the leaves dried up and curled and fell, leaving only a wooden skeleton behind them, diminished by the shedding of its heritage. The bare tree shrank further, branches folding down into the trunk, trunk sinking into the ground, splitting at the base to form legs, arms, a head.

A man stood where the tree had been, his feet rooted firmly in the earth. He lifted them with a great effort and looked at Hugo. He had a close-clipped beard the color of oak, and a young face. Hugo thought he must be barely old enough to grow a beard like that.

"Lignumis?" Hugo said again.

The young man reached out, gripping Hugo so tightly that he could tell the strength of the oak was still in him. "What did you say?"

Hugo spoke the name again and the young man cocked his head, tasting the word as if for the first time in a long time.

"Yes," he said after a moment. He spoke slowly, with the care and patience of a much older man. "No one calls me that here. I buried that name so deeply that years later, when my strength came, even I could not find it."

Hugo nodded, looking around at the darkness. "I can see why you would want to hide who you are here. How did you survive?"

Lignumis released his arm. He touched his face with his hands, felt his beard, and smiled. "I have not taken my own shape since the Magemother told me to hide."

"What?" Hugo asked in amazement. "Never?"

Lignumis shook his head. "Never. She told me to hide, told me that Lux was lost, and that I would not be safe until my power had grown. I was old enough to find my own hiding place, she said, so I went looking for one, and was captured by the Janrax instead."

"You got caught by the Janrax?" Hugo said. "That shapeshifter?"

Lignumis nodded. "I was trying to get across the bridge into this place," he said, waving an arm at the trees. "Foolish of me, really. I told myself the Ire would be the last place Lux would look for me, but I was really just curious. I think it was the forest calling to me. I needed to see it. I couldn't get across the bridge by myself, of course, but the Janrax helped me.

"How?" Hugo asked.

"He was the one who made the medallions that Shael has been using to get across the bridge to the Wizard's Ire. He tried to take me straight to Shael as soon as I was in here, of course, but luckily I was able to escape."

"And they never found you?" Hugo asked, impressed.

Lignumis frowned. "I forgot my own name, to make sure they never did. I knew that there were things in this forest that would see through the shapes of trees and shrubs and pine needles and see a man. I wanted to make sure that when they did, they would not recognize the man as me." He paused, considering. "I always remembered that I had something important to do, and that I must hide myself from the darkness that lives here, but until you spoke my name, coming out of hiding was not a possibility in my mind. Will we go now? Has the time come for me to return?"

"Yes," Hugo said. "I mean, you can go. I have to stay a while. You can head for the bridge, and I can call the Magemother and tell her you're coming. Make sure you throw the medallion back through for me or something."

Lignumis gave him a questioning look. "You will not return with me?"

Hugo shook his head. "I have something else I need to do. I need to get back to that box."

Lignumis frowned. Something of the oak's hardness entered his expression. "That is a fool's errand, brother," he said. "No one who sees the box or its guardians survives."

"I have to," Hugo said. "Besides, I'm not going for the box. I'm going for the trees."

"The trees?" Lignumis asked. "The twistwoods? You should not touch them."

"Look," Hugo said impatiently. "It's a long story, but I know what I'm doing, okay? I won't be gone long."

"There is no reason that you should go alone."

"Yes, there is," Hugo said. This was what he was trying to avoid. He had to do what he had to do, but he didn't want to hurt anyone else along the way. Not if he could help it. Besides, someone needed to take the naptrap back. He couldn't risk that getting into the hands of Shael. He pressed it into Lignumis's hand. "Take this," he said. "Keep it safe. Give it to the Magemother. It is very, very important. Don't ask me why. She'll tell you. I can't bring it with me."

"Are you sure you don't want me to go with you?" Lignumis asked.

Hugo thought about it for a moment. He didn't like the thought of visiting the twistwood trees alone, but he didn't have many options. "I don't know how long I can keep control of Molad here. I haven't been very good at it so far. It doesn't make sense to risk anyone else's life."

"How very brave of you, boy," Gadjihalt said from behind them.

Hugo jumped, reaching for his sword as he turned. But he had given it to Gadjihalt already. There it was, in the big man's hands as he approached.

"You're a slippery one, I'll give you that," Gadjihalt said. "Might not have found you if it hadn't been for the leaves." He stuck his thumb behind him, indicating the long trail of leaves from Lignumis's hedge. "Don't go anywhere," he added, pointing the sword at Hugo. "No quick movements this time, or we'll kill your friend here." He pointed behind him and Hugo saw two more men, bowmen, with arrows trained on them. "Lignumis, right? Heard rumors you were here. The master's been looking for you too."

Hugo searched for a way out but couldn't think of one. He could let Molad out, but as far as he could tell, Molad wanted to be captured anyway. Why else would he have brought them to the Ire?

"No way out," Gadjihalt said. The big man was tying Lignumis's hands behind his back now, and the archers were only feet away. "You're coming with us. Definitely in a bag. I tried to be nice, but you obviously can't be trusted to walk."

"Where are we going?" Hugo asked, already knowing the answer.

"To the master," Gadjihalt said. "Where else?"

❖ ❖ ❖

"Kneel." Gadjihalt's powerful hands clamped around Hugo's shoulders, forcing his knees to buckle and bang into the dirt. Lignumis was right beside him. They were in the horrible clearing again, four large, terrible, twisting trees before them, their branches cradling a dark iron box. "We found him just after he found the wood mage," Gadjihalt said.

To Hugo's horror, a voice came out of the box. "Search him," it said.

It was sweeter than he had imagined it, almost frightfully so, and quiet too, barely louder than a whisper.

Hands rummaged through Hugo's pockets, finding nothing. Hugo breathed a sigh of relief. If he hadn't happened to hand the naptrap over to Lignumis earlier, things would have just gotten much worse. Hopefully they wouldn't think to search the other mage. Hugo had been dreading just such a thing since they had been captured, but evidently Gadjihalt had orders not to harm them, though that hadn't kept them from putting a knife to Lignumis's throat the entire way. Gadjihalt had wanted to make it quite clear what would happen to his friend if Hugo chose to escape.

Now, in this place, with guards all around and Gadjihalt at his back, Hugo couldn't imagine escaping. His head was practically bursting at the seams with pain as Molad struggled to break free. Hugo didn't want to think of what would happen if he let him. Then again, it might not make much of a difference. Things were looking pretty bad. Unbidden, Cannon's voice echoed in his mind. "Stories, Hugo. Stories." Well, this would be a good one, if he lived to tell it.

"Ah," the voice said wistfully. "The youngest Paradise brat. Kind of you to join us. Do you know why I brought you here?"

The voice made Hugo's skin crawl, though he couldn't put his finger on why. It sounded normal enough, if sickeningly sweet. Then he realized what it was. Molad loved the sound of that voice. He was practically basking in it. Hugo attempted to ignore him.

"You brought me?" Hugo asked, trying to be difficult.

"Yes," the voice said. "Of course. That dark twin of yours is an old friend of mine, you know. We've accomplished much together in the past, including bringing you here."

"What?" Hugo felt sick. He searched his memory, analyzing how things had unfolded. Molad had been helping Hugo, hadn't he? Sure, he was evil, but he wasn't conspiring against him. When it came to the bigger picture, Hugo had always been in control.

"Did that darkness of yours not bring you here?" Shael said. "Did it not plant in you a desire to stay? Give you a reason to come here? You came for Gadjihalt's sword, did you not? I can only imagine that that dragon is behind it. Why? Does he have some piece of information that you require? Some memory, perhaps? Do you hope that he holds the key to defeating me? I can assure you he does not. I defeated him."

Hugo breathed a sigh of relief. For a moment there, he was almost sure that Shael knew what he was after. Not that it mattered, really. It didn't change the situation one way or the other.

As if reading his thoughts, Shael said, "It does not matter. You are here now. Here to stay."

"Why?" Hugo asked. "What do you want with me?"

The voice laughed. "I need you, Hugo. It's hard to admit it, but I do. Do you know how long I worked, how hard I worked, just to let my voice escape this prison? Too long! And it has nearly ruined me. My strength is spent. I will get no further on my own . . . that is why I need you."

Hugo laughed. "I'm not going to help you get out of there," he said. "You can kill me if you want, but I won't do it."

"Oh, I don't want you to let me out," the voice said. "I want to let you in."

Hugo blinked. What? What had he said? Let him in? That didn't make any sense.

"Do you know how a Panthion works, Hugo?" the voice said. "Of course you don't. Let me show you. Gadjihalt, open the box."

Gadjihalt moved to the Panthion and, to Hugo's astonishment, opened the lid.

Hugo gasped. It was supposed to be locked. It was supposed to be an inescapable prison. He winced, waiting for Shael to leap from the box, but nothing happened.

"Look!" the voice snapped. "Look inside!"

Gadjihalt pulled Hugo to his feet and forced him roughly to the box. It was empty. Just an empty stone box. Gadjihalt closed the lid.

"You see?" the voice said. "That is how a Panthion works. It is a prison, after all. Easy to get in. Hard to get out."

Hugo still didn't understand.

"Do you know who can open this box, Hugo?" the voice asked. "I mean really open it? Enough to let me out? Do you know who the only person is?"

"No," Hugo said honestly.

"The Magemother. None but she can open it."

"I see your problem," Hugo said, smiling. This had been a terrible day, true. He was likely going to die—maybe be tortured first, but Shael was not going to escape. Brinley would never let him out.

"Yes," the voice sneered. "She is not likely to release me. She would never open it for me . . . but I think that she will open it for you."

With a sudden rush of understanding, Hugo realized what Shael's plan was. "You want me to come in there with you?"

"You see the beauty of it?" Shael said. "She will open the box to free you, and she will free me as well. She will not want to do it at first, but she will in the end. She cares too much for her children. That is her weakness. In the meantime, there is much that I will be able to discuss with you, one on one. Just you and I. I daresay you are in need of a decent tutor."

"What makes you think I'll let you?" Hugo growled. He wouldn't, and that was the end of it. He would die first. He would run first. Shael was locked in there. His voice was out, sure, but obviously his power was not. Gadjihalt could not force him to do anything.

"Let me speak to your twin now, Paradise," Shael said. "I'm sure he will be more accommodating to my wishes."

Molad surged so violently within him that Hugo nearly blacked out. It was as if Shael was calling to him. Like a dog, Molad rushed to answer. It was all Hugo could do to hold him back. He tried not to let the strain show on his face. It wouldn't do to let Shael know how close he was to getting what he wanted.

"No," he said. He had meant to say something grander, something threatening, maybe, or something funny, so that Shael would think he wasn't afraid. The problem was, he *was* afraid.

"No?" Shael echoed. "Very well. Then I am afraid I will have to cut your friend's hand off. Maybe then you will reconsider. If not, he has another one. Two feet, too. I'm sure you will agree eventually. Unless you have the desire to watch a mage die slowly."

One of Gadjihalt's men forced Lignumis's sleeve up, brandishing a knife.

"Stop!" Hugo shouted, and the man stopped. For a moment, everything was quiet. He closed his eyes in pain as Molad made another effort to escape. There was sweat forming on his forehead now. He was losing. Losing this battle, and he knew it. He couldn't watch Lignumis get tortured. Couldn't watch him die. He couldn't hold out against Molad all night either.

"Fine," he said. "But you let Lignumis go free first."

There was a short silence, then the voice came again. "Very well. He goes free."

"And safe back to the bridge."

"And safe back to the bridge," Shael agreed.

"And before he goes you give him a piece of bark from that tree," Hugo pointed at the twisting black behemoth beside the box.

"Excuse me?" Shael said.

Hugo smiled. "So that after the Magemother frees us, I will have a weapon to kill you with."

Shael laughed. "Fair enough, Hugo. Whatever you wish, though I think you may be disappointed if ever you face me in combat."

"We'll see," Hugo said.

He watched as Lignumis was released. He watched in satisfaction as Gadjihalt cut a piece of bark from the tree, wrapped it carefully in a strip of fabric from his shirt, and gave it to Lignumis. That had been some of the quickest thinking he had ever done. He almost couldn't believe that it was working.

But it was. Lignumis was turning to leave. Hugo caught his arm. "Make sure you get that bark to the Magemother," he whispered. "She's expecting it."

Lignumis nodded. "I won't forget this," he said, casting an almost guilty look at the black box in the trees. He released Hugo's arm and left. Hugo was pleased to see Lignumis disappear at the edge of the clearing, turning into a network of vines that swung from tree to tree, making a quick path out of the forest. He would get back safely.

Brinley! he called. *I found Lignumis.*

What?

I'll explain later.

Where are you? We'll come and get you!

No, Hugo said. *Go. Get out of here. We'll be along in a moment. Just leave the medallion on the bridge for us. Toss it back after you're through.*

Hurry, Brinley pleaded.

"Now," Shael said, "your turn."

Gadjihalt put a knife to Hugo's back with one hand and reached around with the other to open the lid of the box again. "In you go," he said. "Just your hand will be enough."

Hugo swallowed. He thought of Brinley, remembering the way she had looked the last time he saw her—pretty, comforting, bending over him and taking care of him. He'd give anything to be back in that room now. He thought of Cannon and his surprising loyalty. Surely he didn't deserve it. Now he wouldn't ever be able to repay it.

"In," Gadjihalt grunted, pressing the knife hard enough to break the skin between his shoulder blades.

He wasn't coming back from this one. But, if he did, somehow . . .

Stories, Hugo. Stories.

He placed his hand in the box.

Chapter Twenty

In which a package is delivered

BRINLEY TOOK THE SMOOTH black stone out of her pocket and fingered it absently as she waited at the top of the bridge to the Wizard's Ire. Hugo had dropped it by accident, or Molad had cast it aside during his escape. She wished that it was still in his possession, instead of back in her own. She tried to feel the peace within it, but it was out of reach.

She hoped that Hugo would come back. He had to come back, and not just because of his own life. He had her mother in his pocket still. She thought Hugo would have had enough wisdom to give Cannon the Naptrap before barreling off into the Ire on an unexplained wild goose chase, but apparently he didn't.

She winced at the thought. What was coming over her? More than likely, he didn't have a choice in the matter. Even if he did, it didn't matter. Now, he was almost certainly in trouble, and all she could do was sit and wait.

It seemed like forever since they had all—Animus, Tabitha, Cassis, the Swelter Cat, not to mention the captain of the guard and his band of rather nervous-looking soldiers—settled down to wait for Hugo.

She returned the stone to her pocket bitterly. If Hugo didn't come back, it meant that Shael had captured him, and Hugo would certainly need some peace if that happened, not that her stone was likely to help anyway. If he didn't come back, she might never see him alive again. If he didn't come back, her mother was as good as dead.

Her fingers brushed Maggie's button again and she pulled it out. She smiled bitterly. The world might fall apart, her mother might die, Shael might return, and Hugo might be lost, but as long as Brinley could find a bit of spare time while she was trying to save the world, Maggie wouldn't have to freeze to death when winter came.

Brinley checked the sky. How long had they been waiting? She was tired. Tired enough to sleep, but she knew sleep was a bad idea. She dreamed nearly every time she slept now, and this would be a terrible time for dreams. She flexed her fingers, trying to wake herself up, and then tried to think of a way to start a conversation with the group, but nothing came to mind. They were all lost in their own thoughts, it seemed. Lost, the way you get in dreams . . . She wished she had a safe place to dream, a place where nothing could follow her. A place where nothing bad could get in.

Brinley stepped through sleep to the halls of her palace on Calypsis. They seemed to go on forever: halls of white stone and golden floors that were warm under her feet, and door after door that opened to new sights, each more beautiful and wondrous than the last—hanging gardens of purple vines and vivid blue pools of clear water, kitchens full of all her favorite baked breads and fresh fruit (she thought she could hear her dad whistling somewhere, just around the corner, most likely making pancakes), a corridor with curved walls and ceilings all painted with birds that looked so real they almost sang, and a dark room larger than the night itself, where the sun was a lamp in one corner and the floor was a beltway of stars.

As she walked, she heard knocking. It was quiet at first, barely noticeable, but it grew louder and louder as she continued. Finally she gave up on her walk and returned to the front door. *Who could it be?* she wondered. Who could bother her here? This place was safe. As safe as the inside of her own head—safer, maybe. She opened the door, and the man with the head of a snake stared back at her.

"Let me in," he said.

"Why?" she whispered, hiding behind the door as she looked him up and down. He looked more tired than evil now that she saw him in the light, but she still didn't trust him.

"You have to let me in," he said.

"To Calypsis?" she asked. "Why?"

He shook his head. "To your mind," he said. "I can't help you unless you let me in."

"Help me with what?" she asked.

"Everything," he said. "Don't you need help? Your mother sent me."

He drew a silver pocket watch out of his pocket, checked the time, and began to swing it back and forth casually. She had seen that before, hadn't she? A silver orb swinging back and forth, back and forth? A pocket watch? She shook her head. The only one she knew with a pocket watch was Archibald, and this person was certainly not Archibald.

The man checked the time again, his snake tongue darting out his mouth, nearly licking the face of the watch. "Won't you let me in?" he said.

She eyed him cautiously. "You don't look like someone my mother would know. Why should I trust you?"

"Because I am here." he said. "You said yourself that this place is safe. Nothing can harm you here."

She thought about that for a moment, then slowly opened the door the rest of the way. "That's true," she said. She stepped back and let him in.

Brinley jolted awake just in time to witness a tall young man with a light beard stumble through the gray curtain of mist. It had to be Lignumis. Hugo said that he was coming.

"Lignumis?" Animus said, catching the younger mage by the shoulders and holding him steady. "Lignumis, is that you?"

The man called Lignumis nodded slowly, staring at the ancient mage. "Animus?"

Animus chuckled, and the sound of it did something to relieve the tension that had been building up among the waiting crowd. "You look different," Animus said, clapping Lignumis on the back and bringing him forward. "Grown up, I dare say, and about time, too."

Lignumis gave a weak smile. "You look the same," he whispered.

Animus laughed again, and Brinley felt herself start to smile. Animus had a wonderful way of making people feel courageous in terrifying situations. Hugo was still in there, doing who knew what. They didn't even know if he would make it back. She clutched her bag tensely. He had taken the naptrap—no, Molad had. That was in the Ire, too. What was he doing with it? It was all that she could do not to rush back in there herself. She was eyeing the medallion still clutched in Lignumis's hand, but Animus took it from him before she could decide what she wanted to do.

The ancient mage took one look at her and tossed it back through the mist.

"Was that wise, Animus?" Cassis said, cringing. "We don't know who might be there. Anyone could pick it up."

Animus swept the onlookers with a stern look, holding up a finger for emphasis. "We do know," he said. "Hugo is still coming. We have to trust that. We have to believe in him."

The crowd was silent. Nobody knew what to say, probably. Brinley certainly didn't. He was right, of course. Animus was usually right. Deep down, they all knew that their fate rested in large part upon the head of the Mage of Light and Darkness. That was the way it had always been.

But in the past, things had always gone wrong. The Magemother had been there to save them all last time. But what could Brinley do? She was powerless, especially now that Animus had thrown the medallion back through the portal. There were no others. According to Cannon, Hugo—or Molad, rather—had thrown the first medallion over the edge of the bridge on the other side. All she could do now was wait like everyone else and hope that Hugo knew what he was doing. Not a pleasant thought, since he had made some bad decisions lately.

"Magemother?"

It was Lignumis. He was standing alone now, hands folded awkwardly before him, as if he was unused to being around so many people. How could she have forgotten him? She had gotten carried away in her own thoughts again, when she should have been caring for another. She felt selfish.

"Lignumis," she said, holding her hand out to him. "I know I'm not the Magemother you remember, but I'm very glad to see you. We have much to discuss. Are you all right?"

She indicated a line of blood on his neck. It was bleeding in a steady, slow stream.

"Ah," he said. He put a hand on it and came away with red fingers. "Yes. Gadjihalt wanted to make sure Hugo did not try to escape."

"Where is he now?" Brinley asked. She couldn't help noticing that every eye was trained on Lignumis now, every ear straining to hear them.

Lignumis hung his head and began to speak.

Brinley felt her last vestiges of hope slip away as she listened to his story. He told them how Gadjihalt had taken them to the Panthion. He told them what Shael had demanded and how Hugo had bartered to save him.

"He's going to imprison him?" Brinley asked, horrified.

"Are you saying you actually heard Shael's voice?" Animus demanded. "He spoke from within the Panthion?" The mage's face was a mix of worry and consternation.

"Did you see an army?" the captain of the guards asked, pushing Cassis aside to get a better look. "Is he going to send troops across the bridge? Did you find out how he has been crossing it?"

Lignumis's eyes went wide with panic. "Thousands," he whispered.

"Thousands?" the captain demanded. "Are you sure? Have you seen them with your own eyes?"

Lignumis paled searching for words.

"He spoke from within the Panthion?" Animus repeated. "He has been leading his troops this whole time?"

"Hush!" Tabitha yelled. She stepped around Brinley and placed herself between Lignumis and the others, hands on her hips, face determined. "You're scaring him half to death. One at a time, or no one at all. Brinley first," she said, motioning them away. "Give them some room. Go on. Shoo!"

Brinley covered a smile. "It's okay, Tabitha," she said. "Why don't you take Lignumis down to the medical tent and have that cut looked at? You can bring Cannon back with you when you come, and then maybe Lignumis will be ready to answer our questions."

"What are you going to do?" Tabitha said to Brinley, taking Lignumis's arm.

"We are going to wait for Hugo," she said firmly. "I'm sure he'll be back soon." But she didn't feel sure. What if Hugo couldn't get away? What if he really was forced into the box with Shael. But why would Shael want that? What did he gain by it?

"Hugo may make it out yet," Animus said, reading her thoughts.

She looked at the ancient mage, searching his face for the same fear that she felt. "Do you really think so?"

He looked down. "We must hope."

The man called Lignumis ducked out of the back of the medical tent as soon as no one was looking. That apprentice, Cannon, was being treated for hypothermia. Luckily, he was serving as a convenient distraction.

He made his way as quietly and quickly as possible down the streets of Ninebridge. Soon, he found himself alone on a dark street and changed shape, becoming a mangy gray dog. He sniffed the air. She had to be close. She was supposed to be in this part of the city. There was once a time when he could smell a witch a mile away, but that was before.

He found her in the basement of an old church. It was the type of place where you might expect to find an old woman selling used clothes for pennies, which was apparently the exact front that March had set up for herself.

He crawled through a half-open window and padded across a dingy floor, skirting racks of clothes as he went, leaving dirty paw prints on the floor. He found her at last, scowling down at him with those squinty eyes. She seemed about as pleased to see him as he was to see her, which is to say, not at all. But desperate times called for disagreeable company.

She glared at him for a long moment, perhaps wondering if he was a dog she could kick out of her home or an ancient sorcerer that had just enough of his power left to make it unwise to kick him. He waited longer than was necessary, letting her squirm. Finally, the Janrax turned back into himself. Not the tall, oak-bearded mage that he had been playing, but the thin, ancient wisp of a man, skin black, features rotted with age, his back bent nearly in half by his long years.

March breathed a sigh, whether of relief or disgust, it was hard to tell. "It's you again," she said.

"Indeed," he muttered. He dug in his pockets and held out the things that Hugo had given him, one in each hand, a small crystal vial and a piece of bark from the twistwood tree, wrapped carefully in the cutting of Gadjihalt's shirt so as not to touch his skin. Even for him, powerful as he was, that wouldn't be a good idea. "I followed the boy mage as we planned. When the moment came, I impersonated the Mage of Wood and led him to Shael."

March surveyed them thoughtfully. "The Mage of Wood. Yes, that was wisely done. From within the circle of mages it will be easy for you to strike at them when the time comes, and as we both know, there is no chance of them finding the true Lignumis."

"Those were my thoughts as well," he said. Then he offered her the items he had been carrying. "He gave me these to take to the Magemother."

"Bark," she said. "From the twistwood tree? Why?"

He shrugged. "Said he wanted his revenge on Shael later. Said the girl would be expecting it, too."

March frowned. "Perhaps you should deliver it to her, then. They can talk to each other over great distances, it is said. It's possible he told her that he was sending it with you. We wouldn't want to risk her suspecting who you truly are." She waved away the piece of bark, and he replaced it carefully in his pocket. "And what of this?" she said, taking the vial out of his hand. "Well, I don't believe it." Her face broke out in a grin. "This is the work of that fool sister of mine. One of her specialties. Naptraps, I think she calls them . . . used to transport her stupid creatures from one place to another or some such. What would the Magemother want with it?"

"Don't ask me," he said. "The boy didn't tell me. Seemed awfully worried about it though. Made sure I knew to give it to her."

March cocked an eyebrow. "And did he say she was expecting this too?"

"No. Just told me to give it to her."

March smiled. "Let's keep it, then. See if you can find out what it is. It might be something important. Tell her you don't know what she's talking about if she asks you. How could you? Hugo never even mentioned it to you."

"I know how to play my part," he said with a sneer. "I don't need pointers, least of all from you."

"Time will tell," she said dismissively. "How is your other work progressing?"

He smiled. "Very well. The Magemother took her haunt, just minutes ago, in fact."

"Then the way is clear for you to attack the others," March said. "You must be quick. We have only days before the attack. You had better get back now before they wonder where you have gone."

He shifted and became the dog again, then turned on his heel, dodging a kick from March as he padded out of the room.

❖ ❖ ❖

Brinley's head snapped up when the next person stepped through the mist.

It wasn't Hugo. She didn't know who it was, for she could not see his face. He wore black clothes that draped about his frame loosely and made him look bigger than he already was, and a black hood over his head with holes for his eyes. It took a moment of him standing there before everyone realized what had happened. A few people, like Tabitha, had nearly drifted off to sleep while they waited, and they were most surprised to look up and see the great hulking shape standing so close to them.

The man had no weapons, only a small black box held between his large hands. It was the size of a shoebox, made of smooth black metal that did not reflect the light. He bent forward very carefully, almost gingerly, and set the box on the ground in such a way that made Brinley think it must have weighed a great deal. Then he pulled out the gold medallion that they had thrown through the mist for Hugo and set it on top of the box. Setting his boot against the box, he pushed it over the line of warding, then backed away without a word and disappeared into the mist.

Everyone exhaled at the same time. "That was unexpected," Cannon said, shifting beneath the warm blanket that he had brought from the medical tent.

"Cryptic," Archibald murmured, staring intently at the box.

"There's a note." Animus said, and he picked up a small black roll of parchment from off the top of the box.

"What does it say?" Tabitha asked.

Animus's eyes danced across the page, his frown deepening the longer he read. Finally, he read the note aloud:

Magemother,

I, Shael, have taken Hugo Paradise, Mage of Light and Darkness and heir to the throne of Aberdeen, into my custody. Unless you open the Panthion and release us both in three day's time, he will be destroyed.

The inhabitants of the Ire are in turmoil. They seek to escape from their confinement and wish to overrun your land.

If you choose to release me, you have my word that I will return peacefully to the Wizard's Ire and maintain order there so that our two lands may continue to live together in harmony.

If you do not, the whole of the Wizard's Ire will move against you.

I trust that you will make the right decision.

I place my fate into your hands.

Nobody spoke.

Slowly, every eye turned to Brinley. "Hugo is in there?" she said softly. "In there with him?"

Animus picked up the box with some effort, examining it. "This truly is the Panthion," he said. "Who is inside, however, there is no way to tell."

"Without opening it," Archibald muttered.

Lignumis was on his feet. He pointed at the Panthion. "That's the box that was talking to us. A voice was coming out of it, talking to Hugo. It said that it was going to take Hugo inside." He looked down. "I thought that he would get away. I thought that he was bluffing when he agreed to go in there, so that I could go free." He sat down, covering his face with his hands. "I'm sorry. I'm so sorry."

Brinley placed a hand on his shoulder, slid it down his arm, and pulled him gently to his feet again. "I want to show you something," she said. She turned him around and began to walk him down the bridge. The rest of them followed silently, not knowing what else they should do. Animus brought up the rear, his expression dark, the heavy box floating before him on a cushion of air.

"I have a place that I go to when the world seems completely unfair," Brinley said. "When everything I am trying to accomplish seems like it is sure to fail. I want to take you there. I have many things to think about now, and only three days left. My friend may be suffering every minute as we decide how to act. Suffering, every minute, as we prepare for what must come . . . but there is nothing that I can do about that just now. There is something that I can do tonight, though, and so I will do it. And you can help me, if you wish. You all can," she added, looking around at them.

"What?" Lignumis said. "Name it, and I will do it."

Brinley looked up at him seriously. "We can finish building a house."

Chapter Twenty-One

In which there is a home

"WHAT IS SHE THINKING? Why did she send us here alone? And why didn't she let him out? She's got to let him out of the Panthion, no matter how long she sits and stews about it. I mean, I don't like the idea of Shael released and free in the world any more than the next person, but he has forced her hand. I don't understand what she's waiting for."

Cannon's voice echoed around them as he and Tabitha wound their way through the dark tunnels beneath the dungeons of Thieutukar's castle. Brinley had taken the others to go and help her finish Maggie's house, and sent Tabitha and Cannon to bring Gadjihalt's sword to Kuzo. The big sword felt heavier and heavier in her hands the longer she carried it. It was an ugly, brutish thing, and she could barely bring herself to hold it. It was better if she didn't think about the great curving dragon's spike on the end of it, or how a beautiful creature had been killed to put it there.

"Ouch!" Cannon said. "You poked me with the sword again! Will you just let me carry it?"

"No," Tabitha said. "Brinley asked me to do it, so I am going to do it."

Cannon's hand reached out, feeling awkwardly in the darkness. When it met her shoulder, he grabbed her arm and led her around him. "You go first, then," he said. "I'm tired of you literally stabbing me in the back. I didn't come all the way through the Wizard's Ire just to be killed walking down a flight of stairs. Mind you, I expect that we will be killed at the bottom. It was Hugo that saved us last time, and though I'll do my best, I don't know how much I can do with wind against a dragon in the dark." Cannon sighed. "Why did Brinley send us to do this? And why can we not let Thieutukar do it for us? He said he was willing. Is there something you're not telling me? Something that everyone else knows that I don't know? Because let me tell you, Tabitha, I've been here before and this dragon will probably eat us when we can't do that dragon dance thing of his. Can you do it, Tabitha? Can you? Because I certainly can't. I think what we will have to do is—"

"Enough!" Tabitha rounded on him, bumping him with the flat of the sword again, mostly by accident. "Brinley knows what she is doing. And I'm sure you would do a lovely dragon dance, but that won't be necessary. Kuzo will speak with me." She returned to the stairs, and Cannon kept his peace for the remainder of their descent.

"Back again," Cannon whispered when they reached the bottom. His voice echoed about them differently, revealing a massive chamber ahead.

"Who is there?" a voice said from out of the darkness. "Name yourself." A little ball of light glinted suddenly out of the sea of black, growing larger as it approached them.

"Oh, no," Cannon said wearily. "Here we go again."

Tabitha squared her shoulders and strode towards the approaching figure. It was a man, she saw. Tall and slender, with hair that glowed like fire. He was Kuzo, the last dragon of Aberdeen, and he was about to know her name.

She changed, her skin shimmering, her body lengthening, growing scales and claws and wings. She felt the now familiar sensation of heat in her belly, the desire to release it into the blackness and bathe the dark in her light.

She roared and loosed a pillar of fire into the air above Kuzo's head, casting sudden light upon his startled expression. She heard a yelp and a thud from behind her, but she didn't dare look away to investigate. Cannon had probably not been expecting her to change into a dragon. She had forgotten to tell him.

The surprise faded quickly from Kuzo's face, replaced by a look of intrigue. "A masterful thing," he said quietly. "To take the shape of a dragon. Few have ever done so. None that I know of now live."

"My name is Tabitha. I am the Magemother's Herald," she said, and she roared again for good measure, making the air shake. When she had finished, she looked down at him. "I brought what you wanted." She raised a giant foreleg and slammed the sword down at Kuzo's feet.

The dragon's eyes widened, staring at it. His jaw loosened, his mouth falling open in surprise as he bent to pick it up. "My Anorre," he whispered. He broke the spike off the end of the hilt with a firm twist and dropped the blade on the floor, kicking it away in disgust. Then he looked up at Tabitha, fingering the spike in his hands tenderly. "You have done me a great favor. What do you desire in return?"

Tabitha shrank back into her own form, and Kuzo watched her, his expression unchanged as he looked down at her. It was the first time anyone had ever looked at her like that. It made no difference to Kuzo, it seemed, what she looked like. To him, she would always be a dragon.

"I want what Hugo wanted," she said. "Tell me what you know about Chantra."

The dragon nodded. "I did not hide her."

Tabitha held her breath. Was that all he had to say? Had they come all this way, sacrificed so much, for *this*?

"But I did help her," he went on, and Tabitha relaxed. "She was trying to help me, help me get my fire back." He looked down at the spike in his hands. "I told her that the only way was to get Anorre's spike. To burn it. To put her soul to rest . . . But Chantra had other ideas."

He glanced up at Tabitha. "None of them worked, of course. But I didn't mind. I was happy just for the company." His face twisted distastefully. "She was the only person I ever saw in this place who didn't want something from me.

"We became friends, in time. And friendships between humans and my race are very rare indeed. But Chantra was special. We spoke of treasure, and I told her of my adventures. She had a strange passion for rubies. Her brother, the Mage of Metal, even tried to teach her how to go inside one. That was her dream. Her secret ambition." He looked down. "Such a wonderful child."

He glared up at Tabitha. "Then the Magemother told her to hide. Once again, the Mage of Light and Darkness had lost his mind and threatened to destroy the other mages. Chantra came to me that day, in secret, terrified. She did not know where to run, where to hide."

Tabitha took a step toward him. "What did you tell her?" She looked around the room, wondering if, perhaps, the Mage of Fire was crouching in some dark corner, still hiding from the darkness that she had run from years before.

"I gave her a gift," Kuzo said. "The last of my possessions."

He smiled faintly at a pleasant memory. "When I was imprisoned by the gnomes so long ago, they searched me for treasure. A dragon never goes anywhere without a little treasure, you know, just in case. I let them find it, take it from me, so that they were satisfied. But they did not find it all." He grinned deviously. "I had one gem left . . . a ruby."

He bowed his head. "I gave it to her that day, just to calm her. But then an idea struck me. What better hiding place for her than that? Inside a stone. Who would ever look there? And this was the perfect stone for it. It was uncut, you see, a rough, dark gem. To most people it would look like a plain old rock. But inside! Inside, she would have the palace of her dreams."

"So did she do it?" Tabitha asked, eyes bulging. "Did she get inside?"

Kuzo nodded. "Not at first, but we practiced together, right here, until she could achieve it."

"Where is it?" Tabitha asked, taking another step forward.

Kuzo smiled, folding his arms across his chest. "I do not know," he said. "I told her to take it somewhere safe. Somewhere that nobody would think to look. Not even me. She said the Magemother would know where to hide it."

Kuzo stared at her for a long time, but Tabitha was at a loss for words, unsure what to ask next.

"Go," he said finally. "I have what I want, and you have what you want. And tell the king of the gnomes that I will not be his prisoner for much longer." He smiled, looking down at the spike, then changed in the blink of an eye into his true form.

"One thing more," he rumbled, his giant head swinging down until it was level with Tabitha. "You owe me one last thing, for helping you. One last thing, if you want to leave this room alive."

He dropped the spike at her feet.

"Burn this for me."

❖ ❖ ❖

Brinley twirled the thick wooden button between her fingers, and after a moment, replaced it in her pocket. She was watching the night sky for Cannon and Tabitha, but there was no sign of them yet. She hoped that they were okay. It had seemed like a good idea to send Tabitha to speak with the dragon, since she could turn into a dragon herself. But then again, just because an idea seems good at first doesn't mean it turns out well in the end.

She returned to the clearing where the mages were working and put a hand on Lignumis's shoulder as he bent over a thick length of wood.

"Lignumis," she said kindly. "Let me give you your power back. I daresay you could move that wood more easily as the Mage of Wood."

He took a step back, looking shocked, but then nodded. She motioned for him to kneel, then placed her hands on his head as she had done with Unda.

Before she could get the words out, he grabbed her wrists. "Wait," he said. He stood up, shaking his head. "Can we just wait for a little while?" He rubbed his eyes. "I'm not ready. Not feeling good. I need some time to adjust. I—"

"That's okay," Brinley said in a soothing tone. "I understand. You've been in the Wizard's Ire so long."

"It isn't that," he said quickly. "I mean, I just need a little time. So much has happened in the last few hours. I just feel . . .wrong. I want to be ready, when I receive my power."

"You need to get your head in the right place?" Unda said, making them both jump. He had come up behind them, and there was a strange look on his face. If Brinley didn't know better, she would have thought it was suspicion.

Lignumis relaxed. "Exactly. You put it just right. I just need to get my head in the right place." He smiled weakly and put a hand on Brinley's shoulder. "Give me one day, Magemother, maybe two, and I promise I will be ready.

Brinley nodded, glancing back and forth between Unda and Lignmuis. Something had just happened, she was sure of it, but she didn't know what it was. A second later, Unda had swept the strange expression from his face and he was walking Lignumis back to the house.

"Don't feel too bad," Unda said, clapping the other mage on the back. "You weren't ever very powerful anyway."

"Unda!" Brinley said, "That's not helping."

"He knows I'm kidding," Unda said, slapping Lignumis on the shoulder. "You did get big, didn't you! Grew like a weed these last few years . . . of course, you *would* grow like a weed."

Brinley was about to scold Unda again, but Lignumis was chuckling now, so she let it go. The three of them joined Cassis at the front of the house, where he was pulling nails out of the ground as if they had fallen there. He was making them from what ore there was in the soil beneath their feet, she knew, but it looked like he was just picking them up. Since Lignumis was unable to control the trees to make wood for the house, Brinley had been forced to make some changes in her design, but the one thing she wouldn't give up was a good, solid front door made of wood. Cassis had made them tools to work with.

"I'll fix it later," Lignumis said, mumbling over several nails clamped between his lips. "We'll make it look good in the end, after I figure out what's wrong with me."

"There's nothing wrong with you," Brinley said, but Lignumis just gave her a skeptical look and kept pounding nails.

"Brinley," Animus called, and she went to him.

He was sitting at the edge of the clearing, apart from the others. He had been sitting on the Panthion, head propped on his fist, lost in thought the whole time they had been there. Now he looked as if he had made up his mind about something.

"I think you will have to let them out," he said. "I can't find a way around it."

Brinley nodded. "I know."

Animus straightened. "Oh," he said. "I did not realize you had already made up your mind."

She sat on a rock across from him. "I have. I'm going to let them out, but not until the last possible moment."

Animus nodded slowly. "That will give us time to prepare," he said. "There is much to do if we are to be ready to face Shael, or war, in three days . . ." His eyes flitted to the house behind them. "Is our time spent wisely, just waiting here?"

Brinley smiled at him. "I don't know," she said. "But this is where I come when I don't know what to do. So far it seems to be working." She turned to survey the house. "And we're almost finished. I can't stop now, Animus. I might never get it done. I may not survive the next three days."

Animus laughed grimly. "True enough." He glanced around. "Where did that cat get off to?"

"He went with Archibald to get Maggie," Brinley said. "They shouldn't be much longer. I just hope we're done before they get back."

Animus pointed at the sky. "Someone is back."

It was Tabitha. The black swan descended and changed into her friend as soon as Cannon had stepped down from her back.

"Tell me," Brinley said without preamble. "What happened? What did you learn?"

"Well," Cannon said, "for one thing, we set a dragon free. He blasted out of the tunnel right behind us. Don't think Thieutukar liked that very much . . ."

"What?" Animus said, rising to his feet.

"And we learned where Chantra is hiding," Tabitha said eagerly. Her face fell. "Well . . . sort of."

"From the beginning," Brinley said, struggling to maintain her patience.

When they had finished their story, Animus and the other mages started pestering Cannon and Tabitha with questions, so Brinley strode toward the house, lost in thought. Where would her mother have hidden a ruby? Somewhere on Calypsis? Somewhere in Caraway Castle? Those were the two places that she had called home, but would they be the best place to hide something? Probably not. She sighed. Tabitha would have to look for it while she went to find her father. Maybe the other mages could help in the search too.

She smiled at the house. At least one thing was coming together. Cassis had made a roof of stone and filled the windows with sparkling, clear glass. Belterras, upon learning that Lignumis was unable to use his powers, had summoned a team of beavers to help them cut logs, which they had then stacked against the outside walls to give the house a warmer appearance. Birds sang cheerfully from their tiny, colorful houses in the yard, and wildflowers bloomed in a little patch of soil under the kitchen window, as if the gods had looked down on her efforts and decided to help. She certainly hoped that they were pleased with it. This was, perhaps, the only responsibility that they had given her as Magemother that she was fulfilling with any measure of success: caring for those who could not care for themselves.

She smiled at the house. It was almost done. She picked up the hammer that Lignumis had been using earlier and drove a single nail through the wooden button, fastening it firmly to the center of the door. "There," she said with satisfaction. "It's finished."

"It's lovely," Tabitha said, drawing up beside her. "She's going to love it, if she doesn't think it's too big."

"Oh, I'm sure she will think it's too big," Brinley said. "But she'll get used to it. She needs the extra space for visitors."

Brinley glanced around, looking for Unda. "Wasn't he going to build a fountain?"

Tabitha nodded. "He is. I told him to do it out back so that the birds could have some privacy when they bathed. I'll show you!" She grabbed Brinley's hand and pulled her around the house. Sure enough, Unda was standing in front of an intricate fountain of rocks and polished stones and tiny waterfalls. But something was wrong; some of the waterfalls were falling up instead of down.

"Oh my," Tabitha said, putting a hand over her mouth and walking to the fountain. It was as if Unda had lost concentration halfway through and turned the laws of gravity upside down. He was standing in front of the fountain with his hands folded across his chest, deep in thought, staring off into space as if he wasn't aware of the fountain at all.

"Look," Tabitha whispered to Brinley. She was gesturing toward a particularly interesting portion of the fountain, where two waterfalls met. One was falling down, and one was falling up, and where the two streams of water met, they swirled around each other in a dizzying circle that seemed to run in two directions at the same time. "Ooh," Tabitha said, going slightly cross-eyed as she stuck her hand into the center of it.

Unda jerked out of his thoughts and pulled Tabitha out of the fountain as the water began to snake around her arms like little glistening serpents. "Careful," he said. "Sorry. Got distracted. Thinking, you know."

"What's bothering you, Unda?" Brinley said.

The young mage cracked his knuckles thoughtfully. "Lignumis."

"What about him?" Tabitha asked.

"He isn't quite . . . how I remember him. That's all."

"He looks different," Brinley said. "He's much older now, isn't he? You are too."

Unda shook his head. "Not that. He talks the same, acts the same. But there is something different about him." He glanced up at Brinley's worried face and smiled. "Don't worry about it," he said. "I am always thinking too hard about something or other."

"Oh, it's perfect," Tabitha said, and Brinley turned to see her placing Miah the toad in the center of the swirling fountain. "You'll love it here, Miah," Tabitha said, and patted the toad on the head firmly, as if to reinforce the notion that it had arrived at its new home. "And you'll love it even more after Unda un-confuses your fountain."

Unda grinned.

"They're here!" Belterras bellowed, and they hurried around to the front of the house. "They're coming up the hill!"

"Positions everyone!" Tabitha called, herding people into the house. They had decided that everyone would wait out of sight, so as not to overwhelm Maggie with too many people at once.

Archibald entered the clearing, followed by Maggie and the Swelter Cat, who trotted happily beside her. She reached down with one hand to adjust one of her colorful socks, the other hand clutched tightly around the tin that held her treasures.

"And then when I was forty-nine," she was saying to Tobias, "I met a cat so fat and blind, he couldn't find his own behind." The Swelter Cat purred appreciatively, nodding several times.

"Whose house have you brought me to, Archie?" Maggie said, peering suspiciously at the little dwelling. "Oh," she said, flattening her dresses with her hand. "It's Magemother Brinley."

"Hello," Brinley said. "I have a surprise for you, Maggie."

"Oh?" Maggie said nervously. "No, thank you. I don't like surprises." She looked around. "Where is Apprentice Tabitha? I would like to play a game of War Hands with her. Just one, if she has the time. Best of three, you know."

Brinley grinned. "She's inside your house," Brinley said, nodding at the little dwelling.

Maggie peered around Brinley suspiciously. "My house, you say? Where? That's not my house."

"It is now," Brinley said. "We built it for you." She put her hands on her hips firmly. "You need a warm place to sleep, Maggie, and space of your own, so that we can come and visit you."

"But—" Maggie spluttered.

"And there's a workshop in the back, if you want to start your own business, though I daresay Jaship will let you keep your job if that's what you really want."

Maggie said nothing, just stared blankly at the house.

"It's nice and quiet here . . ." Brinley said softly, "and you're not too far from the city. Do you like it?"

Maggie threw her arms around Brinley. "It's wonderful!" she said. "What's that on my door?" She marched up to the house and touched the little button. "Ah! See, I told you. A lucky button, indeed." She threw the door open excitedly. "Luckiest button I ever—AAAHH!" She leapt back from the door, pointing at the inside of the house. "It's full of people!"

"Just me, Maggie," Tabitha said, stepping out of the doorway. "Me and all the mages, of course." She stepped aside and they all filed out of the house after her.

"Oh my," Maggie said. "All the mages, in my house! How wonderful!" She took Tabitha's hand and led her back inside, slamming the door behind them. A second later, her voice came drifting out of the house, muffled slightly by the door. "I'm going let all of my street friends move in with me, Apprentice Tabitha, and that way we can all have a real house together, and we can make our own money in the workshop to buy food with. We'll probably have to steal a few tools to get started, but not for long, and we'll give them back once we have money to buy our own."

Cannon slapped his face with the palm of his hand, shaking his head, and Belterras chuckled heartily. "Honest, isn't she?"

"I think maybe I should make her a few tools before I leave today," Cassis murmured thoughtfully.

Animus was looking at Brinley. She cleared her throat, and the mages all looked at her.

"Thank you," she said. "I couldn't have done this for her without all of your help." She shuffled her feet nervously, then calmed, realizing what she wanted to tell them. "This is what we do," she said, pointing at the house. The door opened a crack, and she thought she saw Maggie peeking out at her, but she continued. "This is who we are. You exist to serve this world, and I exist to serve you. There is much to be done, and none of it is easy, but we can do anything together."

She paused, her eyes drifting to the cold black box that sat at the other end of the clearing. "In three day's time, I will open the Panthion. By then we must be ready. We must return Shael to his prison after Hugo is free. I don't know how, but we must do it. We must prepare the kingdom against an attack from the Ire. We will save Hugo. We will save my mother, and we will save the kingdom. I cannot do it alone, but we can do it together, as a family . . ."

She trailed off, feeling foolish. That was more or less what she had meant to say, but it had sounded much better in her head than it did out loud.

Maggie flung her door open and began to clap enthusiastically. "That was a *very* nice speech, Magemother Brinley," she said. "Now, come inside, please, so that I can show you my house."

❖ ❖ ❖

Brinley and Tabitha sat on log stools across from Maggie's little stone kitchen table, upon which she had proudly set her treasure tin. Brinley was watching the others through the window.

"It's a lovely home," Tabitha said, smiling pleasantly at Maggie.

"Thank you, dear. It was a gift from the Magemother, you know."

Tabitha grinned. "I know."

"Not the first gift I've been given from the Magemother, you know."

"I know," Tabitha said. "I remember."

"Not the second gift either, dear."

Brinley turned away from the window. "Really?" she asked. "Did my mother give you something? Did you know her?"

Maggie nodded. "Oh, yes," she said. "I've lived all over this world, you know. Met all sorts of people. All sorts of people, high and low, and almost everyone has met me." She took the lid off the tin between them and motioned for Brinley. "It's time for you to pick a gift again. Since you returned my last one."

Brinley grinned sideways at Tabitha, who looked rather jealous. "Any advice?" she said, remembering what had happened last time.

"Yes, in fact," Maggie said. "I think it's time you took back the gift your mother gave me." She reached into a corner of the tin and drew a rough-looking rock out from among the other odds and ends. Brinley remembered seeing it last time. It didn't look like much, but if her mother had given it to Maggie . . .

"It is a ruby, I think," Maggie said, handing it to her. "Uncut, of course, but someday it could make a beautiful piece. It's the most valuable thing in the tin, but nobody ever wants it."

Brinley's eyes had gone wide.

"Ooo," Tabitha said, pulling on the sleeve of Brinley's shirt. "Ooo, Brinley!"

"I know," Brinley said, holding the gem up to the light. She closed her eyes and reached into the stone with her mind. It was a vast, beautiful place, a palace, just as Cassis had described.

Chantra, she called.

And Chantra came.

A thin line of red, like molten metal or a thread of fire, fell from the stone onto the floor, becoming first a pair of feet, then legs, then the torso of a young girl, older than Brinley, but still vibrant with the strength of youth. Her hair was raven and her eyes were a warm brown, tinged at the edges with red. Her arms were folded tightly across her chest, and as soon as she had emerged from the stone she began to shake. Her eyes rolled backwards into her head, and she toppled over. Tabitha caught her just before she hit the floor.

"What's wrong with her?" Tabitha said.

"Magemother?" It was Belterras. He stepped through the front door with Animus following behind. Chantra was convulsing now, legs twitching back and forth, eyes rolling back and forth.

Brinley was propping her head up with Tabitha's coat to prevent her from striking the floor. "Turn her on her side," Belterras barked. "No! Don't hold her down."

"It's the pain," Animus said. "It's too much for her. I feared this would happen. Magemother." He shot Brinley a meaningful glance. "It is time."

Brinley laid her hands on Chantra's head and whispered in her ear, feeling once again the surge of power, the lifting of weight.

Chantra stilled at once, but she did not wake. Her eyes closed and her jaw slackened, and she would not respond to her name. Belterras opened one of her eyes and examined it.

"Well?" Animus said, leaning in to have a look for himself.

"I think that she is no longer in pain," Belterras said. "But she is no longer with us."

Brinley gasped. "Dead?"

"No," Animus said, and Belterras nodded in agreement. "Not dead. But barely alive. Not asleep, not awake. She has . . . gone away. But she will return. Her body needs to rest. She will likely wake in a matter of hours. A day or two at the most, as long as she is well cared for."

"She can stay right here," Maggie said. "I'll look after her."

Belterras eyed her thoughtfully. "I will come and check her myself from time to time. And I may ask Habis to come and stay with her. She is good with remedies, or so the animals have told me."

A swallowing sound made Brinley turn around. The Swelter Cat was sitting in the front doorway, preening himself. He must have come in when she wasn't looking.

He cleared his throat when he saw her watching him. "This is no time to stand and glance," he said loftily. "It's time to go. It's your last chance."

"What is he talking about?" Animus said.

"My father," Brinley said. "He's in Inveress, and I have to go rescue him. I have to go now, I'm afraid. There is. . . something that I want to ask Cyus as well."

"Inveress?" Animus said. He searched her face for a moment. "Very well," he said. "I see that you have already decided. Will you allow me to accompany you?"

Brinley shook her head. "I need you here. There will be much to do in preparation for the war."

"War?" Tabitha said, glancing up from Tobias. She had begun to pet him, and he was glaring at her.

"Yes," Brinley said, bending to help Belterras lift Chantra onto the table. "Three day's time, that's what Shael said."

Cannon, who was now leaning through the kitchen window, gave a low whistle. "Three days," he said. "I'm not going to lie. I wouldn't mind being somewhere else when Shael comes. No matter how ready we are, it's not going to be pretty if he really can get his armies across the bridge. Can he?"

Animus nodded. "I think he can. I do not think we could stop him from doing at least that, even if we all attempted to overwhelm him the moment he emerged from the Panthion. I have no doubt that he will come out fighting. We cannot expect him to keep his half of the bargain. If you let him out, he will not go quietly back into the Ire. He will pick up right where he left off, and he will destroy this world."

"What?" Brinley said.

Animus hesitated. "I said, if Shael gets out—"

"Not that," Brinley said. "Cannon. What did you say?"

"Uh, me?" Cannon asked. "I said it won't be pretty if Shael's armies get across the bridge."

"No," Brinley shook her head. It had been something else. Something important, that nobody had noticed. "You said you wished you could be someplace else."

Cannon flushed with embarrasement. "Well, I mean—You know I'm not one to run from a fight, Magemother. I was just saying—"

Brinley held up a hand. "Shh," she whispered. "There is something in that. Something important." She closed her eyes, trying to catch a glimpse of it. Someplace else. What if they could be somewhere else when Shael came. Out of reach. Safe . . .

She smiled. "I intend to be ready for Shael when he comes. I will wait until the last possible moment to release them, but in three days's time, we must be ready."

"Ready?" Cassis said. "To face a full-scale invasion of the Wizard's Ire led by Shael himself? We will need more than three days to prepare for that!"

"Then we had better get started," Brinley said. She laid a hand on Chantra's chest. "Belterras, you will care for her?"

"Not just him," Maggie said. "I'm going to make up the most comfortable bed a person could ask for, and that's where she'll stay until she has mended."

"Good." Brinley took Tabitha's hand and stepped to the door. She paused on the threshold to address Animus again. "How long would it take you to gather every king in the land and meet me in Ninebridge?"

"With the help of the others," he said, "three hours. Maybe less."

"Good," she said. "Do it."

"They will not all like being summoned like this," Animus said. "What shall I tell them?"

Brinley thought for a moment, trying to think of something impressive. Eventually she settled on the truth. "Tell them that we have a world to save, and three days in which to do it." She hesitated. "And tell them that I have a plan."

He raised an eyebrow. "Do you?"

She took the little silver summoning bell from her bag and twirled it thoughtfully. "Maybe . . ." she said. "Maybe when the fight arrives we can be somewhere else." She replaced the bell and took a step towards the door. "I have to go speak with someone now. Gather the kings for me, Animus. Summon the Mages when you have them, and meet me at the Bridge to Nowhere."

Epilogue

In which there is darkness

HUGO PUSHED HIMSELF UP onto his hands and knees, rubbing them gingerly. They had been torn by the rough stone floor from his fall. How far had he fallen? It was hard to tell, but it had felt like several feet, and his legs were definitely going to bruise. He took his eyes from the rough gray floor and felt his stomach turn over. He had never liked heights much, or darkness, for that matter, but the space he was in had plenty of both.

The tiny gray platform he had landed on was one of many, sticking up out of the immense blackness like odd bubbles rising from a bottomless glass. Long, narrow staircases led up and down from each platform, long lengths of steeply angled steps, leading into darkness. The other platforms were empty. He couldn't imagine what they were for, except perhaps for catching people when they fell in, but he didn't think that happened very often.

Someone spoke his name, someone very far away, by the sounds of it. He crawled to the edge of the platform and peered into the darkness below him, straining to see the man he knew would be there. Shael. He was locked in here with a madman.

Hugo wondered if he was really going to use him as bait to force the prison door open, or if he had simply been lured here to die. It didn't matter. He didn't have much of a choice in the matter. If he had it to do over, he would let Lignumis go every time.

"Hello?" Hugo called into the darkness. "Who's there?" Stupid question. He knew the answer. Who else could it be?

Pain lanced against the inside of his head, forcing a moan from him.

We're here! Molad cried in jubilation. *We're here at last!*

Hugo bit his tongue, focusing on the pain, forcing that into the center of his attention, drawing the power of his mind away from Molad. It wouldn't do to give up just yet. Maybe he would get lucky. Maybe this wouldn't end as badly as it was promising to.

"Hugo."

His name echoed out of the depths again, mixed with the sound of dripping water, as though there were a great tangle of pipes just out of sight somewhere in the darkness. Hugo forced himself to his feet, eyeing the stairs with reluctance. It *had* to be a great dark palace of floating stone balconies and rickety stairs with no rails, of course. A nice warm room with bars on the windows and a plushy armchair or two would have been too much to ask of a legendary magical prison box. Well, at least it was spacious.

"Hugo," the voice floated up again.

"Yes," Hugo mumbled. "I'm coming."

He started down the stairs, hoping beyond hope that he might find something in the darkness below him other than the stuff of nightmares.

END OF BOOK TWO

People and Places

Aberdeen The lands under the rule of King Remy, consisting of the countries of Caraway, Aquilar, Hedgemon, Chair, and the Greggan States.

Archibald The most trusted advisor to the king of Caraway.

Animus The Mage of Wind.

Aquilar A country in Aberdeen.

Belterras The Mage of Earth.

Brinley The main character. If you don't know who she is, you should probably just start over.

Calypsis The moon of Aberdeen. The location of the Magemother's castle.

Cannon The apprentice of the Mage of Wind.

Caraway The most powerful country in Aberdeen. The king of Caraway is also the High King of Aberdeen.

Cassis The Mage of Metal.

Chair A country in Aberdeen.

Chantra The Mage of Fire.

Cyus An exiled god. He lives in Inveress and serves as the scribe of the world.

Gadjihalt Chief servant of Shael; the commander of his armies.

Greggan States Ganna, Garra, Galla, Gappa, Gassa, Gatta. Together, they form one of the five countries in Aberdeen.

Habis One of the oldest and most powerful witches in Aberdeen. Sister to March, and daughter of Shael.

Hedgemon A country in the north of Aberdeen

Hugo Paradise The Prince of Caraway, and heir to the thrones of Caraway and Aberdeen. Son of Remy Paradise. The new Mage of Light and Darkness.

Idris A type of evil giant that can take the form of a child.

Inveress A magical realm beneath Aberdeen.

Janrax An evil shapeshifter. Formerly the wizard Maazan Dow.

Kokum The witches village. Located in the Moorwood, near Cemlin.

Kutha A giant owl. Evil creature that serves Shael.

Kuzo The last dragon of Aberdeen.

Lake of Eyes A lake in Pine Forest, close to Tarwal.

Lewilyn Brinley's mother, and the previous Magemother.

Lignumis The Mage of Wood.

Lux Tennebris The second Mage of Light and Darkness.

Magemother The guardian of the mages.

Magisterium The ancient school of wizards. Located in Tarwal.

March a.k.a. The March Witch. One of the oldest and most powerful witches in Aberdeen. Sister to Habis, and daughter of Shael.

Ninebridge An important city in Caraway. The location of the nine magical bridges that lead to major cities in Aberdeen.

Panthion A magical prison box.

Pilfer Archibald's pony.

Remy Paradise The King of Caraway, and the High King of Aberdeen.

Rift A deep, magical gorge or canyon that separates Aberdeen from the Wizard's Ire.

Shael An evil wizard of ancient date who was confined to the Wizard's Ire.

Swelter Cat A magical cat. The servant of Cyus.

Tabitha The Magemother's Herold. The Apprentice to the Mage of Earth.

Taluva The first Mage of Light and Darkness.

Tarwal A city in the south of Caraway. Location of the Magisterium.

Thieutukar Manisse a.k.a. Tuck. The King of the Gnomes.

Tobias See *Swelter Cat.*

Unda The Mage of Water.

Void A place of emptiness. Generally, it separates different worlds.

Wizard's Ire This is the nasty bad place where Shael, and other evil creatures are imprisoned. It is separated from the rest of Aberdeen by a deep, impassable canyon.

Acknowledgements

Thank you to . . .

. . .Spencer Bowen and Spencer Bagshaw once again, for suffering through my first draft with me.

. . .Katie Babbit, John Bigelow, Shannon Forslund, Isaac Reyes, Amanda, Charlene, Ron, Jamie, Rebekah, Jeanine, Shari, Anna, Jennifer, Tanya, and Robin. I couldn't do it without your support.

. . .And as always, to God.

Made in the USA
Lexington, KY
24 September 2017